"Why don't you come over here and keep Nattie company?"

He got to his feet, hesitating a bit, kicking off his shoes. She gestured to him, a come-hither motion of her free hand, took a last delicious gulp of her drink, and set it down on the floor under the couch as he came over to her.

Their eyes never left each other until he had knelt on the floor next to her and bent his head to kiss her. Then he closed his eyes as he opened his mouth and enclosed her in his embrace.

It had been a long time since she'd had a lover this deliberate, this searching, this slow. . . .

EVERYTHING IS BETTER AT THE BEACH.

Also by Marcia Rose
Published by Ballantine Books:

ADMISSIONS

CHOICES

SECOND CHANCES

CONNECTIONS

Summer Times

Marcia Rose

BALLANTINE BOOKS • NEW YORK

To
the best of women—
all of us

Library of Congress Catalog Card Number: 85-90705

ISBN 0-345-31854-4

Manufactured in the United States of America

First Edition: August 1985

❀ 1 ❀

A Day in the Life

Natalie glared at her boss as hard as she could, but Peter Marcus bent his head and became extremely busy pretending to read one of the papers on the top of his very large, very shiny, very modern rosewood desk. She was left glaring at his carefully barbered salt-and-pepper curls. That thick, wavy silver-gray hair was supposedly the reason he was known up and down Madison Avenue as the Silver Fox; but she knew better. It was his feral eyes and that sly little smile, not to mention his foxy smarts, which included an instinct to go for the jugular. Oh, he was presentable enough, even handsome. Sort of. And he had a kind of animal charm. But what a lot of people didn't realize was that Peter Marcus was not to be trusted.

She knew Peter; she knew him almost too well. Now, for instance, he was magically making her go away by pretending she wasn't there. Well, goddammit, she would *not* go away ... not after what he'd just done to her! Heart pounding, she drew in breath.

"Save it, Natalie, darling," he growled. "I don't want to hear it."

"How the hell do you know what I'm going to say?"

Now his head came up and those pale, implacable eyes bored into her. "Nattie. Darling. The thing is done. Face it, deal with it, accept it. It's not so terrible. You have plenty of other accounts, most of them bigger than Ali Baba Bread. No, don't say a word. I know exactly what's in your mind. First, you'll get all nostalgic and emotional because the pita bread account was your first and your favorite. And then you'll start to cry because you and Paul Hasahni used to have something going and giving the account to Martha J was his idea. And then you'll stop crying and get mad and you'll curse and holler and threaten to quit. Well, don't bother. I might just accept."

He raised his eyebrows in that irritating way he had. And then he waved her off, as if she were an annoyance. Waved her off! Damn him! She was Natalie Simon, Executive Vice-President and Creative Director of his lousy ad agency, not some little clerk-typist! Dammit, he'd known her for too many years, and too often, he took advantage of it.

She could feel the heat of her hurt and fury climbing in her face; and now tears were gathering in her eyes. She wasn't going to give him that satisfaction, damn him! Without another word, she turned on her heel and marched out, slamming his door as hard as she could and sailing by his secretary, her nose firmly in the air.

She didn't even pause as she came out into the hallway. Her own wonderful corner office with its skatey-eight windows and its drop-dead view of Manhattan was just a few steps to the right. So she turned left and went striding down the hall, toward Martha J's office—her own old office, her beloved old office, the one she'd had when she was *young* and on her way *up*. Not like now, her favorite account yanked away from her without warning, and without apology! Dammit! Martha J was going to hear about this! She needed to get this said.

She also needed a drink; but it was still too damn early. Never drink before noon was her rule—rarely broken. She hurried down the hall, bending her head, pretending to be deep in thought so nobody would stop her or try to engage her in conversation. Let them think she was in "creative mode"! Creative! What a joke! Right now, she'd be hard pressed to give her own address.

God, she hated feeling pushed around! She liked being in control, and up until ten minutes ago in Peter Marcus's office, she'd thought she was, dammit! Hell, she'd been *positive* she had everything under control.

Hadn't she just brought in the new orange juice account after months of hard work? It was no fun, going out to dinner with the Dorsey twins, two identically fat men who had two topics of conversation: orange juice and race horses. Race horses! Neither Tim nor Tom Dorsey could ride—hell, there wasn't a horse in the world that could take their weight—but they could talk horse all right! And talk and talk and talk. When they finally called Peter to say Sunshine Orange Juice was now in the M & M Advertising stable, Peter asked her what she wanted as a prize—"Name it, Nattie, and it's yours." She'd grinned and said "Twelve hours of silence and sleep, please. And a diamond ring."

Now, barely two weeks later, he was waving her out of his inner sanctum, dismissing her! Yes, he was right, Ali Baba was only one account and she held eleven in her hot little hands. All the food accounts. Not to mention that she was creative director—what she liked to call "head of all creation"—and every goddamn campaign came across her desk at some point or another. Come on . . . she was Big Stuff in Marcus & Morisey. . . . She didn't have to worry her head over one little account!

But, in this business, you had to run very fast just in order to stay in the same place—like Alice in Wonderland. You could not afford to lose even the tiniest bit of business; it was a sure sign to everyone that you were losing your grip. Particularly, Natalie thought, since she was well aware that Peter was still quietly buying up large chunks of Steinberg & Epstein, the public relations firm. And furthermore, that Steinberg & Epstein had one of the hottest young VPs around and her name was Daisy Villiers. She didn't want to think about it, but she knew with a cold chill of certainty that Daisy Villiers was the main attraction. And the worst of it was A Secret . . . Peter had only told his top people, so she couldn't confide her horrid fears, not to anyone. And there they sat, making her break into cold sweats.

So, yes, Ali Baba was only one account, but the cold lump in the pit of her stomach would *not* go away. Was this just the beginning? No, she would not think that way . . . although, it had to be faced, she *was* forty-four almost forty-five. Oh Jesus, forty-five! That was halfway to fifty! And *fifty*, that was halfway to oblivion!

Stop it Natalie! Oblivion indeed! She knew damn well that at thirty paces, she could easily be taken for a woman of thirty.

Well . . . make that fifty paces and a woman of thirty-five. But hell, she looked *good*. Her hair was still dark, almost black, curly and glossy with only a stray white strand or two; she didn't have a weight problem, was still built small and taut, thanks to good genes and a habit of running several miles a day; and dammit, she passed the acid test—she could get away with a bikini. No raving beauty, she, but then, she never had been. A short, dark, somewhat older Meryl Streep: that's how she liked to think of herself. And actually, what Jake had once described as her "peculiar brand of glamour" was still operative. She could still turn men's heads . . . and still did so! What difference did the actual number of years make? She was young— dammit, yes she was! Young and vibrant and sexy not to mention successful, scintillating, and single. Well . . . almost single. About to be officially single. Just as soon as the papers came through. Oh, lord, could she use a little drink right now. It would settle her right down. But no, a rule was a rule.

Jerry had accused her of being alcoholic. No such thing! Oh, she knew she sometimes drank a teeny bit too much; but, hell, it had been years since she'd needed that shot in her morning orange juice to clear her head. Nobody could say, these days, that Nat Simon couldn't hold her booze. She never got what you would call drunk. And anyway, Jerry had a nerve calling her anything at all. Hell, he'd called himself a husband, hadn't he?

She'd been living alone in a sublet apartment since February, two months now. But even before she'd moved out, their marriage had been all sham and pretense. He hadn't made love to her for three years—no, more like four. Four fucking years! Ha, more like four fuckless years—at least with him.

They had what the world liked to call "an arrangement." She slept with other men, and he didn't object as long as she was discreet. Ostensibly, it was all a deep secret in order to spare their daughter; but for Christ's sake, Melissa was fifteen, dating, and a typical New York City kid: sophisticated, shrewd, and knowing.

Natalie, as a matter of fact, had been thinking more and more that it was time to stop pretending for Melissa's sake;

time to get Jerry alone one evening and make him see it her way. "It's stupid to pretend we're intimate," she had planned to tell him. "It's stupid to keep on pretending that we have a marriage at all. Let's move into separate rooms." That was her plan and then, when Melissa went off to Miss Porter's in her junior year, they would try a separation. But the bastard beat her to it!

It was so like Jerry: the careful throat-clearing, the careful closing of the living room doors, the careful preparation of his pipe. She sat at the edge of her chair and drummed her fingers on the table, watching him tamp down the tobacco, noisily suck on the pipestem, light the match, puff and puff, take it out of his teeth and eye the bowl. She watched the whole goddamn ritual, holding in her temper, sipping her drink to keep from snapping at him to get *on* with it, for Christ's sake! Everything about him irritated her that night. Come to think of it, everything about him had been irritating her for quite a while—even the way he looked. And, the way he looked was why she had fallen for him in the first place. Jerry Weber was a solid, broad-shouldered, shambling big bear of a man, thirteen years her senior. When she'd first met him, she was a newly minted copywriter of twenty-three and he'd seemed so grown up and glamorous. Sitting at his ease in his big leather chair, calm and soft-spoken, yet full of authority, he had looked to her like the epitome of strength. And the pipe!—the wonderful professorial pipe constantly clamped in his even white teeth, sending up little clouds of blue smoke!—that was part of the picture.

Now she looked at him and noticed the ash that constantly sprinkled his chest from that wonderful pipe. Now she looked at him and saw wattles, wrinkles, bulging belly. From dynamic big bear, Jerry had aged into slovenly fat. As far as she could see, his appearance mirrored his mind. He had become more and more the self-assured and boring pedant, pontificating to her about every goddamn thing at stultifying length until, these days, she winced if she saw him preparing to speak. It had got so she could hardly bear to be in the same room with him.

Where had it all gone: the high hopes, the dreams, the plans for their future?

"You look like a fossil," she said; and when he shot her a questioning look, added, "You must be the last man on earth who still smokes a pipe."

He replaced the pipe in his mouth, puffed it, and talked through it. "You know, sweetheart, that's so typical"—puff, puff—"I hate to say this, but you do tend to get"—puff, puff—"nasty when you've had too much to drink."

"Oh, for Christ's sake . . . a lousy glass of wine is too much to drink?"

He smiled gently. "That's your sixth."

"But who's counting, right?"

"Sweetheart, sweetheart, I'm only talking to you because I have your best interests at heart. You're my wife, after all. . . ."

"In name only!"

He shrugged. "That's true. But beside the point. I still care about you. You're the mother of my child. And, in the eyes of the world, you *are* still my wife."

"Oh, God, Jerry! Get to the goddamn *point*, would you?"

"All right, I will." Suddenly, the pipe was in the ashtray. And suddenly, those soft eyes were flinty and the soft voice went hard. "The . . . ah . . . goddamn point, as you so delicately put it, is that your drinking has escalated. No, no, don't argue with me, I've been keeping very careful track. In fact, it's right back to where it was the last time we discussed it four years ago."

"You're wrong, Jerry. All right, maybe I'm drinking a *little* more than usual. . . . There's stuff going on at M & M I haven't told you about yet. . . ."

"Stuff?"

"Like Peter's talking acquisition of another agency." She was damned if she'd say word one about Daisy Villiers. Nor was she about to mention Peter's lecture to her about how four vodka martinis at lunch could be dangerous to life, limb, and career.

"Another agency? I doubt it. You know how Peter runs off at the mouth."

"I don't know, Jerry. He told all his VPs. He sounds serious. He *acts* serious. And my job might very well be on the line. No, I can't just ask him. He's so damn volatile, you never know what's going to set him off. And anyway, I don't want him to know that I'm worried about it. You know Peter: The minute he thinks you're vulnerable..." And she drew an imaginary knife across her throat.

"But that's beside the point, also, Natalie. I'm sorry you're having problems at the office, but I made it very clear to you, four years ago, that I didn't want Melissa forced to contend with an alcoholic mother—"

"So holier than thou. How about Melissa's learning that a proper mode of behavior for a woman is to never get laid by her own husband? Huh? How about *that*? You think that's healthy?" And the minute it came out of her mouth, it was like a revelation. Goddammit, she had just, in a moment of anger, said a great truth. It was awful for Melissa to be living there and thinking that this sterile sham was a real marriage. Suddenly, it became very clear that divorce wouldn't destroy Melissa. Missy was a big girl now; she was a teenager! It would be much better for Melissa, she suddenly decided, for them to split now and be finished with it. And then, just like that, it became a decision, it became words coming out of her mouth, "Okay, Jerry, out I go." She delighted in his astonishment, quickly covered. Aha! she thought, gotcha!

"You don't mean that," he said.

"Oh, yes I do. Let's talk to Melissa right now. And then I'll move out."

Well, she'd done it, she'd done it right away. It had all been finished and over with very quickly—almost too quickly? She sometimes wondered if perhaps she had panicked a bit, fearful that if she didn't move instantly, she might never move at all. But, what difference? It had to be done. The marriage was dead, and it was time she got out.

To hell with Jerry! She didn't have time to waste thinking about something that hadn't been viable for years. However, now her anger at Peter had drained away.

Never mind that she felt vulnerable; never mind that she

had her doubts about herself. She knew how to hide that stuff. She stopped in the hall a few steps from Martha J's office, rearranging her face and her mood. She had to be very careful. She was not going to let her old protégée see her looking less than supremely confident. It wouldn't pay to go in there and yell or cry. First of all, it wouldn't look good. It would make her look weak. And second, Martha J's secretary, a would-be actress, would have a complete performance of the entire incident worked out for the lunch-hour crowd. The gory details would be all over the agency (and back to Peter) at the speed of light. This time she would behave.

She took in a deep breath and marched to the office door. She was going to behave, yes, but goddammit, she'd *made* Ali Baba Bread! All by herself, with her brain and her energy. She'd taken four brothers and six cousins sweating in a tiny bakery on Atlantic Avenue in Brooklyn, and she'd turned them into a multimillion dollar business with distribution from coast to coast and their name (not to mention their bread) on everybody's lips. And in one moment it had been taken out of her hands, given away to someone else! She would hide it, okay, but she was hurt and mad.

She felt the usual nostalgic pang as she walked in—even though the decor had been altered, to say the least. In place of Natalie's favored plants, wicker, and basketry, there was black leather, African masks, zebra rugs, and a seven-foot palm. And standing next to the tree, looking almost as tall, hand on one narrow out-thrust hip, resplendent in a white jumpsuit with a red snakeskin belt and matching high-heeled snakeskin boots, was Martha J Jones herself.

"Well, hi there, boss lady," she said in her slightly husky voice. Mild as milk—chocolate milk—but was there something in her face, something uneasy, something guilty? Hard to tell. Martha J had the definite angled bone structure of an African mask. In repose, she looked cool, remote, and unreadable; in fact, if she didn't want you to know what was on her mind, you never found out. When she smiled, of course, it was very different. Her smiles spread across her face and crinkled her eyes. When she smiled—and she was smiling now—there was nothing to do but smile back. Natalie smiled back.

"You're a helluva lot faster than I am," Martha said, coming over to embrace her.

Against the smooth copper-colored cheek, Natalie said, "How so?"

"I was just on my way over to see you. . . ." She pulled back, radiant with pleasure. "I owe it all to you, you know."

Now she could *never* admit to Martha J that she had been, even for a split-second, mad as hell. God, no. There was more than a bit of hero-worship in Martha J. Natalie had hired her when not a whole lot of major middle-sized ad agencies were eager to take on black women. How well she remembered the fight she'd had with the other account executives, even Peter briefly. In high dudgeon, she'd gone home to tell Jerry. He'd certainly be on her side; he'd hired *her* when nobody wanted women period. And anyway, she wanted his input; he'd spent about a million years with M & M and he knew everybody inside and out.

But he had surprised her. Puffing on his pipe and frowning, he'd said, "Oh, I can see their point. . . . Now don't get in a huff, sweetheart, listen for a minute. We're talking about a beautiful young black woman. That means a lot of people perceive a problem for each of those attributes. (A) black—'They all have a chip on their shoulder'; (B) woman—Not all women are as clear-headed and businesslike as you are, Natalie; (C) beautiful—Well, you know full well what happens when a good-looking young female comes into a group. . . ." And he gave her a fatuous grin.

Oh, she knew what he meant. He was reminding her that years and years ago she had seduced him away from his boring wife, when she was his young good-looking copywriter and he was Jerry "Big Daddy" Weber, her copy chief. Yes, she remembered, but she was too annoyed to smile back at him. "Well, I don't care if they have more points than a porcupine, Jerry. Guess what? I'm going to have her!" And she had. She had prevailed and made them all sorry they had ever protested.

Three years ago, when Peter had given Martha J her own

group, her own accounts, and told her to hire her own secretary and a copywriter, too, Natalie had taken her out for a celebratory dinner. And over their third cocktail, Martha had said, "I know how you stuck your neck out for me when you hired me. ... No, no, don't pretend. I've got me a seventh sense that tells me every time someone is thinking 'nigger.' I know how you fought every-goddamn-body and I want you to know I'll never forget it. Look at me, do you see that?" And she pointed to the one fat glistening tear that was sliding down her cheek. "That's a rare diamond, Natalie, 'cause I hardly ever cry."

And, Natalie, fighting her own tears, had raised her glass and said, "Just make me proud of you, Martha J. That's all the thanks I'll ever need." God, she had been eloquent! But the sentiment was sincere. And now, it would be so unattractive for her to stamp her foot and whine.

"You've made me very happy," Natalie lied.

Martha J laughed her throaty laugh. "Oh, Jesus, you have no idea how relieved I am that you feel that way. God! I was so nervous, you can't imagine. Calvin yelled at me all yesterday. He kept telling me you wouldn't take it wrong. 'A together lady like Natalie Simon?' he said. 'No way, honey.' But you never said a word about it; so when I saw you appear in my doorway just now ..."

"You thought I was coming to yell and scream and stamp my foot and carry on?"

"Something like that. Silly, huh?"

"Yeah," Natalie said. "Silly." She silently congratulated herself for being smart enough to keep her mouth shut. It happened rarely enough these days!

"And besides ..." Martha J turned, went to her worktable, and picked up a printed sheet. "Besides, *this* came out this morning. ..."

"What? I hate to admit this, Martha J, but from this distance, I can't read a damn thing, not even that big red headline."

Martha J smiled. "That's not a big red headline, that's the big red name of the newsletter. You know: *The Ad Game*."

"Oh, yeah, I know it. Mostly gossip and every once in a while an interesting article ..."

"Everyone reads it; that's all *I* know. Not that anyone likes to admit it." She laughed. "Like all the people who read only the *Times*, but when they quote something, it's always the *News*. Anyway..." And she held it out. Natalie took it and Martha added, "Page three."

Natalie scanned page three, which was mostly a column called "Galley Proof," boxed with red lines and featuring the picture of a broadly smiling female face with a lot of curly hair, à la Harpo Marx. There it was:

Martha J Jones, one of the copy chiefs at M & M is flying mighty high these days... and we don't mean to imply an airline account. She's just taken over Ali Baba Bread, the pita company that's been growing as if someone put extra yeast into its dough, and will next be moving into the franchise business. Everyone in the biz knows Martha J is an expert on franchising, ever since she made her mark with those Romance Bookmobiles you see everywhere these days.

"Very nice," Natalie said. "How did this blond broad find out so fast?" And then, of course, she knew. "Oh, Martha J! You didn't!"

"I confess. I did. Not on purpose, Nat. I know her—her name is Bambi Hirsch; by the way, she *owns The Ad Game*. ... Anyway, we were having lunch a couple of weeks ago and I was all excited about it and—I hope you're not mad at me."

I wish you hadn't, Natalie thought; but aloud she said only, "Of course not. Don't worry about it." Then she had to leave quickly because she was getting mad again.

She zipped on down the hall, telling herself, Look, Nat, you've been in this business thirteen years, give or take a century, and nothing yet has ever been able to keep you down, nothing! And nothing ever would. She wouldn't allow it. Arriving at the test kitchen, Natalie sailed right past Barbara's assistant who was fussing over a dozen dishes of butterscotch pudding and wouldn't have noticed an atomic explosion. She headed for the big Garland range where Barbara stood studying batches of bubbling pancakes.

"Mix me up one recipe of poison—" she began; and then stopped abruptly. Barbara, calm, collected, motherly, serene Barbara, was standing there, her head bent, dripping tears onto the griddle. You could hear them sizzle as they dropped. "Barbara! What's the matter?"

"Oh, damn," Barbara said. "Can you believe this? Hal and I broke up two months ago and—for two months, I've been waking up every morning and crying. This morning, no tears. Hooray, I said, it's over, the period of mourning is over. And now, out of the blue, out of nowhere, I swear I wasn't even thinking about him, just watching these damn buckwheat pancakes do their thing . . . and boom! Or rather, drip-drip." She sniffled a little and gave Natalie a wan smile.

Even with her lips quivering and her eyes red-rimmed, Barbara was undeniably lovely. Natalie marveled. There was something about Barbara beyond beauty. She was womanly, that's what, but just in case anyone might think that "womanly" meant "matronly," oh, no. Barbara had her own kind of appeal. How well she remembered her first meeting with Barbara, four years ago, the day she hired her as a food assistant. She had been so impressed with the woman's composure, with her sense of herself—something Natalie often felt she herself lacked.

Not to mention the even, all-American features: the tilted eyes, the regular nose, the thick, shiny dark-blond hair. Not to mention her body, which was full breasted, slim-hipped, and long-legged—all attributes the young and not-so-young Natalie Simon had yearned for. What was really wonderful about Barbara Valentine, she suddenly thought, was that her insides matched her outsides. She was as nice as she was pretty, and she was always a good friend. God, how many hours had she spent listening to Natalie's woes, and never never making judgments.

"Where's your supply of cooking wine?" Natalie said. "You and I both need, and want, and deserve a drink."

"Natalie! a drink! It's not even 9:30."

"Well, damn the sun and damn the yardarm and anything

else you can think of." She went poking into the cupboards, opening and closing doors impatiently. "Where is it?"

Barbara did something or other with a spatula and said, "Wait a second. Let me turn off the gas and then let's talk seltzer. Or Perrier. Or . . . I know!" she said brightly. "Sunshine orange juice! That ought to set us up! Your nice new account . . . Peter must be so pleased with you. It's the biggest new one since the mattress account came in, and that was months ago. So how come you're dying to poison him this morning? If you'll pardon the pun."

"I'll pardon the pun. But Peter's a different matter. Peter is a royal pain . . ."

"So what else is new?"

"What's new is me losing an account: my oldest, my dearest, my most precious account, might I add."

"Oh, Nat. No matter how well prepared we think we are, change is always so hard."

"What do you mean: *prepared*? It was sprung on me just this morning! Martha J, my very own protégée who should be on her knees kissing my feet for Christ's sake . . . she took it away, she connived with Paul Hasahni and she took away my baby, my Ali Baba bread, of which 'forty thieves couldn't steal the flavor . . .'" She stopped, a bit choked. "I remember when Grandfather Hasahni *gave* us that slogan, Barbara. That's *my* account and Martha J stole it."

"Is that what Peter told you? Because, if so, then Peter is up to his old tricks, playing with people just to see what they'll do under pressure. . . . Is that really what Peter told you? I'm having Perrier. You really don't want cooking wine, do you?"

"No, I'll have good old Sunshine OJ. As good old Tommy Thoms always says . . ."

"Client loyalty above all else," Barbara finished in a sonorous tone that was a not-bad imitation of Tommy's fruity Connecticut speech. "Oh, we shouldn't pick on poor Tommy; he *is* one of our better account execs. . . ."

"At least one of our longest-lasting account execs," Natalie said, taking the glass and sipping. Then she dragged in a breath and admitted, "Actually that's not what Peter told me. What he actually *told* me is that Paul Hasahni asked for the transfer—"

"But Nat—"

"Let me finish. Paul *asked* for Martha. It seems I'm too damn high-powered, high-priced, and high-everything to spend enough time on it. And also..."

"And also?"

Natalie took a sip of the juice. "And also, it was Martha J's brilliant idea to put them into the fast-food business with her Pita Parlors—and so she gets the whole damn account—after my thirteen years!"

"I understand why you're upset, Natalie. But that's not unreasonable. The Hasahnis apparently want to put all their efforts into making Pita Parlors a chain across the country.... The original one in Wall Street did so well."

"I don't care. Goddammit, that was *my* account. The least Paul could have done was to tell me, to *warn* me, to give me a hint at the very least—" She stopped suddenly at the puzzled look on Barbara's face. "What's the matter?"

"Natalie." The puzzlement turned to pain. "He *did*."

"Who? Did what?"

"Paul. He *told* you. I heard him, we all heard him."

"When?"

"At the Christmas party—don't you remember?"

Natalie felt a cold chill creep down her spine. "I—I—no. No, I don't."

"He said, 'If this goes, Nat, I'd like to take it off your shoulders—' You really don't remember? Because, when he said he didn't think the franchise fast-food business was quite your thing, you said, 'Right you are, Paul, as usual.' You don't remember any of it? And then he kissed you and said, 'I'm so glad you see it that way. Martha J will be perfect. And after all, why not, look who trained her!' And you turned to us and said, 'I may cry, everybody. Isn't he a doll!' I'm sorry, Natalie, but that's exactly what happened."

"Oh, shit!" Natalie groaned.

There was a pause, and then Barbara said, very carefully, "You really don't remember."

"That's right. I really don't." They eyed each other for a moment. Natalie forced a laugh and quickly added, "Not only do I not recall, but I can't believe it. 'Isn't he a doll!' Oh, really!" She rolled her eyes. "No wonder I don't want to remember! Me saying something that flirty-poo. Ugh!" This made them both laugh. Then Natalie, in an entirely different tone of voice, said, "My memory's none too wonderful these days . . . age, I guess."

"Don't be ridiculous! You're the same age I am and I'm fine, so that means you are too, so there!"

"You're a good friend, Barbara."

She made some more polite noises and began to back out of the test kitchen. She might have promised to have lunch the next day; she couldn't be sure. Her mind was dithering with panic. Oh, my God, I forgot an entire conversation, *the whole damn thing. Again.* She fought off a feeling of dizziness, gulping in deep breaths as she hurried down the hall, head down, thoughts racing. Oh, my God, it was happening too many times. How many?— Never mind. Never mind, she didn't want to know. She wanted to get back to her office, back to where she could lock the door and be by herself and fight off this growing terror.

It was frighteningly like that night. In March, she was letting herself into her sublet apartment, feeling just fine, a little tired, that's all, but feeling fine. She was groping in the dark for the still unfamiliar placement of the light switch, swearing a little and laughing a little at her ineptness. And suddenly it hit her. She was not coming home; she was coming to someone else's apartment with someone else's history and someone else's memories. If she couldn't find the damn light switch, she'd never be able to find her way across the room. Because it wasn't *her* room. She was in a totally strange place.

Frantically, she searched and at last found the switch. And with the lights on, her heart sank even further. God, what a horrible place! The rooms were too small and the ceilings too low, and, what made it worse, all the walls were painted either black or dark purple, with carpeting to match. It was positively funereal. What the hell was she doing here, in this gloomy place, sitting on someone else's dun-colored sectional, staring at someone else's depressing artwork, sleeping in someone else's too-soft bed? What ever had possessed her to try to make a home in this weird godawful place? This was no home. Hell, she *had* no home any more.

That's when the bottom had fallen out of her stomach, the same feeling as being on a plummeting elevator: gasping for breath, empty and sick. She was surprised at herself. . . . Surely, after all these years of fooling around and thinking of Jerry as that pain in the ass who lived in her apartment, she should be elated. Instead, the only feeling she could discern was emptiness.

Now the future loomed before her, a long dark featureless tunnel, the mystery wrapped in an enigma at the end. What was left for her, in her life, at her age? Already she could see the signs: the small network of lines that radiated out from her eyes. . . . Oh sure, now she could cover them up with W-1 Camouflage Cream; but that wouldn't work forever. And then there was the way she had to hold paperwork out at arm's length to read it . . . that hint of a pot belly that absolutely would not flatten out, no matter how much she ran or how many extra situps she did. Soon, *no* man would look at her with interest. Already, she had noticed that her younger copywriters, the boys in their twenties, didn't see her as an interesting female. She had become transparent, a pane of glass. She was the "boss lady," she was good old Natalie, she was—to her horror, over-heard late one afternoon—"the old lady." They should only know, those puppies! In their wildest dreams, they should only find a woman half as exuberant as Natalie Simon!

That's right! Natalie Simon! Who always got what she wanted, sooner or later. Come on, Nat, she thought, none of this gloomy stuff. So, she didn't have Ali Baba Bread any more, so what? Maybe it was time to let it go. Maybe it was fated. Maybe it was time to concentrate on bigger, more important accounts. So, she was having a few minor lapses of memory. Of course she was; she was under fantastic stress. On the stress scale, number one was loss of one's mate by death or divorce and number two was moving . . . or maybe it was number three. In any case, there she was, right on top of the chart. This memory thing would pass. In the meantime, she'd cut down a bit more on the drinking. What the hell. She was single, she was free, she was smart. And she was Natalie Simon, by God, the indomitable.

As she passed Peter's office door, she gave it the finger, and laughed out loud.

❀ 2 ❀

Little Natalie

Larry was sitting at his desk in the anteroom outside her office, his back as straight as a soldier's, typing so fast his fingers were nearly a blur. Even though she didn't feel like talking to anyone, Natalie came to a halt. Larry wasn't just anyone; he was a blessing, a gift from the gods, and also her very efficient, very quick-witted, very motherly secretary. Strange, but wonderful how Larry took care of her, fending off unwanted visitors, keeping track of her appointments, and checking her health on a daily basis.

Today he looked up at her, stopped typing, and said, "So? Did you remember to add those iron tablets like I told you? And the extra Cs? Just because it's getting onto summer, doesn't mean we can't catch cold."

Natalie smiled at him. TLC certainly came in odd packages these days. Larry was totally bald, with a weightlifter's body, a five o'clock shadow even early in the day, and a diamond stud in his right earlobe. Not everyone's notion of Mother! No, nor even everyone's notion of secretary! Ever since he'd started working for her, she'd been getting the business—mostly from men. "Have your boy call my girl" . . . "Your . . . ah . . . *secretary*?" . . . And, from Tommy Thoms, who was so WASP-y as to be a caricature of himself: "Natalie, are you sure this is an appropriate choice?" She loved him; and, incidentally, he was one helluva secretary! Her instincts, at least, were still good; she could still spot a winner. "Yes, yes, and yes," she said. "And that's right. And I'd like an hour of privacy. Think you can arrange that?"

Larry gave her a shrewd look. "What did he *do* to you?"

"Who? Oh . . . Peter?" She shrugged. "Come on, Larry, since when can I not handle Peter Marcus? Hell, I've known him practically forever and what's more I taught him everything he knows."

"God, Natalie, don't ever admit that to anyone else! He's awful!" Larry gave a shudder. He was not a Peter Marcus fan, probably because when he was first hired, Peter bluntly demanded: "Does the earring mean you're gay?" Of course, Larry hadn't batted an eye, but had blandly answered, "I like to keep my options open." Which had made Peter laugh. Oh, now Peter liked Larry, thought he was a super worker—which he was. But Larry had never forgiven him.

"Now, Larry," Natalie said, a warning in her voice, "remember. Peter is the Marcus of Marcus & Morrisey. Catch that name? the one on all your paychecks?"

"Gotcha, boss. But . . . why an hour? Usually you only need about twelve minutes to recoup from one of your meetings with him."

Oh, he thought he was so clever! "I'm not going to drink, Larry. I promise. Never again before noon."

But once inside, with the door firmly closed behind her, sitting in her soft leather chair and gazing out the window down onto Madison Avenue with its wall-to-wall traffic and hordes of pedestrians, she immediately thought, But I could sure use a drink. She could almost taste it, feel its friendly bite on the back of her tongue, its friendly warmth in the pit of her stomach.

But no. There was nothing worse in this world than a woman drunk. Oh, lord, she thought, swiveling in her chair, that's what Dad told me the first time I came home from college; and I've never forgotten.

She'd come back from Syracuse for the Thanksgiving recess, and, in fact, it was at the big Thanksgiving meal that she felt his eyes on her. There were always bottles of wine on the table at state occasions like this; and she was helping herself, feeling very much like a bigshot. She had just learned how to drink beer at various fraternity parties—in her high school, only the very bad kids, the greasers, drank anything stronger than Coke—

and it made her feel very grown-up. She liked the taste of the wine, too; it was much better than beer, she thought, sweet and real good.

She might have had two glasses, maybe three, when he spoke, his deep voice carrying easily down the table. "Haven't you had enough, young lady?"

"Who, me?" She really was startled. And a bit miffed. Hadn't she been on her own, the past two months? "I can hold it."

"You're not old enough to know if you can hold it or not."

"Oh, Dad! . . ." It was getting embarrassing, and all her cousins were finding this conversation very fascinating.

"Never mind 'Oh, Dad.' I'm going to tell you something, and I want you to remember it. There's nothing worse in this world than a woman drunk."

"I'm not drunk, for God's sake!"

"I know that, sweetheart. I just want you to be careful. You're my little girl."

Quite without warning, anger gripped her. "Oh really?" she snapped. "That's funny. Last night, when I wanted to talk to you about something, I was adult enough to handle it myself. And now, when it suits you, suddenly I'm a little girl."

"Natalie! for shame!" That was her stepmother, always on Dad's side, didn't matter if he was right or wrong.

"This isn't any of your business, Beth!" She watched with a kind of pleasure as the color drained from her stepmother's normally ruddy face. It was so easy to wound her; it was almost not fair to do it. On the other hand, she hadn't asked for a stepmother; a stepmother had been thrust upon her. And she certainly wouldn't have ordered this one: a plump, young, doughy nobody, straight off the farm.

"Natalie," Dad said, very even, very calm. Dad made a point of never losing his temper. "That was very unkind."

"That's me!"

He shook his head sadly and said, "You've become hard, Natalie, you've become cruel." And hanging in the air between them were the unspoken words: "ever since your mother died."

He was only partly right. She had changed since then, but

so had he. *Everything* had changed. She was startled—no, more than that, she was stunned—that Dad, who knew everything, never seemed to realize what he had done to her, how he had deserted her. Her perfect father, her beloved Dad, had this huge area of stupidness. She could hardly believe it.

Her earliest memories of childhood had to do with him and with his office, the big storefront office of the *Hampton Herald*, her town's weekly newspaper. Jonas Simon, Editor and Publisher, it said in carefully painted gold letters on the big plate glass window.

How well she remembered that office: the bare, worn wooden floors, the oak file cabinets, the desk right at the front where Mrs. Carpenter sat, taking classified ads, a telephone at her elbow. The afternoon sun would stream through the big window, illuminating dancing dust motes in the air and casting shadows of the gilt letters onto the floor. It was very clear in her mind because, from toddlerhood, she was brought there to play, sitting on the floor with the end of a roll of newsprint and a bunch of crayons, listening to the sound of male voices, punctuated by Mrs. Carpenter's typewriter, telephones ringing, and in the background the steady clack-clack of the big press.

She loved the *Herald* office. Everyone was nice to her there, and it was there that she learned that her father was probably the most important man in the world, if not the universe. Everyone came into that office, sooner or later, from the mayor to Doc Smith, the druggist, to Drunk Eddie, the local vagrant who came in to cadge a dime or a quarter nearly every day. Dad would always give Drunk Eddie his money, and always with the proviso that he spend it on food: "Food, Eddie, something to eat, not cheap muscatel." It didn't occur to her until years later that Dad knew Eddie wouldn't buy food, that it was just an old refrain.

As she got older she preferred going to the *Herald* after school rather than go home, where her mother would be busy painting a picture or practicing a sonata or digging in the garden or vocalizing or pinning fabric onto a dress dummy. Her mother would give her a vague smile and a light kiss and ask her if she had homework and would turn away, very involved in her creativity. Natalie no longer sat on the floor, but was given one of the scarred old oak desks to work at—one of the reporters' desks, her father used to say. Here she would do her homework and sometimes make up her own newspaper and later on, when she was eleven or twelve and it became apparent that she had writing talent—"a chip off the old block," Dad would brag— she even wrote simple stories for the *Herald*. She remembered very well the thrill of seeing her own words appear as if by magic in type on the page, telling the world that Mr. and Mrs. Simpson of Clark Street had had relatives visiting over the weekend, or that Jim Conroy was the bowling champion of the Masonic League, or even, once, how the local cop had chased a speeding driver all the way to Grove's Corners.

Even today, she could evoke the smell of the place: a mixture of printer's ink, dust, cigars, bay rum, and Mrs. Carpenter's talcum powder. She had only to close her eyes to see Dad, in shirt sleeves and vest, leaning back in the big oak swivel chair, running his fingers through his thick, dark hair, crinkling up his eyes to little slits when he laughed, which was often. He was some laugher. He loved a good joke. He loved to fish and to hunt, he loved billiards, he loved a good joke and a good story and a good cigar. Everyone said wasn't it a shame Jonas Simon hadn't had a son. She heard it all the time. It struck her only years later how often adults either forgot she was there or thought she wasn't listening; or didn't know that it might bother her. Dad certainly didn't have the least notion that it hurt her feelings, because he always gave them the same answer: "Natalie's as good as most boys."

And she had loved that! She had felt it was praise above and beyond anything she could possibly deserve! To be as good as most boys! And to be thought so by Dad! It always made her feel so proud, and for a while after she'd heard it, she'd strut around like she saw boys doing.

One day her mother caught her walking like a boy and called her over, and asked her why she was walking funny. She was terribly embarrassed, but she finally admitted what it was. "You don't want to walk like a boy, Natalie. You're eleven years old and you're a girl. Soon you'll be a young lady and you'll want

to walk gracefully, like a lady." Like fun I will! Natalie thought.
If there's one thing I never want to be, it's a lady. She knew
what ladies were like and it was boring. Ladies always dressed
up, if they weren't in their aprons, and they behaved and they
never ran or skipped, and they stayed in the house a lot and
when they talked, they either whispered, which was annoying,
or else they talked about you and how you were growing and
all your personal business, or else about dumb stuff like babies
and cooking and stuff like that. No way was she ever going to
grow up and be like that! When she grew up, she was going
to be a newspaper reporter or a foreign correspondent. And
then her mother said something that caught at her. "Ladies are
gentle and ladies are soft and ladies are pretty," she was saying.
And Natalie said, "Mommy, am I pretty?" and her mother
paused for just a moment too long before she answered, "You
have beautiful eyes."

That's when she first realized she wasn't pretty. She knew
she was skinny; everyone was always saying they couldn't see
her at all if she turned sideways. But heck, she was as good
as most boys.

And pretty *didn't* matter to her, not at twelve and not at
thirteen and not even at fourteen. Because she was Dad's fishing
companion and his bowling companion and his movie companion—especially after her mother became ill and began to
spend a lot of time in bed, even during the day.

It all changed so suddenly. One day, when she let herself
into the *Herald* office after school, it was empty. Mrs. Carpenter was not at her desk smoking Camels one after the other.
None of her father's cronies was hanging around. Even George
and Frank, the two printers, were missing and the big press
was quiet. Dad had his dark suit on, and he looked strange as
he told her that Mommy was very very ill and Natalie was
going to stay with Grandma Simon out at the farm for a little
while—at least until Mommy was better. There was something
strained about his voice, and when Natalie asked what was
wrong with her mother, he became angry and told her she was
asking too many questions. And when she went to him for a

hug, he shook his head—the first time she could ever remember it—and said, "Not now, Nattie. I just can't."

She didn't come back from Grandma Simon's until her mother's funeral, that horrible, bleak, black day, and then he wouldn't allow her to stay home. He looked gray and drawn and so far away. She really could never remember much about that day or the four months that followed when she stayed with her grandmother. It was as if she had wiped that time completely out of her memory.

Her next vivid image was of her father, facing her in the back hallway of their house, of how strange it looked to her because she had been gone so long, and his saying, "I have a surprise for you, Natalie," and there, suddenly, behind him, was a plump little blond woman, smiling and flushed. And clinging to her leg, a little boy, also blond, with a smudge on his chin. That smudge was probably etched forever into her consciousness; she must have stared and stared at him. Her father was going on, saying, "This is Ralph. He's your brother now." "He's my what?" "Yes, yes, Natalie," Dad said, impatient. "Haven't you heard anything I've said? This is Beth, my wife. This is your new mother."

Then she'd suddenly come to life. Something, a feeling of sickness, rose in her throat. She'd thought she would choke on it. She stared at this strange woman and her little boy. Mother? "No, she's not!" she shouted. "She's not, she's not, she's not! She'll never be my mother!" And she'd run upstairs to her room, ignoring Dad's angry commands for her to stop this instant, to come back this instant, to apologize this instant, and she'd slammed the door as hard as she could. And when a picture on her bedroom wall fell to the floor, its glass shattering into a thousand pieces, then she'd begun to cry.

It must have been some weeks later—she would never be sure because everything blurred into everything else during that strange, dislocated time—that she had let herself into the smoky newspaper office, put her books down, and headed for the press room. She'd been hanging out with the printers ever since she was old enough to learn the California Job Case, and George, the boss printer, let her set headlines by hand sometimes.

This time, though, Dad's voice had halted her. "Hold on there, Natalie. Where do you think you're going?"

"Just in back, to mess around with George and Frank."

Her father cleared his throat. "Come here, Natalie." And when she was standing in front of him, he cleared his throat again. "Your mother and I . . . *your mother and I*, she *is* your mother now . . . are concerned about you . . . um . . . messing around with Frank and George."

"Why?"

"Natalie, you're a young lady now."

"Oh, Dad, I'm exactly the same as I was last week."

"No. No, you're not. It's been pointed out to me that . . . um . . . that you're no longer a child. . . ."

"Yeah. And so?"

"And so it's not right, it's not a good idea, for you to hang out in the press room. Hampton's a small town; people will talk."

People will talk? she remembered thinking, very puzzled. "What will they talk about?"

"Was that a wisecrack?"

"Wisecrack! No, I just don't get it."

He heaved a great sigh. "Dammit, I wish your mother would have talked to you about this . . . your stepmother . . ." There was a long pause, and then he said, "You know . . . you have the body of a woman. . . . You . . . you're beginning to grow up, Natalie. You're not a little girl anymore. You're . . . well, you're a young woman . . . attractive to men."

"Frank and George don't think so."

His lips thinned. "It doesn't matter, Natalie. I forbid you to go into the press room any more."

"But why?"

"Oh, hell, Natalie. You know what I mean."

"But what you're saying—it's silly."

Then he got angry. "You're being a fresh-mouth and I don't appreciate it. If you can't show me the respect I deserve, maybe you shouldn't come here at all any more."

Tears sprang into her eyes. "That's not fair!"

"I'm warning you, young woman . . ."

"Well, it's *not*! Ever since Mommy died, you've been terrible to me!"

"That's a lie!" he thundered. "You apologize for that!"

"No, I won't! It's true, it's true!" She whirled and dashed out of the office, slamming the door behind her, heart hammering with fright. Surely, he would come after her. He would be furious . . . maybe. And maybe he would be sorry . . . maybe. But surely, surely, he wouldn't let her leave him like that. They had always been able to talk things out; he had always told her that she should count him as a friend—"No matter how old you get, Nattie, remember, you always have your old Dad." And she had hugged him that time, saying, "You're not old, you're not!" She remembered thinking fiercely to herself that she would never allow him to get old.

She had walked as slowly as she could, up North Main Street, past the feed store, past the creek, past Llewelyn's Ladies' and Children's Clothing, past the high school. And her father never came after her. With every step she took, she felt sadder and sadder.

When she heard her name called, she turned quickly, smiling. But it wasn't Dad; it was only Jack Henderson who sat behind her in English class. He had his bike, walking it along, slightly out of breath. Her first reaction was disappointment; then she was annoyed because she didn't particularly want to make conversation. And then she saw something in his eyes, something new, she thought. Without really putting it into words, she realized that this boy, a boy she had known her entire life practically, found her pretty. He was *interested* in her, she knew suddenly. He was flirting with her. He was asking if he could walk her home, a good mile. And suddenly she wanted him to. Couldn't hang out with the printers any more? So what? Her father didn't want her in the office at all? She didn't care. Jack wanted to know if she'd like to stop for a Coke at the drugstore and she found her heart lifting. Sure she would. Maybe Dad didn't want her around any more, but Jack liked her company. Okay, Dad. Mentally, she thumbed her nose at him, at him and all the stupid people in that stupid town and their stupid talk. She'd give them something to talk about!

* * *

Her private phone rang shrilly, jolting her. God, she'd been really lost in her memories. She could, even now as she picked up the receiver, smell the *Herald* office smell . . . and the entire building had been torn down as part of urban renewal years ago. "Yes," she said, into the phone.

"But you don't care . . . nobody cares." Jake Miller. Of course Jake Miller. Nobody else would begin a conversation without preamble, without a hello; nobody else would just start in, as if he had just been talking to you a minute ago. It was one of Jake's very favorite *shticks*. Truth be told, it was one of *her* favorites, too. It never failed to charm her, and it didn't even matter what the hell he said. Or even that it had been two weeks since she'd left a message on his machine to call her immediately.

"Oh, Jake! Of course I care! I always care!" God, it was good to hear his voice, to have him carry on the way he always did. He always made her laugh. Of course there were moments when she did not appreciate that. There were moments when she wished to hell he would be serious about something for a change, instead of hiding behind a barrage of mockery and jokes. But she meant it; she did care about him. He was her favorite male person in the whole world . . . in spite of the fact that she must have been involved with a hundred and fifty men in her lifetime, in one way or another, mostly another, beginning with Jack Henderson and ending only God knew where or when.

"You don't care, you don't. I'm gonna prove it." He was grinning; she could hear it in his voice. "Bet you don't know what day it is."

"What *day*? Is it something special? You tell me, Jake. I *think* it's Thursday, and if it's Thursday, then this must be Marcus & Morrisey, purveyors of dreams and dealers in nervous breakdowns. But what else, I—"

His voice was lugubrious, as only Jake could do it. "Natalie. Be kind. It's . . . oh, hell, it's my birthday."

"Impossible! You don't have birthdays! You're Peter Pan and you never have to grow up."

"Fifty, Nat! Fucking *fifty* . . . and what the hell do I have to show for it? Two divorces, no kids, not even a dog to lick my boots! The apartment I live in isn't *mine*. . . . It's a depressing rental, Nat! And here I am, fifty fucking years old and you didn't remember. Well, at least tell me happy birthday."

"Oh, Jake darling! Let me meet you at the Silver Streak and buy you several thousand drinks and wish you the happiest of birthdays ever!"

"Shit, no, I *hate* birthdays! Especially mine! Especially when I'm fucking fifty! Why'd you have to mention it, anyway?"

"Jake, for God's sake!"

"I'm depressed. Oh, Jesus, I'm so depressed. . . ."

She did not say, That's how our last telephone conversation ended. She did not say, Grow up. She did not say, So what else is new? She didn't say any of the things she should have said, including, And why do you call me if you don't want to be nice? Instead, she cried: "Oh, Jake, I just had the most wonderful idea!"

"I hate wonderful ideas, especially when someone else has them."

"Jake, just listen to me for a minute. You're gonna love this."

"I hate love . . . well maybe not hate."

She sucked in a deep breath and let it out very very slowly. He *was* her beloved Jake, she had to remember that. And it *was* his fiftieth birthday—fifty! she couldn't believe it! So, very sweetly she said, "Listen, darling. I actually bought that house on Fire Island. . . ."

"What house?"

"*You* know . . . oh, Jesus, now don't tell me you hate houses on Fire Island. Just shut up for a minute. I'm making you an offer you can't refuse. I bought this house, and how about you sharing it with me? For the summer. The *whole* summer."

He laughed. "Can you promise to keep your hands off me? Because I just now came back from church and I've made a solemn vow to St. Jude or St. Jew, I never can remember, that I'll never have anything to do with women again as long as I live or until I'm fifty-one, whichever comes sooner. . . ."

Now she spoke through gritted teeth. "It wasn't a joke, my dear. I thought you might possibly enjoy spending a summer on beautiful, elegant, very desirable Fire Island."

"Enough! You just said a bad word. Desirable!"

"Oh, Jake, is it that bad?"

"Oh, don't worry about me, Nattie baby. I *shtup* . . . I shtup plenty. They're all after me, Nattie. I've grown into a fantastic and fascinating "older man." There are times I think I'm the only straight male left in the city of New York!"

"Look, Jake, what if I tell you I don't care if you're as crooked as a bobby pin. Come meet me at the Silver Streak and we'll have a drink. I'll talk you into coming to Fire Island, and you'll feel better. Honest. For you it's a chance to have a whole summer on Fire Island with all the pretty people. For me, it's a chance to pay my bills. What could be better?"

There was a long, long pause. Then, he said in a slightly muffled voice: "You know I hate the beach." He did not hate the beach—on the contrary, as she well knew.

"White man speak with forked tongue," she said as lightly as she could manage; but she was gripping the phone so hard her hand hurt.

"Ah, Nattie. I can't live with you all summer."

"Why the hell not? We were lovers for umpty-ump years. We've been friends just about forever."

Jake's voice changed slightly. "It's different now, Nattie honey." Now he was going to tell her he'd found his one and only love yet again.

"What do you mean . . . *different*?"

His laugh sounded self-conscious. "Well, see, now you're separated, Nat. When you were married . . . well, it was for fun, but now . . . Gee, Nat, you might propose to me. And we can't have *that*, can we?" He laughed again.

She sat very still in her big leather chair swiveling from side to side, trying not to hurt so badly.

"That's right," she said in her lightest tone. "I'm not married and you're not married, so what do you say I take you out for a drink? I'll even spring for dinner, since it's your natal day."

"Nah . . . can't. I have a date. In fact, I'm a little late for a meeting right now, so I gotta run."

Natalie held on to the receiver, listening to the hum of the dial tone, seething.

Share a house with Jake, indeed! What could she have been thinking of? Who needed it? He was such a big baby, such a royal pain. Besides, the whole point of her buying a house out there was spelled M-E-N. Oh, yeah, and it was also nice to have the sun, the sand, and the surf, if you cared for that sort of thing.

But she had to be crazy to bring a man out there. How would she ever meet anyone that way? No, no, if you felt you were going to have a problem paying your mortage—and she definitely felt she was going to have a problem—then the thing to do was to get another lady. Preferably another attractive lady so as not to scare the quarry away.

Another lady! Of course! What an idiot she was! It was right there, in front of her face the whole time, and she was just too damn dumb to see it.

She punched one of the multitude of buttons on her phone, and when Larry's gravelly voice said, "Yeah?" she twirled her chair around, smiling to herself in glee.

"Larry," she said. "Get me Barbara Valentine!"

❀ 3 ❀

In Paradise

"Isn't this lovely!" Barbara, hunkered down on her haunches in front of a round metal table which was half faded-green and half shiny-white, put down her wet paintbrush and threw her head back, eyes closed, sniffing in the salt air.

"That makes the three-hundredth time you've said that," Natalie laughed. "And once again, yes, it is. Isn't it lovely here!"

They were on Natalie's deck, the side facing the ocean, in jeans and T-shirts, painting the deck furniture, sipping large Bloody Marys, and exclaiming to each other over the delights of the Fire Island air, the Fire Island smell, the Fire Island sun, the Fire Island beach, the Fire Island dunes, the Fire Island surf, and the Fire Island peace.

"Yes, it is," Barbara agreed; and then added, "We've got to stop doing that."

"No, we don't," Natalie said. "Keep on saying it. God knows it's costing me enough. I want to be conscious of enjoying every second. So tell me again . . . isn't it lovely? Did I make the right decisions? Wasn't I wise to pauper myself, put myself in hock, and get in way over my head? Huh, Barbara? Wasn't I?"

Natalie reached over for her drink, sipping it with pleasure. She applied some white paint to a chair and then put the brush down, her eyes drawn once again to the view spread out below. Her little house sat directly atop a dune, and from this part of the deck, she could see a mile and a half up the beach and way out to sea to where the ocean blended in a band of haze with

31

the sky. Seagulls were wheeling and dipping near the shore, now gray, now flashing white as they turned in a group, crying out together. God, it was gorgeous—and it was all hers! And the bank's, of course.

Yes, she'd gotten in over her head; that was true. If she lost her job—God forbid, bite your tongue, don't even think it— but if she l—t her j—b, she'd be up shit creek without a paddle. She had to earn what she was earning, just to make the payments, and it wouldn't hurt if she got a raise. Then, maybe, she could start to go to the movies and eat out in a restaurant from time to time. It was really very tight. Dumb of her. Dumb, but maybe understandable.

All those years since Melissa's birth, she'd begged Jerry to rent a little house on the beach for the summer; but old stick-in-the-mud wouldn't hear of it. The sun wasn't good for him, there was poison ivy all over, and he hated the way people on Fire Island carried on. Now, goddamn it, she didn't have to ask him. She could do whatever she pleased.

And what she pleased was to take herself out to Fire Island on a bright chilly absolutely gorgeous day this past March. She was the only passenger on the tiny ferry that bounced through the Great South Bay. She watched the peaked roofs and undulating dunes of Paradise rise up, like a vision, right out of the water. The closer the boat came to the shore and the more detail she could see, the more enchanting it all appeared to her and the more excited she became. All that light and air and space and freedom . . . to be on an island, far far from her real life, from all those frustrations, from Jerry's elephantine and suffocating presence. She knew before she landed that she was going to find a house she loved, and as soon as she did, she was going to rent it.

It turned out she was the only prospect to come out to the hamlet of Paradise that Sunday . . . something about a bad weather forecast and she seemed to be the only living New Yorker who had missed it. The real estate agent, a plump woman in her fifties named Margie who laughed every other sentence, was delighted to show her everything. Deserted now for the most part, Paradise looked clean and crisp and vivid, like a picture on a postcard. Like Paradise, in fact. The air smelled fresh, and the houses all spoke silently of long summer evenings, lazy days on the sand, cocktail parties on the deck when your skin tingled pleasantly of sunburn, and lovemaking to the thudding rhythm of the breakers.

The insides of the rental houses were not so promising though: musty, damp, crammed with ugly old maple castoffs. One after the other, she looked, shook her head, rejected them, feeling let down and disappointed. Until the agent chirped, "Well, Ms. Simon, that's about it. I do have one for *sale*...."

"I wasn't really thinking of buying."

"Well, maybe the owner would consider a rental with an option to buy. It's a charming house."

"No, no. I'm not in the market to buy."

"Ms. Simon, you owe it to yourself not to leave Paradise without seeing it. I've been watching you today.... You've fallen in love with Fire Island, haven't you?"

"That's right. Of course, I've been on Fire Island before."

"Ah, but there's a light in your eyes, Ms. Simon. I've been selling real estate out here for thirty years, and I know what people want, sometimes before they know it themselves. I get the feeling you're ready to put down roots.... So many of my fast-track women clients feel that way. I think you'll want to see this house I'm talking about."

Now, how could anyone in advertising resist that pitch? So, within ten minutes, she was being marched up the ramp of a smallish, modernish, grayish house perched atop a dune. Natalie looked at it as carefully as she could and found herself wondering what the shouting was about. It was nice—not too big, and a peek through the windows at the front showed lots of neat built-ins—but what was the woman waxing so poetic for?

And then they walked around the deck and there it was: white sand beach, white-capped surf, white-clouded sky—all of it spread out as far as she could see.

How wonderful it could be, living here all summer long, with the quiet and the space and the ocean and the sky. And the men. Because Margie, the real estate agent, was saying, "And there's a lovely singles community here in Paradise—

not the kids, Ms. Simon, oh, no, but older, successful executives, like yourself." Natalie's imagination immediately put a group of silver-haired broad-shouldered executive types right here on the deck, lounging on black and white striped deck chairs—she'd recently seen them displayed at Jensen-Lewis—sipping their tall drinks and fighting ever so subtly for her attention. She had to smile at this idyllic picture. Still...

"Let me see the inside," she said.

"Oh, I knew it. I just knew it!" Margie crowed.

Inside it was neat and open and flooded with light. One wall was all windows, overlooking the ocean. The living room flowed into the dining room and kitchen, and everything was white and pale oak... very different from the big, warm, rambling apartment near Central Park West where she and Jerry had lived for so many years.

Margie was going on and on about the view, and the workmanship and the convenience and... "But where are the bedrooms?" Natalie asked. They were down a curving flight of stairs, which for some reason charmed her. In fact, she was becoming more and more charmed by the whole idea with every passing moment. In fact, she was falling in love.

What in the hell was she doing, falling in love with an overpriced house on Fire Island, a house, furthermore, totally different from any place she had ever lived! But already she was seeing herself in it, seeing herself so clearly. Her own house! Hers! And in a community where it would be simple to meet people.

One of the scariest things about being separated was that she was on her own, naked in a way before the world. Funny how easy it was to hide behind the safety of being Natalie Simon, Married Woman, Wife of Jerry Weber. What it meant was that no rejection need be a real rejection... because, hell, she had a husband, and anything extracurricular didn't matter really. She could run around as much as she liked, put herself out there, and if someone turned his back on her, to hell with him, she *had* a husband, she'd already proved once and for all that she was desirable.

Now, as she had painfully discovered, she was simply Natalie

Simon; and the few times that she'd come on to a man and bombed . . . well, she had not been prepared for the agony. She hadn't realized how much of a cushion the fact of Jerry had always been for her, like a big warm quilt that kept her from feeling the chill of "No thanks, you don't appeal to me."

If she were here, in this house, in the town of Paradise, Fire Island, she would be Natalie Simon, Homeowner, Resident, Taxpayer. She would belong, automatically, without having to work at it. She could just imagine the looks on people's faces when she casually asked if they'd like to spend a weekend with her in Paradise. Oh, it was too good to turn down! And never again would she be tempted, as she had been last week—for five minutes—to go back to Jerry. She had thought at the time that what she missed was not the warmth and comfort of his embrace, but rather the warmth and comfort of her leather couch and her big rolltop desk and the Oriental rugs she had bought at auction.

And now she was sure. Of course, that's what it was. She was missing a place of her own. And here was her golden opportunity, right here, this day, this hour. Oh, the parties she would throw! She'd make this house the center of activity, she'd make this house the place everyone wanted to come to, she'd make this house special. Already, just thinking about it, her heart lifted. Who the hell cared about eggplant-colored walls and other people's depressing taste? None of it would matter when she had her own house on Fire Island!

"How much?" she heard herself ask and never even listened to the answer; because, if she had, she would never have said "I want it." Would she have? But say it she did, and it was only a matter of weeks until she was driving out on the Long Island Expressway for the closing, sweating in the rented car, struck with the sudden realization that she was now beholden to Emigrant Savings Bank for the next thirty years, for a sum of money each month that could probably support the entire nation of Liechtenstein.

"I certainly made the right decision, didn't I, Barbara?" she repeated now. "Reassure me."

"I only wish I had the money to get *myself* a house. It's so love— No, I have just made myself a solemn vow I'm not going to say how lovely it is, again. Not today. We have a whole long weekend ahead of us; I want to save a few superlatives for later. I *hope*." They both laughed.

"Oh, I understand there'll be plenty of men at Happy Hour. Which reminds me, you won't forget about my age?"

"Your age? Oh, you mean, your *new* age."

Natalie gave a little snort of laughter. "I never thought I'd stoop to that kind of stupid social lie. Honest Nat Simon, right? But it's different, being there. I've read the personals in *New York* magazine and now I know the revealed truth of the 1980s: Nobody Wants a Woman in Her 40s. So, okay, I feel dumb about it, a little, but please remember, okay?"

Barbara laughed. "Of course, Nat. Thirty-nine and holding. I don't know . . . it's beginning to sound good to me. Maybe I'll decide to do it, too. Oh, hell, let's just hope it doesn't come up. Look, grown-up men just don't go around peering into women's faces, saying, 'How old are you *really*?'"

"From your lips to God's ears, Barbara dear." Natalie sipped her drink and picked up the paintbrush again. But she was feeling restless, somehow. She didn't feel like painting. "Let me refresh those drinks," she said. "And maybe I'll find some music on the radio."

As she stood up, stretching her legs out, a voice pierced the quiet. "Yoo-hoo, up there! Yoo-hoo!"

It couldn't possibly be for her; nobody in Paradise knew her except for Margie, the real estate lady. She looked toward the voice and it insisted: "Yes, Natalie Simon of M & M! Hi there!" Down on the boardwalk, at the foot of the ramp, stood a blond woman and two men, all dressed alike in tight designer jeans and Merona Sport sweaters. "Look at that, Barbara, the Bobbsy triplets," Natalie said quietly.

"What?"

"Didn't you hear that? That woman down there just called my name. She knows me. But I don't know *her*. Do *you* know her?"

Barbara got up, massaging her lower back with her hands,

and said, "I don't think so. . . ." But instantly, the voice caroled: "And Barbara Valentine! Oh, good! We'll all eat splendidly this summer in Paradise!" Tinkling laughter followed.

"Who the hell is she and how does she know us?" This was said through a big smile as she waved down at the trio. "And who are those guys?"

"Search me."

Barbara waved, too, which the trio down there seemed to take as an invitation, because they all started up the ramp. And when they got halfway up, she recognized the woman.

"That's Bambi Hirsch," she said. "You know. The owner and editor of *The Ad Game*, the newsletter that comes around every week."

"Of course," Natalie said. "She looks just like her picture, doesn't she?"

Barbara had to smile at that. *The Ad Game* specialized in photos of Bambi Hirsch smiling broadly in the company of whatever advertising celebrity she could snag. She was a public relations natural. Barbara had seen her, very casually, at a couple of business functions: a seafood press party; an autograph session in Barnes & Noble—stuff like that. Bouncy and blond—of course, you couldn't miss Bambi Hirsch. She was the supreme mixer, always with a glass in her hand, whizzing around chatting people up, flashing that big broad smile. And laughing. Almost always laughing. She had a rather loud laugh, Barbara recalled. Not exactly her own style, but, come on . . . it took all kinds. It was admirable, actually, throwing yourself out there with such persistence and enthusiasm.

"Hi there! Welcome to Paradise. Owning or renting?"

"The ramp is mine," Natalie said. "The rest belongs to Emigrant Savings Bank."

Bambi laughed and said, "That's cute! Isn't that cute?" and Barbara had the feeling she didn't like Natalie's quick clever answer.

"I'll answer that," Natalie said. Oh, that Natalie, you couldn't outmaneuver her; no way! "That's right. I'm known far and wide as Natalie Cute."

The two men laughed with pleasure, and the shorter one.

the fair one, the one with the beard, stuck his hand out and said, "And I'm Fred Adorable; this is Jay Fantastic and Bambi Ebullient. You *are* cute. Will you marry me? No? Well, then, will you come to Happy Hour with us?"

"Do I only have those two choices?" Natalie's voice had changed—not a lot, but it was now just the least little bit throaty. Not only that, Barbara noted, but she was tossing her head and opening her eyes wide. In short, she was a woman flirting. Well, why shouldn't she be? That's what they were out on Fire Island for! But it had been a long time since Barbara had watched Natalie Simon in action. She wasn't sure she liked it. It looked a little silly, actually. Was it possible that this guy, Fred, would go for it? He certainly seemed to; he was doing his own little dance, crinkling his eyes, and laughing a bit too loudly. Was this how fast social life here was going to move? Because it if was, she wasn't at all sure she could handle it. She'd done it before, after she'd left Mark; she'd done it and she hadn't liked it then. The plain truth was, she wasn't very good at flirting, at coming on to a man, at making herself unutterably desirable and wonderful. Maybe she wasn't competitive enough. . . . It didn't matter. It made her uncomfortable. For the three years she'd been out there on her own after the divorce, she had finally ended up only going out with men she met through her friends or through work.

And that's how she had met Hal Pedersen: at the Food Show in Washington. She'd fallen for him, immediately and completely—a dumb thing for a grown woman to do, probably. After their first meeting, she hadn't had a shred of doubt; either that, or she hadn't allowed herself any doubts. She had often wondered: Why then and why him? He hadn't bowled her over with charm and wit. All he'd done, really, was a very simple thing: He'd picked up some papers she had dropped and returned them to her. But oh, the way he did it! Smooth.

She'd kind of noticed him all day—very tall, very nice-looking, bearded, and tanned—as their paths crossed; but no bells rang.

And then, suddenly, he'd just materialized in front of her,

saying, "Hi, Barbara." She remembered thinking, Have I met him and forgotten? Oh, no, couldn't be. Her mouth must have been hanging open, because he laughed aloud and held out a sheaf of papers saying, "I figured you'd miss these, sooner or later." It was a bunch of her own scribbled notes, on her own FROM THE DESK OF BARBARA VALENTINE memo paper. And then she had thought, How clever of him. And it *was*. In any case, he was willing to put forth a bit of effort; and she remembered very clearly that, at that precise moment, she thought, Well, well, this might turn out to be *something*.

She babbled, "Oh thank you . . . yes . . . yes, I would have . . . missed them, that is. Thank you, thank you." And thought: Shut up, Barbara, that's three thank-yous and that's quite enough.

And then, he grinned down at her—*down* at her, she who was five feet seven in her stocking feet—grinned down and said, "That's three thank-yous and I only did one thing. And that means I owe you two. How about a drink and dinner?"

The rest, as the saying goes, was history. Here at last was a man who was in charge, who was ready, willing, and able to take matters into his own capable hands, thank the lord. The men she'd been dating lately, it seemed to her, were all so passive, to the point of being wimpy. She was tired of dealing with depressed men, absolutely exhausted. Hal seemed a dream come true.

And now Natalie was poking her, giving her a funny look. "Barbara? Are you with us?"

"Sure, sure." She put on her best smile—she hoped. What was the matter with her anyway? There were two attractive, presentable, apparently decent men standing on this deck, and all she could think of was how much she missed Hal and how much she would appreciate it if those two men and Bambi Hirsch and Natalie would only all go away to Happy Hour and leave her alone. But that was stupid. She was out here so that she wouldn't be all alone in her apartment, weekend after

weekend, wallowing in self-pity. She was here to meet people.
She broadened her smile.

"Sorry . . . what were you saying?" she asked in her brightest
voice.

Natalie said, "We were saying we're all going to go together
to the local watering hole, Bob's Bar, and see what's doing."

"You guys go ahead. I'll finish painting the table."

"Barbara!" Natalie gave her a hard look. "The painting can
wait; our social life won't. Come on, let's change to *our* brand
new white pants and sandals!"

"I'm kind of tired, actually."

"Well," Natalie said, an edge to her voice, "I'm certainly
not going without you."

That was a bit unfair, Barbara thought. She really didn't feel
like going out to a strange place to drink too much and make conversation with a whole bunch of strangers, the object: to find a
man. And now she *had* to; there was no gracious way for her to
say no, not when Natalie's going depended on her. Damn! Later,
they'd have a talk, she and Nat. They couldn't do the entire summer in lockstep! Natalie was newly separated and in the market,
as it were, for a boyfriend. For herself, it was a very different
story. They'd have to talk it out and come to an understanding.
But in the meantime . . . there were the three people, still on the
ramp, looking eager and expectant, all combed and brushed and
washed and polished and ready for the singles scene. Oh, hell,
she couldn't spoil it for all of them.

Making her voice very bright, she chirped: "Well, then, I'm
going. Just let me get rid of some of this paint, okay?"

New drinks were concocted in the neat little galley kitchen,
and the two men ambled out onto the deck. Bambi Hirsch,
however, followed Nat and Barbara downstairs. Barbara didn't
quite know how to ask her not to. She wasn't *doing* anything,
just hanging around. But it made her uneasy that Bambi was
wandering around her room while she was in the shower, fin-
gering her photos and looking over her clothes. She changed
in the bathroom, feeling like a jerk, but unwilling to get dressed
and undressed in front of this total stranger.

And when she got back into her room, all finished except

to rebrush her hair and twist it up and find her sandals, there was Bambi, lounging comfortably on her bed.

"Oh, there you are. Natalie finished showering five minutes ago. Are those your children? They're awfully good-looking. And I love your clothes. It must be wonderful to be so tall; you can wear anything! When you're teensy-weensy like me, honestly! Everything in the world has to be custom-tailored to fit properly, just taken in and taken in!" Barbara swallowed a growing irritation and tried to smile with a whole heart.

She was relieved when Nat came in. Let the two of them chatter and leave her alone. She concentrated on doing her French knot, casually watching the two of them in the mirror.

"So Natalie, you're an owner here. From what I hear, that's the only way to go. From what I hear, you don't get invited to the good parties out here unless you're an owner. You've been around awhile; what made you decide now to go for the mortgage bit?"

The nerve! Barbara thought. Why, she as much as told Nat she's an old bag! She tried to catch Natalie's eye, but Nat was too busy telling Bambi the story of her separation, with its usual tagline: "It's a trial separation. He's a trial, so I'm sep-arating."

Bambi laughed. Of course; everyone always laughed. And then her face became very serious and concerned, and she jumped up from the bed to give Natalie a one-armed hug. "But I know just how you really feel, Natalie! It's so lonely and empty when you lose your dream!"

Locked into the hug, Natalie slid her eyes to catch Barbara's. As soon as their glances met, she waggled her eyebrows—a gesture so reminiscent of Jake Miller that Barbara had to strug-gle not to burst out laughing. Of course, Bambi didn't know Nat Simon; she had no way of knowing that Natalie Simon's favorite dream was to get as many different guys into the sack as often as possible. As for her husband: It was ludicrous to think of big, silent, slow-moving, slow-talking Jerry as any-one's dream!

"I'm ready," Barbara announced; but as the three of them

made their way up the stairs to the main floor of the house, she knew she was lying.

Bob's Bar was the one and only commercial establishment in all of Paradise. It sat, square, white-painted clapboard at the edge of the bay, just a few steps from the dock. At eight o'clock of the Friday of the first weekend of "the season," the noise of merrymakers floated out of all the windows as well as the big front door.

Inside it was indeed crowded, although it was kind of hard to tell when you first entered, in the dim light. The five of them hung around the entrance for a few seconds, not sure where to go. Natalie hated that feeling; she liked knowing her way around. But there was a first time for everything, wasn't there? Once her eyes became accustomed to the place, she could see that most of the tables were filled already. Of course they were. What else could have caused the din that filled the room and leaked out all over town?

Bob's Bar, she noted quickly, was of the let's-pretend-we're-aboard-a-jolly-ship genre, complete with captain's chairs, lots of mahogany, ships' lights, lanterns, and behind the bar, an enormous old carved wooden figurehead in the shape of a naked and very buxom lady. "I wonder if that's Bob?" Natalie murmured and was rewarded with laughter from her group.

Of course, every head in the place had turned to look over the newcomers. Natalie did her usual number. She drew in a deep breath, stood up as straight as possible, and stared back. Lots of men. Good. She spotted a couple of tables of women. Were they pretty? Were they *young*? You couldn't tell, in this gloom. A *frisson* of fear ran down her spine. What if every other woman in this town was in her thirties! What if she looked too old? Well, to hell with it. Just give her a drink and give her a chance.

"Me for the bar," she said.

"Then our back will be to all the action!" Bambi protested. "If you're going to do the singles scene, Natalie, you have to be center stage!"

Where *I* am is center stage, Natalie thought a bit belligerently; but aloud, she said, "I'll go with the majority."

And then Barbara did the right thing, as usual. She read Natalie's mind and went along. "I'm for the bar," she said firmly and went, seating herself on a stool. "Let them find *us*," she added. There was nothing to do but join her; and they all did.

Natalie was preparing to sit down when something large lifted itself from the floor directly in front of her, making her gasp. Then it shook itself and revealed itself as a very large and shaggy dog, which now opened its large mouth and yawned. "Get this monster out of here!" she snapped. She did not like dogs, especially not giant-sized.

"Oh, sorry, honey. Beat it, Annie, you're keeping the paying customers away." The bartender, a little leprechaun of a man, complete even to the pointed ears and curly fringe of red hair, leaned way over the bar and snapped his towel at the animal, who gave the man a look of disdain and ambled away toward the other end of the bar. "What'll you have?" said the bartender. "Name it, it's yours. On the house."

"Oh, well, then. Vodka on the rocks. Hell, I'd even sit down with Annie for a free drink!"

"Hush now . . . not where Annie can hear you. She'll hang around all night if she thinks she can get a drink."

Right at Natalie's elbow came Bambi's breathless gurgle. "Oh, don't tell us that dog *drinks!*" Her laugh ran merrily up the scale.

He slid his glance over to her and then jerked it back to Natalie, smiling. He got points for that, she thought, even if he wasn't playing the game. "Sandy taught her," said the bartender, laughing and gesturing down to the shadows at the other end of the bar. "Led her down the path of perdition and turned her into a goddamn drunk." He leaned closer to Natalie and said, "Nothin' uglier than a drunk woman." She pulled back a little. He'd better not think he could get instant intimacy with her on the strength of one free drink.

"Good evening." The voice was deep, rich, basso profundo, a voice which Natalie knew she could fall immediately in love with. She was a sucker for deep male voices—witness her unfortunate marriage to one. She squinted at the figure down there, only dimly discerned, and had to smile to herself. So what else is new? she thought. Cut from the same cookie cutter as Jerry . . . perhaps a tad heavier and with thicker hair and maybe taller. But, essentially, she was looking at another Big Daddy just like Jerry Weber or her name wasn't Natalie Simon. Stay away from him, she warned herself. But that voice!

She reached out for her drink and sipped it, turning in her stool to look into the center of the room. People were moving around from table to table, chatting and laughing; and the dance floor, a tiny space about the size of a telephone booth, was crowded. For a moment she felt lonely, looking at the scene and yet apart from it. How many weekends would it take, she wondered, before they all came to where Nat Simon was sitting to joke and gossip? If she faced it, this was really her debut into singlehood. All those years of fooling around didn't really count, because all those years, she knew Jerry was there. In fact, right after Jake took off for the West Coast, three years ago, she and Jerry had had a brief kind of honeymoon time, when he'd actually laid her a couple of times. And when she'd actually *wanted* him to!

But this was now and now her moment of truth had arrived. She was in debt and on her own, in Paradise on Fire Island; and her heart was hammering and her palms were clammy with sweat. Lunacy! If she should turn to Barbara now and tell her how scared she was, Barbara wouldn't believe it. "Who, *you*?" she'd say. "You, who told me how to put myself out there, who taught me the meaning of fearlessness?" That's right, Barbara, me, because you know what? Don't tell anyone, but I've been holing up in my dreary little sublet more than I care to admit and you know why? Because every time I put myself out there in Singlesland, I look around and everyone there is thirty-two years old!

And here was cute little Fred, jumping up from his stool next to her, bowing low and asking her to dance.

"Dance?" she repeated. "You mean, like when I hold you and you hold me and we move around to the music? Like that?"

"Like that," he agreed, laughing. Yes, she thought, if I live to be a hundred and I'm still single, it'll be okay, because I'll always be able to make 'em laugh.

She moved out onto the tiny space with him, thinking, God, I hope I remember how. Social life on Madison Avenue, which consisted, for the most part, of dining and wining clients you normally wouldn't be caught dead with, did not include tripping the light fantastic. And away they stumbled, she and Fred. And then, miraculously, after a minute or two, she was dancing, actually dancing. And doing nicely, too, to her surprise.

"Say, you must be Ginger Rogers."

"I am if you're Fred."

"And I am," he admitted and they both laughed. It wasn't so hard, she thought, not in Paradise. You just put on your tightest jeans and made believe you had never been rejected in your life and lo and behold, a nice guy came up and asked you to dance and seemed to like you and there you were!

The pressure at the small of her back startled her. She had thought she knew exactly where Fred's hands were. She turned to see who the wise guy was and damned if it wasn't Bambi, one arm around her and one arm around Fred, dancing along with them.

"Hi there," Bambi said. "May I join you? I can't find a partner of my own and when there's music, my feet insist upon dancing!"

Natalie glanced up at Fred to see what he was making of this. But he wasn't looking at her at all. He was looking down at Bambi, laughing as if she'd just made the best joke in the world.

Well! to laugh at Natalie Simon was one thing. Natalie Simon was a funny lady. But to laugh at *everyone's* little sallies was something else. Or was this the way it worked in the Land of the Singles? She didn't know and what's more, she didn't care, either.

"Bambi, here's Fred and Fred, here's Bambi." She gave them her best bright smile and broke away.

"Oh, but wait!—" Bambi called. "We can *all* dance!"

"Hey, it's okay, Bambi. Not to worry. I remember about

cutting-in. He's all yours." Then she gave Fred a grin. "For now," she added, feeling very goddamn proud of herself. As much as she might want to, she hadn't decked that pushy little blonde.

Two hours later, flushed and breathing hard from the umpteenth bunny hop, she grabbed Barbara and said, "For God's sake, unplug that jukebox, would you?" And made all her nearest neighbors laugh. It had been two hours of constant movement and frolic, during which time she had gotten to know just about everyone in the place by their first name, danced with most of them—both male and female—drunk with all of them, ditto, agreed to meet each and every one of them on the beach tomorrow, and had a vague recollection of agreeing to play on a volleyball team.

And now the leprechaun bartender—whose name she now knew to be Irving . . . *Irving*?—was declaring Happy Hour to be really, no kidding around, no fooling this time, no more extensions, period, exclamation point, absolutely and positively *over* and now, ladies and gents, you pay two-fifty for your drinks instead of a buck I'm sorry but do you want me to go out of business or what?

Natalie ended up sitting with Bambi and the two guys and Barbara at one of the big oak tables, watching the place magically empty out and toasting everything they could think of, including her volleyball team called The Miltons because, as someone explained, "Paradise lost." And everyone groaned. She was feeling mellow, real mellow and pleased with herself. Barbara was all for going back to the house and scrambling an egg; but she didn't want to leave just yet. What was the point of being single if you had to go home and scramble an egg?

"Say, Irving," she called, "can we get something to eat around here?"

"Ask Sandy; he cooks occasionally."

She had noticed before that both the man called Sandy and his big dog had disappeared from the end of the bar. But there they were again.

"Sandy?" she called.

"Arf."

She threw her head back and laughed. Sandy . . . and his dog named Annie. . . . Oh, my God! *Little Orphan Annie!* "That's so bad, it's good," she said; and in answer, he heaved himself up and strolled on over. Well, she'd been one hundred percent correct. He could be Jerry's twin, almost. It was the same big, broad-shouldered build, the same shambling walk, the same extra flesh through the middle.

"What can I do for you?" There came that voice, deep, sonorous, dramatic.

"We're hungry."

"Okay. I can give you a burger . . . a hot dog . . . a ham sandwich . . . a cheese sandwich . . . a ham and cheese sandwich . . . a cheeseburger . . . a ham and cheese burger . . . a—"

"Enough," Natalie said, smiling up at him. "Five burgers, medium rare, toast the buns, okay?"

Before you knew it, the hamburgers arrived on a huge wooden tray, smelling and looking fabulous. Sandy was surprisingly deft for such a large man, bending easily and moving quickly around the table, handing out the plates with a flourish.

Natalie took a big succulent bite of hers—it was delicious— and she smiled up at him. "We are hungry," she said around a mouthful, "and now we're in love, too!"

He patted her shoulder. "That's why I adore cooking for women. They're always so appreciative."

"Hunh," Jay said. "Maybe I should learn how."

"Barbara will give you lessons," Bambi said. "She's a pro."

Sandy looked with interest at Barbara. "Really? A chef?"

"In charge of the test kitchen at Marcus & Morrisey," Natalie said. "And a whiz."

Barbara, coloring a bit under the attention, said, "Well. I've become good at doing four batches of just about everything. But"—and she looked up with a smile—"I've never tasted a hamburger as wonderful as this one. Are you professional?"

Sandy put his head back and laughed. "Sort of," he said. Digging into the pocket of his shirt, he brought out a card and handed it to Natalie, saying, "Pass it around." ALEXANDER Y. LOVALL was in large capital letters in the middle. Sur-

rounding the name, in smaller type, it said: WORLD TRAVELER
BON VIVANT SOLDIER OF FORTUNE CHAMPION OF THE OP-
PRESSED INTERNATIONAL LOVER CASUAL HERO ALL AROUND
GOOD GUY PHILOSOPHER SEEKER OF PEACE PAINTER OF PIC-
TURES REVOLUTIONARY LEADER OF MEN. And then there was
a phone number.

He stepped away, but Natalie said, "Wait. Alexander Lovall.
The man who wrote that card, we want at our table. We can't
offer you food, but pull up a chair, why don't you?" And then
she stopped, mid-thought. Alexander Lovall! *Alexander Lovall!* Where was her brain?

She pointed an accusing finger at him. "Alexander Lovall!
Of course! *Fire Island Fragments!* Jacobson Gallery!" She
grinned at him. "You devil . . . pretending to be just one of the
local yokels!"

He grinned back, his face flushed, enjoying himself greatly,
while the others sat there puzzled and mystified. He looked
Natalie straight in the eye and, still laughing, said "But you
never bought anything!"

"Listen, Alexander Lovall, noted American artist and hamburger king . . ." She had to laugh, too, not only with him but
at Barbara and Bambi and the guys, who looked absolutely
stupefied. Well, who expected to come across one of New
York's currently favored painters in Bob's Bar? . . . Particularly
when he willingly took himself out into the kitchen and cooked
for you? "Never mind, never mind! all I want to know is, how
do you find time to cook *and* paint? And *sit*, for God's sake,
will you?"

He pulled up a chair next to her and produced, seemingly
out of thin air, a small spiral pad. "Actually," he said, "I usually
draw."

There was a chorus of squeals and protests. "Not *us*!" Bambi
shrieked through a mouthful.

In answer, he flipped the pad open. Natalie pushed her plate
into the middle of the table to leave room for it as he silently
turned the pages. Amazing, absolutely amazing. There, in quick
pencil sketches, they were. Fred was the first, looking pensive.
He turned the page and there was Jay scowling a little into his
drink . . . and Bambi, laughing, Barbara, looking up suspi-

ciously. That made them all laugh and Barbara said, "Well, some guy must have been giving me a line! Enough of them did! And I think it was all the same line!"

And then he turned another page and there were three men swiftly sketched, seated at a table, laughing. And there were sketches of various couples dancing. But he hadn't, Natalie thought with some asperity, drawn her. She fought feeling hurt.

"But you didn't do Natalie!" That was Bambi; well, thank you, Bambi.

Alexander Lovall turned in his chair to smile into Natalie's eyes. "Do you think I forgot you, Natalie Simon?"

"Never mind that. How do you know my name?"

"I knew your name the first time you called Margie . . . the real estate lady. And I knew when you came out here. I knew which house you liked and I knew when you changed from wanting to rent to wanting to buy." He laughed again, "I hope this doesn't make you nervous, Natalie. But now that you're a part of our town, you ought to know there are no secrets in Paradise. At least, not from me."

"You sound like a very dangerous man, Alexander."

"Call me Sandy. Residents get to call me Sandy. Well, I'm either dangerous to know or very good to know. . . . Which would you care to bet on?"

More and more interesting. Natalie gave him a big smile. "Sandy, I'm going to assume it's both."

"Excellent," he said. "You get an A."

"A's are good, Sandy," she laughed. "But where's my picture?"

"Yes," Barbara said, "You couldn't have left her out of your sketchbook."

"You're so right. I've simply saved the best for last." He laughed and added, "Excuse me, I didn't mean it *that* way. I'm not stupid enough, I hope, to say to three beautiful women that one is the best. I meant, I like this sketch the best." And with a flourish he whipped a page back to reveal a drawing of Natalie with a look on her face that could be described only as smoldering. In fact, Natalie thought, the only time I've ever seen myself look like that is when I've looked in the mirror while I was making love.

"Jesus!" she breathed. "What was I *doing*?"

"I don't remember," he said. "No, really. I mean it. It's how I saw you, that's all. First impressions. That's what I draw."

"But you make Nat look so *angry*!" Bambi said.

"Not at all, not at all. I sat there at the end of the bar, watching and listening and sketching, and I like to think I know my people." He stared down at his drawing, and then said, "Angry? No, I think what I saw at that moment was Natalie's intensity."

"Stop right there," Natalie ordered. "That's a word I like. Intense."

"Of course," Bambi said. "Intense. That's really what I *meant*."

"And what *I* really meant to do, ladies and gentlemen, was to invite you to the summer's first big Event." You could hear the capitalization in his voice. "People," he intoned, getting to his feet and bowing a little, "I invite you all to come with me for the First Annual Walk on the Beach Beneath the Summer Stars."

There was a flurry of activity as chairs were scraped back and sweaters grabbed and wallets dug for . . . at which Sandy held up a hand and announced that the last round of drinks and the burgers were all on him. "This time only," he said. "And I have an ulterior motive, so don't think too well of me."

He held out an arm for her to take, and Natalie felt a lift, that nice warm feeling when things were going right. Famous artist or not, Sandy Lovall was a sweet guy and a helluva good hamburger cook, too. And hell, she was lucky to get picked right up by one of the locals—especially Sandy—and pulled right into the community. She made herself a little silent vow that she wasn't going to let anything get in the way of a perfect summer on Fire Island. Not Jerry, not Peter, not Martha J, not Paul Hasahni, not anything, not even her own fears. She was there for the express purpose of not thinking about any of that. She was there for the express purpose of . . . well, actually, she wasn't sure what the express purpose was. But the First Annual Walk on the Beach Beneath the Summer Stars was close enough.

It was a bit chilly, but the night air was soft with the promise of summer. And it smelled delicious, Natalie thought, absolutely wonderful—of salt and seaweed and fresh air. They walked at the edge of the ocean. A pale half moon hanging low in the sky cast a bluish glow on the sand and the surf as it foamed under their feet. Natalie kept up a little hop-skip-and-jump step, avoiding the water, hanging onto the solid, sweatered arm offered her by Sandy Lovall. Behind them, the others giggled and shrieked as the icy cold tide surged in, soaking the bottoms of their jeans and their socks. For the first time since she'd closed on the house, Natalie felt light-headed, lighthearted elation. It made her want to run down the beach, fling her arms out, laugh, and shout. Of course, she didn't. She walked side by side with bulky, solid, comfortable Sandy Lovall and felt happiness slide over her and said to him, "It's all so beautiful!"

He tucked her arm under his more tightly and said, "I know. I've lived here all my life and it still gets me. And the ocean here is only half the picture of Paradise. Wait till you walk around the bay side. That's where the true beauty is, at least in my opinion. It's so still there, so peaceful. Some days the Great South Bay is so calm, it's like a giant mirror flashing light back into the sky." Now he laughed. "Don't get me started. I'm emotionally involved with every square inch of this land. My house is on the bay. Actually, it's the family house. My grandfather built it." He stopped walking and gestured toward the dunes behind them. Dimly Natalie discerned a flight of wooden stairs three stories high at least plunging down from dune top to beach. Sandy said, "Come on, everybody! Let's sit for a minute and contemplate the ever-changing ocean. We can sit on the stairs." To Natalie, he said, "And anyway, these are the last stairs in Paradise. A little bit further and you're in Beach Haven."

"And we don't want to be in Beach Haven, do we?" Natalie said it as a joke, but he answered solemnly, "That's right. Beach

Haven is nothing these days but a collection of renters. And renters are—never mind. Present company excluded, of course. Over here, everyone!"

They straggled over, slogging through the thick, damp sand, enjoying being the only human beings out in the darkness, and arranged themselves on the steps. For several minutes, they were all silent, sitting very still and staring out at the half-visible rhythmic crashing breakers. Natalie and Sandy were sitting high up on the stairway, and she looked down at the others, wondering about them.

One she knew, the others were strangers. And yet, already they were sitting here in some intimacy. This, she knew, was the way of summer resorts. Like cruise ships, you realized you had been set adrift from your real life and so you could do what you wanted and never have to pay for it. Perhaps someone on this island she hadn't met yet would end up being a dear friend. Or her lover. Or an enemy.

And then Sandy Lovall broke the silence. "I never tire of this place. And up until now, it's been left untouched."

"Up until?" Bambi said. "It looks pretty untouched to me."

"Ah, yes," Sandy sighed. "Here, you'd think we'd be safe from intrusion. But even the ocean is being threatened with pollution. You've all read about that in the papers. Human beings can be disgusting creatures: trashing their own planet!"

"What can you do?"

"Yeah, you can't police everywhere at once."

"What you can *do*," Sandy Lovall said, his voice taking on an edge, "is fight intrusion and pollution wherever you can. I myself am presently involved in trying to stop intrusion and pollution here. Some might say it's a small thing. But not to me."

"What?" Natalie asked. "You sound . . . so committed."

"Precisely!" He reached over and squeezed her shoulder. "There's a small freshwater pond on the bay side of Paradise."

"Fresh water? In the middle of the ocean?" That was Barbara.

"Very unusual, quite right. That's why I'm fighting to save it. What's happening is, someone has come in, bought the property containing the pond—Halfmoon Pond, that's what it's called—and is putting up a monstrosity. They plan to drain the pond and change its contour and—I don't want to bore you people with this. It's very close to my heart, and I tend to get carried away. But I feel it's important to everyone who loves the peace, the quiet, and the unique beauty of Paradise. You, Natalie, you've just bought a house. You have a right to a community that stays the way you first saw it. If they go ahead and build this thing—"

"Who is this 'they'?" Natalie asked.

"I wish I knew," Sandy Lovall said and heaved a great sigh. "I wish I knew. They're hiding behind a meaningless corporate name: Halfmoon Associates, may they rot in hell." Now he laughed. "And there I go again. I warn you: I am fast becoming a fanatic on this subject. In fact, I've appointed myself chief fanatic in charge of protesting this. You'll be seeing a lot of me over the course of the summer, handing out leaflets and making speeches. I hope that perhaps one or two of you will join me...."

Not on your life, buster, Natalie thought with some asperity. This is my vacation and I was never very big on political stuff anyhow.

"I will!" Bambi volunteered. "I'm in favor of ecology!"

There went the ballgame. If a renter was going to get involved in his protests, then probably she ought to, hadn't she? How annoying!

Aloud she said, "You mean I finally take a deep breath, take the plunge, and buy myself my very first personal piece of property...and in five minutes I find out that Fire Island is about to be ruined." She laughed.

Sandy Lovall patted her hand. "Not *that* bad, Natalie, not if we all fight. In fact, I've even been able to halt construction until there's a hearing. I mean, legally anyone who wants to build in Paradise must hold a public hearing. We're a wilderness area...almost. What they want to do to the pond will ruin its ecological balance forever! It's a crime, that's what it is! Natalie, the next time you hear me start to go on and on, poke me, will you? And if you happen to meet my brother, don't listen to him. He'll try to tell you that any building is good for the economy. God, how I hate developers, they have no heart, no soul, no feeling, and no love for the land. They care for nothing but profits."

Dryly Natalie said, "I take it your brother is a developer."

"My brother," he said in a similar tone, "is president of the construction company in charge of the project. God, I'd give my right arm to know who he's building for. Just one name, that's all I need. But don't ask me to ask him. We don't talk to each other. We haven't exchanged a word since Christmas of 1981. All I know is what I hear through the rumor mill."

There was an edge to his voice that made Natalie a little uneasy. And in fact, it seemed to have made the rest of them uncomfortable. They all began to get to their feet, stretching and chattering and making little jokes. She was a little tired of them all. The thought of curling up alone in her bed under the quilt and falling asleep was very appealing. Then she laughed at herself. Only six or seven hours on Fire Island and already she was sick of group living!

Sandy Lovall walked them all home, regaling them with hilarious stories about his eccentric family and what happened to them during the Great Depression. The man's family, apparently, had been on Fire Island for practically forever. He had a right to get upset. Hadn't she and Jerry formed their own block association on the West Side to fight gentrification? You had to defend your own turf. And now this town *was* her turf. She turned to Sandy and said, "Hey, I'm a resident here. I'll help you. I'll fight those black hats. And I won't listen to your brother if I happen to meet him."

"Is that a promise?"

"That's a promise."

She could feel his approval and his growing affection, like a wave of warmth. He reached out with both hands to grasp her shoulders. "You're okay, Natalie Simon. And to show you how I feel"—and he laughed a little—"I'm going to invite you to the opening of my new show in the city. Yes, and maybe there'll be a surprise, just for you. Will you come?"

Was he kidding? After such a special invitation? Of course she would, no question.

❀ 4 ❀

Works of Art

"Some special invitation!" Natalie groused; but when Barbara turned to look at her, she was smiling. "Just you and me and Sandy Lovall and three hundred of his intimate friends."

It was true, Barbara thought: the main room of Jacobson Gallery was packed with humanity. A good thing Nat had insisted they stop at the Silver Streak for a quick drink; no way would they ever make it to the bar before next Thursday! Well, who cared? Just looking at the mob scene made her feel tired. She was overcome by lassitude. What she longed to do more than anything was to turn around, walk out of there, and go home and cry. Tears were prickling at her eyes even now, even though she was carefully turned out in a favorite silk dress, her hair twisted into an impeccable French knot, looking, as she damned well knew since she had checked herself in a hall mirror not three minutes ago, perfectly wonderful. She looked like a woman in charge of her life. She looked like a woman who could get whatever she wanted. She looked like a woman who had come to her middle years pleased with herself. All lies. Well, what mattered was that nobody besides her realized it.

Natalie was raring to go, obviously. "Let's fight our way to the bar and get a drink. Of course, we'll have to call in the artillery, but what do you say?"

"Oh, Nat, I say it's spinach and I say to hell with it." She tried for a light laugh, but it came out choked.

"Come on, it'll do you good. No? Well, I need a drink."

"Go ahead. I'll catch up with you."

Natalie hardly paused. Well, who could blame her? That's why this horde was here: to drink, to chat each other up, to flirt, to meet people who might do one good, and incidentally maybe cast a glance to the paintings and drawings on the walls. Natalie was doing what was expected of her: putting herself out there. "Okay," she said now, patting Barbara on the shoulder. "'Cause there's a muscular redhead with an RAF mustache I want to check out. . . ."

"Good luck," Barbara said. That Natalie! She'd probably still be checking out interesting-looking men when she was ninety! Well, she looked good, she didn't look like a woman in her mid-forties, not unless you studied her face closely. Small and tight-knit and athletic, she wore clothes beautifully. Tonight, in a bright red knit with very high heels and her hair, blunt cut to chin length, caught back on one side with a red comb, she could pass—from here anyway—for twenty-five. And a good thing, too. Barbara had also noted the redhead, and he couldn't be a day over thirty. Well, more power to her! I wish, Barbara thought, I had half her energy. And as she watched, the red figure disappeared, sucked into the crowd without leaving so much as a pink ripple.

Barbara edged herself over to one side, where she could lean against the wall, looking around to see if there was a familiar person nearby to talk to.

"Beautiful Barbara! I've been looking for you!"

Oh, lord, Jay from Fire Island. She liked Jay, she liked him fine, he was a very nice guy for an accountant—sorry, all you accountants, but some of you are D-U-L-L—but he was ena-mored. Lord, if there was anything she did *not* need in her life right now it was a six and a half foot tall enamored accountant who knew all three of her phone numbers and used them with persistence. Lately, she had her assistant screen the calls in the office, and, at home, well, she was always on her way to the shower or standing there dripping or with a wet head.

"Hello, Jay." She smiled at him; she hoped she was smiling at him. He was a sweet man, gentle, a bit shy—the way he described himself was that he'd been born two drinks under par—nice-looking, neat—oh, hell, he should have appealed to her, but he just didn't. What was wrong with her, anyway? Look how nice he was; he held two glasses of wine. One was for her. Too bad she didn't want it. But that was the story of Barbara and Jay. Or of Barbara and just about anyone, these days.

She took the offered wine and sipped it, and he said slyly, "I'm on my third; I hope I'm now in the proper shape to charm you. And you do look wonderfully clean."

"Ouch," she said. "I *am* sorry. . . ." Maybe now that it had been said, he would go away.

But no. "Perhaps I can talk you into a little dinner at Piro's tonight. You can't tell me now that you're almost into the tub."

Ouch. What could she say to him to make him stop? If only he weren't her neighbor on the weekends. Maybe then she could brush him off. As it was—

"My darling! or is it Dy Marling?" A whirlwind topped with red-gray curls swooped down on her, throwing its arms about her and kissing her noisily on both cheeks. "Excuse me, sir," it said, offering a hand to shake. "Have I interrupted something fabulous? I cannot apologize; I am carried away."

"Oh, Jake." She had to laugh at him; he could be so unself-consciously exuberant, like a small boy. Even Jay was smiling at him, poor Jay, who had hoped she would at last go out to dinner with him. And now—

"Oh, Jake!" she repeated and gave him a big hug. See that, Jay? Hint, hint, Jay, go away.

He went away—fairly gracefully, she thought, pretending he saw someone he knew at the other side of the room. She regarded Jake, still skinny, still all arms and legs, and it seemed impossible he had just turned fifty. And when she looked at him, she felt nothing but affection. No lingering after-effects from their very brief affair, if you could call it that. She had run away from home, to Jake's place, and had ended up living there for six weeks before she realized that she was never going to really love him . . . not that way. Could you call six weeks of playing house an affair? She wasn't sure.

"You no-good," she said affectionately. "You stood me up for lunch!"

"When? When did I do such a horrible thing?"

"A month ago last Thursday, but who's counting? And by the way I haven't heard from you since."

"Now you have. Here I am and didn't I just rescue you once more from the clutches of a horny male?"

Barbara had to laugh. He was reminding her of an office party four or five years ago, when she was first at M & M, and found herself with Peter Marcus at his wiggiest and randiest. Oh, she remembered that time, all right! There she had been, brand new to the business world, unsure of herself, standing frozen while her boss held onto her left breast, and chatted on and on. Yes, Jake had come to her rescue then, he surely had, deftly taking Peter away and then escorting her, semi-catatonic, to a corner where she could recover.

"Yes, you did, you rescued me once more. Of course, this is a very nice accountant and not the old Peter..."

"If he's such a very nice accountant, then why did you have that panicked look on your face?"

"Oh, Jake. He's told me fifty times that we're about to have something special. Well, maybe *he* is, but he's going to have to special it all alone. I'm not in the mood. I'm in terrible shape."

Jake waggled his eyebrows and looked her over. "You don't look it," he said in his best Groucho voice. "No, scratch that, I apologize. Tell me."

"No, you tell *me*. Tell me a funny story, Jake. Tell me something happy that will make me laugh."

"Sorry, Barbara, I'm all out."

Now she looked at him sharply. Jake "Laugh-a-minute" Miller, all out of funny? He was *never* all out of funny, not in all the time she'd known him.

"What is it?" she asked and put a hand on his arm.

"You know I got married out there in Lotus Land...of course you know. Well, I got married out there." He paused, a very long pause, gazing out into the distance. "Yes. Well, I ruined it. There it is, not a funny story, not a happy story. I ruined it and she left me and now she's fucking someone else, someone younger, handsomer, smarter."

"Nobody in the world," Barbara said firmly, "is younger, handsomer, or smarter than you. You go right back there and *get* her." He shook his head and she persisted. "Look, even Mark and I made a stab at getting back together." She laughed a little. "That should prove that nothing is impossible. So, go for it."

A look of pain passed over his bony face. "Shit, Barbara, she's *pregnant*. Pregnant by him. It's too late, too goddamn late."

"Oh, Jake . . ."

"She wanted to have *my* baby, that's the hell of it. And I? . . . I refused. Do you believe that? I told her, 'Are you kidding? I can't even take responsibility for a dog, for Christ's sake. How do you expect me to think about a *baby*?' And she left me and she went with this guy and now she's going to have *his* baby. And here I am—free as air, right?"

"Oh, Jake!"

Quite suddenly, he grinned at her, all the sadness wiped away in an instant. "And while we're on the subject, who's that cute little blonde with Natalie?"

Oh, Jake. "*Were* we on the subject of blondes?"

"You know me: I'm always on the subject of blondes."

"Well, I'd guess that cute little one with Natalie is probably Bambi Hirsch. . . ." She craned to look and caught a glimpse of that familiar curly head. "Yep, that's her. She owns that newsletter, *The Ad Game*."

"Bambi Hirsch . . ." Jake said. "Very interesting . . ."

What fun! Bambi thought. She loved big gatherings like this, loved to see who was with who and who was pretending not to be with who . . . whom? she wondered. Grammar was not her strong point. Not missing anything was.

"Everyone in the art world was at Jacobson's Tuesday night," she wrote in her head, "to see the work of artist Alexander Lovall (those of us who know him call him Sandy) and surprise, surprise, who should appear in a pencil sketch but M & M's very own Creative Director, Natalie Simon (those of us who know her call her Ms. Popularity)." Yes, that would be good.

"Galley Proofs" was harder to fill up than anyone could possibly realize. She had to be out every single night, just about, not really enjoying herself until she had made sure she had enough items.

This party normally would not have given her much for the column because it wasn't the ad business. But Sandy had asked them—she and Natalie and Barbara—to invite anyone they knew who might be interested in art—"in buying my art, is what I mean," he had added with a laugh. Well, they all knew that! What else was an opening for?

Standing with Natalie was a good idea. Natalie knew a lot of people in the ad game. When she first came in tonight and had spotted Nat, she'd laughed and said, "Nat Simon! Always right next to the bar!" and Natalie had answered, "Sooner or later you see everyone if you stand near the bar." Her tone was rather sharp, Bambi thought. Well, no reason to get mad at her; she hadn't said anything so terrible.

Oh, pooh, what did she care? If Natalie took an innocent comment all wrong, that was *her* problem. Natalie Simon tended, she had noticed, to be just a little irritable with women. She'd have to watch that. Especially now that Bambi Hirsch knew her. Bambi Hirsch was the eyes, ears, and voice of Madison Avenue, didn't she realize that? Didn't she realize how many people would read that little item next week in *The Ad Game*? How many people would see her name in print? My God, she couldn't *pay* for that kind of publicity. And she was getting it for free, just because she was a friend of Bambi Hirsch's. She ought to watch her temper.

Now Bambi nudged her and, when Natalie turned, gestured with her head. "Isn't that Jake Miller of Reynolds Associates? Over there, talking with Barbara?"

"Is it, that rat? Yes, by God, it is. He'd better not get near me or I'll kill him."

In her head, Bambi wrote, "What has a certain creative director, female, got against a certain VP, male? Could it be professional jealousy? Or is it personal?"

Natalie laughed and said, "Don't print that. Oh, Bambi, I can hear your brain clicking. Jake's an old friend of mine. And of Barbara's, for that matter. We're always threatening to give him cement sneakers."

Hear my brain clicking? Bambi thought, annoyed. That's what *you* think. You don't know anything about me, Ms. High and Mighty. But she knew all about Natalie Simon! Natalie Simon slept around. . . . Natalie Simon had married her copy chief, stealing him away from his wife. . . . Natalie Simon was ready for anything, any time. That's how she got where she was! By screwing! Sure! While someone straight, like Bambi Hirsch, had to work and slave for every little thing.

She might have said something, might have told Natalie off right then and there, except that, just then, she caught sight of a man coming over to them. He was the most sexist-looking man she'd ever seen, she thought. He fairly reeked of self-assurance. He was small and slim, the way she liked them, with a craggy narrow face, intense eyes, and thick, wavy graying hair; and he was wearing a linen jacket with the sleeves rolled up and pleated pants she knew were custom tailored. Why did he look so familiar to her? She grabbed Natalie by the arm and said, in a whisper, "Natalie. Who is that man? Why do I think I've met him somewhere?"

Natalie laughed. "That, my dear Bambi, is the one and only Peter Marcus of Marcus & Morrisey." Then, she peered at Bambi and laughed some more. "If you could see the look on your face!"

"Introduce me! Please!"

"Hey! don't clutch at me. This material wrinkles if you look at it. I'll introduce you. I think he's heading for us, anyway."

"Oh. I hope so!"

And then he was there and Bambi was looking right into his eyes and, oh, it was special, she just knew it. Oh, my God, she hoped he hadn't heard her, or maybe she hoped he had.

"Good evening, ladies," Peter Marcus said. "Since you are so conveniently near the bar, perhaps one of you will hand me a glass of something light? Natalie, why don't you, you know what I like." He leaned across Bambi to take the glass of wine she chose, and she could smell his cologne, which was absolutely delicious.

She was ready to faint, in any case, because all the time he was talking to Natalie, he was looking at *her*, at Bambi Hirsch, looking at her and smiling.

"And now," he said, never taking his eyes from her, "who is *this*?"

"I'm Bambi Hirsch," she said, a bit breathless. And then, hardly able to believe her own audacity, she added, "And I think you're the most attractive man I've ever seen."

Natalie watched the two of them do their mating dance and resisted the urge to make a witty remark. Peter had not been exactly thrilled with her lately and discretion was undoubtedly the better part of valor—particularly when he was taking himself so seriously. Just look at him, all charm and smiles, hovering over her. And just look at her! all dimples and blushes and eyelashes batting away! And that birdlike trilling of laughter—it was to gag. She had seen Bambi do her number several times now, and it was always the same. Couldn't Peter smell a line?

Oh, lord, that's all she needed: to have Peter coming out to visit Bambi on weekends. She'd *never* have a rest from him! But on the other hand, maybe it would be a help. Bambi was, to say the least, lively and maybe she was just the one to handle him. And, who knew? maybe if Peter was getting laid regularly, he'd be easier to get along with. She could sure use *that*!

Well, to hell with them both. This was an art show opening, and so far, she hadn't even given a glance to the art. Nobody had, really. She turned away from the now-engrossed pair and got her glass refilled, and then pushed through the packed bodies. It was becoming difficult to make anyone move, as people became intent upon their conversations. She could hear snatches as she shoved her way along. It was all business. To hell with that. She was getting just a little sick and tired of being expected to do business at every social function in Manhattan. So she ignored the high sign she got from a guy who wanted M & M to take on his breakfast cereals. Let him call her at the office, goddammit. She was going to go look at Sandy Lovall's paintings!

She strolled by a long row of beachscapes, each painted at

a different time of day...or maybe different time of year. They were all oil paintings, of course, but the light in them was so true, so clear, they seemed to have been captured on the spot in luminescent water colors. The thing that struck Natalie was that if someone had asked her to guess, she'd have said a woman painted them.

On the end wall were drawings—well, the pictures were in black and white, anyway. And when she looked, she gave a little gasp because there, enlarged and done more carefully, were those sketches of them, the ones he'd done during Happy Hour. And then she giggled because the artist had entitled them "Happy Hour at Bob's." What fun! She'd have to get Barbara and Bambi. She'd have to show Jake. There they were, on the wall, and there were the dancers and the groups at the tables, Annie sleeping by the bar. They were really good; she could recognize every face. She scanned the wall, looking, of course, for her own portrait.

And, wonder of wonders, a beautiful young man was standing in front of it, chin in hand, pondering it. Quietly, she moved next to him. What a good joke! Not even glancing at her, he said, with a British accent, "I love his line work...prefer it, actually, to the painting." And she said, noncommittally, "Um."

"Yes, it's crisp, clean, and it captures everything one feels, with such acuity."

"Um?" Natalie said. Better and better!

"Just look at this. Beautiful, isn't it? So complex, so... human. It makes one wish one could know that woman."

"Oh, really?" Natalie said.

Now he turned and, to her delight, did a double take. "Oh, my word! It is *you*, isn't it? Yes, it is, of course it is. How lucky." His head swiveled back and forth between the framed picture and her. And then he laughed. "He certainly has caught the bone structure. But somehow, you look...different."

Dryly she said, "I'd had three or four drinks, and it was a weekend."

"Yes, well...you know the artist, then."

"We both have houses on Fire Island."

"Very interesting, very interesting." Again, he looked at the drawing and murmured, "Beautiful, beautiful..." smiled at her, and said, "It's been a pleasure." And strolled away.

Natalie stood very still, her mouth open. He raves over the drawing and then looks right through the real thing! How insulting! Probably a fag. Oh, shit, she thought, you promised yourself never, ever, to think that about a man just because he doesn't drag you off by the hair, remember?

Sorry, fella, she thought, but in *my* movie script, in *my* scenario, when I came upon you gazing enraptured at a drawing of me and said quietly, "Hello, there, I'm the woman in the picture," you were supposed to gasp and swoon and throw yourself at my feet. Oh, well. You can't win them all... I guess. But she gazed after his sleek young head thinking it would have been nice. She hadn't been laid in quite a while ... too long, in fact. In the old days, there was always Jake.

Speaking of which, where the hell was he? She'd invited him to this thing. He might at least have said hello when he got in. There he was. All the way across the gallery, naturally. She tried to catch his eye—the crowd seemed to be thinning a bit—but he was too busy entertaining a small group of younger people with one of his *shticks*, she was sure. If she stood there and watched his hands and facial expressions long enough, she'd know which story he was telling. She'd heard them all, more than once.

Okay, the mountain would go to the goddamn Mohammed. Tonight, she needed him. The last thing she wanted to do after this opening was to walk out alone and go home alone and be alone with those black walls. Okay, so Jake tended to be a pain in the ass; at least he was *her* pain in the ass. They could go out and have a few drinks, eat a little dinner, *shmooze* a bit, play "Can You Top This?" and make believe they were feeling terrific. Then, by the time she got home, she'd be tired; she might even be able to fall asleep, for a change.

Carefully, she edged her way along a wall, not in the mood for pushing and shoving through a thicket of bodies. Suddenly, there was an eddy in the midst of the throng, instantly noticeable, so she stopped to look. And there, sweeping into the room and parting bodies like Moses with the Red Sea, was ...

well, she didn't know quite what to call it. Woman, she guessed. About half a ton of woman swathed in fuchsia silk that billowed about her and wearing a hat with a brim the size of a small island in the Caribbean. She had a stunningly gorgeous face all but buried in an excess of black eyeliner and bright pink blusher. Like the Queen Mary being brought into berth by half a dozen tugboats, she was surrounded with a coterie of short blocky men.

"Thandy, *darling!*" The voice was husky, warm, and carried exceedingly well. "Where *are* you hiding?"

Natalie found herself turning to follow the progress of this remarkable-looking creature, and noted that everyone else in the place was doing likewise. Who *was* she? And what was she to Sandy? And would she appear in Paradise? Natalie had a sudden vision of this gargantuan lady swooping down onto the beach, wrapped in yards and yards of gauze, exclaiming over the "thand, the thun, and the thurf." And even as she thought it, she looked around to see if Jake by any chance was looking in her direction. This was too good to keep to herself. . . . It needed sharing.

She spotted the bright billows of silk, off in a corner, and yes, there was Sandy, his cheek to hers, kissing the air next to her. Who *was* she?

As soon as Natalie reached Jake, she said, "Who in the world is that . . . magnificent creature?"

"Who? Oh, the fat lady? I don't know. You know how art openings are: filled with hangers-on and lookers-on. I'm with the last-named group. And who are you?"

"You were late, as usual."

"Call me *pisher*," he said.

"Oh, very original, Miller."

"Get off my case, Nattie, would you? You're getting to be a regulla pain in the ass."

"But at least I'm *your* pain in the ass."

He shrugged irritably. "I'm not in the mood, Nat."

"You were in the mood a few minutes ago, convulsing the crowd with your rapierlike wit. How about telling *me* a funny story?"

"You're the second lady tonight who's demanded that I play the jester. Did you ever figure I might not like it?"

"Jake! What in hell is the matter?"

"I told you. I'm not in the mood. In fact, I think I'll go home now." Finally, he looked at her, trying to smile at her and failing rather miserably. He looked awful. "I'm sorry, Nat. I had planned to be ebullient, charming, delicious, and etcetera, just for little you. But I can't. No. I can't explain it. No. A drink at the Silver Streak won't help. No. I don't want to sit and *shmooze* with you and make it all better. I'm sorry. . . ." He blinked very rapidly and looked away.

For an instant, she was at a loss. Jake funny or Jake angry or Jake sexy, she could deal with. But Jake sad made her feel terrible and lonely. If only she could get him to laugh.

"Listen, Jake, this will give you a giggle. I think Peter's in love!"

"Come on, Nat, give Peter a break, will you? He deserves to fall in love. You're becoming a termagant in your old age."

She forced a laugh. "Smile when you say that, stranger. But what's really a scream is *who* he's decided to fall in love with. A slightly ditsy little blonde who's my neighbor on Fire Island. God, Jake, think of it. If it works out, I'll probably have to see him every weekend, too!"

"That little blonde is your neighbor out there?"

"Yes. You know who she is; she owns and writes that newsletter we all get, *The Ad Game*. You've probably seen her picture over her column every week."

"All I know is, I had my eye on her and Peter Marcus beat me out. It's just not my day. You know how I'm a sucker for blondes!"

"Good-night, Jake. Call me when you feel better." She turned on her heel and walked away, not thinking or caring about where she was going. Just away from *him*, the insensitive bastard. And after about six steps, she knew where she was heading and that was straight for Sandy Lovall, who had spotted her and was gesturing her to his side with big motions of his hand, calling out her name, and shouting, "Come here, there are some people who want to meet the model!" Her heart warmed, and she felt a real, a genuine, smile—not the stiff, pretend one she'd put on for Jake—spread across her face.

And now, she'd get to meet the fabulous fat lady, who had been seated on a very large hassock and was holding forth, Sandy's hand grasped firmly in her own beringed one.

As Natalie approached, she husked, "Thandy, I inthitht upon being the firtht to be introduthed."

"My darling, your wish is my command, as always."

"Never mind, you're much too thlow. My dear, the drawing ith beautiful . . . and tho are you. I'm Thelma Fabricant."

Oh, Christ. Was the woman's name Thelma or Selma? Best not to call her anything. "Ms. Fabricant, it's a pleasure. And I'm Natalie Simon."

"Natalie Thimon. I'm glad to meet *you*. Thandy here has done a lovely portrait of you. And it's the very firtht thing thold, too. Terrific, no?" Her voice was a magnificent instrument, rich and deep and enveloping. In spite of the lisp, you could just listen to the sound of that voice, on and on.

"Sold?" Natalie said, turning to Sandy.

"As Selma says," he answered with a shrug and a smile.

Aha! It was Selma with an S. "But . . . who bought it?" she asked.

"The buyer wishes to remain anonymous."

"Not fair, Sandy!"

He pulled his hand from Selma's and came over to her. "But the artist is pleased," he said, putting an arm across her shoulder. "I hoped you would be, too."

"Well . . ." It was nice standing next to him, leaning a little into his solid bulk, belonging there somehow, part of this group of people who were all feeling good and probably interesting all of them.

And her portrait, sold. It was intriguing. Who, in this mob, had seen it, loved it, wanted it, purchased it—all so quickly? Jake? Not a chance. Barbara, as a surprise for her? Probably. Oh, that Barbara, it was so much like her. But her birthday wasn't for months. And what if it wasn't Barbara? Who, then? It didn't really matter. What was important was that, right now, she was feeling better than she had in ages.

And now Sandy was introducing her, much too quickly for her to remember all the names; although she did catch that one of the guys was Bert and another was Ernie, something she tucked away to tell her people tomorrow morning at breakfast in the office. Her copywriters were all young, and although they might sneer at Hemingway and ask who the hell Nellie Lutcher was, surely they all remembered Sesame Street's Ernie and Bert!

She'd have quite a few good tales to tell tomorrow morning. For just a moment, fleetingly, she wondered why it was so important to her to entertain the troops all the time; and then she let it go. Because Sandy Lovall was inviting her to dinner... "and Barbara, too, if you can find her in this mob, and any other of your friends, Natalie. We're going to the Grove Street Health Food Restaurant. It's really much better than it sounds...." And she felt very very good. "And," he added, laughing, "they always treat us right when they see the Lady Selma!"

"*La Exigenta*, that's Selma," someone said, and Natalie asked quietly. "Sandy, who is she?"

He threw his head back and laughed. "Selma? She's my agent. And, Natalie, believe it or not"—he bent his head close to her ear—"my former lady wife."

❋ 5 ❋

Brainstorm

Natalie walked into the boardroom and immediately noted that Martha J was sitting next to Peter, on his right. Not that there was anything *official* about sitting next to Peter at a brainstorm; but nobody would dare do it unless specifically invited. Up until this very day, the person on Peter's right hand at a brainstorm had been none other than hers truly, Natalie Simon.

She plastered a look of professional blandness onto her face—at least she hoped to hell that's what was showing—and tried not to care. Martha J and Peter were deep in conversation when she walked in. She stood at the doorway, a bit undecided, and Martha J looked up, right at her. She flicked Natalie a wave and turned her eyes back down again. Stung, Natalie thought, Well, at least she has the grace to look embarrassed. And then, quickly, she scolded herself: Grow up, for Christ's sake. What has she to look embarrassed about? She's sitting next to her boss—your boss, too, in case you'd forgotten—doing regular business, during business hours, and at his invitation at that. So, come on! If it meant anything at all, it was Peter's little message, not Martha J's; and if Peter was trying to tell Natalie that he was miffed at her, so what else was new?

"Hey, Nat! Good!" That was Evan Goodman, standing by the coffee urn. Evan was copy chief of what was generally known as the men's accounts: tires, tools, cars, and computers. He was such a sweet guy, Evan, big and handsome and very happily married. She'd come on to him once, at a Christmas party, back in the days when Christmas parties were your one big chance to act on all the fantasies you'd had during the rest of the year. Well, forget it! He'd chuckled and given her a big bear hug, all in the best possible humor; but it was no go, no *way*! They were the best of buddies, nothing close really, but whenever they had reason to be together, they had a helluva good time.

"Natalie," Evan was saying loudly, "you gotta sit next to me and feed me ideas, so Peter won't catch on that I don't even know what a loofah *is*." He guffawed, throwing his head back. "It sounds to me like a social disease!"

Everyone in the room laughed at that, including Peter, who then said loudly, "Never mind that, Evan. Natalie had just better keep her ideas for herself." He paused and then added, "Because I'm keeping score."

Again, everyone laughed, including Natalie. But inwardly, she winced. It sounded a little nasty, like he meant it. But she knew better than to ever show him he'd scored off her. She grinned her broadest grin and said, "You got yourself a deal, Evan m'boy. Just bring me some caffeine, would you?" And she sat herself in the chair next to his well-worn herringbone tweed jacket, greeting the others at the big round table.

Barbara was there, and Tommy Thoms, who was busy talking to Jeff Lawrence. Jeff gave Natalie a very brief hello; you'd never guess, Natalie thought, that once upon a time he had eagerly backed her up against her own desk and given her the screwing of a lifetime. But he'd been younger then, four years younger, and a copywriter, her copywriter. Also, she reminded herself, she had been four years younger; now, she doubted he'd bother, even if she did a striptease in front of him. When he looked at her nowadays, there was no sign of that sly, secret sexiness. Oh, stop it, she told herself. It wasn't that she had lost her appeal; it was Jeff who had changed. When he left the creative end for account executiving, he'd somehow lost all his juiciness. To hell with him. She shifted her glance.

"Joe Hernandes, as I live and breathe!" This was cried dramatically. "I thought we weren't inviting the art directors any more."

Joe, a small dark man with a lovingly combed and waxed mustache he curled up at the ends, gave her a big smile. "Oh, yeah? How come you thought that, Nattie?"

"I thought the last time we had an AD at a brainstorm, he never opened his mouth, just sat and doodled. Remember, Joe? You turned out twenty-seven pages of beautifully rendered mice in sexy underwear?" There was a ripple of laughter around the table. "I thought then that we all joined hands and took an oath. No more ADs because they're visual, not verbal."

"Half right. . . . We're not verbal," Joe quipped. "We're oral."

As everyone groaned at this sally—everyone, Natalie noticed, except Peter and Martha J who were still eyeball to eyeball—Evan came to sit down next to her, remarking, "That's the other reason we decided never to have an art guy again. You guys have filthy minds."

Natalie laughed with the rest, but her mind was really focused on the pair of them, so ostentatiously busy over there, their heads close together, speaking so low that nobody could hear them. Surely, she'd never been that rude when she was sitting next to Peter at a brainstorm! Irritated, she picked up the sheaf of papers neatly laid out in front of her, held in place by a loofah sponge. There was a similar bundle at each place; and in fact, at this very moment, Tommy and Jeff were examining and discussing their loofahs earnestly. Natalie turned hers over and looked at it. It looked like a sponge, nothing more, nothing less. Yet, there were three typewritten pages in front of her, headed "THE LOOFAH STORY: A Miracle of Nature."

"Do you believe," she murmured to Evan, "that twelve or thirteen grown-up people are going to devote several hours today discussing this . . . miracle of nature?"

"Miracle of nature?" Evan murmured back. "That's funny. Looks exactly like a sponge, to me."

They were giggling together when Debbie and Bob came sauntering in. They were part of what Natalie thought of as the New Wave of copywriters, translation: *young*. Debbie, she knew, was still in her mid-twenties; Debbie had, in that other, former life, been her secretary, fresh out of secretarial school. She had proved so bright and so creative that, of course, Natalie encouraged her to try writing copy; and she now wrote under the tutelage of Martha J. Bob, fresh out of NYU, was so young as to be almost unthinkable. He was Evan's newest writer. Come to think of it, Natalie mused, hadn't she seen Bob and Debbie together an awful lot lately? Of course, he was a doll; he looked like everyone's dream of a college jock. She wouldn't mind having a go at him, herself. He looked strong and muscular and tireless, just the way she liked them. And then she reminded herself, Jesus, he's even too young for Debbie! Half your age, Natalie, shame on you! And wasn't that a sign of advancing years, when you found yourself eyeing younger and younger men? Well, nobody was going to catch *her* at that!

Debbie was learning from Martha J. She had taken to dressing in her own very unique and attention-getting style, which consisted of old clothes from the fifties done with great panache. She stood in the doorway for a moment, posing a bit, Natalie thought, and then burbled, "Oh, Bob, we're in luck. We're going to brainstorm with all the best of the old-timers!"

Natalie whirled in her chair, looking frantically around the room. "Where!?" she shouted. "Where are they?"

This brought down the house. And then Peter banged on the table and said, "Come on, everybody. We're here to work . . . and so far, I haven't noticed anyone reading their background material."

"His or her," someone corrected *sotto voce*; and when he glared around the table, Martha J said sweetly, "Buzz, buzz, Peter. I see you thinking negative thoughts." It took a beat and then he laughed. And Natalie couldn't help think that for years, *she* had been the only person able to jolly Peter out of his little snits. It looked as if she had been well and truly replaced; and for an instant, there was an empty, yawning, sinking feeling in her stomach.

"As for you, Natalie," Peter said in a mild voice, "try to hold it down, would you? We all love your clowning, but come on, this is serious business. Nature Boy is one of our most valued clients."

"Who, me!" Natalie protested. She threw up her hands and gave him a mock-innocent look.

"You know you're always carrying on at brainstorms. Which is why you haven't been welcome lately, by the way."

There was a small but meaningful silence at that one. Suddenly, everyone was very intent upon their loofah sponge saga.

As sweetly as she could manage she said, "Would you like me to leave, Peter?" Her heart was going so fast that she was sure everyone could see it. Or hear it.

"Hell, no. You have too many good ideas. But please, Natalie darling, don't make the price so high, there's a good girl."

She longed to say "Yowza boss," like she used to in the good old days when he found her endlessly amusing. But she did not have a death wish, and she knew damned well that he was not going to find her amusing today. If ever.

She was just wishing that someone, anyone, would look up from the sponges and look at her, when someone did. Of course it was Barbara. Barbara's eyes were brimming with laughter, and she was trying very hard not to giggle aloud. Natalie stared at her friend in a kind of daze. Barbara thought it was all terribly funny! Maybe they all did. And maybe—the thought was chilling—it *was* funny, and she was the only one in the room who thought differently.

Well, no time to conjecture now because Peter was running through the Rules of Brainstorming, which signaled that it was beginning. She only half listened; she knew the rules by heart. She'd been one of the first people in advertising to be in on this spectacular new idea: the idea that a bunch of people getting together and just spinning out their thoughts about a product without anyone saying "No, it won't work" or "It's been done before" or "That's stupid" or "It'll cost too much," might come up with a winner.

She knew she didn't always treat brainstorm sessions with respect. But that didn't mean she *had* no respect. The notion of putting aside all negative thoughts for a time was a workable one. She'd seen plenty of good campaigns, nifty marketing ideas, and terrific slogans come out of brainstorms. If you allowed the creativity to flow, as it were, allowed the chaff to come out along with the wheat, you ended up with much more wheat. And they could be fun; often they were; and surely, they should be.

Of course Peter could have picked a better time than one o'clock on a Friday afternoon in June in the middle of an unseasonal heat wave. But, what the hell. The sooner they got on with it, the sooner she'd be sitting on her deck, drink in hand, all cares thrown overboard on the way over.

"Today, we will work on different ways to market Nature Boy's loofah sponge," Peter was saying. And there went young Bob Wagma, first crack out of the hat, saying, "How the hell do you tell a Nature Boy loofah from any other loofah!" and a delighted smile spread over Peter's lean face. He loved ringing that bell. He did it now, banging on it with fervor. "Uh-oh," he said, shaking his head. "Somebody has forgotten rule number one."

"Sorry," Bob said, his face becoming positively crimson. "No negative thinking. I'll remember."

And then they were off and running, as Peter monitored the tape recorder. "Dye them a bright color!" "Yes, something unusual, like puce!" "Like hot pink!" "Like stripes!" "Polka dots!" "Ns and Bs for Nature Boy!" "Or give them a name, like Lucy Loofah!" "That's like Chiquita Banana!" DING DING DING went Peter's bell. "Slit them and put soap inside!" "Put bubble bath inside!" "Cut in shapes and sell as bath toys!" "Cut into shapes according to use, like boats for the bath and pots for the kitchen!"

During a longish pause in the proceedings, Peter looked over at Natalie and said, "You're terribly quiet today, my dear. Is that the way for the creative director of my agency to act in a brainstorm?"

Dare she? She looked him straight in the eye. "Buzz buzz, Peter. Or ding ding." She had to remember that, boss or no boss, she had known him when he was in diapers, practically. If she ever let Peter Marcus terrorize her, she was finished. And he dearly loved playing terror games. Well she remembered the couple of years when he fired her regularly every Friday, only to call her over the weekend and plead with her to return. She had promised herself when he stopped that she'd never let him jerk her around again.

He gave her a look, but said only, "I thought I was saying something positive, cheering you on, as it were."

She took in a breath, and rapidly recited: "Cut it into a loaf shape and call it Loafa Loofah. Glue it onto a stick like a bathbrush. Back it up with terry toweling for the complete rubdown. Package it with Nature Boy's body lotion. Put all the odd shapes left over in a mesh bag and sell it as Odds and Ends of Loofah. . . ." She paused and smiled at Peter. At that moment, someone chimed in with something else, and quickly the room was once again filled with the sound of voices. Natalie kept her eyes on Peter's. His face was bland and blank, but she could have sworn there was a gleam of disappointment in those deep-set eyes.

Once again, her heart began to hammer painfully. Dammit, she wished she knew why he had it in for her. He kept intimating that she was losing touch. But that was nonsense . . . wasn't it? Hadn't she just shown that she was still full of ideas, *good* ideas? Did she have to keep proving herself, over and over and over? Jesus, as creative director of M & M, she ought to be in a position where she could relax a little! Instead of that . . .

Irritated with him, annoyed with herself, she said loudly, "Excuse me, Peter, but it's now 3:45. *Pee em.*"

"Yes, and?—"

"And it's Friday."

"So?"

"And it's summer. Didn't you send out a memo two weeks ago, setting up summer hours for Friday? We were going to close at 3:30 on Fridays, I thought."

Peter gazed at her. There was something implacable in his look, something that gave her the feeling he was about to say something horrible, something that would hurt her, something she really didn't want to hear. But all he said, after a moment, was, "You know something, Nat? Once again, you're absolutely right. It *is* 3:45 pip emma, it *is* Friday, and it *is* summer and I *did* send out a memo. . . . And you're all excused, boys and girls, with many thanks—Nature Boy will be delighted with all these ideas—except for you, Nat. If you don't mind, I'd like a word with you."

And why the hell did she feel precisely like a juvenile delinquent about to face the judge? She sat, her eyes fixed firmly upon the table, while everyone bustled out, chattering and laughing, free. When Barbara stopped by, she muttered, "Go ahead, wait for me in my office, I'll be right there." And felt somewhat ashamed . . . Why couldn't she say it right out loud, like a regular grown-up person? That's what Peter could do to you . . . *if* you let him.

The room emptied quickly, but Peter kept right on talking softly into the tape recorder, casting his eyes heavenward from time to time as if waiting for the gods to speak to him. Honestly, he was a pain sometimes. She recalled that he ignored her this same way when his father brought him into the agency one day. . . . God, it was years and years and *years* ago and he was a snotty teenager; and he very carefully buried his head in a book or something while she waited to get his attention. His father had said, "Teach him, Nat." And she damned well better. But the young Peter didn't like the idea, not at all.

"Peter?" she said now. "Didn't you want to speak to me?"

Just as all those years ago, he brought his eyes up to look at her, vaguely, questioningly, as if he'd forgotten exactly who she was. "Speak to you? About what?"

"*I* don't know, Peter," she said, in her best patient voice. "I thought perhaps you'd like to tell *me*."

"I can't think what . . . Oh hell, it's gone, that's all."

Through gritted teeth: "Then am I excused?"

"Natalie! Of course! Since when do you have to ask? Have a nice weekend! Say . . . didn't you just buy a house on Fire Island? In Paradise? What a name!"

"Yes to all three."

He smiled enigmatically. "Then I'll see you. I'll be visiting Bambi again . . . Bambi Hirsch."

"I didn't think there was another Bambi out there, Peter."

He waved her off, narrowing his eyes at her for a moment. "Spend some time out in the sun, Natalie darling. You've been looking awfully . . . *tired*, lately."

She left without another word, hurrying to the ladies' room. She knew what *tired* meant. She leaned on the sink, giving herself a quick appraisal in the mirror. Yes, she knew what that meant.

She looked *old*.

❀ 6 ❀

The Bay Witch

It was a relief to get out of the hot train and then out of the hot taxi and, finally, at last, onto *The Bay Witch*, the six o'clock ferry to Paradise. It was jammed, of course; it always was. "Dammit," Natalie said to Barbara, dumping her duffel into the luggage pile and heading for the bow, "if Peter had let us out when he was supposed to, we'd have been able to make the five o'clock. . . . Oh, well, nothing's ever a total loss." She lifted the plastic glass of vodka and tonic she was holding and took a sip. "We did have time to stop off at Bailey's."

Barbara leaned on the rail next to her, tucking her hair behind her ears. Casually, she said, "I thought you said last week that you weren't going to drink before seven o'clock."

"I *wasn't* going to. But extreme pains in the arse call for extreme measures. That meeting!—"

Barbara laughed. "For the sixteenth time," she said, "shall I remind you of our promise to each other on the train and in the taxi and at the bar? . . ."

"The promise that we wouldn't talk about business any more for the remainder of the weekend? *That* promise?"

"The very same."

"But I'm not talking about business, Barbara." She took another swig of the drink. "I'm talking about *me*. You see how Peter picks at me all the time."

"Pick at you? No he doesn't! What I heard was him telling you how smart you are."

"In that way he has that says you'd better not *be* so smart."

79

"Oh, Nat! Don't be silly. Why in the world should Peter put you down?"

"Since when has Peter Marcus ever needed a *reason* for doing *any* goddamn thing?"

"Come on, Nat, that's not fair. Peter's much different now. . . . Oh, yes, he is, admit it. God, when I first came to work for M & M, he was as wiggy as could be. And he just got crazier and crazier . . . remember? But after his breakdown, after he got shrunk, you know as well as I do that he's been just fine."

"Depends on what you consider fine," Natalie said. "He's great at getting business, yes. Hey, come on, nobody ever said Peter Marcus was *stupid*. But he's after me. He's playing games with me. . . . Oh, don't give me that look. I haven't had *that* much to drink."

"Well, I just don't see that he did anything at all to you today at that brainstorm. I was there and what I remember is him praising you. Oh, he did ask you to not act up. But, you know Natalie, you *do* carry on sometimes. And you know how seriously Peter takes his brainstorms. If I were you, I'd just cool it during brainstorms, period. I hope you don't mind my saying this, Nat, but you're just a little too casual with Peter, a lot of the time."

"What is *that* supposed to mean?"

"I'm sorry, Natalie, but Peter's the president of M & M. No, wait a minute. You're always telling people, like a joke, that you taught him everything he knows. And it's true maybe; but maybe it's not funny to him. You're so off hand with him sometimes . . . as if he were your kid brother, instead of your boss."

"Well, that's how I feel. And as far as I can see, he hasn't grown up all that much since I saved his hide four years ago. Dammit, he never, ever said 'thank you.' And when he got back from the funny farm . . . remember? . . . for a long time he just wandered around like a faint gray ghost. While yours truly ran the whole place. And then, all of a sudden one day, he appeared in my office, all spruced up, in a brand new suit— with a vest, yet—and, I'll never forget it, he leaned on his hands, way over my desk until we were nose to nose, and he grinned at me and said, 'Hi there, Nattie. It's me! I'm back in the world. And back in charge of M & M.' Well, I guess he *is* in charge and he's good at a lot of stuff and he's brought in a lot of new business. But, I don't know . . . I still feel protective, I guess."

"Isn't it the Chinese who believe that when you save a life, you owe that person forever?"

"Well, I'm not Chinese, but that just about says it. I just wish I knew what the hell was in *his* head . . . why he's giving me the business."

"And *I* say you're imagining it. Come on, Nat, Peter loves you! He knows the agency would fall on its face without you."

Natalie made a deprecating gesture, but she smiled. "And just to make matters worse," she said, "he already announced to me that he's coming out here again to see his beloved."

"That didn't take long, did it? They really are going at it hot and heavy."

"I find it irritating."

"Irritating? Why?"

"Because for one thing, I don't believe all their romantic twaddle, not for a minute. Come on, she's so crazy about him, supposedly, but she's still after any man who looks at any other woman. She can't leave *anyone* alone!"

"She's not married to him; she can do what she likes."

"Yeah, well, she's got someone. Let her leave the other men for the rest of us!"

Barbara laughed. "Natalie, Natalie, I do believe you're a bit green-eyed. But she can't hold a candle to you. In fact, there are very few of us who don't pale in your bright blaze."

"Many thanks, friend." Natalie drained the glass and stared pensively out toward the horizon for a moment. "But you know, I'm no kid any more. Not even after lopping six years off my age!" She laughed briefly.

"That Bambi! Can you believe . . . last week, on the beach, she was carrying on at length about how she *adores* being quote an older woman unquote . . . how every line in her adorable little face bespeaks the love affair that put it there . . . how now, at her advanced age, she finally feels womanly and so-phisticated and experienced and exciting! And, goddammit, Barbara, this so-called older woman, this aging coquette, this experienced old babe, is all of thirty. *Thirty!*" This last was said with such deep disgust that Barbara shrieked with de-light.

"Not funny, Barbara! Bambi is very well aware of my age . . . well, my new age, anyway. But even with the lie, I'm ten years older than she is. And she kept giving me these sly little looks."

"Oh, Natalie! Honestly! You're beginning to sound posi-tively paranoid!"

"Part of growing old. Don't you dare laugh, Barbara. Dam-mit, every time I look in the mirror, I see another wrinkle, another crease, another crow's foot, another sag, another bag. And it's showing up in my social life, too. Fred took me out once and that was it. That guy, what's his name, Barry, he took me out once and I haven't heard from him, either. It's damned depressing."

"Ho, ho," Barbara said, holding onto the rail tightly as the boat made its sharp turn in toward Fire Island. "And who was it who told me, very seriously, a couple of days ago that the trouble with most women is that they're waiting for a man to complete their lives?"

"I'm *not* waiting for a man to complete my life!"

"Oh, Nat! you're always looking *at* men and looking *for* men!"

Natalie laughed and held her skirts, which were starting to blow about in the sea breeze. "Want to sit below? Me, neither. I'd rather get blown to bits than swelter . . . especially after the week we just had. . . . I ask you, 104°? New York has the most impossible weather! What were we talking about?"

Barbara laughed. "What else? Men!"

"Oh, yeah. Well, of course I always look at men. But I don't want to *marry* one! Come on, Barbara, dating is one thing and a permanent relationship is something altogether else!"

She laughed again, ruefully. "All I want is a good time, nothing serious."

Barbara tied a scarf around her head, leaned on the rail, and said thoughtfully, "You know, you're lucky to have that attitude. I think it makes the single life so much easier, being able to just . . . well, have a good time whenever the mood strikes you. I tried sleeping with a lot of men. But it doesn't work for me. If I'm going to make love to a man, I just have to be in love . . . or in like . . . or in-volved."

"Don't tell me you want to get involved again! Jesus, Barbara, you just got through with an involvement and it did nothing for you except give you pain, grief, and misery. I can tell by that sheepish look, you're ready to do it again, as soon as Mr. Right comes along! Jesus Christ, Barbara, what is wrong with women? They keep on looking for the one wonderful relationship with a man that's going to make them okay! It's a crock, Barbara, can't you see that? It's a canard, a trick, and a trap! Why, why, *why* do women think they're worthless if they don't have a quote relationship unquote with a goddamn *man!*"

Barbara was laughing hysterically. "Hey, Nat, you're a woman too, remember? And everyone's staring!"

"Fuck everyone! It's true, goddammit, it's true, and we're *all* dupes, every goddamn last one of us. Including me. So what's so funny?"

"I'm laughing on the outside, crying on the inside," Barbara said. "You're one hundred percent right and here I stand, Exhibit A! I *am* still looking for Mr. Right and shame on me! But . . . I just like being married."

Oh, the look on Natalie's face! It would have curdled milk, as Barbara's grammy always said. Maybe it *was* kind of the wrong thing to say to a woman who was just getting out of a marriage that didn't work. But, Barbara thought, she herself had been divorced for three years now and she knew one thing: She didn't really care for the single life. The world traveled in couples, there was no way around it.

Her relationship with Hal had filled her with hope and with relief. No need to be alone any more, to be single, to be empty.

And Hal was a lot of fun. He was so eager for them to do things together. He got her to try squash—she was awful—and he taught her how to play bridge. She had the makings of a really fine player, he told her, if she would only concentrate. And he insisted she should just try, just *try* to learn how to play chess.

"Anyone who is as logical and organized as you are," he said, "will certainly be able to play a good game of chess."

She really did try to understand chess. But she couldn't get much further than memorizing the moves: knights, two up one over or one up two over and pawns straight one square at a time and bishops diagonally any number of spaces. She couldn't seem to keep it in her head, and Hal just couldn't understand it. "You're so intelligent, Barbara. You're the smartest woman I've ever known. I think it's a matter of not caring enough." And she didn't say, as she wanted to: "Why should I care about a game? especially one you win by killing off your opponent?" Instead, she tried harder, and he was so delighted when she seemed to catch on. "You're learning," he crowed when she managed to make two good moves in a row one evening. "You're learning!" And he leaned over to kiss her. He was so pleased with her! And she wondered why that didn't make her feel better.

Of course, as she couldn't help noticing, Hal was somewhat rigid. Not as bad as Mark—good grief, nobody *could* be— but he had his particular ways and he didn't like them messed with. He liked to think he was an adventurous diner, and it was true that he would try anything once. But once he liked a given dish, woe betide the woman who changed a single ingredient. "What's *wrong* with this chili?" he would demand. Or, "What have you done to this veal?" Putting her on the defensive when she had nothing to be defensive about.

And he also had the endearing habit of insisting upon absolute silence when he was playing the stereo. You couldn't ask him if he wanted something. You couldn't even say, "I love you." You had to tiptoe around while he sat enthroned in an easy chair, eyes focused on something far far away.

She knew these little things were not important, not really;

but they nagged at her. And then one Sunday, they were sprawled on her living room rug, in front of the fire, reading the Sunday *Times*, sipping wine, feeling cozy and comfortable, and he did it again. He handed her the magazine section and said, "Read this 'For Men Only.' It's wonderful." She did so and then handed it back to him, eager to discuss the article. But he frowned at her and said, "You can't be finished already."

She laughed. "Yes I can. You know I read fast."

"You read too fast."

She found herself getting irritated. "What do you mean, *too* fast?"

"Just what I said, Barbara. You read too fast. You couldn't possibly get it all when you skim like that."

"I don't skim. I simply read quickly."

Then he laughed, condescending and disbelieving. "Call it what you like, darling." He spread his arms wide as if to ask the world's indulgence.

She found herself becoming enraged, unable even to speak for fear her voice would shake with it. She couldn't look at him.

"Here," Hal went on, totally oblivious, "let me test you. We'll see how much you got, reading that quickly."

That brought her to her feet, fighting mad. "Who do you think you *are*?" she managed, her voice sounding choked and strange in her ears. "Who the *hell* do you think you are, to test me and test me?"

"Barbara! Barbara!" He leaped to his feet and wrapped his arms around her, murmuring little comfort noises, kissing her on her neck and her nose and her cheek and her eyelids. And of course, it ended with them making love. It always did. And, dammit, she still missed it . . . all of it. Even the testing.

Now she took in a deep breath, let it out, and said, "The truth is, Nat, I miss being married."

"Yeah, well, all *I* ever miss is being laid."

"Oh, Nat, I don't really believe that."

"Believe it. That's all they're good for really. That's all you can count on from a man."

Barbara put an arm around her friend's shoulder. "Oh, Nat, you can't really mean that."

"There's not a man in this world who can be trusted to be there when you need him."

"Now I *know* you're making it up. How about Jerry? Don't try to tell me he can't be trusted, that he's not dependable. My God, isn't that exactly why you married him? Didn't you tell me? And, furthermore, isn't that exactly why you finally couldn't stand him any more, didn't you tell me?"

Stubbornly, Natalie answered, "Jerry, too. Jerry couldn't be trusted to be there when I needed him." There was a long pause, and Barbara was able to hear the people behind them, laughing about somebody's hat blown into the water.

Then Natalie continued: "Yes, I married Jerry because . . . I don't know, really, because he was fatherly, I guess. I thought he was so much older and wiser and smarter and calmer than I. And he was, I guess. But . . . you know, he wasn't much of a lover, Barbara. He wasn't very interested in me sexually. Oh, I was a good faithful wife, I really was, and I really wanted to be. The first time I . . . strayed, was with Jake. And that was special. I mean, I loved Jake, I always loved him. After that, though, it just got easier. Jerry made me feel undesirable, unpretty, unwanted, unsexual. I'm not sorry I fooled around; he deserved it.

"The horrible part of it is, he never said a word about it. Not one goddamn word. He just went on in his elephantine way, pretending it wasn't happening, puffing on that fucking pipe and calling me sweetheart and giving me husbandly kisses good-bye when I left for the office each morning." She made a face. "Agh! I kept wanting to say 'Jerry, I fuck other men. *Do* something. *Say* something. *Kick* me out or get me back!' Never mind . . . it didn't happen. We went on pretending to have a marriage. You know, seven years ago I told him never to touch me again and you know what he said? He said, 'Whatever you want, sweetheart'!"

Barbara said, "What? No rape scenes in the middle of the night? Oh, God, I'm sorry, that wasn't nice."

Natalie gave a short laugh. "It's okay. No, no rape scenes

on the living room couch. That would have been much too
assertive for our Jerry! No. He didn't *care* about the marriage,
he didn't give a goddamn how I really felt about him or what
was really happening between us. Just so long as it all *looked*
good. Just so long as nobody in the world knew what a failure
we had. In public, you know—well, of course you know
because you saw us together—in public, he was the Complete
Attentive and Contented Husband. It made me so goddamn
mad, Barbara. It was so fake and so phony and I just longed
for him to face facts, just once, just for a minute! I wanted
something real, for a change. But, no, he'd rather look away,
he'd rather not deal with it, he'd rather pretend that nothing
was happening. Just like my old man—" She stopped abruptly;
and then said, musingly, "Jesus, I hadn't thought about that,
for years."

"What?"

"Nothing, just something about my father. Ah, look, rising
out of the sea, as it were. Over there, on the horizon. Paradise."
As she spoke, the ferry made its final sweeping curve, and the
town of Paradise seemed magically to appear out of the bay,
half-hidden in a pearly band of mist. Little sailboats bobbed
gently at their moorings, and there were four clammers in
T-shirts and shorts bending and dipping into the water. Idyllic,
Natalie thought. Instant calm, better than Valium.

Barbara said, "You never told me before...that Jerry
accepted not sleeping with you. Nothing could be more opposite than the marriage I had with Mark. We had very little
except sex going for us."

"And we had very little sex, period," Natalie said.

Barbara waited a moment, uncertain of Natalie's mood.
Then she said, "You're probably not going to like hearing this
again, Nat, but—"

Now Natalie laughed. "Don't you say it. Sandy Lovall is
not another Jerry! They just look alike, that's all. They're as
different as night and day. Hey, I ought to know, right?"

"I know you *ought* to know. What continually surprises me
is your obstinate denial. Sandy Lovall is Jerry Weber in a curly
wig and Hawaiian shirt. I don't know why you won't see it."

"Because, dammit, Barbara, it ain't so. Sandy is funny, gentle, caring, patient, and above all, creative."

"Oh, and Jerry Weber is rough, crude, and self-centered? And he's not creative? What's he doing in that den of his, sitting all day at the typewriter with pages coming out of it? Making borscht?"

"Enough, enough," Natalie said. "It doesn't matter. I'm not going to marry Sandy Lovall. For Christ's sake, it isn't a romance! In fact, if you want to know the truth, he's never touched me. In fact, he's more affectionate to Annie than he is to me."

"All the more reason for me to lecture you, Nat. Ah..." The last was said as the boat engines were reversed and the water beneath them began to churn. "I can't wait to get to the house and shuck these city clothes. Anyway, what I'm saying is, since you've been spending every free moment lately with Sandy Lovall, it's *stupid* that you're not even having a romance. Because, if you keep it up, you'll be cutting off your other options—and for nothing!"

"At least he's involved with his community—*my* community, too, I might add. And besides, Barbara, I know damn well what you mean when you say 'options.' A man I can marry, *that's* what 'option' means! Well, I've told you a million times, I don't want to get married again, *ever*. Therefore, it follows, as the night the day, that I don't want to find a man to marry."

The boat bumped to a halt against the side of the dock and the engines were cut abruptly, leaving a ringing silence.

Barbara laughed. "Take a lesson from me. Hal was a variation of Mark. But I've learned. I'll *never* do that again!"

Natalie grinned and picked up their two cases, handing one to Barbara. "Wanna bet?"

● 7 ●

The House That Jack Built

They opened the door to Bob's Bar at five after five and already the place was waist-high with cigarette smoke and a din of voices. "Yuck," Natalie said, wrinkling up her nose. "Saturday!" And Barbara laughed. "Since when does Natalie Simon every say yuck to Happy Hour when drinks are two for the price of one?"

"Not tonight, Barbara. Not with *him* holding forth." She gestured to the middle of the room, where one of the round tables was surrounded by a tight jam of chairs with Peter Marcus, impeccable in white, officiating. "I've had just about all I can take of Peter Marcus," she said sourly.

"And so has someone else, I think," Barbara said, indicating a rather sullen-looking Sandy Lovall slumped on his usual stool at the end of the bar, frowning in Peter's direction.

"I don't want to deal with either of them," Natalie said, making up her mind all at once. "I have my drink. I'm going to take a walk, okay?"

"Oh, Natalie . . . don't let Peter get to you. I'll be fine; I'll go sit with Sandy and cheer him up."

Natalie took herself off, not caring where she went.

What a day! Beautiful beach weather . . . She had gotten up this morning thinking she'd get out there and work on her tan and forget her troubles. And that's how it had started: She and Sandy and Barbara with their cheese sandwiches and flask of margaritas and book of crossword puzzles, lying side by side on the warm white sand, chatting, relaxing, giving each other words. Until after lunch, when she and Barbara became a band of two, handing out buttons and pamphlets emblazoned with the *leitmotif* of Sandy's obsession: "Save Halfmoon Pond . . . Forever Wild." He buttonholed—belly-buttonholed was more like it!—everyone on the beach, giving little pep talks and lecturing small children about the importance of wetlands until they looked as if they wished he would sink into one and disappear. He hadn't been kidding when he promised to make a pest of himself this summer. By two in the afternoon, she'd had it up to *here* with the ruination of Halfmoon Pond.

So when Peter and Bambi appeared, loaded down with gear, she gave a shout of welcome and motioned them to come sit next to their blanket—a move she soon had cause to regret, because Peter wanted a touch-football game; and when Peter wanted something, Peter nudged and cajoled and argued and begged until he got it. In fact, most people wanted to do what Peter suggested because he got so enthusiastic that it always sounded like the best fun in the world.

She was the lone holdout, and of course, Peter Marcus was not going to put up with anything so antisocial, not on *his* beach. It maddened her how quickly he was able to make this section of the beach his very own—and the man wasn't even a resident, he was just a lousy visitor.

"Come on, Nattie, you're on my team in the city, and I insist that you be on my team here."

"Peter. Darling. Read my lips. I don't want to play touch football. It's not my sport. Snowshoeing is my sport. Hanggliding is my sport. You want to join me hang-gliding with snowshoes on, swell. But football? Nyet."

"Team! I implore you! Convince this woman. We need her to run interference. She's all muscle. Look at those legs. Look at those arms."

"Look at this fist!" Nat laughed.

But Peter did not find this amusing. "Nobody loves a smart-ass, Nat," he said warningly and those closest to this scene began to look uncomfortable.

Then Sandy Lovall looked up from his sketchbook and said, "Hey, stop picking on the lady. First of all, she's petite, and second of all, we're not in the office now, we're on the public beach, and third and most important, I happen to be drawing her and I don't want her to move." He'd been lying, of course; actually, he had been sketching Peter. But it did shut Peter up for the moment. Not that he was about to let it go; not Peter. Peter loved to say that he didn't get mad, he got even. So he kept on yelling things about how Natalie could have got *that* one and Natalie would have caught *that* one and pretty soon, she was laughing helplessly and helplessly picking herself up and going over there and playing touch football. This, in spite of the fact that Sandy said, "If you crumble, if you let that overgrown brat euchre you into doing something you don't want to do . . . then don't expect me to take your side again."

When she got up, she grinned at Sandy and said, "You don't know what's been going on in the office, but believe me, it's important that I play football right now, if I value my job. I know it's dumb and I know it's childish and I know it's cowardly. But there you are."

"He's a pain."

"Well . . . he's *my* pain . . . and I have to handle it."

When the game was over, after they all—at Peter's insistence—had run into the waves and splashed each other and she had come back to the big blanket, Sandy had just shaken his head sadly at her and without a word handed her a fresh drink. "I hope he's not here for the entire summer," he said. "Because he's not my favorite person."

"From your lips to God's ears," Natalie laughed. "But I think it's a vain hope because I think cupid's arrow has struck once more." And they both looked over to where Peter and Bambi stood, arms wrapped tightly around each other, gazing intently into each other's eyes, occasionally kissing, murmuring all the time.

Barbara, who was oiling herself again, looked up too and laughed. "Bambi's nose is out of joint. Oh, lord, she couldn't stand it when Peter was teasing you!"

"See?" Natalie demanded. "That's how clever he is. You think he was joshing me in a cute, friendly way. And that's what it looked like. But I know, I know Peter too well, and I know damn well he's putting me down. 'All muscle'! What

kind of a thing is that to say to a woman? Made me sound like
Mean Joe Green . . . whoever that is!" And then they all laughed
and the subject was dropped.

But, Natalie thought, walking along the bay, listening to
the sounds of lapping water and distant music from someone's
deck, I can't drop the subject because the subject is me. Why,
she wondered, did she always end up with men who eventually
wanted to humiliate and dump her?

Jack Henderson . . . God, it was all so long ago, and yet
every once in a while, his face appeared before her, vivid with
detail, as clear as if she'd seen him yesterday. Jack Henderson,
her first love. Her first lover, if you could call their brief
grapplings in the back seat of his father's car, on top of a
scratchy Hudson Bay blanket, lovemaking. Looking back on
it, she realized later that it was unsatisfactory, too fast and
fumbling. The first time, in fact, she lay in the dark, eyes wide
open and staring at the felt ceiling in the car, thinking to herself,
Is this *all*? Is *this* what all the fuss is about? And that night,
when she got home, she stared into her dresser mirror because
all the Frank Yerby novels she loved reading said that the
woman was supposed to look different, somehow. But all she
saw staring back at her was the usual, regular face with the
too-long nose and the too-round eyes and the too-thick-and-
unruly black hair. She finally said, in her most solemn voice,
"You are not a virgin." But in truth, she didn't feel the least
little bit changed. All she knew was that she must be in love
with him, if she did it with him. That was the revealed wisdom
and she managed to believe it, right through her junior year in
high school and the next summer and the year after that. She
and Jack Henderson were a "couple," they were going steady,
and her father muttered and mumbled about them being too
young . . . and several times when he and her stepmother came
home earlier than expected, nearly caught them in bed together.
And once, when they were squirming around on the sofa in
the living room, there was the awful sound of her father's key
turning in the lock. He must have seen their distress and di-

shevelment; he must have! But not by look or word or attitude did he ever admit it.

Come to think of it, her father *never* allowed himself to recognize that she was sexually active—and she certainly was, all through college and beyond. He had to know what was going on when she didn't come home until six in the morning; he had to have been told by her snoopy stepmother that she had a diaphragm. God, he had to know! She had made a decision that she was going to do what seemed right to her and that she wasn't going to make excuses for her behavior . . . and that when he confronted her with it, she was ready to stand up for her convictions. "Sex isn't okay just for boys" she was going to tell him. "The double standard stinks." She had a whole speech prepared. But she never got the chance to give it.

Because her father never said a word, never showed by the slightest flicker of an eyelid that he had any idea at all what was going on right in front of him. The coward! Her relationship with her father had gone downhill very rapidly after he remarried; and by the time she came home for Thanksgiving, her freshman year at college, she had ceased to think of Hampton as home. She hadn't *had* a home, till she went to work at M & M.

Walking along the edge of the bay, staring sightlessly out over the still water, Natalie stopped in astonishment. Good God, M & M was home to her, not a job, but *home*! It was where she had proved she was a grown-up; it was where she became successful. Not to mention it was where she met Jerry, where she met Jake, where she met Barbara. It was the center, the core, of her life, in fact. Why the hell hadn't she ever seen that before? What a dummy! No wonder Peter held so much power over her. No wonder she crumbled when he frowned. No wonder he could make her stomach knot up so easily. No wonder she jumped when he said jump and played touch football when he said play. He was Daddy, in her mind, just as Old Man Marcus had been. God, of course! She'd been the favored child of Old Man Marcus; he used to say proudly, putting an arm around her, "This is my best investment, this little girl." Just like a father with his daughter. And then he

had died and Peter had taken his place and . . . oh, lord, it was
ludicrous! Peter as the father figure! She took a sip of her drink
and laughed aloud. It was a goddamn joke and unfortunately,
the joke was on her. Because it was her palms sweating and
her heart quaking and goddammit, it was *her* job on the line,
her life that was falling apart.

She shook herself in exasperation and turned to the left. She
didn't care where she went, really, just so long as she could
keep moving. Yeah, Natalie, she twitted herself, and maybe
that's the story of your life, right there in that sentence. Maybe
that's why you've come to in your forty-fifth—woops, thirty-
ninth and holding—year, facing a void. Never mind where,
just stay in motion.

The path took her into a forest of high dune grass, stained
pink by the lowering sun, rustling gently in the breeze that
always sprang up in the early evening. Natalie swung along,
breathing deeply. She loved being in the thick of the tall, pale
grasses, having the rest of the world shut out, closed off from
view. She liked being able to hear only the wind and the faint
cries of seagulls. It was nice to be so utterly safe. . . . She even
walked along for a minute or two with her eyes closed.

Safe. Yes, of course. Her life wasn't really falling apart,
even though she got to feeling that way. It was just all the
changes in her life, the separation, leaving the apartment and
the neighborhood and then, having this gut-wrenching feeling
that Peter wanted to dump her—that's all it was. Just everything
happening at once—and her fertile imagination, making it into
a melodrama.

In reality, she wasn't losing everything, not at all. Didn't
she have her own house? Yes, she did. She had her own house,
the first house in her life since she'd stopped thinking of the
rambling Victorian on East Main Street in Hampton as home.
She'd even decorated it in her head. She had never been big
on interior decoration. She'd always left that to others: her
husband, her roommates, her secretaries. But with this house,
suddenly, she was moved to nest-building. At least in her day-
dreams. She'd never gotten around to actually *doing* anything

about it, of course, and actually, it was Barbara who was buying fabric and rearranging furniture and deciding on color schemes.

But she loved that house. She stopped in her tracks, in the middle of the dune grass, and smiled to herself. She hadn't thought about it too much, but, yes, she loved the house. Every Friday, when she got on board the little ferry at Bay Shore, she felt her spirits lift immediately, almost automatically. The house in Paradise meant fun and freedom and peace and quiet and respite from the hurlyburly.

Peace, quiet, respite: Weren't those the reasons she had bought a house on Fire Island at a price that still gave her a bellyache? To have peace and quiet, some change from the constant crisis atmosphere at the office, some fresh air and space and—and then she laughed right out loud. Because of course, that was *not* why she had beggared herself and given herself the job of traveling two hours just to get to a ferryboat so she could travel another thirty minutes so she could get here. She was here because she'd fallen in love—with a *place* this time, and with a house and with a rather weird fantasy that managed to include peace and quiet with lots and lots of partying.

So what if Peter threw her out? She was well known, hell, she was *prized*, in the ad game. Not a month went by that she didn't get some kind of offer for work! Well, maybe not exactly lately, but she wouldn't have any trouble at all, making a good living. She could freelance. She could come out here, live here all year round, buy a little car and drive into the city for meetings. She could see it now: watching the snowflakes drifting by the big picture window . . . hearing the wind howl outside while a merry fire blazed in the fireplace . . . striding, scarved, sweatered, booted, and looking like a Ralph Lauren magazine ad, down a windswept, wintery beach, a big beautiful Golden Retriever by her side.

"Oh, come *on*, Natalie!" Once again, she stopped in her tracks and, throwing her head back, began to laugh. What kind of fantasy was she spinning, complete with a Golden Retriever! She didn't even like dogs!

The well-trodden pathway took a sudden twist, and there, quite suddenly, was a rather large crescent-shaped pond with lilypads crowding its edges, cattails rearing up in silhouette against the graying sky. A beat later, she became aware of the sound, not at all typical of the beach: the grunts and croaks and peeps of frogs, a sound, she realized with a smile, she hadn't heard since childhood, lying in her bed of a hot summer's night. So this was Halfmoon Pond, Sandy's cause and mission. It was lovely; it was totally unexpected here in the middle of Fire Island. And, yes, Sandy was right: It was special.

And then she noticed all the insults to this beautiful and peaceful scene: pilings set out on the far side; browning, decaying heaps of cut-down grass; ugly bald spots in the natural growth. And, worst of all, the shiny metal retaining wall that cut across the still water, and behind it, a wheezing, pulsating pump, which she could not hear. Christ! they were going to ruin this whole area, she could see that. Anyone with half an eye could see it! Damn real estate people! She'd watched them swarm all over her beloved Upper West Side, gentrifying it right out of existence, boutiquing it to death! They never gave a damn about who lived there or what changes might do to them!

From across the pond, a very loud, very male voice yelled: "Goddammit all to hell, anyway! You fucker!" followed by frantic splashings and more cursing . . . and then the sound of machinery, turned on, chuck-a-chuck-a-chuck, and a flock of startled small birds took sudden flight, rising in the air in graceful arcs and then flying away in a flutter.

"Hey!" Natalie shouted, indignant. "You! What do you think you're doing! Hey! Show your face!"

And then she saw him, almost directly across the pond, oblivious to her, tramping around, cursing loudly every time he sank into the muck at the pond's edge. His denim workclothes were splattered with mud and grease, as were the high black rubber boots.

He looked up and saw her, finally. "Get outta here!" he called. "You're trespassing! This is private property!"

"Not where I am!" She deliberately took a sip from her glass, glaring at him over the rim.

"Halfmoon Associates owns it all, lady! You're trespassing! Get the hell outta here!"

"How very polite!"

"Oh, you want polite? Okay. *Kindly* get the hell outta here." Meanwhile he made his splashing sloppy way over toward her. "Come on, lady, don't make trouble, okay? Beat it!" And he made that shooing gesture with both hands.

"This is public land."

"Oh, you think so?" He was getting very close, and it was making her very nervous. Let him stay over there, where he belonged! Now she could see how big he was. Not so terribly tall, maybe five ten; but blocky and very strong looking. "You want me to *escort* you to the topographical maps?" he said.

And then she started to giggle. His face was smeared with mud, muck, and grease. You couldn't possibly tell what he looked like, except good and mad. The clay-splattered face, the yellow hardhat, the whole macho aspect of him was ridiculous. She really ought not to laugh; he looked *furious*, and furthermore, he could pick her up and throw her into the goddamn pond if he took a mind to! And there *she* stood, defiant in her black and white print jumpsuit, armed with a glass of white wine! The two of them made some picture! She bit her lips frantically. She must *not* laugh.

He glared down at her, hands on his hips. "What's so goddamn funny?"

"You. Me. Us." She couldn't help it. The laughter was pushing out.

For a minute she thought he was going to explode. And then, instead, he began to laugh, not timidly like her, but great big guffaws. Finally, he wiped his eyes with the back of his hand, streaking even more muck around, realized it, pulled his hand away as if it were burning him, and said, "Oh, shit!"

Now that he was smiling and a little more relaxed, she could almost see what he looked like. Nice. Squint lines around the startling green eyes, deep smile grooves either side of the generous mouth. About her age, she guessed. Not a *pretty* man. Rugged. Solid. Nice.

"What do you think you're looking at?" It was a challenge.

"A good-looking guy," she shot back . . . and then smiling, added: "Who needs his face washed."

Involuntarily, he swiped at his face again. "Agh! I've been working."

"So I see. . . . Doing terrible things to the environment."

He grinned at her. How white his teeth looked in the middle of the mud. "You one of those ecology freaks?"

"Why is it that when people band together in a common cause, their adversaries immediately label them freaks?"

"That makes . . . lemme see . . . four, maybe five big words, in a row. So I'm dealing with a smart lady."

"Smart enough . . ."

"Smart enough to what?" Now he was grinning in a way she could only call wolfish.

"Smart enough to smell a line coming from about a mile away."

"Who, *me*? Not me, lady. And anyway, who says we're doing terrible things? This place is going to be better than ever."

"Oh, really? Ever hear of a wetland?"

"I know that's what you people call it—but I call it a goddamn mosquito-infested swamp, which is what it is. That's what I hate about you ecology freaks: When you want it saved, you call it by some fancy name. Just hang around. When it gets darker, you're going to see a helluva lot of mosquitoes around here!"

"A few mosquitoes won't make me love what you're doing! *That* thing for starters!" She gestured at the snoring machine across the pond.

"That *thing*," he said, "is a pump, see? It's going to pump all the excess water outta here and then this place won't be a swamp anymore, see? And people like you will be able to come here and walk in their fancy clothes right to the edge and not sink into ooze up to their knees. See?" And he held up a leg so she could look at his muddy hipboot.

"Some of us," Natalie answered, "*want* this to stay a wetland for the wildlife that lives here."

"You're talking about that through your hat. You don't know anything about it."

"How would *you* know? Some guy pays you to keep a pump running and chase people away, and you automatically parrot his views."

There was a tiny pause. He opened his mouth and then closed it and then opened it again and said, "Maybe. All I know is, if the boss heard you mouthing off, he'd kick you out himself."

"Oh, really? Where is he? I'd like to hear what he has to say. Lead me to him, why don't you? I know who he is. I've met his brother Sandy." He ducked his head, adjusting a buckle on his boot, and muttered something. "Come on," she insisted, "I just want to hear his side."

He laughed then. "I know his side as well as he does. I've heard it often enough. You just ask me *anything* and I'll tell you. We could discuss it. And who knows?" He grinned at her. "Maybe you could convince me of something."

He really *was* coming on to her. Good. He was cute and she hadn't had a blue-collar lover in fifteen years, not since the telephone repairman came in one morning and found her, hung-over and horny, in bed. He had been something else, that Carlos. She wouldn't have minded seeing him again. She remembered very clearly how he lifted her up in the air, as if she weighed nothing, then let her down very gently, right onto his big hard cock, and damned if he didn't screw her that way, standing up, his trunklike legs planted firmly apart. He never even swayed—that she remembered. And he didn't come for almost an hour—that she remembered, too. That was some experience. Later, after Carlos had left, she lay curled up in her bed, exhausted, laughing at it all, falling deeply asleep all of a sudden. And when she awoke, several hours later, not only did she feel satisfied, but the hangover had disappeared. The next day, she had told Jake about it—he was the only other person in the entire world who knew. How he had howled with laughter. "Great! Great!" he'd cried, holding his sides. "Nat Simon's System: Fucking for Fun and Fitness! If we could only sell it as a hangover aid . . . but no, it wouldn't go in a family newspaper!" That Jake!

Too bad Jake had decided he couldn't come visit them this

weekend. Too bad about Jake period. Dammit, she could never think about him, even a funny memory, without some sort of pain. Her best friend—or so she had thought—a man she'd known practically forever, her former colleague, her sometime lover, her wonderful, dear, funny, endearing Jake. Oh, yeah, but he hadn't been able to take it, when she became creative director (and his boss) four years ago. "Call me piggie-wiggie, Nattie, but it goes against the grain." And away he went, not to another agency on Madison Avenue, not Jake. Oh, no, he had to take a job in San Francisco! He'd taken a job, taken a plane, and then, that rat, taken a wife: a very rich, *very* young person of the beautiful blond persuasion, who had then dumped him after two years and sent him back east sulking and sullen.

After his rotten behavior to her at Sandy's opening, she'd let a week or so go by without calling him. The rat, she wasn't going to run after him, not at their age, and certainly not after all the years between them! But she had softened this week, and she had called him and she had cajoled him and charmed him and humored him and in the end, she had invited him out. And he had sighed and said, "Nattie, Nattie, I'm worthless to you right now. Don't ask me why and don't ask me how. Just believe me, okay?" And he'd hung up.

What were you supposed to do with a guy like that? She no longer knew. And, right now, dammit, she didn't want to be thinking about it.

"What's your name, anyway?" she said. To hell with Jake! She had a live one here!

"The boys call me Mr. Dee."

"I'm not one of the boys!"

"I noticed. *You* call me Ben."

"You didn't ask, but I'm Natalie, and the boys call *me* Ms. Simon."

He grinned again at her, and said, "You know what? You're a very cute lady."

It was happening. Waddaya know, it still works! she thought. She was going to go for it!

"Ben, you were right, the mosquitoes *are* starting to bite." And, actually, they were. In the dim light, she couldn't see

them, but she could hear their irritating whine. And feel them!
"Why don't you come back to my house . . . and what the hell,
you may be ruining the environment, but I'll give you a drink
anyway."

"Tell you what, Natalie Simon, since I'm a filthy mess, you
come with *me*. You may be an ecology freak, but I'll give you
a drink anyway." He twinkled, and added: "Don't worry, it's
safe. And it's not far. . . . See over there? That house."

Well, it was rapidly getting dark, and she couldn't see which
house he meant; but what the hell. "You're on."

They moved off single file, saying little as they made their
way back on the narrow dirt path.

His house sat high on a dune overlooking the bay. It was
one of those "summer cottages" from the turn of the century
with about thirty-seven rooms, four attics, and probably a real
basement, too. It was an anachronism, it was excessive, eccentric, and absolutely beautiful. But a hardhat living in a mansion?

She turned wordlessly to look at him; and, as if he could
read her mind, he said, "We'd better use the service entrance,
okay? The boss doesn't like dirt on the rugs."

So. It *wasn't* his. It belonged to the Big Guy. "It's hard to
believe," Natalie said as he ushered her in.

"What's hard to believe?" He sat on the stairway and pulled
off his boots, then his hardhat, and quickly stripped the sweater
over his head.

"That your boss actually lives here on the island and yet,
he'll gladly spoil the natural beauty of Halfmoon Pond."

He made a rude noise with his lips. "I have a rule, Natalie
Simon. No fight talk in the house. Okay?"

"Hell," Natalie laughed, "if we can't fight, what are we
going to do?"

He paused, in the middle of unbuttoning his shirt. "Oh,
we'll find something. . . ." And he smiled into her eyes until
she thought her heart would stop completely. She could hardly
wait to see that face, all washed and clean. "But in the meantime . . ."

"I'm sure," she murmured; and meekly followed him up
the steps into what turned out to be a gigantic slate-floored

kitchen, a kitchen so huge that one half of it was a sitting room. He gestured to the cupboard. "Help yourself, Natalie. And make me a scotch, will you? On the rocks, a little water."

"Oink, oink, oink," she muttered, but he was already gone into another room. In a minute, she heard the splash of water and smelled the strong soap; and quickly, she reached up for the scotch and the vodka. She had two tumblers all fixed up in a minute and sat herself where she could see him through the open doorway, standing at the sink, the water running full blast and steaming. He stood stripped to the waist, scrubbing vigorously, and Natalie sat very still looking at the play of muscle in his upper arms and his back. He was already quite tan from working outdoors. He had a very nice back, very nice, and a lot of curly hair on his chest—not too much, nothing apelike, just a nice mat. White, too, like the thick hair on his head. Interesting. Sexy, in fact. As she watched he shampooed his head, then ducked it under the splashing faucet in the sink, rubbing at his hair vigorously. Everything he did was energetic, almost explosive. *That* might be interesting too, Natalie thought. Especially in bed.

But he mustn't catch her sitting there licking her lips like a cat eyeing the cream. She allowed herself to sink back, drink in hand. After all the activity today, it was a pleasure to just sit and think about nothing.

The water was turned off at last and here came Mr. Possibility, pulling a red polo shirt over his head. He was very cute, she could see now, *very* cute, flattened nose and all. "My drink?" he said and she reached for it, holding it up. "Come and get it!"

He plopped himself down at the other end of the couch, turning to face her, reaching out for the glass. When he got it, he took a hefty swig and then sighed deeply and said, "So here we are, *Ms*. Natalie Simon."

"Your memory is terrific, Mr. Dee. . . . And what does that Dee stand for, anyway?"

"DeLuria."

"Italian."

"Oh, really? No kidding?"

"I'm sorry," she said. "I wasn't trying—"

"Hey." He reached over and put a hand on her arm. "Don't mind me. My sense of humor is a little rough. I'm around guys all the time on the job, you know? I'm not used to talking with ladies."

"Oh, I do love being called a lady!" Natalie laughed. "For the first time in my life."

They continued with the light chat and banter, something that took only a small portion of her brain anyway, while she sipped at her drink, looking him over, and enjoying it. He was looking her over, too. She could swear there was an impish twinkle in his eyes, but she couldn't be sure. Patience, she cautioned herself. Patience, my good woman. Maybe this is how they do it in the lower classes. Slowly. Very slowly. *Too* slowly, if you asked her!

"Tell me something about yourself, Natalie. You interest me."

"What do you want to know?"

"What are you looking for?" Aha. The pitch. At last. They'd been sitting here for over an hour. It was about time!

"What do you mean?"

He grinned. "In life, Natalie, in life. You say you're a VP. Looks like you've made it. So . . . what's next?"

She sipped her drink slowly and regarded him. Did she dare? Was her name Natalie Simon?

"What's next?" she answered, smiling. "What's next, I *hope*, is that we make love."

He stared at her for a moment, dumbly, and then began to laugh. "You really are something, you know that? But it sounds good to me! Come here . . ."

The next thing she knew, she was stripped naked, head whirling, lips tingling, flat on her belly on his big bed while he bit at her back, working his way down to just above the buttocks. A convulsive shiver ran up her spine. She moaned and wriggled, trying to get closer to those caressing lips, that seeking tongue . . . but he laughed and turned her over onto her back, kneeling above her, grinning with pleasure, his eyes alight.

"No, I've had enough of that side for a while. Now let's see what we can do with the front."

Natalie looked up at the rugged face, flushed with lust, and chortled. "Do your worst. . . ."

He laughed. "My worst is my best, sweetheart. Are you ready for that?"

"God, I'm ready for *anything*."

"Good, 'cause that's what I had in mind." And he bent to bite at the soft flesh of her belly, little nips in an ever-widening circle, until she was writhing around in an agony of ecstasy, screaming at him to put it in, for Christ's sake, put it in before she went crazy!

"Beg me, beg me!" He lifted his head and laughed into her face, holding her wrists down with his hands. "Go ahead, goddammit! Beg me!"

"Give it to me, you bastard!" She struggled to free her hands, fighting her laughter. His delight was so infectious! He was wonderful, he was fun, she wanted to feel his cock deep inside her, she *needed* it. . . . "Goddammit, you bastard—"

"Beg, beg!"

"Woof!" Natalie said, and he chuckled, letting one of her hands go. She immediately reached down and grabbed him. "Yum, yum . . ." He felt enormous, hot, and very very stiff.

The look on his face changed, and the eyes gleamed ferally. "Later, baby, later we'll do yum yum . . . but now—" And with a grunt, he rammed into her.

Natalie gasped and then gave herself totally to the sensation: the feel of him as he pounded into her, as he pulled it out, as he teased her by keeping it just at the edge, then pushing in deeply. And then, he grabbed her buttocks, holding her close into him, and started to pump quickly until she felt his already-swollen member swell with that final tension, felt it filling her, stretching her, more and more and more and then he yelled, driving himself deep into her and she could feel the pulsating and the quivering that said it was over. For this time. For this time.

There *would* be a next time, she promised herself fiercely. There had to be. This she had to have more of. This was the

best stuff—wild and free and uninhibited. Not like the last few
guys she'd been with. He had collapsed onto her, and they still
lay closely entwined, relaxing. She could feel his strong heartbeat gradually quieting down, slowing to a regular rhythm.

He finally pushed himself away from her, giving her a light
kiss on the lips. "You gotta watch that stuff with old guys like
me. You could give someone a heart attack."

"I guess that's a compliment," Natalie said, pushing her
fingers through the mat of curly chest hair. "Don't tell me if
it isn't. I prefer to think it is."

"Of course it is! You're terrific!"

"Never mind the compliments. A repeat performance is all
I require."

"Now!?!" he squawked and then he laughed. "You always
so blunt about what you want?"

"That's right. Any objections?"

"Nooo . . . I guess not. If you don't mind waiting. I mean,
I'm not Superman."

"You coulda fooled me. . . ."

He laughed again, patted her hip, and heaved himself up.
She watched him, taking pleasure in watching the solid muscles
of his buttocks as he strode away. And she stretched herself in
the rumpled bed, luxuriating in the tingly sensation still left
between her thighs. There had been a few other interludes
lately, but she'd been a little too looped. So when he came
back, handing her a chunky tumbler full of vodka and ice, she
smiled and said, "No thanks. I don't need that."

It was past midnight when the two of them left the house,
and she, for one, could hardly keep her eyes open.

"Too bad you're going back to the city tomorrow," he said.
"But how about next weekend? It's the Fourth. . . . Same time
. . . Friday . . . you know, around Happy Hour. When I finish
work."

Hosanna! "Sure," she said, trying hard to sound supercool.

"Good." He leaned over and let his mouth rest for one heart-
stumbling moment on hers. His lips were firm, soft, warm;
she longed to bite them. And then they were gone. And she
was breathless. She hoped he couldn't tell; she hoped it didn't

show on her face. There was a moon rising in the sky and enough light for her to see the smile on his lips.

"So long for now . . . Ms. Simon."

"For now, Mr. Dee."

She stood, like a teenager, gooping after him; and at the end of the walk, without turning around, he lifted the flashlight in a jaunty farewell salute.

Natalie laughed aloud. That bastard; he *knew* without even looking that she had been staring after him. And if he knew that, he knew he had her. And she wasn't at all sure how she felt about *that*.

❀ 8 ❀

Women's Lib

Natalie let herself out onto the deck, gently slid the door closed behind her, and let out a sigh of relief. Alone at last! Away from Jennifer Valentine! Go harangue your mother, Jennifer, go lecture all of womankind—but leave *me* out of it! I've got a daughter of my own to give me a hard time, and I sent her away for the summer just so she couldn't. I sure as hell don't need somebody else's teenager on *my* case.

It had begun innocently enough over orange pancakes and orange juice—Sunshine orange juice, of course, her own and newest client. She and Barbara were laughing over Peter's latest notion, which was that there *had* to be a way to combine all the house food accounts into a complete cookbook. Since all the food accounts consisted of a baking mix, orange juice, salad dressings, pita bread, sardines, assorted nuts and beans and tofu, California pistachios, and eggs, this was no easy task. In fact, it was proving pretty impractical.

"Can you see it now?" Barbara was laughing so hard that she couldn't take another bite of her orange pancake. "This is good, but how about OJ and sardines."

"Or tofu and beans and orange juice en casserole."

They had gone on and on a bit, inventing more and more incredible combinations, when Jennifer, who had been eating quietly, said, "I don't see why it's so funny. Nobody really wants you to make up a recipe with sardines and pistachios and orange juice."

Natalie, choking with laughter, said, "Peter does!"

"Then just tell him the whole idea's ridiculous. And then Mom can go on doing her good stuff."

Patiently, Barbara said, "Darling Jennifer, you haven't been in the big world long enough to know, but the reason we don't simply tell Peter his idea is ridiculous is because he's the boss."

"But that's toadying!"

Said Natalie, "One hundred percent correct. When you work for Peter Marcus, you learn very quickly how to toady . . . and kowtow."

"And genuflect," Barbara added. They both laughed, while Jennifer sat at her place at the table, a little frown between her eyes.

"That's what's wrong with you," she announced when they had calmed down. "You play games with men. Even your boss." She shook her head sadly. "You don't want any man to get mad at you."

There was a full minute of stunned silence. And then Barbara said, "Yep, you're probably right."

"But that's *awful*, Mom!"

"Well, but Jen, our generation was brought up to believe that we women are the ones who smooth things over. We don't tell silly men that they're silly; we cajole them out of it. Well do I remember, when I was first sent to work at M & M, Peter Marcus, who, as you may know, is something of a flake, came storming into my kitchen. I forgot now what it was about. And the only way I got him to calm down was *not* by telling him that he was behaving irrationally, which was the truth, but by getting him to talk about *lentils*, of all the damn things. And in the end, Jen, he went away thinking I was a culinary genius and therefore worthy to work in his agency. I see that look on your face, Jen, but there's nothing wrong with being nicely subtle rather than brutally honest."

"Well, I don't agree. If you can't have honesty, you have nothing, that's how *I* feel."

Natalie could take no more. "Look, Jennifer, when I first went to work at M & M, I was the second woman they had ever hired in a creative capacity. That's how little they thought of women. In no time flat, I discovered I was smarter and better at my job than most of the men. Do you really think I would have done myself any good, running around announcing this? No, I had to play dumb, to a certain extent. It would have been self-destructive to do anything else. And now, because I played a certain number of games back then, there are plenty of high-ranking women at M & M."

Jen turned a stormy face on her. "You're as bad as my mother! Maybe worse! She just lies down and allows men to walk all over her. But you do it and you still think you're *superior* to men! You're just fooling yourself."

What a nerve that kid had. It was Natalie's house and she was a guest and only a kid at that. But Jennifer didn't care. Oh, how satisfying it must be to be young and so sure of your rightness.

"I suggest, Jennifer, that you withhold judgment until you've been on your own long enough to have had a relationship. Or two, or three, or a dozen. With so-called grown-up men."

"There! You're doing it again!"

"Damn well told!" She laughed at the intent, serious look on the girl's pale face. "All based upon experience. But at least I still have a sense of humor." Which, she added silently, is more than *you* have, my young woman.

"Agh!" Jennifer made a disgusted face. "I was listening to you two on the ferryboat yesterday on the way over. Honestly! The girls in the dorm never went on about boys the way you and Mom do!"

"Jennifer!" Barbara objected. "That's not true! Natalie and I talk about everything!"

"Sure," Jennifer countered. "Everything called Peter and Mark and Jake and Jerry and Tom, Dick, and Harry."

Natalie exchanged a glance with Barbara. It was uncomfortably true, what the kid was saying. They had begun talking about one of their clients who wanted "new ideas" and wanted them yesterday, never mind that the big Fourth of July weekend was here and not a soul would be left on the island of Manhattan—at least not a soul in the ad business. And before you knew, it, the conversation had drifted to Tommy Thoms and from Tommy to Larry Jordan with whom Tommy was carrying on a kind of feud, to men's ridiculous territorial behaviors, their lack of feelings, their denial of intimacy.

And of course that brought them quite naturally to the men they knew best. Well, not quite. Because Barbara carefully avoided the subject of Hal Pedersen. Evidently she didn't want to hear Natalie say, once more, that she was better off without him; because it still hurt her too much. Poor Barbara . . . it was her bad luck that she knew no emotional middle ground. It was always love forever, with her, when she got interested in a man. Like a schoolgirl, she would just fall head over heels. Well, if you did that, you were bound to get hurt all the time.

And then it occurred to her that she probably ought to be taking that warning to heart, her own self. No, no, she wasn't going to call it love—ugh! nasty word—she wasn't going to call it anything at all. But. But she found herself waiting impatiently for the phone to ring. And when it did, found her heart thumping painfully. And when she answered and it wasn't Mr. Dee, found herself sunk in disappointment. Over a man she'd gone to bed with exactly once, last weekend. Over a man she barely knew! She kept thinking about their lovemaking and getting breathless. There was something about him . . . and in the back of her mind, came the naggy little question, Could this one be the one, perhaps? Shit, she never allowed herself this sort of self-indulgent fantasizing! She made herself *not* think about him, about the full-lipped mouth, the thick white hair, the hard, hot, curved rod. She forced herself not to think about any of that. But she was unable to resist.

And last night, after Barbara and Jen and Martha J had all gone to sleep, she tippy-toed upstairs—sneaking around in her own house!—carefully avoiding the two squeaky steps near the top, and very very quietly dialed his number. She let it ring twenty-seven times. Dammit! he said he was out here for the summer, where the hell was he at 11:07 P.M. Why wasn't he home, where he damn well *should* be?

It was that sort of thing that made her very angry with herself. This was not how Natalie Simon did it. Natalie Simon was too careful. And on the ferry, although she was dying to talk to Barbara about him, about her feelings, yes, about *all* her feelings, she didn't. Like Barbara, she chose careful avoidance of what was most important to her.

But it *was* true that she and Barbara talked a lot about the male of the species. So she laughed at Jennifer's sally and said, "She's right, Barbara, only she forgot Larry and Tommy and Jeff and George and Phil and maybe a few dozen others!"

Jennifer sniffed. "What you two need is to learn how to feel worthwhile without a man!"

The little pisser! Lecturing them; she, who had probably had one and a half boyfriends in her whole life! She wanted to give the kid hell, but then decided not to. Martha J was still sleeping beautifully downstairs. So instead of yelling, she smiled very politely and excused herself very politely and went out onto the deck to lie in the sun and let her blood pressure simmer down. Blessedly alone.

As she glanced back into the living room, there was Barbara, being her usual calm, motherly self, not getting excited, not getting mad. She should *get* mad, Natalie thought. She should demand that Jennifer respect her feelings. Well, she hadn't done enough of the tough stuff when Jen was younger, and as a consequence, Jennifer at twenty-two was undisciplined, unfocused, a kid who went from feminism to vegetarianism to reincarnation to yoga and back again with the greatest of ease. And even worse, she felt herself qualified to lecture the world on any one of them. Or anything else for that matter. Okay, right now, her stance was feminist. She disdained women who felt different than she did; she disdained anyone's life experience. She disdained her mother, even though Barbara had made it possible for Jen to pursue feminism with such ardor.

Almost worse, as far as Natalie was concerned, was Jennifer's utter disdain for what she called "Servitude to Men's Ideas of Beauty." What she meant by that was bras, pretty clothes, good haircuts, makeup—anything that might make her attractive. That was a shame, because she was not a natural beauty. She was too thin by far, and she had inherited her father's strong Mediterranean features. On him, they were handsome; on the rather wispy Jennifer, they just didn't work. What a contrast to Natalie's own Melissa, whom she laughingly

referred to as Bloomingdale's Class of '86 or Ms. Saks Fifth
Avenue. The thing about Missy was, she was so damn normal
for her age. She would go miles to get the perfect haircut and
was an indefatigable shopper. If she wanted a black and white
plaid skirt that came to the middle of her knees and had exactly
twelve pleats, she would hunt and search and hunt and search
until she found it. And it took her a full twenty minutes each
morning to apply her makeup so that she didn't look made up.
And the wonder of it was, she didn't look made up. Every
morning, Melissa Weber set off for school looking absolutely
up to the minute. And gorgeous. Yes, gorgeous, at fifteen. It
should only have happened to *me*, Natalie often thought, recall-
ing her own teenage years of despair whenever she looked into
a mirror and saw her oval face with its large heavy-lidded eyes
and bumpy nose. She hadn't realized then that she was going
to look exotic and sexy; she had only known that she wasn't
pretty, the fate worse than *anything*. Lucky Melissa.

And lucky Melissa's mommy, who had sent her daughter
away to France—to France, imagine—to spend her summer
learning French and absorbing culture, instead of coming out
to the beach and bothering Mommy. If there was one thing she
didn't need during this, her thirty-ninth—nobody better laugh,
she thought—summer, it was a mouthy, intrusive, demanding,
fussy teenager.

So she had shipped Missy off only to be forced to deal with
someone else's pain in the arse. Well, this was the last time,
the very last. She simply had to say something to Barbara about
it; she couldn't let it go. In fact, if it were anyone but B.
Valentine, her old and dear and trusted friend, she'd be sorry
about now that she'd ever taken a housemate. But it *was* Barbara, so she'd swallow her annoyance for the moment and take
herself for a walk.

Where to, this time? Not the ocean; it was already too hot
in the open sun, and there were people all over the place setting
up for tonight's fireworks. No, she'd head for the bay, maybe
stroll over to the pond and see if she could catch sight of *him*.
And maybe not. She shouldn't even be thinking about a man
she'd only met last weekend. He *had* made a date for this

weekend; she had no reason to think he hadn't meant it. Still . . . it would have been nice if he'd called her during the week. She just hadn't been able to get him out of her mind.

At the harbor she stopped, because there, coming into the dock, throwing up spray as it plowed slowly through the glassy water, was the one o'clock ferry. She loved boats, even this little one. And apparently she wasn't the only one. Six children appeared, seemingly out of nowhere, complete with dogs, gazing intently upon the slow ballet of docking, disembarking, and unloading.

There was something about the arrival of even this poor excuse for a ship that created an aura of expectancy. Natalie scanned the passengers sitting tightly packed along the railing, faces turned eagerly into shore.

Was that Mark Valentine? Yes, it certainly was. She hadn't seen him in years. He really *was* a handsome man; and for a fleeting moment, she recalled lying on the floor, him on his knees above her, his face twisted with lust. That had been some night! Of course it was long long ago—four years, wasn't it?—at least four. And they had never repeated it. Too bad . . . in a way, too bad.

And who was that with him? Tall, very young, very good looking, familiar looking. Well, of course, he was familiar looking! He looked like Mark and that meant it was little Scott, no, scratch that, great big Scott. Great big beautiful Scott, in fact.

"Mark! Scott!" she called as they came off the ramp, laughing at the surprise on both their faces when they spotted her. "What are you doing here?"

"Business," Mark said. "What are *you* doing here?"

"I've bought a house here." It surprised her, how much pleasure it gave her, saying those words.

Scott laughed. "I told you that, Dad. Remember? Mom's in Natalie's house . . . right, Natalie?" His voice was a deep baritone now.

"Yeah, and so is Jen," Natalie said. "Where are you guys staying?"

"We plan to go back on the last boat tonight," Mark said.

"Oh, yes we do, Scott," he added, as the young man made a face.

"Aw, Dad, it's such beautiful weather. We might as well stay overnight and catch some rays tomorrow. God, we've been working like madmen ever since I got home from school. And it is the Fourth of July weekend!"

"We're here to work," Mark said and then, relenting a little, "All right, maybe we'll stay until noon tomorrow. We'll see how it goes."

"I have beds in my house," Natalie said; and then regretted her impulse.

Mark gave her a funny look. "Thanks, Natalie, that's very kind. But if we stay, it will be with . . . my client. He has plenty of room."

"All right. So just come over now for a little brunch or a drink. Oh, come on, Mark. Barbara would never forgive me." She laughed, looking him straight in the eye. "I *think*."

"No problem. We're quite amicable these days. Well, what do you say, Scott? Would you like to see your mother? I know I'd be interested in seeing Natalie's new house."

"Oh, it's not so terribly *new*, and it's not a spectacular house—not to an architect—but it *is* Natalie's!" she said.

Scott laughed, but Mark, stiff as ever, quickly said, "Now, Natalie, I'm not going to look at your house with a critical eye. Just because a man is an architect doesn't mean he thinks of nothing else, you know."

"Just so you know not to expect anything spectacular."

Mark looked Natalie over—unobtrusively of course—as they walked along. The woman was amazing . . . must be pushing fifty and she talked and walked like an ingenue. Dressed like one too; just look at her, in a sunsuit or whatever they called them and unless he was going blind, no bra. She wasn't going to be able to get away with that much longer. Someone ought to tell her. But, as he well remembered, nobody could tell Natalie Simon much of anything. He had just a flash of memory then, of her smooth skin with her firm muscles moving under his hands. And then it was gone.

He took his eyes away from her and focused on the town, the hamlet, actually. It was pleasant enough, in its low-key way; but look at those open dunes, for instance, nothing guarding them but blue sand fences. Everyone knew they weren't enough to protect the beach. They needed sandbagging.

He was walking behind Natalie and Scott—the boardwalk wasn't quite wide enough for three of them—lost in his own thoughts. The sound of idle chatter was pleasant background noise.

And then, she stopped and said, "Here we are."

She was right: It was a very ordinary modern house, two levels, bedrooms and shower on the ground floor, the public rooms upstairs with the deck, to take advantage of the view over the ocean. A nice little beach house, but she probably paid too much money for it. And, of course, she had to do some kind of wise-ass thing. There were two horrible cheap garish pink plastic flamingos stuck into the sand right in front. He tried very hard not to show his annoyance at them, but she gave him a little nudge and when he turned to her, she was grinning like a monkey.

"That's me. Tasteless and cutesie-pie, right?" She laughed and Scott joined her. The years hadn't done much to improve her personality. Once a ballbreaker, always a ballbreaker. Then she put a hand on his arm, and said, "Aw, Mark. Don't get mad. I'm sorry. Come on up and relax. I didn't bring you here to give you a hard time."

Maybe not, but he'd love to know why she *had* invited them over. If she thought she was going to see some kind of explosion between him and Barbara, she had another think coming.

Jesus, there were enough people on the deck! eating and drinking and talking, all at once. That's what he hated about Fire Island—all this enforced gaiety. They were all high, of course. They'd probably been drinking those Bloody Marys all morning. He knew about Fire Island. Where was Barbara, anyway? He wanted to see her, not all these hairy men. And Jen, of course, he wanted to see Jen, too. The lousy kid wasn't even answering his phone calls any more. Who'd she think paid all the bills at Tufts all these years? And where did she think graduate school was coming from, for Christ's sake, thin air? She could talk to him once a week; it wouldn't kill her to show a little respect.

And then he spotted Barbara, lying back in a lounge chair, in a black swimsuit, all oiled and shiny, her hair piled on top of her head, looking gorgeous. Well, Barbara had always been a sexy woman. He just didn't care for the way the big overweight old guy was leaning over her, popping grapes into her mouth, one at a time. Barbara's eyes were closed and she was smiling. Jesus, he remembered seeing that smile with her eyes closed from before . . . and it was always in bed! She had no business looking like that in public!

"Look who's here, Barbara!" Natalie caroled. "A surprise! Two surprises, in fact!"

Barbara said, "Hold that grape, Sandy," and sat up, squinting. Then she smiled broadly. "Mark! Well . . . this *is* a surprise." She swung her legs over the side of the lounge and, lifting her arms to her son, said, "And Scott! No, don't anybody say the obvious. I know I look too young to have this great big handsome man for a son. But it's true. And the other gentleman, the one who looks like Scott, is Scott's father."

The overweight guy, the one who had been feeding Barbara those grapes, shambled over, thrusting out his hand. "If you're Scott's father, and Scott is Barbara's son, that I figure you must be the former Mr. Barbara Valentine."

Mark felt his back go up. *Mr. Barbara Valentine!* Even as a joke, it wasn't funny. But he smiled in his pleasantest way and shook hands with the guy. "Mark Valentine," he said.

"Alexander Lovall," the old guy answered, and Mark's eyes opened wide.

"*The* Alexander Lovall?"

The guy grinned. "If you mean am I the picture painter, yes. Guilty."

Mark pumped his hand. "I'm delighted to meet you. I did the Schaeffer's new house in Greenwich."

"Ah . . . Jake and Pauline, yes, of course. They own five of my pictures."

"Six," Mark corrected; and Lovall grinned even more broadly.

"Six. You're right. I keep forgetting the one they bought last summer. It didn't go through my gallery; they bought it at auction somewhere. You know, now that I think of it, how come we artists don't get residuals? Huh?" And he turned, laughing. "Martha J? How come?"

Then Mark saw her, sitting at the picnic table, reading the *Times*. Without looking up, she said, "Sorry, Sandy. Not my line."

She was lovely for a black: tall and slender and elegant. Her face was rather bony, copper-skinned, with large luminous deep-set eyes. She didn't *look* black, that's what it was. Indian, maybe. He only knew she was Negro because Barbara had mentioned it, years ago.

"Scott," he said, "did you ever meet your mother's co-worker, Martha . . . uh . . . Jones? That's right, isn't it?"

She flashed him a gorgeous smile and said, "You get one hundred percent." She was sexy, all right. Wow!

The boy was a chip off the old block. Didn't hesitate, not even for a second. Went right over, stuck out his hand, smiled, smooth as you please, and said, "I'm sorry to say no, I haven't." She looked charmed, as well she might. And, say what you would about colored people, good-looking was good-looking! He wouldn't mind crawling into *that*, oh, no. You know what they said about black women . . . always hot, always ready for a man. Well, you never knew whether those stories were true, of course, but the way she painted her full lips bright red, and the short shorts that showed off her long slender legs—well, it was an open invitation. Come to think of it, he'd never had a black woman. Scott better watch out; she was strong stuff. He eyed his son carefully as the boy chatted and smiled. What were they talking about? He couldn't hear. And then Natalie said something to them, and Scott turned away from Martha and, laughing, began to talk animatedly to Natalie. Better a ballbreaker than a black cutie who was probably dying to get her hands on a cute white boy like Scott.

And now he decided he might as well have one drink—just one—as long as he was here. He walked over to the big table and poured himself a Bloody Mary, wondering if it was the wrong time to talk business with Sandy Lovall. There was $25,000 budgeted for art in this new project. Who better than an artist known for his Fire Island landscapes? And maybe, now that he'd met Lovall, they could get a lower price. Buy directly and skip the whole gallery scene.

And then his attention was caught by his son's voice, very serious for a change, very low-pitched. "But wouldn't I really need an agent?" And Natalie laughed and said, "Wait until you've *finished* it, Scott. *Then* think agent." And he said, "Maybe I should squeeze in a night course in creative writing."

What in hell was all this writing talk about, anyway? Scott had finished his fourth year in architecture at MIT. It was all decided; he'd come right into the firm next year, after he graduated. Hell, that's what he *wanted*! But, wait a minute, now she was saying, "Of course I'll read it. I'll be happy to read it. I have a half-finished novel myself; I'd love to see one finished, *anyone's*."

Novel! He shot a hard look at his son, but the boy was either so engrossed that he didn't notice or he simply wasn't having any. How the hell could he maintain his GPA at school if he was writing a stupid novel, for Christ's sake!

It must be Natalie. She was such a ballbreaker, she probably got the kid talking about writing whether he wanted to or not. And he was too polite to be rude to a woman. Hell, of course he was. He learned from his old man, after all!

There was the sound of a door sliding open and when he looked over, who should be standing there, looking scruffier than ever, but his daughter, Jennifer. Goddammit, he was ashamed sometimes to call her his daughter. Just look at her with her hair hanging all stringy; and no bright-colored shorts and T-shirt for Jennifer, oh, no, that might be too flattering. No, she had to wear baggy sweatpants and three cut-off tops about seven sizes too big, hanging off her shoulder. Jesus Christ!

"What're you auditioning for, Jennifer?" he said, maybe a little more loudly than he had intended. "Bag lady?"

Every head turned, of course, and she gave him her usual sulky look and usual sulky answer. "I like it."

"Well, I don't."

"I think it's neat," Scott put in quickly. Scott always *had* taken her side against him. "I like when people use their clothes to express themselves." He looked at his sister and they both grinned. "And besides, everyone knows you need to keep warm on the Fourth of July, right, Jen?"

"Yeah, well, it's pretty icy here right now," she said. Oh, very clever, Mark thought. God, they were both so irritating. But at least it had gotten Scott to his feet and away from Natalie. If there was one thing he didn't want, it was to have *her* messing with his boy, either! And, as he knew well, she was quite capable of doing so . . . of doing *any* goddamn thing!

God, that time in her apartment! He hadn't intended to do it, he didn't even *like* the woman, for Christ's sake! He'd been looking for Barbara, mad as hell. It was the beginning of Barbara's pulling away from him, working late all the time, never telling him where she was, carrying on with Jake probably! He was beside himself that night. Couldn't reach her at the office, which was where she was *supposed* to be. Couldn't get Natalie on the phone either, and somehow that maddened him. He went tearing out of his house and drove like a maniac to her place.

He remembered how it was when he first came in. She was so startled that she didn't know what to say. She, without words! It was wonderful. He was convinced by this time that she was hiding Barbara and he went tear-assing around her apartment, looking for her.

How did it begin? He was all het up and excited, and she laughed at him, made some kind of stupid joke, and suddenly he had to get her, had to have her. He reached out to shake her and found himself kissing her instead.

What a hot number she was! She didn't even pretend to push him away. The minute his hands were on her, the minute his tongue went into her mouth, she was ready, rubbing up against him, moaning, making little noises, getting him hotter then he could ever remember in his life.

He had stripped quickly. The bitch hadn't been wearing anything but a little nightshirt anyway, and when he put his hand down on her, she was soaking wet. Jesus! it had seemed forever until he could get all his clothes off and throw her down. He took her right there on the living room floor, in a frenzy, pushing it in as deep as he could get it, hearing the sounds of his own grunts as he crashed into her. He felt so good, he felt so strong, as he battered his hips into hers, hearing her cries with enormous pleasure, moving faster and faster, into that pulsating wet warmth, deeper and deeper. And then came like he had never come before, soaked with sweat, almost unable to breathe. And even then, she wasn't through with him. She held him close and got him hot again, so he really did her good. He licked her body, her belly, her breasts, her pussy, until she was screaming for him to give it to her, give it to her and so he did. God, what a night! He'd never told Barbara about it, of course not, no matter how angry she made him. There was no reason to. He'd never told her about any of them.

"So that's your ex," Jay murmured, leaning very close to Barbara's ear. "How come you left a hunk like that?"

"Because," Barbara said lightly, "hunk is as hunk does." People never believed her when she told them she was delighted that she'd done it: left him, left his house, left his bed, and had never regretted it.

Never regretted it, maybe, but she had apparently never freed herself completely either. Because there she was, last month, finding herself sliding right back into wifedom-serfdom.

She had prided herself on their amicability since the divorce. She called Mark whenever she had a question to put to him; and he felt free to call her too. They had been together for all family celebrations and had deported themselves with grace, being very pleasant to each other.

So it came as no surprise when Mark, having finished with the main subject of his phone call, began to chat about the new renovation of his brownstone in Brooklyn Heights. And somehow or other, his chat led inevitably to something he needed desperately—and it was available only in a shop not two blocks from M & M.

"Say, would you mind?"—At that moment, she should have

yelled, "Yes. I mind. Very much." But of course, she said
nothing because she was talking to the great Mark Valentine
and she had had twenty-odd years of bending before his will
and catering to his whims and it didn't even occur to her that
she could just hang up on him. Instead, she waited and sure
enough, his next words were: "... ambling over there at lunchtime and checking it out? I have the style number right here
in my wallet."

"Oh, Mark. Surely there's someone in your office who could
handle this for you. Your secretary, perhaps?"

"I never ask my staff to do personal things. You know that."

And for reasons too numerous and painful for her to look
at, she had agreed to do his errand. Inwardly furious, she had
written down the number and said the requisite number of "Unh-
huh's" and had dutifully gone out that very day during her
lunch hour, her previously overcrowded lunch hour, and checked
it out. Just as the boss had ordered.

When she got back to the office, she sat down at her desk
and began to cry. Dammit, Barbara, she told herself, you've
been divorced three years; and you've even been involved with
another man, with *lots* of them. But whenever Mark says jump,
you still jump as high as you can. That isn't good for you,
Barbara, it's not productive, hell, it isn't even *sane*! Maybe,
she told herself, it was just because of her recent breakup, with
feeling lonely and alone. In any case, she had promised herself,
he was out of her life, really *out*! That's all she needed now:
to take Mark back on the rebound! She'd sooner slit her wrists!

She eyed him sitting so uncomfortably on the deck, looking
tight and overdressed and as if he'd love to be somewhere else,
and she thought: Yes, in spite of it all, he *is* a hunk. The years
since their breakup had only improved him, put a sprinkling
of distinguished-looking white at his temples, interesting planes
in his face, pleasant crinkles at the corners of his eyes. Too
bad, she thought, that passing time had improved his looks but
not his attitude toward women. She hoped he hadn't passed on
every bit of it to Scott . . . a vain hope, probably. It was hard

to tell with Scott, who was not very forthcoming. At least, not with her.

Just look at him now, though, head to head with Natalie, totally engrossed in what appeared to be a very serious conversation. Thank God he was capable of opening up to *some* female, she thought; and then she looked more closely at the two of them. Were they being serious or something more . . . intimate, perhaps? Oh, really, Barbara, what nonsense! *Natalie?* Never in this world would Natalie, at her age, even *think* about coming on to Scott!

"Don't you think so, Barbara?" Sandy Lovall shouted to her, and she came out of her reverie with a start.

"Yes. Think what about what?"

"Think it's a damn shame, what's happened at my pond? I'm telling you, Mark, something's got to be done before the entire island sinks into the sea from neglect, and too many people."

They all hooted at Sandy, Barbara, too. He was at everyone, every minute, if you let him. It was important to save the ecosystem, of course it was, but he didn't have to go on and on about it all the time! If he weren't so talented and charming . . .

Right now he was laughing with the rest of them, holding up hands in surrender. "All right, all right, I won't bother Mr. Valentine with our problems . . . not yet." And when they all applauded, he added, "But in return, I'm going to need each and every body on this deck at this moment—not to mention a few hundred more—to be on the beach two o'clock sharp. We need everyone we can get and that includes our two lovely visitors." He made a little bow to Jen and Martha J. "And by the way, speaking of lovely, where is Bambi this morning? She can usually smell a gathering from three miles away."

Natalie answered him. "Look for the great God Peter, and there, at his feet, in total adoration, you will find Bambi."

To which Fred said, "Do I detect a note of disapproval, Natalie?"

And Jay added, "Or dare I say . . . jealousy?"

"No, men, what you hear is a note of feminism. I mean,

my God, Barbara and Martha J and I *have* to bow at his feet; that's what he pays us for. But here we have an intelligent, attractive, live-wire woman who *chooses* to do so. As far as I'm concerned, it's beyond belief."

"What's beyond belief," Sandy said, "is that it's now one-fifty-five, time for all of us to get down there, pronto."

Nobody questioned him. They just all stood up prepared to do his bidding. Mark and Scott quickly left at that point; they had to get to the bay. And Martha J had to change. But the rest of them, lugging their beach gear, followed him obediently off the deck, down the ramp, and headed for the ocean.

❀ 9 ❀

Martha J Jones

Well, would you look who's strutting down this fancy Fire Island beach, dabbling her toes in the Atlantic Ocean and wearing a seventy-five-dollar bathing suit made of two strips of cloth so small . . . hmm . . . makes the cost about ten dollars a square inch! Me, that's who! Martha J thought and giggled.

Hard to believe, sometimes, that little Martha J Jones from Newark, New Jersey with her corn-row hair and neatly ironed dresses and skinny legs could have ended up the way she did: twenty-eight years old, on the Madison Avenue fast track, happily married to a big, tall, handsome rich man, on her way to having it *all*. Maybe even pregnant? She put her hand on her very flat belly, wondering. She'd missed her period. It was only three days late, but she was usually regular like clockwork.

She decided it was time to turn back. She'd long since gone past the big octagonal house that, she'd been told, marked the end of Paradise. Paradise! what a name. But, in its own way, it *was* Paradise here. The place smelled of money: money and success and suntan oil. She headed back the way she'd come, walking at the very edge of the water so that the waves coming in could nibble at her toes. The sun on the water was dazzling; it was a gorgeous day, bright and clear, the sky very intensely blue and the sand very intensely white. A very good contrast, she thought with a smile, for her own self, brown as she was and getting browner every minute. The heat of the sun on her shoulders felt wonderful, felt like melted honey. The gulls swooped and cried and on the open beach—nothing like Coney

Island crowds here, oh, no!—half a dozen children, toasted
like cookies, built a sand castle, their voices high and tinkling.

She'd only been there twenty hours, and it was amazing how
time had slowed for her. There was no sense of urgency out
here on Fire Island. Fire Island was for sheer pleasure. It sat
with the Great South Bay on one side and the Atlantic Ocean
on the other, no cars, no trucks, no noise, no pollution, no
nothing but eating and drinking and sunbathing and all so upper
class and elegant. Did she love it? Yes, she loved it!

Wouldn't it be fabulous to have a house here? Martha J
thought, looking away from the lazy surf to the dunes with
their few houses sitting in scattered splendor. Wouldn't it be
lovely to sit with Calvin and look out *their* big picture windows
at the scene below, like Natalie could do from her house. Damn,
she wished Calvin were there . . . but, no, that damn company
had to send him to Atlanta. "It's not that I want to go, honey,"
Calvin said. "I don't particularly want to be far from you on
the Fourth. But that's when this deal can go through, so that's
when I've got to be here. You go visit Natalie and come back
on Saturday and we'll go out to your mother for the rest of the
weekend."

Oh, hell, she understood. But it still made tears come to
her eyes. Damn, she didn't like being without him on family
holidays. Wasn't it bad enough that they both worked so hard.
Some weeks they hardly had a chance to do more than kiss
each other hello/good-bye, it seemed like. She was jealous of
every single weekend moment. And the Fourth had special
childhood memories for her. It was always the big fun holiday,
with a gigantic picnic. Lord, everyone showed up at that picnic.
And there was a big softball game and horseshoe pitching and
someone with a guitar and food, food, food! It would last long
past dark—when she was real little, that was the best part:
being safe there in the dark, giggling with her sisters and their
friends, singing with everyone, watching the fireflies and smelling burnt marshmallows.

How different was this scene, here in Paradise, with its
miles of open beaches, the blue sand fences up on the dunes,
the endless ocean tumbling onto the shore. Next stop, Portugal,

that's what they all said; and that thought somehow kept tugging at her. Next stop, Portugal, and here was little Martha J Jones, who could *go* to Portugal if she wanted. Who could do anything and go anywhere. Her grandmother would not have been able to believe her eyes, if she'd lived to see this. Martha J smiled to herself, because she knew what her grandmother would have said: "That's not for black folks, honey!" Well, yes it was, oh, yes it was! If there ever had been a time when it paid to be black and female and smart and not bad looking, this was it!

Now she had to walk away from the water's edge onto the hot sand that burned the soles of her feet to get around the silver van that had been parked there since early in the morning. She'd seen it at eight o'clock from Natalie's deck with four people hard at work setting up the fireworks for tonight. As she strode by she idly wondered how much this was costing the good citizens of Paradise. Sandy Lovall said it was a fabulous display, ending with a waving American flag, with skyrockets going off and pinwheels, everything red, white, and blue. It cost a fortune, she decided, that's what it cost. Well, St. Laurent had done it, to announce Opium. And didn't some bank or department store or somebody sponsor one of the city fireworks displays?

Fireworks. Well, the Hasahnis didn't have that kind of dough. Still . . . who else? She'd talk to Peter about it, after she'd worked out a few thoughts. It paid to always have a new idea or two around him. She'd learned that real fast, once he'd made her his favorite, his *new* favorite. She mostly liked her special status. And yet there was a certain amount of stress: She was constantly expected to perform and she was endlessly on display. Peter was creative, himself, and what he expected from his people was nothing short of genius. At any hour, as she had also learned. Never mind if it was past five o'clock and your husband was going to be waiting impatiently for his dinner at six-thirty. It was time to change your dinner hour, that's all.

And there they all were, that whole gang of them, their blankets and beach towels all pulled up in a circle, like the settlers protecting themselves against the Indians. Who, she wondered briefly, were the Indians, around here?

The first thing she saw, of course, was that yellow head of curls. That Bambi! For a little gal, she certainly knew how to make herself visible. Well, hell, so did Martha J Jones. She knew her way of dressing caused constant comment. That's why she did it. Nobody was ever going to be able to forget Martha J Jones, once having seen her. And it was a damn good way to make sure you were never confused with anyone else.

Next to Bambi was Peter, his head on her lap. Even lying flat on his back on a beach, he was busy; his arms and hands were moving about and she could tell from here that he was talking a mile a minute. The others were there, too, of course. Natalie and Barbara, Natalie oiling Barbara's back. Those two guys, Fred and Jay, one reading and the other talking to Peter. And Sandy Lovall and that big dog of his, with *her* head in *his* lap. And another couple of people she hadn't met . . . leastways, she didn't think she'd met them. She'd had so many glasses pressed in her hand last night, at Happy Hour, that she wasn't quite sure exactly whom she knew.

As she watched, Peter sprang to his feet and clapped his hands. What now? She strolled closer so she could hear him calling everybody to get to their feet for a volleyball game. It was so like Peter. Everyone said no, but that didn't stop him. He just stood there insisting until they stood up. And then he took himself from blanket to blanket, and sure enough, he got that entire section of beach cleared in about three and a half minutes. It was *something*, watching him at work, getting his own way.

She had to admire him, demanding and flaky though he was. He was smart and he was shrewd. The agency just kept growing. And in his own strange way, he was dependable. Just last week, wasn't it? Yes, last week. Peter had told her to call this guy, Sherman Boyd, who wanted M & M to handle his video cassette rental business, wanted someone who had experience with franchises. Okay, so she was the franchise expert, these days, at M & M. So Sherman Boyd called her. Very cultured voice, good English, very chatty, she was even beginning to like him. "I think we'd better get together and talk over lunch," she said to him.

"Terrific! Let me look at my calendar. You understand, our offices aren't in the city. We're up in Chappaqua."

She remembered saying "Um." Who cared?

"Let me tell you, it's night and day. Some of my people are still grumbling about the commute, but at least now we don't have to deal with niggers."

She let some time slide by, very aware of the sudden thudding of her heart. And then, very sweetly, very quietly, she said: "Well, I'm another one you won't have to deal with."

There was an audible *ulp* from the other end, followed by a string of apologies. She couldn't remember at all what he said. It was all mixed together in her memory—the usual garbage about some of my best friends and of course you're different: that crap. She didn't really listen to it, she sat trying to control her rage. And when she discovered that she couldn't, she just hung up, mid-word.

Then, stricken—Jesus, what an unprofessional way to behave!—she ran out of her office and burst in on Peter, who was on the phone. Give him credit, he took one look at her and ended his conversation. "Sit down. Immediately," he ordered. "And tell me what's wrong." And when she gave him the whole story, he sat for a few minutes, cogitating, rubbing his chin and swiveling back and forth in that big leather chair of his. Finally, he said, "I've been sitting here, thinking I'd like to call Boyd myself and give him some more hell. But the more I think about it, the more I come to the conclusion that he's a piece of garbage and I don't *want* to talk to him."

One of the many lights on his console blinked then and when he picked up the phone, he listened for a moment, gave her a big wink, and said, "Mary-Claire? Tell that piece of ka-ka to fuck off. No, never mind, I'll tell him myself."

There was a pause, during which Martha J argued with herself: Would he *really*? No, he couldn't, and then he said, "Sherm? Martha J is with me and here's my feeling on the subject: Fuck off." And he hung up, grinning across that huge rosewood desk, looking precisely like a pleased little boy. And then he said, "There!" and it sounded just like a pleased little boy. Well, she didn't care if, very often, Peter Marcus acted juvenile. All she knew was: He was there when she needed him. She knew damn well how much that account would have been worth!

Well, Peter had done it, he'd got his volleyball game going. It might be a very hot day on the Fourth of July and people would much rather lie on their blankets or swim in the ocean, but there they all were, jumping around after a ball and screaming their lungs out. She had to smile; he really was something else, that Peter. He was in the front, spiking the ball, cheering his team on, the most energetic player of them all. The first time he yelled, "Get the lead out, Nattie!" Martha J searched in vain for Natalie. Where *was* she? And then she saw: Nat was on the other team, that's where she was. She didn't even bother to answer him.

And then a few minutes later, Peter shouted, "What's the matter, Nat? Hung over? I see you sweating. I see you sweating bullets over there!"

Martha J was well aware that people often ragged each other when they were competing. On the tennis court, for instance, Calvin often gave her the business. It was a way of psyching out your opponent. She gave Calvin back double.

But Nat wasn't answering Peter. She was pretending not to hear him. And still, he didn't let up. "Don't do it, Nat! You'll never make it!" he was shouting. And when Natalie, reaching up, up for a high one, missed it, he cackled like an old crone. "Not on your best day, shortie!"

God, he sounded like her and her sisters, when they had all been teenagers. Silently, she told him, Enough is enough, Peter. But apparently, enough was never enough for him. All right, so Nat was the captain of the other team, still . . .

From here, Martha J couldn't hear what went on, of course, but she could guess, because, a minute later, when Peter gave that evil laugh and yelled, "Move your ass, Nattie. Pretend you're in bed!" a great cry went up from the other team, and in a body, they ran around the net, shrieking and threatening and laughing, picked him up and ran to dump him into the

ocean, Martha moved down to join them. She hoped it was all
in good fun; but she couldn't be sure. By the time she reached
the water's edge, Peter had come up, spluttering, and was
wading in to shore. He was laughing and so was everyone else.
Including Natalie, she noted. Good. Then it was only a joke,
after all. Sometimes, she thought he razzed Natalie much too
much and went much too far. Now he had his arms held out,
and he was saying, "You're going to get exactly what you
deserve, Nat Simon . . . a big wet hug!" And Natalie, saying,
"Oh, no! Not this girl!" turned and ran away.

Martha J frowned after her. At Natalie's age and in Natalie's
position, wasn't it too bad she had to put up with this kind of
stuff. And on the weekend! Martha J had never really socialized
with Peter before. If she had thought about it at all, she probably
figured he was somehow different when he left the office.
Calmer, maybe. More level. But he wasn't; he was the same:
impulsive, emotional, erratic.

She had a flash: Peter did this kind of thing to Natalie all
the time. He was always on her case in one way or another.
Stupid that she'd never seen past the joking around before.
Jesus, was that her future at Marcus & Morrisey? She had an
image of herself running faster and faster and jumping higher
and higher in her effort to please him. Oh, no. She didn't do
it for Calvin; she was not about to do it for a man she didn't
even love. Forget it! Now that she was thinking about it, Peter
had already started with her, calling her in any goddamn time
he had a thought and expecting her to drop every other thing
in her life. But wait a minute, she cautioned herself. Not too
darn fast, there, Martha J Jones. Because right now, Peter
Marcus and his agency are your ticket to Paradise!

And then she stopped thinking, because Peter spotted her
and he called to her. "Martha J! Where the hell were you when
I needed you for the big game?"

She just laughed and then it was perfectly natural to just
join all of them walking back up the beach from the water and
plop down with all of them, to lie in the sun. She closed her
eyes, loving the smell of coconut oil and the regular boom-
boom of the waves as they broke, enjoying the sounds of lazy

conversation over her head. They talked about the volleyball game, then they were *arguing* about it; then someone mentioned a show on Broadway and they argued about *that*. And then they discussed the fireworks tonight. And then someone said isn't it a gorgeous day and they all agreed that it was a gorgeous day and they were all so lucky to be here instead of the hot, grimy, sticky city. And then they talked about the situation in the Near East. And when they started to argue about that, someone changed the subject to Sandy's Big Party tomorrow night. And then there was an outburst of smart remarks, one piled atop the other. With her eyes shut, she couldn't sort it out, but it was amusing. This was an okay group. And, she had to admit, this was The Life.

The sun felt so good on her skin, and it was good for her to lie there in the sand listening to meaningless conversations, idly speculating on the personalities of all these strangers. She could just speculate away, guess, dream, drift, and not really get involved.

She was beginning to drift into sleep, when suddenly there was a new, much louder voice from somewhere above her. "Where are my people? I'm looking for my people! Oh, people! People!"

She knew the voice; it couldn't be missed, once you heard it. And she had heard it, making its poetic commentary on moon, sky, stars, surf, sand, dunes, and every other gift of nature for an hour the night before in Bob's Bar . . . not to mention this morning. Sandy Lovall. Amusing enough, but all that flamboyant charm could get a bit wearing. Well, there was no getting away from him if he was looking for them; and he was definitely looking for them.

She sat up, blinking, squinting. He looked almost larger than life, standing there in his terry-lined Hawaiian print beach jacket and old fishing hat, his big hairy belly bulging over his trucks, grinning from ear to ear, putting down on the sand two enormous bulging canvas bags and announcing, "Hello, my people. Your leader is back." She couldn't help but notice that their little group was now the center of attention for everyone within earshot.

Bambi leaped up, holding onto the very tiny top of her bikini, and raced over to him, lifting her face for a kiss. "Oh, leader, I promised I'd help and I will! Just tell me what to do."

Is she for real? Martha J thought, and hoisted herself to her feet. Do I want to stay here for this? And apparently he took her standing up as a signal. Oh, hell, she thought, because he was reaching out, clasping her hands, laughing like hell, pulling her in, and clutching her in a big bear hug that smothered her.

And then he murmured into her ear, "Come on, Martha J. Let's put on a show for the ordinary people." She couldn't help it: She just burst out laughing. He was incorrigible; he was bound and determined to be Mr. Charm. "I know, I know," he said, "I'm so naughty. But I'm also a lot of fun. See?" And he reached down into one of the canvas bags, coming up with a handful of bright scarlet Frisbees. "Toys!" he announced. But when Bambi reached out for one, he pulled his hand back, saying, "But first, a brief refresher on why we are gathered here today.

"Attention! Attention! Everyone pay attention, please! And if you're all good little girls and boys and listen without talking or chewing gum loudly, Uncle Sandy will give you all a lot of nice toys for fun and frolic . . . okay? Okay.

"Here's the story. There's a unique natural wonder in the village of Paradise, unique not only to this little place but to all of Fire Island. It is the island's only natural freshwater pond, with a marsh and all the wildlife that naturally occurs in a marshland. Birds flock here every year on their way south and on their way north to Canada. It is a spot of unsurpassed beauty. . . ."

"Bring on the dancing girls!" a male voice hollered, but was immediately *shushed*.

"Halfmoon Pond," Sandy Lovall continued, undeterred. "The name is not half so beautiful as the place itself. It is wild, in the best sense of that word. It is wild and it is about to be desecrated, despoiled, and destroyed. A group of real estate developers—do I hear hisses for the villains?"—and there were hisses and boos from his audience—"I repeat, my friends, a group of developers so ashamed of what they are planning that they refuse to reveal their names and hide behind a corporate *nom de guerre*, Halfmoon Associates, are going to build what appears to be a very large edifice on the shore of this gorgeous, wild, unspoiled, natural setting!"

Martha J glanced around and saw that he'd caught the attention of nearly everyone. Well, people wouldn't fight the traffic to get out here if they didn't love it. And the price you paid to own or rent or even to just get a share of the most modest house!! You *had* to love the place!

"Fire Island is a sandbar, people! It can't take overbuilding. And there's something fishy about it. We're not getting the whole story, believe me!" Sandy's voice had risen and taken on the rhythm and inflections of a preacher. He was a true believer, there was no doubt about it. "My family's been here, in Paradise, since 1923, when there was nothing here but a couple of cottages, a fishing pier, the beach. No stairs going down from the dunes, people, no sand fences, no nothing but us, and our dreams and our indomitable spirit—and Halfmoon Pond, beautiful glorious Halfmoon Pond!

"And now they're going to desecrate it!" Did she hear his voice break? Could he really have allowed his voice to break? Or did it truly, sincerely break? "They're going to desecrate it."

And somebody interrupted again: "So what else is new?" And again was told to shut up.

"I know many of you are renters. But you come back here year after year! You're not strangers! And look, you pay a lot to come and to stay here, right?" There was a murmur of agreement. "And why is that, people? I'll tell you why. Because Fire Island in general—and Paradise in particular—is one of the most sought-after, most exclusive, most unspoiled vacation spots in the metropolitan area!"

Again there was some applause. "If we all work together, if we all sign the petitions and attend the rallies and bring enough pressure to bear, we can force our unknown despoilers out into the open. That's our first step. We must know our enemy!

"My friends," Sandy continued, his voice dropping and his

stance relaxing, "we're going to fight this thing, any way we can. I have these wonderful Frisbees for all of you. Please, give them to your friends, and pass the word around: FOR-EVER WILD." He held one up so they could all read the big white letters. "Before I give them out . . . I just happen to have a petition with me. Just sign your name, your summer address, and phone number, and I'll be in touch when we need you—probably next weekend, okay?"

"Okay!" It was a roar of approval.

"My assistants will be around with petitions for you to sign." He gave Martha J a great big wink and bent once more to bring out of one of the big canvas bags clipboards, pens attached, petitions clipped . . . and held them out. Natalie, Barbara, Bambi—each held out a hand for a clipboard. Martha J shook her head at herself. She didn't like getting involved, but what the hell, the man was right—and so what if it all harked back to college days with signs asking you to join your local rev-olutionary group, and rhetoric by the barrel anywhere you turned? The man was right. He was right. There should be a law against dumping sewage into a natural pond . . . or hiding your plans until too late for anyone to fight you. And, let us not forget, she told herself, you might be living here yourself one day. All the old juices were running; it made her laugh, it made her feel like a kid again, to have a cause to fuss about. She'd been there; she'd been a part of it. She gave Sandy a big shit-eating grin and reached out for her clipboard.

As she did her thing with the petition, she couldn't help thinking: How absolutely extraordinary, what has happened to this lazy, lounging crowd. They had all been lying around chatting about this and that, and now there was a loud buzz of busy conversation. Everyone was all het up to sign, to somehow fight. She didn't have to say much of anything, hardly even had to offer the petition. It was all but snatched out of her hand, with others waiting impatiently for their turn.

The sound of the airplane was at first just a grumble of sound in the distance, almost like thunder but different. It brought two or three heads up, to see what was happening. But then it got louder and louder and louder and then somebody shouted and pointed and there it was: a little silver plane, propellers flashing in the sun, flying very low over the water, heading their way.

Now everyone stopped to watch. Here it was, and now you could see that it was towing a long banner. And the plane passed, heads swiveled—hers, too—to read the message as it floated by. Someone read, "LET US LOVE THE STRANGER IN PARADISE."

One wise guy shouted, "The lord knows, I've been *trying* every weekend!" But for the most part, there was just puzzled amusement on the beach.

☙ 10 ☙

Bambi's Place

It was, Peter thought, a perfect evening. Bambi's deck was high up, swept by the breeze that flowed from ocean to bay each day at sunset, and now, with the sky slowly darkening, it was nice and quiet. He lay back into the padded chair and sucked in on the joint. He didn't know who Bambi's connection was—he didn't want to know, either—but she always had real fine pot. Right now, after only two hits, he already felt that slight buzz in his head, that need to breathe deeply, that loosening of his mind. Perfect.

Out by the ocean, a fusillade of sharp cracks broke the silence. Bambi, sitting at his feet, squealed with excitement. "Oh, look, Peter, fireworks! I *love* fireworks...oooh!" She was quite right, it was beautiful: a chrysanthemum of dazzling red and pink sparks bloomed in the sky, slowly fading as another, this one purple, exploded higher up. One after the other, they arced into the blackness and burst into showers of light and color, each one punctuated by Bambi's little cries of delight.

"Come here," he ordered, drawing her closer, and she snuggled into him obediently, her curly head on his lap. The fire flowers gave way to rockets and then to whirlwinds and then to galaxies. Peter drew in on the end of the joint. Now his head was light as air, a feeling he relished. He loved being freed up, loved it. He had so many responsibilities: the agency, all those people working for him, his other investments, his plans, ah, yes, his plans, all his plans....

Everything was working out just as planned. It had to work out. Because if it didn't...well, what had Morty the accountant said? "You're . . . ah . . . just the least bit, shall we say, overextended, Peter. So I'd be very goddamn careful, if I were you."

Well, very goddamn careful was not what had got Peter Marcus where he was today. Nevertheless, one paid one's accountant to worry and fuss. So he listened. He didn't worry and fuss, since someone else was doing it for him, but he did listen. He had moved with caution; hadn't told anyone, not a single soul. Of course, he'd had to borrow against the agency . . . maybe that was a little risky . . . but it had paid off! Oh, God, yes, it had paid off—or was about to! Because yesterday afternoon, he'd been given the word. Chambless was coming over to his side! Oh, God, it was wonderful. Chambless was the major stockholder—of Steinberg & Epstein, the PR firm. They were small, but what potential! He, Peter Marcus, had been able to see that, way back last November. And that's when he began his first moves, to buy up stock very quietly, very secretly, in a bid to take it over.

"God, I'm brilliant!" Had he said that aloud? Or was it just echoing in his head? That was the thing about marijuana: It opened up the door between illusion and reality. Well, no matter. "I'm going to own S & E. Own it. Myself!" Again, he wasn't quite positive whether he had merely thought it or said it.

And then Bambi said, "What? Are you, Peter? That *is* brilliant!"

Then he must have said it out loud. He had to warn her, tell her it was a secret. "Bams?"

"Mmmm?"

"Mustn't tell."

"Mmmmm."

She wouldn't. She loved him. She was a good girl, Bambi. He was getting very attached to her. Mustn't tell. Women could be terrible bitches, once they thought they had the upper hand.

Natalie. Prime example. Pop had dragged him into the agency—years ago, of course, years and years ago, but still. He remembered. Pop brought him in, said, "Peter, it's time you saw where all our money comes from. And some day,

you'll be running it, so you'd better learn." And who did he
bring eighteen-year-old Peter to? Not Jerry Weber, not Tommy
Thoms, not a man. No. To little Natalie Simon. She wasn't
that much older than he, and there she was, lording it over
him. Probably humping the old man. He discovered later on,
she screwed around plenty. Everyone but him, everyone but
him. And there was Pop. Beaming at her, squeezing her arm,
kissing her cheek all the time, as if he had invented her, saying,
"Just follow Nat Simon around, Peter, and you'll learn what's
what at Marcus & Morrisey!" God, he'd been so relieved when
she got married and left to have the baby. And then, she had
to come back! Jake insisted. Well, of course, she was good at
her job. In fact, she had really pitched in and helped when she
first came back. And later, when he was going to be in trouble
with the IRS. Well, yes, she had stepped in then, too, but she
had overstepped.

As long as he lived, he would never forgive her for what
she'd done to him. It wasn't bad enough she'd patronized him
when he first came into the business . . . that she'd kept giving
him lip, even after he was president. Then, she had to blackmail
him! The bitch! He'd never forgive her, never, for taking over
the business, for sending him away—he hadn't been *that* hooked
on pills—for controlling his very spending money for months
after he got back! He'd signed the contract making her creative
director, but that was the price she exacted.

And now that price was getting to be too high. Too goddamn
high. In a way, it was unfortunate, his suggesting she rent a
place in Paradise. It had been a devilish thing to do. Just because
he was building a house for himself out here, he had thought
it might be amusing to bump into her from time to time, shake
her up a little.

He didn't know he'd meet Bambi. He didn't know that
Lovall character was going to start a whole brouhaha. He didn't
know Natalie would *buy* a goddamn house out here! He'd just
been having a little fun. He really hadn't intended her becoming
this involved in his life.

But . . . Never mind. It was amusing. It was instructive. It gave him that extra bit of ammunition. He could see very plainly out here how much she was drinking: plenty. Too much.

Pretty soon, she'd be in no shape to handle her job. Already, she was getting into trouble. Yes, pretty soon she'd violate her contract one time too many and he'd be able to throw her out. And then . . . her job would be waiting for a certain party to step in.

Bambi would be wonderful, he just knew it. She was certainly wonderful for him: ebullient, clever, and biddable—all of his favorite things in a woman. She knew just what made him happy, and it made her happy to do it for him, *all* of it. She was perfect, just perfect. . . .

He reached down and dug his fingers into the curly head between his legs, crying her name aloud as he came to climax.

❀ 11 ❀

A Working Weekend

Natalie ran down the beach toward home, keeping to the packed sand next to the receding tide, muttering curses and checking her big wristwatch every twelve seconds. Damn that Peter! He was really and truly beyond belief! Calling her at nine this morning when they had *all* been partying together at Sandy's last night until three! And, of course what Peter also didn't know was that she and Mr. Dee had made a little plan for a party of their own, tonight. And if she didn't hurry, she'd be too damn late!

She had been so nicely asleep this morning, curled up on her bed, having a wonderful dream, loving her sleep, when that damned Peter called, all cheery and lighthearted—as if it were perfectly normal to insist on going to work right in the middle of the Fourth of July weekend. On a Saturday, at that!

"Oh, good. You're up." That's what she woke up to when she picked up the phone.

"Not really," she had answered; but he rolled right over her words. "Splendid," he said. "So listen: about that Lovin' Oven Club you suggested . . ."

"Peter!" she protested. "Wait a minute! What are you talking about? It's Saturday for Christ's sake! And it's—oh, my God— it's only nine o'clock, Peter! Don't you and Bambi sleep at *all*?"

He laughed, so pleased with himself. "I'm not at Bambi's. I'm in Beach Haven, at Gus Whitaker's place. . . ."

Now she groaned inwardly. Gus Whitaker was her client. The Big Boy at Lovin' Oven, the president of the firm, Mr.

Lovin' Oven himself. And he had a place in Beach Haven?
Oh, shit. Beach Haven was only a mile and a half down the
island from Paradise. Even before Peter said anything more,
she knew in her heart what was coming.

Sure enough, he went on to tell her that good old Gus had
brought a batch of work out to Beach Haven with him and had
come across a list of two hundred thirty-four ideas generated
in a brainstorm session last month. She remembered that brainstorm well. She ought to; she had run it. At least two hundred
of those ideas were completely off the wall—well, that's what
brainstorms were for—but good old Gus had seen one he liked.
"I mean, he *likes* it, Nattie," Peter had said, emphasizing every
syllable with great care. "And, believe me, darling, we *need*
your input."

She had heaved a great sigh. It was not productive to fight
Peter. Nevertheless she said, hopefully, "Not today?"

"Today. Now, in fact. There's my good girl!"

So hours ago, on this brilliant blue-sky summer day, when
she should have been lazing in the sun getting more tan—
better yet, still sleeping—better yet, sitting on the deck sipping
an icy, spicy Bloody Mary—on this wonderful summer day,
she had found herself jogging up the beach to work.

Dammit! If she hadn't been so greedy, she'd never have
answered the phone at all this morning. She'd have let the
damn thing ring right off the hook; she'd done that before. But
this time, she was hoping it would be the elusive Mr. Dee.
Well, of course, it wasn't. But if it had *not* been Peter, it
wouldn't have been Ben DeLuria. Dammit, he just wasn't the
eager pursuer type.

Not true of Peter. Peter was precisely the eager pursuer
type. She hadn't even gotten her whole body in the front door
of Whitaker's fabulous boat-shaped house, when Peter had her
sitting at a big table, going through papers, commanding her
to take notes, and questioning her on a brainstorm that had
happened, as far as she was concerned, in another life.

Finally, she said, "Whoa there, buddy, let me catch my
breath, will you?"

Oh, that Peter. Instantly, the parody of a good little boy, he sat down, hands folded in his lap, and said, "Okay, let's talk summer talk. So, how do you like Paradise, Nat?"

Yes, Peter, she thought, I remember it was your brilliant idea. But if you think I'm going to say anything about that, forget it! Instead, she twitted him. "When I'm allowed to be there, I like it fine."

"Since I put you out there, I guess I have the right to borrow you back when I need you."

"Since you're president of Marcus & Morrisey and I'm not, I guess you do."

"Isn't it a pretty little town? And full of single men, so I hear." He gave her that little quirk of a smile that said, I know you so well, Natalie. And to be honest, he *did*, so she couldn't help smiling back. And then she relented.

"Yes, it is. It's beautiful and the people seem very nice."

Peter said, "And in your usual style, you managed to captivate the most important person in the place. You know who I mean."

"Alexander Lovall." Okay, so she was proud of having captured such a big lion, first crack out of the hat. So what? She liked Sandy Lovall for himself, too.

Peter clapped. "Good for you, Nattie. Maybe, now that you know him personally, we can get some commercial art out of him."

Now she laughed. "Fat chance!"

Luckily, at that moment, good old Gus came in with a pot of coffee and the subject could be easily dropped. She didn't like working on the glorious Fourth; but work they did. Worked and worked.

Now, on her way back to Paradise, her head ached and she was madder than ever, although of course, it hadn't been a total loss. Not only did they have a brand-new Lovin' Oven Bakers' Club in the works; but also the basis for next September's new campaign. That was good. Peter Marcus was beaming upon her for a change. So *that* was good. Whitaker had decided that she was a genius and irresistible to boot, and that was good *and* bad. Good because he had okayed, at least verbally, a budget twice the size of last year's. Bad because her poor rear end had been patted and pinched more than she really cared to remember.

She only hoped that there were no bruises. Because what if Mr. Dee did the right thing and she found herself naked with him today? Come to that, she only hoped she could make it to the pond while he was still there. He'd told her he'd be working all day. And here it was nearly five. She had to get back.

Weary as she was, she sucked in a deep breath and lengthened her stride. If she got to Halfmoon Pond and Ben had already left, she'd murder Peter Marcus in his sleep. But no, that wasn't going to happen, she wasn't going to let it. She was going to get there on time, by God, and then? Well, she didn't really care, as long as *something* happened. She made the loop around the end of the island, from ocean to bay and came up on the bay side, running easily, feeling good. And there he was, on the beach, near his house. Her heart speeded. And then stopped momentarily. Barbara!!? No, it couldn't be. It was just a woman—tall and blond and shapely—who looked like Barbara. But, wait a minute, a Barbara look-alike with Mark Valentine? Not bloody likely. And as she got closer to the threesome standing on the beach, talking together, she saw that indeed it *was* Barbara. And Mark. And Mr. Dee. Deep in conversation, laughing. And, as she watched, Mr. Dee reached out and touched Barbara. Natalie was fifty yards away, but she could see the tenderness in his touch. But that was crazy! You couldn't see tenderness close up, much less from this distance. She was jealous! But that was crazy, too. She hardly knew the man; their relationship, or whatever it was, was just beginning. So why, then, did she feel such pain? Why did she long to run over there and snatch him away? Why did she immediately think about that time when her own beloved Jake had fallen for Barbara and dumped her? Why did her chest hurt? Why was she being a total ass?

She had been heading their way, but now she realized that if she ran up to them, she'd probably only make a fool of herself. She hadn't had a real date with Mr. Dee; she had just been taking a chance that she'd see him. She had no right to feel this way, no right at all. Feeling very goddamn foolish, she kept to the edge of the water and ran right past them, hoping none of them saw her.

It didn't occur to her until she was running up the boardwalk to her house to wonder why the three of them had been there together.

❀ 12 ❀

Sandy Lovall

He loved the light on the pond at this time of day: four o'clock on a summer afternoon. The sun was still high enough so that the grasses—what was left of them—cast their long lacy shadows on the water. The Rapido pen fairly flew across the paper. He was so angry. Already the pond was changed. Already the hateful ugliness of construction had intruded. Actually, he did not have to look at Halfmoon Pond in order to draw it. He knew it by heart.

He ought to know it by heart. Right behind him, where he sat on the crest of the dune, was his house, his family's old house, built back in 1911 as an eighteen-room "summer cottage."

His grandfather had chosen this spot for its view of the pond and the Great South Bay just beyond. He'd looked down at this same vista as far back as he could remember. And now that the house was his alone, he'd had the three front bedrooms upstairs opened up onto one large space, his king-size bed on a platform right in the middle, so that the first thing he faced in the morning and the last thing at night was this very view.

He was part of a long history here in Paradise. The Lovalls had been here first. By all rights, it was all theirs to claim. It should have been his today; he was the last of the Lovalls. His half-brother didn't count. *He* was no Lovall!

Once again, he felt the grab in his belly when he thought about the land, *his* land—all gone. His father's complacency had cost them everything. No will for Harold Alexander Lovall, oh, no! *He* wasn't going to die. But one day he swam out too far and he drowned. Sandy was two years old. His mother inherited all the land, and since there was nothing else, she sold it off, bit by bit, every time she needed money, until there was nothing left but the house and the pond and sixteen acres.

That—at the very least—he thought now, sketching quickly, should have been his. It was meant for a Lovall. But she had to go get married again! Weak woman! Pandering to her swampy passions, falling in love—or so she said—with a common laborer and, as if that weren't sinking low enough, *marrying* him, taking his name, giving up the Lovall name. And then, worst of all, she had a child by him. Sandy still remembered— he would never forget—the morning he awakened to find it was already nine-thirty and he was late for school. Where was his mother? She always woke him by coming into his room and pulling up the shades and rubbing his shoulder until he opened his eyes. He knocked on her door and that hated man, her husband, opened it and grinned at him and picked him up and threw him in the air and said, "You have a brother! You have a brother and I have another son!" He hated that man, and from that moment, without having seen him even, he hated that baby. They had never gotten along, he and his half-brother, never. Of course, there were eight years between them, but that wasn't the problem and they both knew it. They were not the same, they didn't share the same values.

And the proof of it was what was happening down there right now. Sandy's hand shook, and a blob of ink shot over the paper. He swore aloud. That low-life! Selling off his share of the land, selling off Halfmoon Pond and not even asking Sandy if he wanted it. How he had smirked that day. "You got the half million to buy it?" he asked.

"Don't lie to me," Sandy had answered. "Nobody is going to pay that kind of money for that kind of land."

"Oh, really? Well, somebody did. And I wasn't about to turn down half a million bucks, Sandy."

"Damn it," Sandy had yelled, "that's Lovall land!"

"Well, you always said I'm no Lovall. You're right; I'm no

Lovall. And it's sold, so quit bellyaching. If you care so much, buy it from *them*."

Well, he had tried, God knew. But they were determined, this group calling themselves Halfmoon Associates, hiding behind a meaningless corporate name. Only their lawyer, a man named Carl Stern, would speak to him, and he said that it was not for sale, no way.

Again, the pen slipped and again, a splatter of ink. Swiftly, without conscious thought, Sandy turned the blots into deepening shadows and smiled at his own cleverness. At least he knew how to turn a mistake into an advantage.

Well, by hook or by crook, *he* would not allow the desecration of his rightful land, his rightful pond. They would *not*, by all that was holy, build whatever it was they were planning to build on his Halfmoon Pond. Already he had begun mobilizing his people, yes, the weekenders too. Much as he disdained their little crackerbox houses and their crackerbox lives, he would use them for a just cause. And they were glad to do it. They were bored, bored almost to death because their little lives were empty and worthless. They didn't have generations of family behind them, of tradition, of land, of property, of belonging to the same place. So they came here, to his island, and turned it into a summer resort. Make-believe people. And when they left each fall, did they know how the real people felt? Did they realize with what joy he watched the last boat leave the dock for the mainland on Labor Day weekend?

Right from the first, though he had thought Natalie Simon would be his main ally. She was smart and she was tough. He liked her, really liked her. Her trouble was, she was too involved in running after men.

Last night, for instance, at Bambi's party. It had been a typical renters' Saturday night bash: too much liquor, too many people, too many decibels on the stereo, too much of everything. He kept himself to himself, as usual, observing everything, being pleasant to one and to all. Natalie began the evening in his company. He didn't escort her, actually, but they were two of the first to arrive and it just seemed natural. Natalie was an intelligent and clever woman. Sometimes a bit abrasive, but it was impossible to be bored in her company. And that counted for a great deal with Alexander Lovall. He thought they were having a wonderful time together; but apparently, dancing was the thing. He of course did not do those gyrations they called dancing nowadays. But Natalie did—and quite nicely, too. She had a neat pair of hips. And her footwork was so smooth that the drink she always seemed to be holding in one hand never spilled a drop.

He kept waiting for her to come back to him. But she didn't. She went from one man to another, her face becoming quite flushed, dancing more and more exuberantly. And, yes, admit it, suggestively. Men liked her and he did not like that. He couldn't go out there and drag her away . . . but he found it appalling, seeing hands slipping down her back and the succession of lips pressing into her neck or her cheek. That was what was wrong with summer people. He'd said it before, he'd say it again. They thought being in Paradise gave them license to act like animals! He wouldn't mind if none of them ever came back, ever. And to hell with the so-called economic benefits to the community! Pah!

When someone finally got that noise they called music changed to Frank Sinatra, that was his chance. Natalie was swaying in the arms of a greasy little man with a mustache— a little man who thought it wonderful to hold her close, resting his hands on her bottom—sipping from her drink now and again. Really, she had to stop drinking. A woman alone: That was her trouble. She needed someone steady and stable; she needed someone like himself. Someone who appreciated her finer points: her mind, her wit, her intelligence. He debated over cutting-in; but was that done nowadays? And he was not a good dancer. He decided, finally, that he would fortify himself with another splash of wine and *then*—even if it wasn't done; did he care what these people thought was In?—then he would cut in and gently suggest that it was after 2:00 A.M. and he'd be delighted to walk her home. But she was gone. Off into the night with that nothing!

He didn't care how often she did it, or really with whom, not really. He was a tolerant man. He didn't feel he had the right to tell his friends how to behave, and he hoped Natalie was his friend. But perhaps, one day, she might be even more than just a friend. He was beginning to have warm feelings toward her. And she cared for him, he knew it. And, perhaps even more important, she cared about the things he cared for. Like the pond. She, too, felt that its change was a desecration. She had loved it at first sight, she'd told him. Not just because he loved it; she had taken the time and the trouble to see it for herself and recognize its uniqueness and its value.

What was happening was horrible. Not only would it destroy the wildlife here, but from now on, for as long as he lived, every time he looked out of those big windows in his studio, he would see something ugly, something unnatural, blotting out part of the bay beyond. And there would be people, strangers, swarming all over; noise, loud music, and parties late into the night. Damn it! nothing would ever be the same. The end of the Lovalls; it was almost more than he could bear.

But bear it he must, bear it *and* fight it. Now he got up, looked over his sketch and gave it a nod. It was fine. He stretched his back, getting the kinks out, and began to think about an ice-cold beer and perhaps some spareribs for dinner.

It was while he was strolling back to his house, and had turned to look out over the bay and its narrow edging of sand, that he spotted Natalie running. From here, she could be twenty. She ran swiftly, her head turned to the water. Maybe he'd call her, give her a few minutes to get home, maybe ask her to have some supper with him tonight. He knew she always stayed Sundays and took the "death boat" Monday morning at six o'clock.

And then he caught sight of his nemesis: his half-baked, half-educated half-brother, standing there, gesticulating with broad clumsy gestures. Even from here, Sandy could hear that raucous laugh. What in the world was he doing with Barbara Valentine and her ex? What in the world could *they* have to talk about?

❀ 13 ❀

Three Couples

What a mistake! Barbara thought. What a dreadful mistake it had been, saying yes to Mark. Because now, here she was, in his bed, in his embrace, opening her mouth to his ardent kisses and wishing to hell she were somewhere else. Oh, lord, how did she get herself into this?—for the third time since their divorce! After two years! And after an involvement with another man! What was wrong with her that made her incapable of saying no to him, that gave out an automatic slavelike response the minute he came on to her?

It had started nicely enough: an invitation to come see his renovation, now that it was complete. "After all," he said, over the telephone, "it's still half your house. I'd like to hear what you think of it." And after she'd said okay, that she'd come over and have a look, he said, "Come after work. We can have a drink and I'll give you something to eat if you like." What the hell, why not? She was safe. He was in no way attractive to her, not any more.

And so there she was at 7:35 P.M., in Brooklyn Heights, at the top of the flight of still-familiar stone steps, admiring the bright polish on the brass numerals and the brass fittings on the front door, loving the quiet and the leafy peace of Orange Street, noting the clean windowpanes and the new pale gray thin-slatted blinds and the new window boxes with their cascades of pink and scarlet petunias. She took enormous pleasure in admiring the perfection of every damned little tiny detail— hallmark of her ex-husband—taking delight in it all because she was no longer responsible for *any* of it.

When he answered the door, coolly neat in an open-collared shirt and chinos, she thought for the one-millionth time how handsome he was. Too bad he was a typical rigid male chauvinist tyrant who thought his role in life was to be a benevolent despot.

"Barbara! Welcome home!" The bastard. He was always denying their divorce one way or another, denying her independence, denying her separateness. He leaned toward her, and she quickly turned her face so that he kissed her cheek. He always did that, too, whenever they were alone. What was he after?

She slipped past him, focusing on the new light fixture—the very one she had gone to get for him, idiot that she was—and exclaiming over the new cream-colored walls and the framed watercolors of Venice. "Don't they look extraordinarily like Turner!" she babbled, not really caring what she said just as long as it was not personal. And then she felt it: felt Mark stiffen; and she instantly knew why. She had just said something about art, probably something intelligent. How he had always hated her to have insight about anything he considered *his* domain! And, sure enough, he mumbled something. These were paintings after Turner that he'd discovered in an antique shop. So she'd been right. Oink oink oink.

He gave her a guided tour of the renovation. It was beautifully done . . . very different from when they'd lived there together. Then, he'd been into restoration, and she well remembered the temper tantrums if heaven forbid she got the wrong period hardware for the kitchen cabinets. Or *any* damn thing. Of course, then she'd been so proud of his interest in their home and his abilities as an architect and even his icky-picky perfectionism. Of course, then, her pride and her very identity had more to do with Mark Valentine than with herself. Silently, as she *oohed* and *ahed* over the new avant-grade furnishings, she thanked her lucky stars that she had finally discovered her own self.

Oh, really? She'd found her identity, had she? Then why was she lying there, skin to skin with Mark, making all the obligatory noises as he pushed into her, groaning with lust. He hadn't *forced* her to strip, to lie down with him, to curve her body into his, to lift her lips for his kiss. Not at all. She'd done it, goddammit, *she'd* done it. Why? Well, she'd had three drinks, two more than her usual. And then, well, he'd presented that feast, all laid out on the coffee table, complete with flickering candlelight, sterling silver, and a branch of cymbidium. It felt so good, having him fuss over her, knowing that he'd done all of this preparation just for her. She had melted, just melted. Well, did that mean she was willing to give her body for a gourmet meal and a bunch of orchids? Of course not!

Habit, that's what it was. Habit, pure and simple. When Mark Valentine wanted her, she was still in the habit of responding. Without thought and without volition. Now, in the middle, as it were, of the whole thing, she realized she hadn't really wanted to make love with him. She was not turned on. She was *pretending* to be turned on and that was horrid. All through their seventeen-year marriage, she had found him the sexiest man on earth. Their sex had always been spectacular. In fact, it was very good—what he was doing right now. He'd even learned a couple of new tricks. He had lifted her legs over his shoulders and was moving in a new and wonderful way. But she felt unexcited. All she could think of was how to get him to come without letting him know what a farce this was. And wasn't that something she and her therapist had wrestled with, time after time? Karen had said, "Any woman should be able to tell a man, 'This isn't good for me,'" and she had agreed. She *did* agree. Right now, she should be able to put a hand on Mark's shoulder and gently ask him to stop, gently tell him that it wasn't working, that she wasn't really *there* for him.

But she couldn't. She just couldn't. She'd been too well trained to make a man feel good, too indoctrinated with the notion of the castrating woman, to do anything quite so honest. It didn't even *feel* honest to her; it felt brutal, she couldn't help it. And, no matter how she disdained Mark, she would not, *could* not, put him down sexually.

However, she *could* bring him to orgasm; she knew how.

She put her hands onto his muscular buttocks and pressed him into her, hard. "Now, Mark. Now!" And, sure enough, it worked, just as it always had.

As he lay collapsed over her, breathing heavily, whispering endearments, Ben DeLuria came insistently into her head, filling her mind. Go away! she thought. Go *away*! This is ludicrous!

She'd just met the man last weekend—he and Mark were doing some work together—and he'd invited them both to his house for a drink. They'd talked for about an hour and a half, total. So it was crazy, what she was feeling, crazy! When you were a grown-up woman, you didn't go around falling for someone so fast, you just didn't. And anyway, that *couldn't* be what it was. It was just summer on Fire Island, with all its implicit promises of romance and excitement and sex. Of course. So why was he once again intruding, uninvited, into her thoughts, even as she stroked Mark's back. It wasn't nice! And yet, she couldn't seem to stop it.

Of course, Ben was extremely seductive. He'd called her every day since that Sunday. Every single evening at six-thirty, when he knew she'd have gotten home from the office. Every day, the phone would ring and when she answered, he would say, "It's me." Even the first time!

The worst part of it was that, even the first time, she knew that voice, knew it by heart. Even the first time, she hadn't bothered to pretend. She'd said, "Hello, Ben," her heart hammering in her chest. She'd felt as if her whole body were vibrating. Later, she could not remember what they had talked about, only that he kept saying, "I miss you," and she, trying very hard to maintain her equilibrium, kept answering, "You can't; we don't know each other," and he kept answering *her* with, "*You* know what happened between us."

Yes, she knew what happened. But it was impossible. Maybe two sixteen-year-olds could base a relationship on ninety minutes of chitchat and a surge of electric attraction. But not Barbara Valentine, forty-four years old, three years divorced, forewarned and forearmed when it came to big, strong, aggressive, demanding men. Pounding heart and sweaty palms notwithstanding, she was *not* going to allow herself to get carried away. She was fighting it with all her might. She said to him, "Look, Ben, I've only recently ended a serious long-term relationship. . . . It wasn't pleasant."

He'd quipped, "Then why did it last so long?"

And she'd said, "The *ending* wasn't pleasant."

And he'd said, "Oh, Christ, Barbara, I knew that's what you meant. I don't know why I said that, I'm sorry. Yes, I do know why I said that. Because I can't stand for you to even talk about being with another man. I'm jealous!" She'd laughed because his blurted confidences made her feel warm and girlish and shivery with anticipation and she didn't want that. She'd wanted to stay safe, uninvolved. So she'd said lightly, "You're forgetting I was married to Mark."

"I'm not crazy about that thought, either," he'd said and then he laughed, too.

No doubt about it, he had endearing qualities. But, no. She was not going to do it. He was just like Mark, just like Hal, pressing to have his way; and she was determined that he would not. She answered the phone, ignoring her racing pulses, and kept putting him off, not responding directly when he demanded to know when he could see her on the weekend. She was in control, her emotions locked away from him and his blandishments.

And then, today, Thursday, he didn't call. At first she had waited patiently; and then not so patiently; and then she had left to go to Mark, feeling cheated and empty. Just because he called her every day at the same time, she'd come to expect it. Dammit, look how fast she'd fallen into his trap!

What a mistake, Bambi thought, eyeing herself in the smoky-mirrored wall in Peter's bathroom. The teddy was gorgeous: satin, cut high at the hip and low at the bosom with teeny-weeny little rhinestone straps. But black simply was not her color. A blonde, even one who wasn't a natural blonde exactly, should have pastels . . . gentle colors.

She turned and looked at herself over her shoulder. The legs were cut so high, part of her backside curved out of the bottom of them. Not a look she liked very much, but if that's what turned Peter on, well, it was his money and his apartment and his show. She knew how to please a man, and Peter was one of the easy ones. He was so insistent about his likes and dislikes, you never had to guess, ever. So, she didn't exactly like the way this looked on her and she would have picked better. So what? Whatever Peter wanted. . . .

Anyway, she knew better than to disagree with him. Peter did not like to be crossed. Look what happened the day she innocently remarked on the scruffy old gray metal file cabinet he kept in his office, his beautiful, beautifully-decorated office. All she did was tell him she'd like to buy him the very newest high-tech cabinet. And my God, he nearly bit her head off. "When I want your help redecorating my office," he'd snapped, "I'll let you know." And he'd given her such a look that she flinched, just as if he had hit her. And whenever they were in his car together, forget it if he took a wrong turn! She was not allowed to say a single word; she was not even allowed to look at him as if she *wanted* to say something.

Bambi sighed, sucked in her tummy, and fluffed up her curls. Well, what were you going to do? That was Peter Marcus: creative, exciting, handsome, sexy, powerful, and rich rich rich. If he was a teeny bit irritable at times, well, that was the price she'd pay. They were spiritual soulmates and that's what really mattered. He was the only man she had ever met who really cared about the inner life. Where it was important, he had it all. And it wouldn't hurt *her* a bit if she became Mrs. Peter Marcus.

She'd promised herself not even to think about that possibility until they had had a couple of months together. And right now, Peter was on the big round bed, waiting for her. Tonight, he wanted to play "Spy." Bambi smiled at herself in the mirror. He really was something!

Yesterday, it had been "Pasha and Jasmine," with her in harem pants and a necklace and nothing else; and him in a caftan. For an hour and a half, they'd done Pasha and Jasmine, with tapes of wonderful oboe-y Oriental music playing. Yesterday, Pasha; today, Spy; tomorrow, who knew what exciting idea he'd come up with.

Again, she sighed. It might be nice if he didn't want sex so much of the time. There were times when she was tired; listen, she worked hard on *The Ad Game*. Peter liked to talk as if she had a whole staff and a great big office, just like he did. But, in fact, there was just her and Denise and the answering machine.

Right this minute, if anyone cared to know, what she really wanted to do was cuddle up with Peter, watch some TV—it was *Hill Street Blues* night—and maybe nibble on some pretzels, maybe drink a little wine. Well, never mind . . . Peter said Spy, so Spy it was going to be. She took one last look at herself . . . she'd do . . . and couldn't help smiling. It would be fun, so what was she complaining about?

But when she sashayed out, hand on hip, she was surprised to find Peter sprawled on the bed, totally dressed. In his street clothes! Well, maybe the part of Spy was stripping him or something. . . .

"I have something to tell you, Bams. . . ." He sat up and patted his knees in invitation, so she went right over and plunked herself in his lap, winding her arms around his neck and resting her cheek on his curly head, the way he liked.

"What is it, Petesy? Is it a surprise?"

"Exactly."

Could it be? A proposal? So soon? This was not the way she'd had Peter Marcus figured. "Tell little Bams," she murmured, nibbling at the top of his ear. "Pretty please with sugar on."

He chortled; there was no other way to describe it. It was a chortle, a gurgle of pleasure deep in his throat. "It's a secret, you know."

"Oh, good. I love secrets. And I'm good at keeping them, too."

"Oh, that doesn't matter. Everyone will know anyway, after Saturday." He paused dramatically; she knew better than to interrupt or press him. And then he said: "Halfmoon Associates . . ."

"Yeah? What about them?"

"Come on, Bams, don't be so dense." He laughed aloud. "It's me!"

"What do you mean, it's you?"

"Me, dummy! Peter Marcus. Me, myself, and I. We're Halfmoon Associates!"

"Oh, my God, Peter. Then..."

"That's right. I'm the ecological villain. But listen... the hated building is just a house for me, that's all. Sandy Lovall imagines a resort hotel with businessmen and their vulgar wives ... or a health spa with a lot of gay bodybuilders. Oh, is he wrong!" Again, he laughed.

Bambi knew that Sandy Lovall didn't want *anyone* messing with his pond, for *any* reason. And anyway, wasn't there something about a court order or something?

"Petesey," she said, giving him a quick little kiss on his head. "You're supposed to stop work at the pond... right?"

"Right!" He laughed again.

"But... there's work going on."

"Right!"

"But... I thought you *had* to stop, if the court said to."

"They can't stop me if they don't know who I am. Oh, Bams, don't look at me like that. I'm going to come out of the closet. I just stayed quiet, hoping nobody would make trouble. I paid for that land. I have the right to do what we want. And I *will*. My lawyer says no reason I can't have my house right there. He's the one who recommended that, on Saturday, I face Sandy Lovall and all those ecology nuts."

"But Petesy..." Bambi was irritated to find her voice squeaking, which it had a tendency to do when she got excited. "*I'm* one of those ecology nuts. I promised Sandy Lovall to help, and this Saturday, I'm supposed to be right up front, next to him, holding the biggest sign."

Peter chuckled and gave her a hug, murmuring into her neck. "I know. I know.... And you go right ahead, Bams, and hold the biggest sign."

"How can I? When I'm your..."

"My *what*, Bams?"

He was such a tease sometimes, honestly. "You know."

"Yeah, *I* know. But do *you* know what you've been? My adorable, sexpot little spy!" And now he just roared.

Bambi bounded right off his lap and turned to him, her fists clenched tight. "You let me tell you everything! About all Sandy's plans and who was on our side and who wasn't and what the attorney said and . . . everything!" He continued laughing, and she stamped her foot. "Don't, Peter, stop that! I'm really upset!"

"I know, I know." He was gasping for breath, holding out his arms. She stood still for a moment. Could she refuse? Could she afford to walk right out? Because damn it, he had used her, *used* her!

"Aw, Bams, don't be mad at your Petesy, come on . . ."

"Is that why you've been seeing me?" Her voice came out high and tight.

"Oh, no!" He leaped up from the bed and zipped over to her, so fast that, one minute she was just standing there and the next minute, she was wrapped tightly in his arms as he kissed her neck and said, "No, no, no. Don't ever think that. No, of course not. You're a very special person in my life, *very*. It was just . . . well, I couldn't tell *anyone*." He pulled back a little, peering into her face. "Give us a smile? Pretty please with sugar on?" Well, who could resist? In spite of herself, in spite of her anger, she found herself smiling and he winked and smiled back.

"Look," Peter said earnestly. "I had no idea my summer house was going to become a cause célèbre. The real estate agent told me that the pond had been on the market forever. Nobody else wanted to sink money into that swamp. It's an eyesore. The people of Paradise should be grateful to me!"

"Does Natalie know?"

Peter shook his head, releasing her. "Nattie. That's a tough one. She does so tend to overdo, you know. But I know how to handle her. She thinks she can take advantage of the fact that she's known me since I was a teenager, but she's wrong.

She thinks she taught me everything I know, and she's wrong there, too. She thinks she owns me—just because she was close to my old man! But she's on the edge, Bams, on the edge. She'd better watch herself, or else. . . ."

"Or else what?"

"Never you mind. Old business. She'd just better watch her mouth and she'd better watch how she behaves with clients. She blackmailed me once, but I'm damned if I'm going to pay for it forever. . . ." His voice trailed off.

Very interesting. "Petesy? What do you mean, blackmail?"

"Did I say blackmail? Just a figure of speech. Nattie gets to me in a way nobody else at the agency does. My old man was crazy about her, did I tell you about that? And then he put her in charge of me when I was learning the business. In *charge* of me. Hell, she was just a kid herself. Did I ever tell you about *that*?"

Only four or five hundred times. "Tell me about it, Petesy."

"Agh!" He dismissed the subject with a wave of his hand. "The point is, she's been out of control lately. Drinking too much. Well, that's always been her weakness, you know. The demon rum. I shouldn't tell you this. . . ." He paused, for a long long time, and Bambi kept as still and small as she could. If she didn't move, he might go on and give something away. It was hell, filling up that column every week. "I shouldn't tell anyone, but, she's been worrying me lately. The work's not quite up to snuff and, well, she's made a few errors of judgment. One client has said straight out that she can continue to write his copy and come up with the ideas, but he doesn't want to see her at any meetings or presentations. Now, that's a problem. I mean, Natalie *is* my creative director. . . ."

"I know. I know. . . ." Bambi murmured.

"Well . . ." He gave a massive shrug and brought his eyes back to her. "I owe her one. I owe her a big one. So I won't do anything right now." Now he grinned at her, really looking at her. "Oh, Bams, if only all women were as understanding and inventive as you! You, now, you'd make a helluva creative director. And I'll bet none of the clients would ask me to keep *you* locked away in your office!"

The hug he gave her now was quite, quite different. He pushed his loins into her so that she could feel the erection, and began to rub her back, slowly, lightly, with just the tips of his fingers. "And now, double oh one," he said, his voice choked with heat, "you will pay dearly for this information. . . . You will serve M and do just as M says."

"Yes, M," Bambi agreed.

"Down on your knees, double oh one. Adore my body!"

"Yes," Bambi said, obeying. A minute later, though, when she had him breathing hard, she paused, looking up at him, and said, "Did you really mean it? about my making a good creative director?"

What a mistake, Natalie thought, staring across the bed at that all-too-familiar and all-too-beloved *punim*. She never should have come to the Alden Hotel with Jake. He was right, he was not in any shape to be any good to anyone. Not sexually, at least. She reached down for the bottle of wine on the floor. As she refilled her glass he glowered at her and said: "Don't you think you've had enough?"

"Not you, too! Dammit, haven't I always been able to hold my booze? Haven't I always known my limit?"

"Nattie, Nattie . . ." His tone softened and he reached over to pat her hand. "You *are* the limit." And instantly, he swung into song: "You're delightful . . . you're delicious . . . you're de limit . . ."

Natalie pulled her hand away. The clown! As always! And, as always, the reality remained unspoken. They had not been able to get it on. He had not been able to get it up. In all their years of hopping over to the Alden for a quickie—and sometimes for a longie and slowie—nothing like this had ever happened. You'd think he'd say *something* about it, but no. She wanted to be angry with him, but she couldn't. He always was able to make her laugh.

She laughed now. "You never change, Jake!"

"You've just said the magic woid! *Now* I want a drink. *Change*. Oh, God, I have changed and you know it. We've both changed, but you seem to get younger and younger, whereas

I . . ." He patted his flat belly and sighed. "*I* get a pot, varicose veins, hemorrhoids, gray hair, wrinkles . . . not to mention a feeling that life is passing me by."

Not to mention, Natalie thought, the unmentionable: that you and I were unable to do our usual mating dance this evening. But she resisted the urge to say something flip. She loved him too much.

"Oh, Jake, that's ridiculous. In the first place, you don't have a pot." She patted his belly briefly. "You still look ten years younger than your age, which I won't mention. And I don't think being executive VP in a major ad agency indicates failure, exactly."

"I'm not."

"What's that supposed to mean?"

"I mean I'm no longer . . . all that, what you said. I've been fired."

"Fired! I don't believe it."

"Believe it. It happened this morning. They're regrouping, and there are too many VPs and I'm the newest kid on the block. So . . . sometime next month, I'll be lining up at the unemployment office."

"And I may be joining you."

"Nattie. You don't have to try to make me feel better."

"I'm not. It's true. Peter's after me, I just know it."

"So what else is new?"

"No, this is different. I feel as if I'm being shredded to death. Dammit, if only he'd come right out with it, let me know what's on his mind."

"I think it's your imagination. He's always acting peculiar, you know that. He's a spoiled brat. Jesus, Nat, I should think that *you* of all people, would know what Peter's like. God, I remember him following you around the agency, back when we still had linoleum floors." They both laughed, remembering M & M as it had been twenty years before when it was known on Madison Avenue as the bare bones agency and its furnishings had been chosen for one reason only: They were cheap.

"Maybe that's the problem. Maybe Peter figures he doesn't want someone around who remembers him following her around. . . . Maybe he thinks I'm too old."

"What nonsense! Peter loves you! Not only do I remember his following you like a puppy, but I also recall the look on his face, which was pure longing. He was hot for you; it was obvious!"

Natalie made a little face and refilled both glasses once more. "He hid it well, I must say. He either pretended to be deaf and dumb to anything I said or he argued with me. God, that was a long time ago."

"You don't tell and I won't tell. But seriously, Nat, what I hear out of the rumor mill is that Peter ain't about to cut back on his staff."

Now she was alert. As casually as she could, she said, "Why do you say that?"

"Well, the word is out that Peter's collecting Steinberg & Epstein stock—all on the QT, of course."

"Oh, really?" She hoped she didn't sound too dumb. Her mind was racing. Where had that rumor started? When Peter had told her his plan, he shook a finger under her nose and threatened her with decapitation, should she ever breathe a syllable. And she hadn't . . . had she? No, she was sure she hadn't. Besides, when she had a bit too much to drink, business was not what was on her mind. No, of course she hadn't let it slip. So . . . who?"

"Stop playing dumb broad, Nattie, it won't wash."

"I'm not playing. I don't know what you're talking about. And frankly, I hope it's not true. What do we want with PR, anyway? It's not our thing."

"Your very innocence has convinced me that it's true."

Quickly, she said, "Never mind rumors, Jake. I want to talk about you losing your job."

"Well, I don't."

"Come on, Jake, it'll take you about five minutes, with your reputation, to find a job just as good or better."

"I don't want to talk about it. Okay?" She reached over to touch him, but he backed away, out of her reach, giving her what she could only describe as a baleful look.

"Later," she said.

"Thank you, but later. I don't want to talk about it. What I want to talk about is the dreams of youth. Remember? We used to walk up to Central Park during lunch hour and sit on our rock and talk about life and love and truth and beauty and our novels and plays? Where are they, the novels and plays and truths and beauties of yesteryear?"

"About truth and beauty, I couldn't say. But as for my unfinished novel, it's on the top shelf of the hall closet in my old apartment. The last time I was overtaken by nostalgia and took it out to read, it was as lousy as ever!"

Oh, good. She'd made him laugh. He lifted his glass and said, "Here's to those golden years, Natalie."

"I'm not going to drink to any goddamn golden years, you nerd. I'm going to drink to now, because the best is yet to come."

"Remember the first day you came to work at M & M?"

"Of course I do. The most important day of my life. It was my first day as a big-time hotshot advertising copywriter. And..."

"Yes, and?—"

"And a gangly redhead with a fresh mouth peered over the partition and did a full-scale production of *Babes on Broadway*."

"Oh, yeah! We'd both seen it on the 'Late Late Show' the night before... I remember. I was absolutely knocked out when you just picked up on it and went along. Jesus, most girls would have giggled and said something meaningful, like, 'Oh, you Jake!' *You* were terrific."

"And you were the funniest boy I'd ever met in my life. I couldn't believe it. I had fantasized that if I ever was lucky enough to work at a real New York ad agency, I'd meet only exciting, terrific, sophisticated, wonderful, delightful, humorous people."

"And all you got was Jake Miller."

"Oh, you Jake!"

Now he reached over and clutched her hand tightly in his.

"Goddammit, Nattie, you are a wonderful woman, you know that? I don't know why I bother with these other babes, I really don't. Why am I so stupid? I mean, here you are and you know me and you love me and you understand me and you know what's good for me." He leaned over to give her a light kiss on the lips.

Now, she thought. But that was all: he sat right back again. That was *all*? Shit. Well, she was horny, and no wonder. She hadn't been laid since the last time with Mr. Dee, and that was too long ago to suit Nat Simon. Nor had she heard from him. Dammit, the last couple of nights, she found herself hanging around her depressing sublet apartment, staring at the walls and waiting for the goddamn phone to ring. Waiting! She kept telling herself to stop doing this. "If he's going to call, he's going to call. If not, not," she told her reflection in the hall mirror. "Waiting here, sweating and pacing won't make the phone ring." But she couldn't bring herself to go out, somehow. Dammit, where the hell *was* he? They'd had super sex together. At the end, he'd whistled and said, "Jesus Christ, lady, you want to give me a heart attack?" She knew what she was like in bed. He couldn't often get it that good. And there he was, stuck out on Fire Island, for God's sake! He couldn't possibly have found anyone else out *there*.

After three nights like that, she got totally disgusted with herself. Forty-four years old and mooning over a guy just because he was well hung? She was Natalie Simon; she could get any guy she wanted. Couldn't she? He'd learn he wasn't the only one who knew how to play cool. And that's when she picked up the phone and called Jake. And now here she was, in bed all right, but a disappointed woman.

What was the matter with all the men she knew? Dammit! But she kept it light. "Okay, so here's my alternative plan. Let's get out of bed and have dinner and maybe take in a movie."

"Sorry. I have a date."

"You have a *what*?"

"Nattie, Nattie, you said a drink, and already we've had

three! A client is expecting me at the Four Seasons in . . . let's see, about an hour."

"You bastard! You didn't tell me? . . . You really take the cake!"

Jake roared. "Oh, God, you're so right. I'm absolutely incorrigible, haven't changed a bit, never will, don't care about people's feelings. . . ."

"Dammit, don't take the words out of my mouth! It's not funny, Jake. Fifteen years ago it wasn't funny, and it still isn't. Goddammit, when are you going to grow up?"

"You're so wonderful, Nattie," he said, and heaved himself out of bed. She longed to slug him. "And in answer to your question, just call me Peter Pan."

And he was gone, into the shower. Well, dammit, she wasn't going to go home at seven o'clock and spend the evening waiting for "Hill Street Blues" to come on at ten. She sipped her wine, wondering what in hell she *was* going to do. And then, it came to her. She reached over, picked up the phone, dialed a number and waited. After seven rings, she began to frown. Him, too? He was in the city and he'd asked her for dinner tonight. She'd turned him down on account of Jake. Shit.

And then the phone on the other end was lifted and the rich, deep voice said, "Yes?" and her heart lifted. There was an evening ahead of her, after all.

"Like the proverbial bad penny," she said, laughing, "I am about to turn up."

"Oh, wonderful," Sandy Lovall said. "I was hoping you'd be free, after all."

❀ 14 ❀

The Ladies Have Lunch

The Cafe de Paris was already crowded; but they knew Natalie there and her favorite table by the window was ready and waiting. "Oh, boy," Martha J said, "even the napkins look edible. I'm so hungry!"

Seating herself so she could look out the window to the bustle of Second Avenue, Natalie laughed and said, "You're *what*, Martha J?"

"Hungry. Lord, I got so busy this morning, finding Calvin the exact tie he had in mind. Honestly, men! Well, it *was* in my closet, since I was the last one to wear it, but still—" She smiled sweetly, waiting for Natalie and Barbara to stop laughing. "Anyway, what did I have here the last time we got together?"

"Softshell crabs," Barbara said promptly. "But who was looking? And that's exactly what I think I'll have today—no, wait. I don't think I want anything sauteed. Broiled sole is more like it." She pointed an accusing finger at Martha J. "It's all your fault! I've put on five pounds since you gave me the assignment of new fillings for pita! But as everyone seems to be saying these days, so what else is new? I've been dieting, girl and woman, since I was five. One more won't kill me."

"I'm not taking the blame," Martha J said, shaking her head. "Oh, no! I just ask you to dream them up; I don't ask you to *eat* them. Let the Hasahnis put on the weight. They try everything out anyway. They don't even care if it sounds or looks weird. Sorry, Barbara, but really, tuna and cheese and *pineapple*?"

"That's not so weird," Natalie said. "When I worked in the college cafeteria, that was lunch every Friday."

"You worked in the cafeteria? Doing what?"

"Spooning out stuff you don't want to hear about. Listen, the ham and cheese and pineapple on soggy bread was the high point of the week in my college cafeteria!"

"Funny," Martha J said, "I never pictured you working. I always figured you for a rich kid."

Natalie laughed briefly. "No, I wasn't. And working in the caf was the price I had to pay for being at Syracuse. My father wanted me to stay home and go to the local college: Hampton College, Hampton, New York, in the pits of the Cherry Valley."

"Hampton's good!" Barbara objected. "Even out in Ohio, we heard of Hampton."

"Yeah, well, to me it was just the local college up on the hill. First of all, it was too close to home. And, I had big ideas. I wanted Syracuse's J-School. My Dad, you know, was the editor and publisher of the local weekly newspaper, and all the time I was little, he and I talked about how I'd take it over one day, you know, be the first lady editor-publisher in upstate New York and stuff like that. But by the time I went to college, I realized he'd wasted his life in that hick town. He was so proud of being one of the bigshots, of being buddies with the police chief and the mayor. Ha! The mayor was the biggest windbag of a real estate broker in town, and running Hampton was a part-time job that made him feel important. I didn't want to spend the rest of my life kowtowing to hicks with delusions of grandeur! I wanted the big time, the *real* big time."

"The Big Apple," Martha J murmured.

"Don't tell anyone, but they didn't call it that, way back then."

A basket of rolls was placed on the table, and Martha J reached in immediately, as did Barbara, saying, "Oh, God, why don't I have more self-control? But I can smell the freshness from here."

"I went to college at night," Martha J said, through a mouthful. "It's a whole different experience."

"It must be," Barbara said. "That means you missed out on

campus life . . . yes, and fraternity parties and dormitory life and serenades and water fights and panty raids." She stopped, laughing.

"I think I'm glad I missed that stuff!" she laughed. "But at the time, what I knew I was missing was sleep. I went to school at night, carrying three courses, and worked an eight-hour day at Johnson Ford, typing and filing and ducking the busy hands of all the salesmen!" She laughed again. "I took it because the money was good, but thank God the next year I found a different job at the same money and no pats and pinches. And then, I got lucky, and landed a job at Rutterman & Rudolph, a little ad agency in Newark. Supposedly I was the switchboard operator and receptionist; but they were so small, I got to do everything: pasteups, calls to clients, space sales, and even—oh, joy of joys—some copywriting. That's when I knew that that was the life for me, having fun and pretending to the world that I was working." All three of them laughed now.

"And then you got your degree," Natalie said.

"Yeah, I got my degree. But I gotta tell you, Mama was a whole lot more excited than I was. I had to make believe. 'Cause I'll tell you something, I didn't feel one damn bit smarter. I must say, that made me an advocate of attending the School of Hard Knocks. I can't see that college taught me a thing!"

"Oh, Martha J!" Barbara protested. "I'm sure that's not so. It's obvious to anyone that you are educated. Now don't make that face at me. It's true, isn't it, Nat. See, Martha J. Of course"—she gave a rueful little laugh—"I shouldn't talk. I met Mark Valentine when I was a sophomore in college, and that was the end of all my ambitions to be a pediatrician or maybe a biologist. In fact, it was the end of all rational thought for a good many years to come. Ask my therapist if you don't believe me. But seriously, the minute I met Mark, I knew he was my future. I switched right into Home Ec, stopped thinking, stopped planning, and began marking time, waiting for my real life to begin."

"Real life?"

"When I would become Mrs. Mark Valentine, of course. Everything else was play. I was at a toy college, going to toy

classes taking toy courses, and having toy friends. Mark alone
was real. It's too bad, you know, because a good deal of my
college years have become a blur in my mind. I can't remember
the names of my professors. I can't remember any of my classes.
But I can recall in every detail what I was wearing the night
Mark proposed, everything including the perfume: Arpege."
She stopped for breath, looking up as the waitress paused by
their table. "Ah, yes. I think we're all ready to order. I'll have
the sole, please, no potato, double veggies..."

They all ordered, then, Natalie asking for a carafe of white
wine, "Right away, please." When it came, she poured, and
when they all lifted their glasses, said, "To us."

"I'll drink to that," Barbara said, sipping, and then added:
"I shouldn't, of course. That was just fifty-five easy calories
that slid down there and landed on my hips. I must keep reminding myself that I have to get into a bathing suit every weekend."
She grinned, and took another sip of wine. "I really must,"
she repeated.

"Go ahead, lady," Martha J said. "You look gorgeous in
your bathing suit."

"We *all* do," Natalie said. "Dammit, I want the world to be
a perfect place and then we ladies would never ever again have
to think about, talk about, or do a diet!"

"Hear, hear!"

"Amen, sister."

"So, Martha J," Natalie said after a moment, "what does
Calvin say about you guys getting a house in Paradise?"

"Oh, Calvin says wonderful. Of course, I'm supposed to
do the looking."

"And, don't tell me, let me guess," said Barbara. "*He* gets
final approval."

"You got it!"

"You mean, even a new liberated male like Calvin?—"

"Some things," Martha J said meaningfully, "never change,
Barbara. In the past, now, forever, on land, sea, or air, at home
or in the office. Honestly, *men*! At home, at least, I only have
Calvin to contend with. In the office, however—"

"Peter!" Natalie interrupted. "He on your case, too?"

"On my case? Like how?"

"You know, his usual: snide little comments, acid asides, unreasonable demands, all that good stuff."

Martha J wrinkled her brow. "No, no. None of that. Peter's been terrific. Demanding, yes. But terrific. No, what I meant was the Hasahni tribe: three brothers, four cousins, six in-laws, a few nephews—and a sister-in-law with a big mouth." She sighed. "Try to get final approval from that group! Just try."

"All I know," Barbara said, trying in vain to stop laughing, "is I cooked up twenty different fillings for those Pita Parlors. I thought they were perfect: delicious, nutritious, easy to combine, and cheap, cheap, cheap. But try to get final approval! Twenty stuffings, and a hundred opinions on each one!"

"That was such a genius idea, Martha J. Doing pocket sandwiches like Steve's does ice cream; pick your own combination. Simple but spectacular." Natalie grimaced a little. "I don't lie when I say I wish it had been *my* idea."

Martha J laughed. "It probably was! I'm merely a chip off the old block, you know!"

"Well, I think it's just too bad," Barbara said. "You think up the good idea and Peter gets the credit."

"And the client," said Natalie.

"And the money," Martha J chimed in. "Hey! I've just had another genius idea. It's called being in business for yourself. That way, *you* have the idea, you gits the credit, the client, *and* the dough!"

"Oh, sure, Martha J. In business for yourself, in New York City! Fat chance!"

"Oh, I don't know . . . maybe not that fat. I mean, Calvin has been making go-into-business-for-yourself noises for a long time now. And I've been thinking about it a lot lately. I mean, if I'm going to work thirteen-hour days, why not in my own office? Maybe in my own home? And besides, maybe—" She stopped abruptly.

"And besides, maybe?" Natalie prodded.

"Nothing. No, not nothing. Something. I'm not sure yet, so I can't say. And, hey! wouldn't it be great if you came and worked with me, Nat! Hey, I'd love that! You too, Barbara. I don't know if I'd have a whole test kitchen, but what the hell, with your brains and your looks, there'd be plenty for you to do."

"I'd *love* to get out of the test kitchen," Barbara said.

"Really?"

"Truly."

"Nat? Would you be game for a try?"

"Is the Pope Catholic?"

The three women stared at each other, eyes very bright. "Oh, my lord . . ." Martha J breathed softly. And then Natalie pounded a fist lightly on the table.

"Nah," she said, shaking her head regretfully, "couldn't be. No way I could afford it. I'm already in hock up to my knees with the house on Fire Island. So I do need that paycheck. Damn!"

"As do I, alas," said Barbara.

"Well, I'm *thinking* about it. I didn't say it would happen tomorrow. I mean . . . it is scary, isn't it? But, I *am* thinking about it. I wish it could be more than that, I really do."

"Hell," Natalie said, lifting her glass. "But it's a nice dream, isn't it?"

❀ 15 ❀

Ben DeLuria

It was dim and cool in Bob's Bar. And quiet. That's what Ben liked about it. At four o'clock on a Friday, the summer people hadn't arrived yet. It was too early. You could still actually hear Sinatra on the jukebox. Nice. He liked Sinatra; couldn't see those noisy groups who shouted into the mike. That wasn't music. "A Foggy Day in London Town"—now ... *that* was music. Made him homesick for London. That was a laugh, because he'd never been to London! He laughed to himself and banged the beer mug on the bar.

"Yo!" Irving shouted and slid a new one down to him. Ben slugged it down; Jesus, that tasted good. It *felt* good, dammit, on a parched throat. He'd been out in that fucking swamp since eight in the morning in this goddamn heat wave, and then on top of everything, a whole boatload of lumber came in and it had to be unloaded and there wasn't anyone else but Ben DeLuria to do it; so there he was, heaving two-by-fours and two-by-fives, sweating like a pig and being eaten alive by mosquitoes.

And thinking about her. Jesus, he hadn't been able to get Barbara Valentine out of his mind since he met her, and that was last Sunday! God, how he wanted her! It was crazy, to have a woman fill your dreams at night and your thoughts by day, when there were plenty of women around, *plenty*, and all very interested in a healthy unmarried man. What was there about her that made her different, that made her special? He couldn't figure it out. He only knew that every time he thought about her, he felt excited. He couldn't wait, couldn't wait to get to know her, to get to see her again, to get her into bed with him. Couldn't wait, couldn't wait, that was the whole thing. All week long, every night, he kept calling her because he couldn't wait until the weekend to hear her voice. Every night he called at six-thirty after he had his shower—funny, wasn't it, that he felt he had to be showered before he talked to her on the goddamn phone, even—and found her just coming in the door from her job, all breathless and sounding pleased to hear his voice. God, he loved talking to her on the phone. He loved making her laugh, loved the way she picked up and said, "Yes?" instead of "Hello."

So last night he was a little late, so he had some things to do before he got into the house and into the shower, and just as he was about to call her, same time as usual, didn't the goddamn phone ring. A minute sooner and they'd have gotten a busy signal. And it was business—he *had* to talk; there was no way he could hang up, and by the time he dialed her number, so okay, it was after seven, so what? She should have been home, dammit, not that stupid machine with its blurred voice saying the same goddamn stupid thing every time you called again. And he did call again, he called every half hour and every half hour he heard that little click and the canned voice reciting once more, "Hi there, this is Barbara Valentine. Not in person, but the next best thing." After the first time, he didn't even wait to hear it all; he knew the fucking thing by heart. And at midnight, she hadn't called back and she still wasn't home and he finally gave up and went to bed, seething. And lay there, talking to himself out loud in the dark like some fool kid in love for the first time. Where was she? Where the hell *was* she, anyway? Who was she out all night with? If he ever found out she was with some guy, he'd kill him; he'd slaughter him. And then he began laughing because, Come on, Ben, what the hell are you thinking about? She's a beautiful dame, sure, and she's got you hot and bothered, but she doesn't belong to you, not yet. Maybe she's been dating somebody. He'd have to give her a chance to get rid of the guy nicely, not come on to her like some street kid. He hadn't even kissed her yet, hadn't so much as held her hand. And he really ought to remember, he'd known her less than a week.

Last Sunday, it was. God, he'd never forget that Sunday, not now, not as long as he lived, not even if she told him to get lost—but she wouldn't, she couldn't. The sun had been low and the shadows were long and cool. It was his favorite time of day—his mother, before she died, used to have tea like the English do at about this time of day, supper really, and it was nice, real nice.

He had been taking a walk on the beach, barefoot, with a can of beer, thinking his own thoughts, and suddenly there she was, standing in front of him—standing next to Mark Valentine, actually. His immediate and very first thought had been, "Shit, some guys have all the luck." And when Valentine said, "I'd like you to meet my wife," he'd really felt disappointed. Even jealous.

He didn't know Mark Valentine too well. The guy had stayed with him a day here and a day there when he came out on the project, but he'd seen enough of him to know he was a cold fish. He didn't deserve something blond and warm and luscious like this. Hell, he wouldn't know what to do with it!

And then she'd smiled at him, at *him*, looking right into his eyes, looking straight into his insides is how he felt, and said, "Not quite, Mark." She still didn't look at Valentine; she was talking to *him*, giving him a message, he knew it. "Remember?" she said. "We got a divorce a few years ago?" And Ben grinned back at her, feeling suddenly . . . happy. Feeling terrific.

"Can you come for a drink?" he'd said.

"When?"

"Right now. I was just going to go back to the house anyway," he lied. "How about it, Mark? Ready for Happy Hour?" He'd felt a little funny; after all, Valentine was staying with him. It was business, of course, but he was still a house guest. And to his relief, Mark had just nodded, hadn't seemed to notice anything at all. And all the way back to the house, Ben was so aware of her, of her scent, and of the softness of her next to him, walking along, not quite touching. He knew how her skin would feel; silky, a bit warm, and his palms fairly itched to touch her.

He hadn't felt like this about a woman in . . . longer than he could remember. Maybe never. Certainly nothing like this had happened with his wife. But of course Betsy had been a tiny, wiry, brown little creature, built like a boy, her curly dark hair cut short, her sturdy legs as muscular as an athlete's. A totally different type. And anyway, he had married her because it was time and she was there and she was suitable and all their friends said they made a nice couple and in those days that counted for a lot. He was twenty-six and he knew damn well he'd gone too long without getting married and starting a family. It was time.

He had thought they were doing real well. He had a nice job, they bought a nice house, she got to pick out all the furniture, she had plenty of girlfriends to talk to all day. They should have been fine; they should have kept busy filling that house up with kids. But it didn't happen that way. He never knew why she ran away—and with a stupid young potato farmer, not anyone special, not anyone handsome or rich or exciting, a lousy potato farmer! As far as he knew, she was still with him, way out on Long Island somewhere. He'd heard somewhere that she'd had four kids, but he no longer cared. He never thought about her anymore. But she was the reason he had steered clear of any entanglements, all these years.

And now, there was this lady in his house, making him feel goofy, awkward, like a teenager. Jesus! He'd gone into the kitchen to pour three drinks and put some frozen cheese puffs into the toaster oven, and even with his back turned, he could still see her sitting there on one of the big sofas with Mark Valentine right next to her, the bastard.

His hands were shaking. He couldn't believe it. He'd dropped the whole goddamn bucket of ice all over the floor, and while he was crawling around trying to get them all before he broke his neck on one of them, the acrid smell of burning cheese drifted down. "Shit!" he muttered, quickly getting to his feet, and of course, he *did* slide on one of those goddamn ice cubes and managed, grabbing onto the counter, to push a glass over onto the floor. Talk about feeling stupid! He'd looked up, and she was right there—she had run over—laughing like crazy, just laughing and apologizing all at the same time.

She'd come around the counter that divided the kitchen from the rest of the room, and when he said, "Be careful, the ice—" she said, "I know, I know. Don't worry," and deftly rescued the poor shriveled blackened puffs, tossing them into the garbage and opening the refrigerator door, seemingly all in one move, talking to herself saying, "Carrot sticks and oh, look, there's some cheddar. That's nice, and raw mushrooms. I'll slice them and make a nice Russian dressing for a dip." She turned her head and gave him a heart-stopping smile. "Okay?"

"Sure," he had said. He would have allowed her anything. And before he knew it, she was slicing and chopping and laying out in pretty patterns the food he'd been planning to use for his supper, but what the hell, who cared! In fact, looking at her, watching her smooth movements and the ripple of light on her hair, he didn't feel hungry, not for food. He was a goner.

He had been dead wrong, thinking Mark Valentine didn't notice and didn't care what was going on. He'd noticed, all right, and he cared. When the three of them were finally sitting together, nibbling and having their drinks, and Barbara sat herself on the other couch, the bastard got up on some pretense or other and sat himself down, once again right next to her. A little too close, Ben thought. Claiming her. And it seemed that she didn't like it, because, very sweetly and very casually, she inched away. And maybe it was his imagination, but it seemed her eyes met his and said silently, "I'm sorry. There's nothing I can do about him right now."

Well, there was nothing *Ben* had been able to do about him, either, although he'd itched to. The bastard had had his arm flung out on the back of the couch, right behind her, his fingers just barely touching her shoulder. Ben could tell she felt invaded. Didn't the guy realize that she didn't want him to touch her? She was almost shrinking from his touch; but she was a lady. She didn't make a great big deal out of it. What a woman! What a woman!

* * *

He signaled to Irving for another one, promising himself that this was going to be the last. When her ferry came in, he didn't want to be smashed. Just enough and not too much, that was the ticket. Dammit, why hadn't he found out where the hell she lived out here? Shit. But of course, all those times when they'd talked this past week on the phone, she wouldn't even promise to see him. He'd been goddamn grateful that she admitted she'd be taking the five-forty ferry tonight. She'd also told him she'd probably be too busy to see him, even if he met the boat, because Sandy was planning a big demonstration at Halfmoon Pond on Saturday—as if he didn't know what Sandy was up to—and she was going to be in the march. It took all his willpower not to tell her what he knew about Sandy Lovall and his so-called ecology kick.

He knew Sandy better than anyone. Knew him real well, real well. He ought to; he grew up in the same house with Sandy. They had the same mother; you'd think that would mean something. Ha! what it had meant was that Sandy hated and resented the baby brother, the son of the despised Italian mason, the usurper. Sandy was one of the Lovalls, the goddamn sacred highbrow, high-class, highfalutin Lovalls who thought they were the next best thing to God. Cold as mackerel, the whole lot of them. Ben remembered them from his childhood: high, tight voices, disapproving stares, a lot of hushes from his mother. Oh, the Lovalls couldn't bear the thought of one of theirs being even a *half*-brother to the child of an Italian immigrant.

His old man was twice the man Harold Lovall ever thought of being. When Sandy's father lost his dough, he lost his nerve. The idiot, getting drunk and then going out to swim! Without a thought to his wife and son. Angelo DeLuria would never have done a reckless thing like that, never. His family came first . . . and that included his stepson, too. He tried very hard with Sandy, very hard. But Sandy was a Lovall through and through. Ben remembered, and it still hurt, watching Sandy flinch away from Angelo's hand thrown paternally across his shoulders—flinch as if he'd been touched by a snake.

How Sandy had hated having to share the Lovall land with

someone who wasn't even a Lovall. But he couldn't do a damn thing about it; their mother had left it to them both—the house and four acres on the bay to Sandy and the pond and its twelve surrounding acres to him. Yes, Sandy hated it with a passion. But the trouble with these overbred types was they didn't know how to take action. When Ben put his land on the market, Sandy was too goddamn proud to come and ask him for it. If he didn't want it badly enough even to find out the price, then fuck him. Well, he did finally say something and then all he could do was squawk. "Half a million! You're out of your mind!" What pleasure it had given Ben to sell it . . . double pleasure, first in getting the money from that flake, Marcus; the second, in being able to give the shaft to Sandy.

Sandy and his ecology and his demonstrations and his marches! Shit! If anyone wanted to know the truth, let them ask Ben DeLuria. He knew what no one else knew: that his half-brother had a hidden agenda. He didn't give a shit about the geese or the frogs; he only cared about his view over the bay and the land he still called his!

Ben drained the last of the beer from the big mug and checked his watch. Five-thirty. At last. He was amazed to find his heart pumping in anticipation. What was going to happen between them? It was goddamn exciting, he had to admit it. And it wasn't just the thrill of the chase, either. No, he knew what that felt like and that could happen with just about any woman he wanted to fuck. This was different. He had a feeling about this one, a feeling that it was going to be more than just a roll in the hay, more than just a passing fancy. Maybe it was going to be forever.

He laughed aloud. Forget that crap, Ben. Come on, first you have to find out if she'll have you at all. That was reality.

He pushed himself up from the bar, throwing a bill down for the bartender. His timing was perfect; he could feel through the soles of his feet, the throb of the ferryboat engine as it slowed down to dock. Here was reality: Barbara, maybe on that boat.

Halfway out the door, he groaned aloud as a thought hit him. Oh, Christ, Natalie Simon. That was a reality he'd tried very hard to ignore this past week; but she definitely had to be faced. Yeah, he had seen her running on the beach Sunday, watched as she gave them a wide berth. He still felt like a shit, not even waving at her; but hell, she didn't wave or give any sign that she was aware of *them*. Agh, who was he fooling? She saw him. It wasn't a nice thing for him to do. She was a terrific little dame, not like Barbara, of course, but she had given him some very nice stuff, the times they went to bed together. He'd have to figure out how he could see her, maybe just for a couple of hours. Make it up to her. Yeah, that's what he'd do.

By this time, he was leaning against a post scanning the faces above the rail as the ferry wheezed and bumped and groaned its slow way in. Where was she? She'd told him she was going to try for the early boat. He really wanted to see her. And then he did, and she saw him and immediately flushed and smiled. He could feel the heat in his own face. Barbara. Jesus, she looked good!

"Shit!" It burst right out of him. Of all the goddamn lousy luck! Because, standing next to her, her dark curly head close to Barbara's blond one, chatting away and laughing, obviously the closest of friends, was Natalie Simon. Oh, Christ! *Now* what? he asked himself. But he already knew the answer.

When Natalie first spotted Mr. Dee, her heart gave a little leap. The sweetie pie, coming to meet the boat. He must be making up with her for not having called. Quickly, keeping her face still, she tried to figure what excuse she could give Barbara for not going to Happy Hour and not staying home either.

So when Barbara said, "Oh, Lord, there he is," she never thought a thing of it, just said, "Who?" without really caring.

"That guy I told you about . . . *you* know, the one who's been calling me every night."

"Where?"

"Right there, on the dock, the one wearing jeans and the red and blue polo shirt. The cute Mediterranean type with the muscles."

She couldn't believe it. She felt like she'd been kicked in the chest; in fact, she put a hand there, as if it were really sore. Mr. Dee! No, it couldn't be!

Barbara was grinning like the Cheshire cat, looking very goddamn smug, blushing like a schoolgirl. Oh, God, Natalie thought, are we going to have teen-age love around here?

"Every night?" When I was sitting home alone, waiting?

"Every night." Barbara giggled. "I don't know whether I like it or not. Do you believe, he insists he's in love with me, that he fell in love with me at first sight? My lord, I haven't heard that since I was fourteen." She giggled again.

"Oh, I can tell you hate it," Natalie said, trying very hard to keep her voice even. In fact, she was trying very hard not to cry. Cry, at her age! Ridiculous! And to cry over a man was even worse!

Barbara, oblivious, was going on and on, leaning into Natalie, talking right into her ear, with her eyes firmly fixed on that tanned and grinning face below them. Natalie could not bear to look at him. "He *is* awfully cute, though, isn't he? And I must admit, persevering. I mean, Nat, after all our talk about passive men, it's a breath of fresh air. There's . . . something about him."

"Sure there is. He's a macho man . . . just like—I won't say it—but it's spelled M-A-R-K."

"Oh, Natalie, they're nothing alike. . . . And anyway, how do *you* know he's a macho man?"

Uh-oh. That was the trouble with secrets: they had a way of worming out at the worst possible moment. Quickly she lied. "Sandy told me about him."

"He's really very sweet, more of a little boy than a macho man. . . ."

Natalie pulled away, angry, under cover of bending over to retrieve a duffel. "I don't suppose he told you which project he's working on! The hated Halfmoon Pond thing! Oh, surprised? Well, so will he be, when he finds you marching against it tomorrow."

Barbara had a little frown between her eyes. "So that's what his company is doing."

"What do you mean—*his* company?" But even before Barbara answered, she knew. That lousy bastard, letting her go on thinking he was one of the laborers, when all the time—

"Babylon Construction. It's his company, he's the owner. He started it right after he graduated from RPI."

Oh, shit, Natalie thought, oh, shit, shit shit shit shit. Aloud, she managed in her second-best breezy voice, "You know what? I'm shot. It's been a lousy week. You go ahead to Happy Hour." And that rotten Barbara, she didn't even pretend to argue. She couldn't keep her eyes off that Italian louse.

Natalie brushed right by him, clutching her two duffel bags as if they were going to save her, and marched herself down the boardwalk toward her house. She stared ahead but saw nothing, filled with rage and hurt. Damn that Barbara, she'd done it again!

She'd never forgot, never in her life, the day Jake had first caught sight of Barbara Valentine . . . how he had come waltzing into her office like a lovesick adolescent, carrying on all starry-eyed about the *shiksa* of his dreams who—miracle of miracles—worked right here, in the agency, at M & M. She had had a terrible foreboding, even as she told herself he was just doing a number, the way he liked to do. And it had all come true. He had fallen in love with Barbara, and he and Natalie had split. It had been awful, the worst time of her life. Okay, so it had all passed; Barbara and Jake had lived together all of six weeks. And in the end, Jake came back to her, to Natalie.

Nevertheless. Goddammit, she liked Barbara so much; they were such good friends. She hated this! Hated hating Barbara over something Barbara wasn't responsible for. Hated feeling jealous. Hated feeling put-down. She found herself walking faster and faster toward the sanctuary of her house, her deck, a drink in her hand. Mr. Dee was not exactly "man of her dreams," but she had thought for sure they had something good going . . . something that might have lasted at least through the summer. Shit. And she wouldn't even have Jake, as it turned out. That bastard had called her this afternoon at the very last minute to say he couldn't make it now, but he'd be out first thing Sunday morning.

As she walked up her ramp she heard the phone ringing, and her spirits lifted. It wasn't Mr. Dee, she knew that now, and it probably wasn't Jake. It was probably Sandy Lovall. She unlocked the door, cursing at the sticky lock, thinking, At least I won't have to be all alone tonight. Sandy was good company, and he liked her. It would be fine. It would be swell. He'd cook—he was a good cook—and she'd allow him to wait upon her. She was good at that.

"Hi there!" she caroled into the telephone.

But instead of Sandy's deep resonant voice, there was a child's high-pitched piping plea, "I want to talk to my mommy."

"Your mommy's not here," Natalie grated and hung up. All that anticipation, for nothing. Nothing. She opened the refrigerator door and brought out the bottle of chilled vodka. Well, not quite nothing, after all.

❁ 16 ❁

The March on Halfmoon Pond

It was beastly hot, even for July. By ten o'clock in the morning, the temperature had already reached eighty-nine degrees Fahrenheit, and a thick white band of haze sat like a layer of cotton over the bay. Not a breeze was stirring anywhere, and now at noon, it was ninety-four degrees and still climbing, the air so saturated with moisture that you felt like you were walking through water.

On the edge of Halfmoon Pond, at the crest of its sweeping curve, the arc that gave it its name, stood a small group of men in shorts, their open-necked shirts already marked with large circles of sweat on the back. They showed no emotion as the raggle-taggle marchers with Sandy Lovall at their head arrived on the scene.

Bambi Hirsch walked alongside Sandy, holding one end of a paper banner that said SAVE HALFMOON POND in large red letters. Jay held the other end, looking uncomfortable. And following them, there were Fred and some city guests; Natalie and Barbara; a contingent of beachniks in their swimsuits; and twenty or thirty local residents, looking a bit stiff and strange. Every person present was flushed with the heat and perspiring heavily. Several looked as if they might faint any minute.

Barbara walked at the back of the group with a sulky Natalie. They were the very last because of Selma, who insisted that she "jutht *had* to make her voith heard, for Thandy'th thake!" But it was hard going for Selma. She was panting painfully—Barbara kept glancing over at her, wondering if she was going to collapse on them—but, dauntless, she kept on going, fan-

183

ning herself with a huge paper Japanese fan resplendent with gilded butterflies.

When she wasn't checking on Selma's heath, Barbara kept her eye on the front line of the march, to make sure her trio didn't wander off. Sandy had said over and over that they should all walk close together, so as to look like "a mob of thousands." So she kept her eye on Bambi's bright red tush—she was wearing a crimson romper today, which could easily be spotted a mile away—and wondered again where Peter was. Peter and Bambi had become, almost at once, inseparable. One day, they met each other, total strangers; and the next, they were a pair, a team, a couple, an Item, in fact. And *The Ad Game* suddenly found a great deal to say each week about Marcus & Morrisey. Barbara's major thought on the subject was that they deserved each other; and actually, they seemed delighted with one another. In which case, where in the world was he this morning? Of course, Bambi was acting as Sandy's right-hand woman. Could it be that Peter Marcus was *jealous*? Of Sandy Lovall? He'd have to be both stupid and blind to think that Sandy was interested in anyone else but Natalie Simon . . . and Peter, so far as she knew, was neither.

Uppermost in her thoughts, she had to admit, was Ben DeLuria. Last night, they had sipped endless glasses of wine and talked endlessly about . . . what? She couldn't really recall; it was all misty and suffused with anticipation. Well, the words he had said were meaningless next to the message in the depths of his eyes. Something was happening between them, and even the thought of it had the power to make her breathless. She had not thought that this would happen to her again, not after Mark, not after Hal. But here it was, once more, that floating feeling she found impossible to resist. Yet, she ought to resist, oughtn't she? He was just another big strong bully . . . wasn't he? None of it seemed to matter, somehow. Oh, lord, she knew she was making a mistake, allowing herself to be carried away. She wished Natalie weren't so angry with her; she could use some of Nat's blunt honesty to bring her back down to earth. She knew what Natalie would say: She'd say, "Come on, Barbara, a lay is just a lay. Don't confuse lust with love; that's for teenagers." Natalie was so right; of course she was. All that was happening was that she was responding to a man who desired her.

And then she pushed through the last of the reeds and suddenly found herself in the clearing, catching up with the rest of the group and facing both men across the curve of the pond. And she knew she was beyond all reason. Her eyes flew to Ben DeLuria's stocky silhouette with the shock of thick white hair and her heart fairly stopped. Mark Valentine, her husband for so many years, might as well have been a handsome stranger who happened to be standing next to the man she was interested in. No contest, not even the tiniest shred of guilt. Mark had been her husband, yes, but it was so far in the past that it had no meaning.

Standing with them was a man Barbara had never seen before, a broad, rather short, shaggy-looking man; and next to him— "Oh, my lord," she heard herself saying and, at the same moment, heard Natalie's *sotto voce* "Shee-it!" There he stood, lined up with the other side, plain as day and pleased as punch—Peter Marcus himself.

"It's Peter who's building. Oh, lord," she said, almost to herself. Because it suddenly came to her that there they all were, all the major men in her life—for now she had spotted her son, standing right behind Mark—all her men, arrayed on the other side, against her. It was ludicrous. If someone wrote this in a book, she thought, I'd say, *Ridiculous*. And yet, there they are and here *I* am. More than ever she wished Natalie weren't so hurt about Ben. They could have a good laugh about this whole scene.

Natalie looked across the haze that lay over the pond and wanted to laugh. Of course! Of course! the quirky little mind behind all this secrecy and hush-hush *had* to be Peter Marcus's. This kind of scene, complete with its surprise, was his specialty. Look at him, so smug and superior and smiling, so delighted to have pulled this stunt on all of them. On *me*, she thought, especially on me. With Peter, it was hard to figure out just what he was up to. Ben, she did not allow herself to look at. Or to think about. He was Barbara's problem now. As was Mark, also standing there looking grim . . . and Scott Valentine, too. Oh, boy, Natalie thought, every man Barbara has ever known practically is standing there, shoulder to shoulder. Idly, she wondered what Barbara was thinking as she looked at them. It was really wildly funny . . . all of it but Peter.

She ran her eyes over the totality of the opposition across the pond. Mark, Scott, Peter, grinning like a Jack O'Lantern, the paunchy sheriff posing, legs spread and hand on holster. And, well well well, a new man. Interesting looking, she thought, very Norman Mailer-ish, an aging gladiator. And then she got a small shock, because all of a sudden his eyes met hers, and instead of looking away, he just kept staring at her. In the end, it was she who averted her eyes, feeling somehow disturbed. Quickly, she eased her way up front, to stand right behind Sandy. This was where she liked to be—where the action was.

"Now, Sandy," the sheriff was saying, "just what seems to be the problem here? These people say you're trespassing on their property with your march."

"That's right. Arrest me."

"Aw, now, Sandy. It's too goddamn hot. . . ."

There was a ripple of laughter amongst the townfolk who were clustered behind, and Sandy whirled around, his face tight with anger. "This isn't funny, people," he said. "This is civil disobedience. These people have been hiding behind a name, afraid to show themselves to us—"

"Hold on, Mr. Lovall. Everybody!" Peter's rather nasal voice with its strong New York inflections carried surprisingly well, Natalie thought. It had a piercing quality. In any case, Sandy turned back around, and Peter used that move to hold his arms out to them all—very like a bad painting of Jesus, Natalie thought—saying, "We reveal ourselves to you now. We wish to show you that you have nothing to fear from us. Here we are, quiet, gentle, harmless."

The gladiator began to speak, and a lady interrupted him. "Just who are *you*, mister?"

"Carl Stern's my name," he said. "Attorney for Halfmoon Associates." He made a small bow and added, "Forgive me, ladies and gentlemen. I have been impolite. This gentleman here is Peter Marcus, President of Marcus & Morrisey advertising agency. And this is our architect, Mr. Mark Valentine, and this is his son, Scott."

"Never mind all that! Just tell us why they hid behind a phony name!" That was Sandy again.

"That's in the past now," said Carl Stern soothingly. "Now here we are and we don't want you arrested. We've asked Sheriff Goodwin here not to do anything like that. We'd rather discuss openly our differences and come to an understanding."

Well said, Natalie thought; but Sandy just rode right over it. "What about the ecosystem in the pond, Mr. Stern? How about *that*? We can discuss it until the cows come home and it won't change the pond back to what it was!" There was a murmur from the group behind him and a couple of fists were shaken.

"It's my understanding," the lawyer answered, "that Paradise has been economically depressed for some time. My client has come in here and employed local workers. Mr. DeLuria is a resident of Paradise and it is his construction company that—"

Sandy's voice now shook. "I know all about Mr. DeLuria," he said, "and his company. *And* his lack of any sensitivity whatsoever to the traditional values of the majority of us here in Paradise!"

Ben DeLuria stepped forward, looking very angry, about to speak. Actually, Natalie thought he looked like he was about to explode. But before he could say even a word, Margie, the real estate agent, yelled out: "Never mind tradition! Let's talk about the pond! Let's talk about the wildlife!" There was an outburst of shouted agreement; and then, a man yelled: "The birds won't have anyplace to go!" And someone else added: "There goes the hunting!" And someone else shouted, "Who cares about your hunting, Les? That's the only freshwater pond in all of Fire Island, that's what matters!"

After that, they all began shouting over each other, until nothing could be understood. And then, holding up his arms for quiet, Sandy said: "The pond, yes, but just as important is the monstrosity this man plans to build here!"

Peter shrugged elegantly. "Who are you to say what's monstrous? You, with your Victorian houses and Victorian ideas! My house has been designed by an award-winning architect and—"

"Yes, well, we've seen the plans," put in Margie. "And it looks like an award-winning bunker from World War II!" There was a great deal of pleased laughter at that one, and Margie smirked a bit and preened.

"Margie has just put it neatly," Sandy said. "That building— I won't dignify it by calling it a house—is totally out of place in this community, on this island. It is an esthetic abortion."

"You aren't the world's authority on esthetics, Lovall!" That was Mark Valentine, who was turning terribly red, Natalie thought.

Peter spread his arms wide and smiled in what he obviously thought was an ingratiating manner. "Please, please," he said calmly. "I am a man of peace. I only wanted to build myself a haven from the rigors of city life."

"That's right!" shrilled Bambi.

Natalie turned to give her a dirty look. And at the same moment, Barbara demanded: "If you're on his side, get over there with the rest of them."

Bambi fisted her hands. "Well, I'm all for ecology. But a man's home is his castle, and it's a free country!"

Peter gestured to her as if to say, "Now there's someone with sense." But Sandy was glaring at her as if he'd like to throttle her, and she said belligerently, "You needn't look at me like that, Sandy Lovall. It's not as if I was a spy or anything. And if you're going to get all mad, then to hell with you and your damn pond." And, so saying, she handed him her end of the banner and marched around the pond's perimeter to stand next to Peter.

"As I was saying," Peter said then, "I am a quiet-living person, looking for some solitude and peace."

"Well, get your solitude and peace in that pillbox in some other town. Don't come in here and wreck ours!"

"Yeah, you people from New York always talk peace and quiet. But we notice what you *do* when you come out here: parties till all hours, drinking, loud music. . . ."

"Yes, and drugs! Oh, right, you think we're a bunch of hicks and don't know what you city people do! Helen, here, has two boys who tend bar at your parties and the stories they tell—"

"Disgusting!"

"Perverted!"

Natalie stood, marveling at how quickly the discussion had escalated from ecology to what was probably the real crux: resentment of the rich city people by the dependent residents.

"Never mind all that," Margie yelled. "That's not fair."

"Fair enough," Sandy said in a controlled, tight voice. "And you better not say any more, Margie, because when the city people come in here and make our little town into a resort, they raise real estate prices. And that's good for you . . . but it leaves a lot of people, a lot of young folks who'd like to settle down here and become *real* residents, unable to afford a home in Paradise. Some of us here today have no particular axe to grind . . . but some of us . . ."

Ben DeLuria shook a fist at Sandy. "You'd better shut your trap! Talk about axes: You're carrying the biggest one of all and I'll bet none of your cohorts knows about it."

"I'm warning you, Ben—"

The sheriff now came up to Ben and put a hand on his shoulder. "Okay, everyone, I think we've all done enough shouting for one day.

"You all might as well go on back home, take a shower, have a nice cool drink, and relax," said the sheriff. "Nobody's gonna get arrested here, and nothing else is gonna happen. Sandy, I'm sorry, but the law's the law and it can't involve itself in a family feud."

Family feud! What family? . . . Whose family? Natalie immediately looked over at Sandy, who glanced at her and then visibly changed the expression on his face from outrage to reasonableness. She watched as his large shoulders relaxed and the big fists opened.

When he turned to talk to his group, it was in an entirely different voice, a kind of folksy drawl. "Oh, hell," he said, "you folks know Ben and me. We haven't agreed on anything, even the weather, since we were kids!" This was greeted with loud laughter.

Natalie stood stock still, stunned. "Sandy . . . and Ben—brothers?" she asked the woman standing next to her.

"Half-brothers" was the reply. "And there's been bad blood between them for as long as anyone can remember."

And now she could see, suddenly, the similarities: the same blocky build, the same heavy eyebrows. Sandy . . . and Ben . . . brothers! Now her eyes met Barbara's, and she saw her own stupefaction mirrored there.

❀ 17 ❀

Enter Carl Stern

There he was. Just as she had guessed. He was sitting at the bar, nursing a tall drink. Earlier, at the pond, she'd heard him tell Peter that he'd be taking the three o'clock ferry back. And where else did you wait, if you didn't have a house out here?

And there he was. Congratulations, Natalie told herself. You're a wonderful detective. And now that you've tracked him down on the strength of nothing more than a long look, what next?

She very nearly turned around and walked right back out of Bob's. But before she could do anything, Carl Stern turned and caught sight of her. He grinned.

"So, Natalie. Why aren't you on the beach?"

This was ridiculous. She felt breathless. But ever onward, ever upward, and into the breach. "I wanted to see you," she said.

"Well, good. Here I am." He patted the stool next to him. "Come talk to me."

She sat, very aware of his solid bulk. He'd taken off his jacket and rolled up his shirtsleeves; and she could see that his arms were thick and muscular, covered with dark curling hair. With an effort, she resisted touching him. She didn't even know him. They hadn't been introduced, even. Which reminded her: "How'd you know my name?"

"Am I a lawyer?" he laughed. "I asked, how else?" He had wonderful eyes, deep-set, dark, enigmatic. He was a sexy man.

"Peter?"

"Peter."

"What did he tell you about me?"

"What makes you think he told me anything? Oh, all right, of course he did. He said, 'Natalie Simon is assertive, imaginative, and independent.' And you've already proved all three."

"Really? How?"

"You came to get me."

She struggled briefly with an urge to deny it. Oh, hell, why bother? It wasn't her style to play hard to get. "So I did," she agreed. "And after all that effort, I sure could use a drink." She laughed and put on her best fake Southern accent. "Hint, hint!"

He laughed again. "What'll you have?" He signaled to Irving.

"The usual," Natalie said and made note of his speculative look, quickly hidden.

"Give Ms. Simon her usual," Carl Stern said. "And I'll have another Perrier."

"Don't you drink on the job?" Natalie said.

"I don't drink. Period. I'm an alcoholic."

Now what in hell was she supposed to say to that? And what in hell was she supposed to *do*? Now that she'd ordered a drink, it seemed a strange thing for him to say.

"Will it bother you . . . if I drink, I mean? Because I'd better warn you, I like to drink."

"I know," he said. "And no, it won't bother me if you drink. It only bothers me if *I* drink." There was absolutely no change in his demeanor. He was still flirting with her.

Did Peter tell him she was a heavy drinker? What did he mean, he knew? And what *else* did Peter tell him? She could just about imagine.

The drinks came and she lifted hers, in a toast. "To . . . what shall it be?"

"To us, of course." Again, she felt that breathlessness. It was really happening, that chemistry, that special electricity.

"To us," she echoed and took a careful sip of her vodka tonic. God, she hadn't tried to behave in a ladylike manner for anyone since the Dark Ages. So much for her so-called independence!

Carl Stern said, "Why are you smiling?"

"I'm having a good time. Isn't that why people usually smile?"

"I'm having a good time, too." He put his hand, for just a moment, on her arm and crinkled his eyes as he smiled.

"You have the goddamnedest smile," Natalie said.

"You're awfully good for my ego, you know that?"

"Hell, I'm a wordsmith, didn't Peter tell you that?"

"You don't have to *say* anything; it's in your eyes, too."

She took a heftier swig from the glass. "That's pretty presumptuous, Mr. Stern."

"You're right. But I'm feeling the same about you, you know."

Jesus. It was unbelievable. One two three, just like that. Eyes meet across a crowded pond, and once more, Nat Simon gets her man. The feeling was delicious; it was the sweet taste of success. So what if she wasn't a kid any more? So what if there were a few wrinkles and a few sags here and there? She still had it!

For confirmation, she looked into the big mirror behind the bar, watching the two of them, leaning just the littlest bit into each other, arms on the bar nearly but not quite touching. It was something of a shock to meet those deep dark eyes suddenly in the glass; in a flash, she saw that he was a total stranger, saw that she knew nothing about him, nothing at all. And yet, at the same time, she felt intimate.

And then he said, "Funny, isn't it, how sometimes two perfect strangers just . . . click?"

She'd always wanted a man who could read her mind. Could it be, at long last?— But she wasn't about to allow herself to build a fantasy. "Funny, isn't it," she mimicked. "Not so funny, since I made a point of tracking you down."

"Hey, Natalie, I was going to call you in the city." And before she had a chance to say zippo, he grinned and recited two phone numbers: her home phone and M & M, both.

"I rest my case," he said as she stared at him without anything to say for once. "Aren't you impressed? Aren't you going to tell me so?"

"I'm impressed. I'm impressed." And, goddammit, she *was*. This man could turn out to be someone very very . . . what? Special, maybe.

And then, dammit, the ferry came in, tooting its goddamn horn. Maybe he'd stay on, maybe he'd say he'd rather be with her than go back to the city.

What he actually did was look at his watch and give her a regretful smile. "Time to go."

"Must you?" She could have bit her tongue out for that one.

"Alas . . . I must. I have business in California. When I get off the ferry, I'll get into my car and go straight to Kennedy."

Keep it light, Natalie. "Oh. Do you travel a lot?"

"All the time . . . well, almost all the time." He looked at his watch again, slid off the stool, stood very close to her. "You interest me, Natalie Simon. I hope you don't forget me before I get back."

Never. But she'd be damned if she'd tell him. "Probably not," she said. "If you don't take too long."

"Don't worry. I'll call you. . . ." As soon as you get back, Natalie thought. But he said only, "Soon." Soon? What kind of word was that? A word of no promise. He put a finger under her chin and, tipping her head up, gave her a light kiss on the lips. And was gone.

And was gone. Story of my life, Natalie thought. Story of my life. She stared at her reflection in the mirror. In the dim light, she looked terrific—even mysterious and almost beautiful. Of course, Carl Stern had been sitting much closer. Oh, to hell with it.

"Irving?" She gestured to her glass. "More of the usual!"

❀ 18 ❀

Scott Pays a Visit

It was getting dark, and still no relief from the woolly suffocating blanket of heat that lay over Fire Island. Natalie sat propped on a pillow on one of her living room couches, feet up, sipping a tumbler of vodka on ice, a small revolving fan blowing a rhythmic arc of cool air over her face and shoulders.

She was just beginning to feel not bad; at last there was that tiny buzz in her head that meant soon things would stop hurting. She lay facing the sliding glass doors through which she saw the sky turn orange, then pink, then purple, and now dark blue.

God, it was hot. Hot and oppressive. Hot and oppressive and lonely. Yes, she could go back down to Bob's Bar and see what was happening. She could also go to Sandy and Selma's party; in fact, she *ought* to go; they were expecting her. But dammit, she didn't feel like pretending to be all up and bubbly, not tonight. In fact, she had taken the phone off the hook so they couldn't get in touch with her. Nobody could. Maybe she should put it back. Who knew who might call? But she knew damn well who might call. Sandy, that's who.

It sure as hell wasn't going to be Ben DeLuria, ever again. The way he and Barbara had looked at each other this morning at the pond . . . the way his arm had gone around her shoulders and she just relaxed right into his embrace, looking as if she'd been doing it for years . . . well, there was no doubt that Barbara Valentine and Mr. Dee—Natalie's Mr. Dee, she reminded herself bitterly—were lovers.

She'd lost a friend *and* a lover all in one fell swoop. Dammit.

And then Carl . . . It just laid her low. She felt as if her whole life were falling apart.

When she had come back from Bob's, the phone was ringing insistently. She figured maybe it was Jake and that would be good news. But the bad news was that it was only Jerry.

It seemed that Melissa wanted to come home from her exchange trip to France. She didn't like her family, he said. Didn't like her family! Melissa had a hell of a nerve, not liking *anything* about that trip. Missy had pleaded and begged and cajoled and argued for months. Natalie knew it would be a mistake; Melissa always got homesick. And now, after being a major pain in the ass, and spending three thousand dollars of her parents' hard-earned bucks, she wanted to come *back*? After only two weeks? No way.

Jerry was all for allowing her back. "I don't want her to be unhappy," he kept saying. The trouble was he didn't want to take responsibility for her after she got back either. He had a four-week commitment on the West Coast. But he had a wonderful idea: Natalie should move back into their apartment, pick up Melissa at the airport, and *she* should take care of Melissa. "No way," she told him. "But, sweetheart—" "You can sweetheart me forever, I'm telling you, *no way*." And she had hung up on him.

And then she felt terrible. What kind of mother would refuse to let her poor homesick child come back? Poor homesick child, indeed! She knew Missy; it would pass; you just had to give her time. Jerry was just being an old lady. It was so like him to take Melissa's side all winter and spring and then to knuckle under the minute she whined or whimpered. Well . . . no way, no way. She was a good mother, she was. Quality time, that's what Missy always had gotten from her. And still would. Anyhow, Jerry was the one who wanted her to come home; he's the one who wanted Natalie to leave in the first place. Didn't want her influencing Missy. Well, then, let *him* deal with this one.

She had enough to deal with at the office. More than enough! Especially now. She went to take a slug of vodka and found the glass empty. Shit. But she had put the bottle and the bucket of ice on the floor within easy reach. It was no big deal to pour it, cube it up, and belt it back. It was so good to feel the sharp edges of life fuzz up. It hadn't been enough, having Peter on her back at the office . . . it hadn't been bad enough, having him out here with that dizzy blonde and bothering her . . . oh, no. Now he had to turn out to be the villain of the piece! She had thought—they had all thought—that Peter had been straightened out, out there in Wyoming or wherever. But it had proved to be only temporary apparently. After three years of relative sanity, he was up to his old tricks again: playing people against each other, telling lies, shafting whoever he thought needed it, hiding his motives. The works. He was as crazy as ever, that's what she thought. Of course, when she said so to Jake, he just raised one eyebrow and said, "Are we a teensy bit jealous, perhaps?"

"Jealous!" she snapped. "Jealous of what? or whom?"

"Of a certain delicious chocolate dish who shall remain nameless?"

"Don't be ridiculous! I love Martha J and you know it!"

Now, in the thick, hot darkness of her house, all by herself, she could admit it. She was jealous of Martha J. Martha J was young, gorgeous, sexy, happily married, and as if that weren't enough to make Natalie cry, she was rapidly climbing up, up, up in the ad business. Her star was in the ascendancy. Her name appeared with appalling regularity lately in that stupid newsletter of Bambi's . . . and even once or twice in the *Times*. She could do no wrong these days; she was the Wonder Woman of advertising. A position that, just a few short years ago, had been held by none other than yours truly, Natalie thought, taking another sip, enjoying her anger, usually kept so carefully in check. Goddammit, just this week, Martha J had captured another account—a string of health clubs—and Peter had been marching around, singing her praises at the top of his lungs. There was talk she'd get a vice-presidency . . . and, as it often did, the fear caught at Natalie's throat. *Was* Martha J in line for Natalie's own job? And was *she* on her way out? He was capable of anything. And now he had become her adversary out here as well! Oh, shit, it was such a mess!

   Nothing seemed to go right, lately. Once upon a time, she
had taken everything in stride. For a long time, she had been
in possession of a magical Midas touch; every goddamn thing
had turned to gold for her. Where had she taken a wrong turn?
What had happened? She was the same person, exactly the
same. Well, not *exactly* the same. She was suffering from the
only malady Madison Avenue cared about: The Thing That Has
No Name except that it does have a name which must never
be spoken aloud lest the beast rouse itself from its cave and,
like the Minotaur, attack and destroy you, eat you up for its
dinner. *Age*. There, she'd actually thought it. Age, the passing
of years, the thing that in Ancient China made you revered but
in modern America only made you a has-been. But, dammit,
she thought, forty-four isn't *old*. For Christ's sake! Is it? Nowadays, she didn't really look at herself in the mirror. She wanted
to skip the lines around the mouth, wanted to slide over the
puckering around her rear end, wanted not to see that she was
losing it all. Her looks, her youth, her sex appeal, her marriage,
her touch, maybe her sanity, her job . . .
   She took another swig out of the nice cold vodka and allowed
tears to leak out of the corners of her eyes. Dammit. Damn
Barbara anyway. Why couldn't she keep her hands to herself?
If not for Barbara, she'd be in the sack with Mr. Dee right this
minute, stark naked, rolling around in his bed, shrieking her
pleasure, instead of getting drunk all by her lonesome, her
clothes sticking to her skin, clammy sweat trickling down
her sides.
   Dammit! *She* should be with him. She knew exactly what
he was doing with Barbara, right now. Holding her hands cap-
tive over her head as she lay on her back, grinning down at
her, shoving that nice big dick of his deep into her, laughing,
asking her if that felt good, if *that* felt good, demanding that
she tell him, describe it to him, his eyes glinting . . . oh, shit.
She shouldn't even think about it. It only made her hornier
than she already was, which was plenty. She should *be* with
him, yes she should. But now she never would be, never again.
She saw the way he reached out for Barbara today, the protective way he pulled her into the shelter of his body. That was

love, ladies and gentlemen, the real thing, the genuine article, and to hell with horny little Nat Simon, good for a roll in the hay, folks, but nothing lasting, nothing more, hell no!

"Mom? You home?" The voice startled her, coming suddenly out of the darkness. It took her a moment to realize who it was, must be.

"Scott. Hi. Come on in. Don't trip; I don't have any lights on because of the heat."

"Natalie? Hold on. I'm not sure I know the way." She reached over and turned on a dim light, and there, suddenly, he was, tall and tanned and handsome and looking awfully goddamn good. She was amazed to find her juices running. She licked her lips. "What a drink?" she asked him.

He walked in, squinting a little, smiling, very much at ease. How did the young do it? just walk in all over the world, sure of their welcome, certain they'd know how to do it, *whatever* it was. "Is Mom around? Or down at Bob's?"

It gave her a certain perverse pleasure to smile up at him over the rim of her glass and then to tell him, "No, sweetie, she's not here, and she's not at Bob's either, and she's not going to come back home tonight."

He looked puzzled and then he colored. "Oh. Yeah."

She heard her voice as if it were coming from someone else. "So, Scott . . . why don't you come on over here and keep Nattie company?"

Scott peered down at her. "You're . . ." he began, letting his voice die away. "You've been drinking," he amended.

"Not a whole lot. I'm not what you could call drunk. Just come have a little one with me. See? I've got plenty of ice."

There was a pause, while he regarded her and she regarded him. She licked her lips again, and he said, "Sure. Okay. Why not?" He accepted a drink from her and then carefully sat on the other couch.

"No, no, Scott, come sit by me."

"There's no room."

"There is if you lie down next to me."

She could hear his sharp intake of breath. Then he cleared

his throat—how boyish and adorable—and managed to say, "You're kidding."

"No, I'm not kidding."

Another pause. "Well, then . . ." He got to his feet, hesitating a bit, kicking off his shoes. She gestured to him, a come-hither motion of her free hand, took a last delicious gulp of her drink, and set it down on the floor, under the couch, as Scott came over to her. Their eyes never left each other until he had knelt on the floor next to her and bent his head to kiss her. Then he closed his eyes as he opened his mouth and enclosed her in his embrace.

It had been a long long time since she'd had a lover this deliberate, this searching, this slow. He had a beautiful mouth, soft and firm and delicious. Without any kind of thought about who he was or what she was doing with him, she responded avidly. She wanted him to keep kissing her and moaned when he pulled away. But he was only changing his target. He kissed the hollow of her throat, then moved over, licking at her skin and murmuring "Mmmm, salt." Natalie arched her back, bringing herself closer to his mouth, closer, closer, closer. His lips were so soft and caressing, nibbling at her skin. He pulled her shirt up over her ribs and bent eagerly to her nipples, stiffly standing in invitation. When he sucked, it hurt, it pulled at her breasts and it pulled in her crotch. She wanted him, she wanted him so badly it felt like pain. And then he tugged at her shorts and kissed her belly, ignoring her pleas for him to stop, to take off his clothes, to get next to her, for Christ's sake to get *in* her.

Her hands plucked at his clothes, and he held them both in one of his. And his mouth moved down. She plunged about like a wild thing, but he did not stop and he did not release her. He pushed his tongue in the moist softness between her legs, making her scream, twisting and turning on the narrow couch while he held her so tightly she knew she could not escape. Sensation after sensation rode over her. "Please, please, please," she was gasping and then there was rapidfire release, her orgasm so strong that it rocked her hips.

"Oh, my God," he said, "you are so damn responsive!" And

in a moment, he had let her go, he was on his feet, stripping his clothes off, flinging them away without looking. He was lean with long muscles, no hair at all on his chest, beautiful, young, firm, and with a huge, hard cock, curving up like a scimitar, making little eager twitches. In a minute, he was on her, his body flung over hers. He was kissing her again and that stiff rod was searching . . . seeking. She reached down and put it where she wanted it, and he groaned as she gave a mighty push and once again, she screamed.

He drove into her without words, moving on her with quick avid movements, thrusting deeply, his brow furrowed with lust, moving faster and faster, their bodies slippery with sweat. She wrapped her arms and her legs around him tightly, loving the sound of his deep-throated groans as he built closer and closer to the climax which came in a burst of pistonlike thrusts. As he came he let out a sound, a yell, a roar. She didn't know how to describe it—it was primeval and it thrilled her. Then they both lay, gasping and panting, clutching each other tightly.

After a moment or two, he said softly, "Oh, my God, I can't believe this happened."

"Are you sorry?"

He laughed. "Are you kidding? I probably shouldn't tell you this, but . . ."

"But?—"

"Aw, I can't."

She reared up on one elbow. "Scott! You just fucked my brains out and you can't *tell* me something? That's funny!"

"Yeah, I guess it is." He was half blushing, looking sheepish.

"So?"

"So . . . it's just that . . . well, I used to—you know—fantasize about you."

"Oh, how sweet—" And then it hit her; he was talking about lying in his bed at night, before he was old enough to get laid. Jesus, how long had she known him? Five years? well, okay, that would have made him fourteen or fifteen, just the right age for sexual fantasies before falling asleep at night.

He laughed again. "Now you're blushing," he said.

"Don't look at me!" But she had to laugh.

"Okay," he said, and reached lazily over her shoulder to turn out the light. "I won't look at you. I don't have to. I have a few fantasies left to try out that really work best in the dark."

❀ 19 ❀

Jake Pays a Visit

Oh, Christ, what a hangover! She'd been up for two hours, and she still couldn't bear to move her head. She stood in front of her bedroom mirror, wondering how it was possible for a human being to be so green, even under a heavy layer of makeup. Her hair was a mess, but when she started to brush it, each hair hurt. To hell with her hair; Jake could just take her with frizzy hair.

Jake. He was upstairs, all full of gaiety and good cheer, waiting for her to get herself ready for the beach. And all she really wanted to do was curl up on her bed over there and go to sleep and make the world disappear.

Oh, Christ, she looked so raddled... so old. She turned away from the mirror, reaching for her dark glasses. She really didn't want to meet her own eyes. Every time she remembered, she felt sick and disgusted. It took only the barest edge of memory to give her that clutch in her belly. Her best friend's son. Oh, God, she'd actually done it. She was really and truly bouncing around on the couch last night, laughing and loving it, with, oh, God, *Scott*. He was probably laughing like hell at her this morning. Oh, Christ, why had she? She wasn't that hard up. Well, of course, she'd been drinking all evening; but that was no excuse. She hadn't been that drunk.

Face it, Natalie, she told herself, you've been drinking too goddamn much lately. Well, but she was under such stress, with her life just slowly unraveling. But Scott, Barbara's son! That was totally off the wall. When she met Jake at the ferry this morning, she'd wanted so badly to tell him. She wanted to tell someone. She wanted someone to reassure her that she wasn't totally out of control. But how in hell could you tell anyone that you fucked your best friend's teen-age son. Oh, God! It really was awful.

She hadn't felt so shaken since that time in Starrett Hall, at college. She was known far and wide as The Wild One; and she kind of liked it. To hell with authority, to hell with rules, to hell with adults who thought they owned you! She was an expert at climbing out of dorm windows, hell, at climbing back at three in the morning. She was expert at all sorts of things, including the silent screw. Her roommates were always in awe of her exploits. They always wanted to hear all the gory details. Well, was she a storyteller, or not? Of course she was and they ate it up.

But that time, that, as it turned out, last time, it was her junior year. They still had curfews: ten o'clock for weeknights, midnight on Friday, one o'clock on Saturday, all that garbage. Hours meant nothing to Natalie Simon. Rules meant nothing. When a guy came along and he appealed to her, and she appealed to him, she went for it. Nothing stopped her! Not Nat!

This wasn't a college boy, not this time. This one was a real man, maybe twenty-five years old, one of the night security guards. He caught her climbing back into her room late one Sunday night—she'd never forget the leap of her heart when she felt his hand on her shoulder and heard him saying, "Aha! Gotcha!" And then when he turned her around, he laughed softly and said, "Well, aren't you the hot little number. What've you been doing out so late?" And he laughed again. Her heart was thudding frantically. Oh, God! She wasn't supposed to get *caught*! They'd throw her out, straight As and all! So she smiled up at him—it wasn't too difficult, since he was kind of cute, big and burly with curly black hair and a nice smile—and said, "Oh, please." And gave him a particular smile. He was shining the flashlight into her face now and he laughed again. "Scared, ain't you? Well, maybe I won't turn you in, if—"

"Yes?" she breathed, trying not to laugh aloud.

"If you give *me* some of what you've been handing out."

He took her to the little guard room in the basement, a bleak little cement block place with centerfolds from *PLAYBOY* all over the walls and a cot against one wall. He didn't even get undressed, just unzipped his pants and sat down with his big purple rigid cock poking up and gestured to her; and she slid off her panties and sat on top of him. He put his hands on her buttocks and roughly pushed her, up and down and up and down, grunting like a pig, his big red face all screwed up, teeth bared. She was forced to look at that face, suddenly hating it, hating having to do this.

She closed her eyes and clenched her teeth and then they both heard it: the sound of footsteps coming rapidly down the hall. He pushed her off so fast, she went sprawling onto the hard floor, hitting her elbows and the base of her spine.

"Damn you!" he whispered, zipping up his pants and getting to his feet. "You'd better think of something damn fast or we're both up shit creek without a paddle."

Me?! she thought. Why me? She wished she had just stayed in her own bed that night, listening to her roommate Laurie snore. She thought she would pass out from fear. And then the footsteps turned and went back. She never knew why, never even wondered. The guard grabbed her arm— there were purple and green bruises for weeks—hustled her up the back stairs and nearly threw her through the first floor door. "You say a word about this," he hissed at her, "you're finished at this school!"

She felt sore and panicked, and *dirty*.

Very like today. Dirty and disgusting, that's how she felt. She glanced once more into the mirror; thank God the dark glasses hid her guilty eyes. As she started up the winding staircase, she heard Jake singing "Where Are You?" at the top of his lungs. He was incorrigible. But he was here and in good spirits, for a change. She had to stop thinking about what happened last night. That was last night. This was today. It was done and she had done it and, let's face it, Scott didn't exactly beat her off. And let's face it, she had been ready, last night, to take on anything that happened to walk in, up to and including Godzilla. Well, maybe not Godzilla.

But now was now and now she had to get out there with a

smile on her face and be adorable for Jake. Not the easiest task in the world, considering how rotten she felt. Of course, he wouldn't notice; he was too full of his own jokes and banter today to notice anyone else.

When she first woke up this morning, moaning and groaning, forcing herself to get up and get moving because she had to meet Jake at the ferry, she'd been looking forward to his company. She'd be able to talk to *him*; they were good old buddies, and she always could tell him anything at all.

But dammit, he wasn't about to allow any real conversation. When she tried, a couple of times, to tell him how she was feeling, he just made a joke and waltzed away, as only he could. He even asked why Barbara wasn't in the house. But when she looked serious, he quickly said, "No, no, don't tell me. I don't really want to know." And, again, when he finally noticed her pallor and said, "Are you sick?" he quickly added, "No, no, don't tell me. I don't really want to know." And laughed, absolutely delighted with himself.

She called him on it. "Dammit, Jake, your trouble is you never really want to know anything nowadays."

He smiled and said, "That's right." And when she protested, saying, "But we used to be able to tell each other everything! And we did!" he just shook his head. "Nattie, Nattie, we did not. Honestly, we didn't. We talked, yes, but it was just the same as it is now! Don't look at me that way. Don't you remember how furious you used to get at me when I cut off your tales of love and woe? Come on, stop living in a dream, will you? Lighten it up. I came out here to have fun and you're not being fun."

You want to know something? I'm sick and tired of always being fun! But she didn't say it aloud.

He was still singing when she came out on the ramp lugging her beach bag with its sun oil, paperback novel, towel, and thermos of screwdrivers; and he threw a companionable arm across her shoulders as they made their barefoot way down the boardwalk toward the ocean.

The long flight of wooden steps down to the beach was the

perfect place to stop, gaze over the view, and declaim. "Oh, ocean! oh, beach!" Jake intoned. "Oh, all that is truth and beauty and love and lust!"

"You just ruined it with that last-named item."

"Lust? What's the matter with lust? It's a good old-fashioned sin, the kind we used to have when we were kids, the kind of sin you could count on, the kind of sin you knew you were sinning when you did it—none of today's ambiguities. Give me yesterday's greed, sloth, and all those other deadly guys!"

"Oh, Jake!" She grabbed hold of his arm and hugged it. "Just like the good old days..."

"Come on, Natalie! Quit it!"

"*That* part I'm *not* making up! Admit it: We always made each other laugh! You've always been the funniest man in the world! Oh, wait till they meet you! Are they in for a treat!"

He laughed with her, but he did not feel particularly amused. He knew what Natalie told people about him. She thought he was Superwit, Superbrain, Superstar; he knew that. Didn't she realize what a strain that put on him? Christ, now he'd have to turn in a *performance* for all her little friends.

They went down the stairs—the beach was beautiful, he had to admit that, the whitest sand this side of heaven, and only a handful of people, relatively speaking. Not like the days of his childhood on Orchard Beach with three million other people. And then they were standing in front of a semicircle of beach towels and he was saying something about the settlers and the wagon train and the Indians and everyone laughed; and the little blonde who did *The Ad Game* stood up and posed for him, pulling in her round little tummy and smiling at him flirtatiously. He knew that look. It said, You're adorable. Only to his amazement, she said it out loud. "Isn't he adorable?" And he thought, But isn't she Peter Marcus's lady? And then, who cares, she's cute and what the hell. He was Jake Miller and he *was* adorable, wasn't he?

And then Nattie spread out their towels and he said hello to beautiful Barbara and a great big guy with a lot of white hair and too many muscles, who was hovering over her. Once he had been enamored of Barbara Valentine and, in fact, she'd moved in with him for a brief time, maybe a few weeks. It was so long ago now, he could hardly remember how he'd felt. Now, she picked herself up and ran right over to him and gave him a big bear hug. And he could see, over her shoulder, that her new boyfriend didn't like that one bit. Tough. He patted her back and said to the boyfriend: "Just practicing!" That got a laugh, although not from the guy.

And then he was so good! He was the perfect friend. He remembered to ask her how her kids were. Of course he didn't remember their names, but what the hell.

But dammit, Nattie had to make a great big thing out of him, looking around so pleased and saying, "Didn't I tell you?" He knew what that meant; it meant he was to be admired. Sometimes, these days, he felt absolutely drained of energy, unable to do that next witty and wonderful thing. Dammit, he was getting too old and too tired to play the clown, didn't Nat realize that? She should! She wasn't getting any younger, either. It struck him now that he didn't know her age anymore. Didn't remember when her birthday was, either. He used to.

Sometimes, lately, he wondered about himself. Sometimes. Sometimes, when he was out with one or another sweet young thing and he was using every bit of charm at his command, he would get a sudden picture of himself: slightly graying, slightly lined, and looking altogether ridiculous as he did his best to seem young and carefree. What the hell was he doing, trying to stay eternally thirty-five? Why couldn't he seem to settle down with a nice young person his own age, like his mother always told him he should? And why, for Christ's sake, couldn't he even think his private thoughts without making a joke of it?

At last, he could sit and stop staring down at all those faces squinting up against the sun, waiting for the show to begin. They were a small companionable group, talking about everything under the sun. Under the sun, get it? yuck, yuck! Any good-looking women? Yes, but they both looked taken. Barbara and her body builder were holding hands like a pair of teenagers. He wished the sight of other people holding hands didn't make him hurt the way it did.

But this was ridiculous. He'd promised himself never to allow himself the luxury of sentimentality. Here he was, in reality, with his health intact, sitting on a beautiful beach with his good old pal Nattie who loved and adored him no questions asked. And who was, in fact, rubbing his pale knobby back lovingly with suntan oil. Who, in fact, didn't care that his back was pale and knobby, loved him just the way he was. God bless, God bless, as his mother used to say. He leaned back and kissed her on her neck where it curved into her shoulder. She smelled delicious, so he burrowed his nose into her smooth skin and said, "Yumm . . ."

"My reputation, Jake!"

He chortled. "Let me ruin it for you, m'dear!"

She sat very still. "Do you really mean that?" Oh, shit, he thought. He'd made the wrong move! Surely she couldn't think—And then, very lightly, she added: "Of course not! You turkey!"

And then he was saved, when Barbara's big boyfriend said, "What do you do, Jake?"

He wasn't planning it; it just came out. "Me? I stand on line at the unemployment office."

"Jake!" Barbara cried. "I thought you didn't want anyone to know!"

"I didn't . . . but once this little lady here printed it up in her newsletter"—he put on a mock growl—"it was all ovah!"

Bambi squealed. "If I'd known it was a secret . . . But when Peter told me—oh, whoops! I'm glad he's not here. Don't anyone tell him. But anyway, Peter thought it would be a help. I don't want to brag, but a lot of people use *The Ad Game* as part of their network. Don't tell me you haven't had offers, Jake Miller!"

"I haven't had offers."

Damn, it felt good, just saying the naked truth out loud. For weeks now, he'd been walking around pretending he didn't mind, didn't care, wasn't affected by it. Hell, wasn't he Jake Miller the Boy Genius of Madison Avenue?

"Oh, Jake, I find that so hard to believe!"

He laughed hollowly. "Me, too. You know, it's funny: while they let me stay in the office, on the nineteenth floor along with all the other superfluous executives, when I still had a secretary answering the phone, saying 'Mr. Miller's office' and taking messages, while I still had a place to put on a suit for and take the subway for, I *didn't* believe it." He stopped and stared out to sea for a moment. Dammit, his eyes were filling, actually filling. He blinked rapidly and went on. "But as of last Friday, Friday last, I've been on my own. . . ."

One of the men leaned forward and said, "I know just how that feels. I've been that route."

"Yeah? How long did it take?"

"How long did what take? To get over it? Or to find another job?"

"Take your pick, brother."

Brother! Natalie thought. He'd never seen Jay before this very moment and he was calling him brother and spilling his guts all over the beach. Whereas, she, one of his oldest and dearest friends, had to pick and pick at him, only to get an old joke for an answer. It made her damned mad! She was supposed to be the one who made him feel better when he was down. She was supposed to be his dear old friend to whom he could tell his troubles.

Jay was saying something about how well Jake seemed to be handling it. "I know how bad it can get. You look at yourself in the mirror in the morning and promise yourself that today, the nightmare will be over."

"Is it really a nightmare?" Barbara said. "Look, Jake, you left M & M four years ago and went to the coast with another agency; and then you changed your job again when you came back. You have a great reputation in the business. Isn't it just a matter of finding another agency?"

"God, Barbara, I only wish." Jake pulled his knees up and wrapped his arms around them, his face serious. "But look at me. I'm no kid. They're telling me now either that they don't hire anyone over forty for creative positions or that I'm over-qualified for what they have available."

"And," Fred added, "that can be true. God, I remember when I was out of work, a couple of years ago, and I had made VP. I wasn't allowed to take a job with a lesser title. . . . nobody would let me."

"Well," Natalie said, "they're afraid you'll leave as soon as something better comes along."

Fred gave a brief laugh. "Yeah, and in the meantime, you can starve, you and your vice-presidency."

"I'm finding out something even worse," Jake said; and they all turned to him. "When I was vice-president and creative director of a big ad agency four weeks ago, everyone wanted to know me. When I had an idea, heads turned and secretaries took notes.

"Yeah, last month, when I called United Artists—and I did—and I was Jake Miller of Reynolds, I got right through to the big boy, no problem, yessir, Mr. Miller, sir. Last week, I called United Artists with an even better idea, only this time I was Jake Miller of Jake Miller Associates and it was 'Who's that? Never heard of him.'" He laughed without humor. "Talk about your naked and afraid in a world you never made! That's how I feel, being only Jake Miller of Jake Miller Associates: naked and afraid."

"That's exactly how *I* feel!" Natalie leaned forward. This was terrific, really talking with Jake for a change. "I was thinking about it the other day: The operative word is naked. I feel naked without the cloak of marriage around my shoulders. It's exactly the same."

To her surprise, she got no answering smile from Jake. And he snapped at her, "It's nothing like, Nat! Nothing!"

Stung, she retorted: "Not as important, you mean! Not as important because women and their relationships don't count as much as men and their work!"

"That's right, toots! Not in the real world, they don't!"

She stared at him, disbelieving. "What about all the years you've been telling me I'm as good as any man in the business?"

"I mean that. Just so long as you think like a man!"

"Jake! I don't believe you said that! 'Think like a man'???"

"Lose your job, Nattie, and then you can come back and discuss this with me."

She almost said, "I might just have to do that, very soon," but then she remembered Bambi, sitting there with her ears all pricked up and her computerlike little brain busily clicking away. And she saw approaching the group, volleyball in hand, Peter.

And then the thought, chilling, struck her. What if the person Peter had in mind for her job was her own beloved Jake? Oh, Christ, she couldn't stand this! Everything that she thought was solid and comforting turned out to be quicksand. She opened the thermos, pouring herself a cupful. This, at least, you could trust.

❀ 20 ❀

A Case of Sexual Harassment

Loudly—and he had a very loud voice indeed—the client called for another brandy. He pulled his chair even closer to Natalie's and, leaning close into her, said, "I have a riddle for you. Oh, this'll kill you."

You said it, buster, Natalie thought. She wished to God she could remember his name. It was either Charles Porter or Porter Charles and she hadn't gotten it quite straight in her head even before they came to lunch. And later he'd ordered three rounds of martinis before lunch and was now on his third postlunch brandy—*her* third, too, she reminded herself rather muzzily. Well, she couldn't remember which way his name was at all. She did remember, though, that he was the CEO of Heartland Dairies in the heart of Minnesota, and that if she did it all correctly, he would be her next, very big, very important client.

She had damn well better remember how big and important he could be and she had damn well better smile at his stupid riddle. He'd been regaling her with terrible poor-taste sophomoric jokes all during lunch; somehow she'd managed to keep a bright smile on her lips. But it was getting more and more difficult as the time wore on and her patience wore thin... and all that booze took effect. Let's not forget that, she told herself.

"A riddle?" she said brightly. "Mr.—"

"Mr. Nothing, Nattie honey! We at Heartland believe in first names. I may be the big boss, but everyone calls me just what I'm called at home...."

Jesus Christ, Natalie thought, after I was so tricky, isn't he going to *tell* me his goddamn name? "And what do they call you at home?" she asked sweetly.

"Why . . . *darling!*" He couldn't stop laughing at his own wit. "But seriously, Nattie, they call me what I've always been called: Port . . . you know, short for Porter."

Natalie nodded solemnly. Okay, so Port it was. But she still had no idea whether it was a nickname for his first or his surname. Oh, well, Larry would know and he'd tell her. Come to think of it, she probably ought to bring Larry on these little jaunts . . . make it more businesslike. She didn't exactly appreciate being called honey by this character; and she appreciated even less the little pats and nudges and pokes she'd had to endure for the past—was it only three?—hours. It felt like three days, three very slow days. Mr. either Charles Porter or Porter Charles was obviously feeling like a smalltown Shriner at convention: let loose, let free, and ready to do his thing now that he was in the Big Apple where everything goes. Well, it couldn't be much longer now. They had a date to see Peter before four o'clock.

"Your riddle? . . ."

"Oh, yeah. Lemme think. Oh. I know the one." He began to laugh. "Who had bigger boobs than Dolly Parton?"

The tasteless boor! Honestly, did she really have to say, "I don't know? Who?" and with half the restaurant listening because his braying voice had gotten everyone's attention? But she didn't have to say it; he could hardly wait to give her the answer.

"Miss Lillian Carter, that's who! She had Jimmy *and* Billy!"

Natalie ducked her head into her brandy snifter. She was damned if she was going to pretend to laugh. This was the worst one yet, and if she had to work with Mr. Porter or Charles himself, she was going to quit.

"Oh, Port," she said, putting a hand on his arm—he'd like *that*, the idiot— "we shouldn't be sitting here having fun, when Peter is back there in the office, just waiting to hear if you like our campaign ideas."

Port put his head down and roared with laughter. "Let him wait, Nattie honey! I told him I wanted a chance at you all alone!"

"And he said yes," Natalie answered, silently cursing Peter. Damn it, Barbara was right. He *was* starting again to play his damned sick games with people!

"Darned right he said yes! Anything I wanted, he said! Clients come first at M & M. That's what he told me." Now he hitched his chair yet closer—she could have sworn it was physically impossible but apparently not—and threw one beefy arm across her shoulder, one beefy hand landing, as if it were totally unaware, close to her breast.

Natalie thought fast. If she removed the hand, he might get nasty. She'd already watched him deal with a waiter who he thought didn't serve him quite right. The waiter might lose a tip, but she would face losing a three-million-dollar client if she made a misstep. She decided that if the hand just stayed where it was, not touching the breast but kind of hovering over it, she wouldn't do anything. If, however, he moved even one quarter of a centimeter . . .

He put his mouth right on her ear and said huskily, "Know what Marcus told me? Told me you're a single woman, told me you're on the loose. Told me you know your way around . . ."

Now, Natalie told herself; but she did not move or answer. Somewhere in her stomach, a fist was squeezing harder and harder.

"So . . . Nattie honey, how about it?"

She smiled. When you were with a client, the motto was: Smile Through Every Goddamn Thing. And Peter had, just yesterday, called her in and very seriously said to her, "You are on probation, my dear Natalie. This client likes you very much—otherwise, I'd close the deal myself—and I want you to watch it, do you understand? Be very nice, very sweet, and very ladylike. In short, Natalie, don't screw up. Okay, darling?"

She had been unable to answer him, so choked with anger was she. But at the same time, she heard him. She knew she'd gotten a few of the clients a bit mad—she only wished she remembered enough to know exactly why—and she was going to behave herself, goddammit, if it killed her.

"My room's right upstairs," Port said, breathing a bit heavily into her ear and now definitely closing in on her breast. Yes, definitely.

Behaving herself was one thing; selling out was another. She was just the slightest bit high, but goddammit she knew she was being treated not like the creative director of M & M, but like a two-bit whore.

Quietly, Natalie said, "Please take your hand off me."

"Huh?"

"I said, please don't do that. You're a very nice man and I like you, but this is business."

"Aw, come on. You're a divorcée. You must be starving for it. I know I am."

"I'm very sorry to hear that," Natalie said. Now she removed his hand, placing it firmly on the table. *"I'm not."*

"You can't fool me. You know you want it."

"In fact, Porty," Natalie said, getting to her feet with as much dignity as she could muster, considering the fact that she was swaying a bit, "I don't want it. What I want, is case you're interested, is for us to get back to the office and work out the details of this deal."

For a minute, she thought she'd done it. For a minute, he looked almost understanding, almost compassionate. And then the lower lip jutted out and the little eyes took on a piggy look, and he said, "Deal? I don't know about that . . . not if you and I can't make one of our own."

"I don't know what they told you about New York, back there in the boonies, Porty, but I'm here to tell you we don't sell our bodies as part of a contract."

She turned on her heel, praying to God she wouldn't trip or lurch and ruin her exit, very goddamn proud of herself. I never even raised my voice, she thought, rehearsing what she was going to say to Peter the moment she arrived back at the office.

"Don't try to tell me *that*, Natalie." Peter swiveled in his big leather chair, scowling mightily and very carefully not looking at her.

"What do you mean?"

"No man in this world makes a pass at Natalie Simon without having been invited!"

"Peter! that's a lousy thing to say!"

"Perhaps..." He kept swiveling; it was making her crazy.

"Not perhaps. Dammit! The man is a boor and an oaf and a churl." Maybe she could get Peter to laugh a little and believe her.

"How many drinks did you have?"

She was taken off balance. "What? You mean, both of us?"

"I mean *you*, darling Nattie. How many?"

"Two or three...I don't remember, exactly."

A sage nod. "I thought so."

Rage now rose in her chest, like a burning sensation. "Quit it, Peter! Just quit it! I wasn't drunk, I wasn't unconscious, I didn't come on to him! I wouldn't come on to a man like him, drunk or sober. So stop it!"

He smiled. "Stop what? I haven't said anything."

"It's all the hints and all the innuendos. It's maddening. I'm telling you exactly what happened. He invited me to his room, and when I said no, he threatened me with his contract. That's called sexual harassment...and believe me, Peter, before he invited me to his room for a little hanky-panky, he was behaving like a swine...oink, oink, Peter...suggestive comments and semidirty jokes and all that kind of thing, complete with winks and leers and busy hands. I'm not making it up, Peter, and I'm here to tell you that all through it, I was calm and I was charming and I *didn't* tell him to take his contract and shove it up his arse, as I had every right to do!" When she finished, she stood, glaring at him, fists clenched, breathing a bit hard.

"That's not the way he tells it," Peter said, sweetly. She longed to throw something at him, something very hard, something that would hurt.

"So it's my word—I, who have known you for years and years—against that pig?"

"You've been getting into a lot of trouble with clients lately, Nattie. This isn't the first time. And frankly, I'm getting just a bit tired of it."

The nerve! The nerve! Natalie took in a deep breath, trying very hard to calm herself, praying that her voice would not quiver with her anger. Her prayers were not answered. Her voice shook like a child's as she said, "And would you care to explain why Porter Charles or Charles Porter or whatever his stupid name is, told me that *you* arranged for him to be alone with me at lunch, that he had requested it and you went along?"

"There, you see? Can't even remember his name. And you expect me to believe that you remember what really happened?"

If ever she had been tempted to kill, this was the time. She was absolutely breathless with rage. Finally, she gritted out, "That was a joke, Peter . . . about his name."

"I can smell the booze from here, Nattie. So never mind the explanations. I don't need them. I know you better than you know yourself. I know what you do with men. I ought to. I remember very clearly how you came on to me when I was sixteen."

"I *never*!"

"Nattie, Nattie, let's 'fess up. You've always been a cock-teaser."

"And you've always been a manipulative little fuck!"

He came charging up out of his seat, hands splayed on the desk, teeth bared. And then, almost instantly, he wiped the anger off his face, sat back down, and began that irritating swiveling, back and forth and back and forth. "Careful, Nattie," he said in his softest voice. "Be very careful. You can be easily replaced, you know."

"By what army!" She didn't give a damn what happened at this moment. Let him fire her! Let him just try to run this agency without her!

"Surprise! because, as it happens, I have someone quite good waiting in the wings . . . just waiting for you to fall flat on your face. I'm not going to fire you out of hand, Nattie darling, first of all, because of our long past history; secondly, I owe you one; and thirdly, I don't want one of those endless suits over your contract with M & M."

Natalie clamped her lips together. She would *not* tell him

to go fuck himself, which she dearly longed to do. If he could erase his anger completely for the purposes of getting her goat, then she could do the same.

So, in her very best sweet and calm voice, she said, "Then am I to take it that you are going to do nothing about Porter Charles and his reprehensible behavior?"

"What I am going to do with Porter Charles, my darling Nattie, is sign a contract." He held up a hand for silence. "The trouble with all you liberated women, Nat, is that you think every little comment is a calculated sexual insult. Come on. You want to be one of the boys, you have to take it like one of the boys."

Natalie opened her mouth and closed it, and he took the opportunity to add: "If you don't feel you can handle the account, tell me now and we'll arrange for . . . ah . . . someone else in the agency to do so."

"I'll handle it," Natalie said. To her horror, she felt tears gathering in her eyes. She wasn't going to stand there and cry for him, goddammit. She wheeled and marched out of the office and straight for Barbara's test kitchen.

They were the slightest bit off kilter, she and Barbara, because of Ben DeLuria, but who else did she have? Who else would understand? Who else would care? And wasn't it just like him not to say *who* exactly he had "waiting in the wings" to take her job? Wasn't it just like him to leave it dangling, keep her guessing, make her suspicious and worried? Who *could* it be? But wait . . . of course! It had to be—

And there she was in the test kitchen: Martha J, all in white from the huge white ivory hoops hanging in her ears to the gladiator sandals that wrapped around her ankles and halfway up her calves. As usual, she looked smashing; and as usual, her makeup was impeccable and her costume the very latest. Almost immediately, Natalie felt ill-kempt and uncombed and old. Dammit, it wasn't fair for Peter to put her into competition with Martha J, whom she loved dearly. But she loved her job dearly, too, and loved the paycheck even more and now, dammit, she *needed* that paycheck more than ever.

Martha J was sipping something from a tall frosty glass—Sunshine orange juice, undoubtedly—leaning against the stainless steel refrigerator looking disgruntled. As soon as she saw Natalie, however, she grinned happily. Or was it just put on?

"Hey, there, lady, come join the bitch session."

Two could play. Natalie grinned back and said, "I'm right in the mood, MJ. Just tell me who we're giving it to."

"This is an easy one, Natalie. Massa."

"Oh. Right *on*! What's he done to *you*?"

"You first . . ." said Martha J.

"No, you." She laughed as lightly as she could. "With me, it's more of the same."

"That good, huh?" Barbara finally turned from the Garland range, and acknowledged her presence.

"It seems," Natalie said, her voice heavily laden with irony, "that the price of the Heartland Dairy account is my own middle-aged, somewhat sagging, but nonetheless desirable body. Would you believe?!"

"So what else is new?" Martha J said with a laugh.

"What does *that* mean?" She didn't intend her voice to come out so sharp-edged.

"Hey, lady! We all get that from time to time. That's all I meant. What the hell did Peter *say* to you?"

Something I can't tell *you*, for sure, Natalie thought. She wished to hell she was absolutely sure it was Martha J he had in mind . . . then she'd say something, right out front. God, how she hated these games. Right now, there was a lump in the pit of her stomach that was knotting up with every passing minute. Who the hell could she trust anymore? Nobody!

Well, on with the games. "You know Peter," she said. "It wasn't the client at fault, hell no. Either I was lying or I had asked for it."

"That's horrid!" Barbara looked genuinely shocked. "I hope you told him in no uncertain terms."

"Of course I told him . . . in no uncertain terms, too. And

he—" But no, that was the forbidden topic, at least until Martha J wasn't around.

"Yes? And he—?"

"He told me to straighten up and fly right," she finished, rather lamely she thought; and she thought she caught a glance flashing between the two women. Was everyone out to betray her? The anger she had felt in Peter's office came rising up once more in her chest, choking her.

Martha J waved a languid hand. "Oh, God," she said, "he's been after everyone lately . . . mean as the devil. Oh Barbara, your stuff . . . your waddayacallit—it's burning!"

There was a flurry of activity, then, with both of them running for the stove, sticking spoons into the big pot, and giggling together like a couple of giddy college girls.

"Do I detect a change in the subject?" she asked, keeping her voice deliberately calm.

"Natalie!" Barbara wiped her hands on her apron. "You really *are* upset. I thought you were used to Peter and his shenanigans."

"I thought so too," Natalie said. "But—I don't know—this isn't just shenanigans anymore. Trust me."

"Nat, honest to God," Martha J said, "it's not just you. I mean, it's unforgivable that he should accuse you of coming on to a client. But, lately he's just been generally impossible. To everyone."

Natalie shook her head. "I'm telling you, it's different this time."

"Shall I tell her?" Barbara asked Martha J, and without waiting for an answer, turned to Natalie. "The other day he called me into his office, Nat, and without any preamble, said, 'Didn't you used to have a thing with Tommy Thoms?' Me! I ask you!"

She and Martha J looked at each other and laughed. "And when I said of course not, in my very best indignant tone, he just pulled back and mumbled something about, oh, yes, of course, it was someone else and waved me away."

"I don't suppose that for one little moment you had a notion who that someone else could be," Natalie said.

"Who, for God's sake? Tommy has got to be the original Straight Arrow."

"You didn't think it was me, not even for one itty-bitty second, right?"

"Natalie! How could you think such a thing?"

How could she? Natalie thought. Well, very easily. They had never really discussed the Ben DeLuria thing, not really. When she had faced Barbara with it, when she'd told her the whole story, Barbara had simply said, "I'm sorry. I didn't know." Not exactly a full-fledged discussion. She was feeling very uneasy about her relationship with Barbara . . . and it wasn't helping for her to come in and find her and Martha J so obviously cozy.

Aloud, she said, "Sorry."

A moment later, when Barbara had gone into the storeroom for a missing spice, Martha J gave Natalie a baleful look and said, "You're being pretty harsh with Barbara, aren't you?"

"You don't know anything about it."

"Hey, don't snap at me. I'm just an innocent bystander."

Where did Martha J come off, sticking her nose in? Bad enough she was after Natalie's job. Did she have to go after her best friend, too?

"I don't know if I'd call myself innocent," she said.

"Natalie, why are you taking that tone with me?"

"You know damn well, Martha J. Don't play games with me."

Martha J let out a sigh, and now, Natalie just couldn't stand it one minute more. How dare Martha J condescend to the woman who gave her everything? "Why don't you just tell me you want my job? I might even give it to you, if you ask real nice."

"Your job! Me? Oh, no, Natalie, I'm not after your job."

"Not waiting in the wings, hoping I break a leg?"

"What are you talking about, Natalie?"

"My conversation with Peter."

"Peter! Don't tell me . . . he did it to you, too. Oh, come on, Natalie, don't look at me like that. What were we just talking about before? He's making everybody crazy! You know how he is: thinks he's got to keep things stirred up, to keep control. You can't mean you're going to really pay attention to anything he said!"

"Stupid me!" Natalie said sardonically. "But yes, Martha J, I *am*. He told me there's someone just waiting to take over as creative director. Now who else could it be? Who's been taking over my accounts, one at a time?"

"Je-*zus*!" Martha J exploded. She began pacing back and forth in front of Natalie, her long legs scissoring. "You're as bad as he is! I haven't been doing any such thing! One account, one lousy account changed its direction and came over to me . . . and damn it, Natalie, you *knew* about it well ahead of time. If it mattered so much to you, why did you smile and tell Paul Hasahni 'No problem'? Why didn't you tell Peter if you didn't like it? Hell, woman, why didn't you tell *me*?"

"Because you're young and ambitious, that's why. Because I remember how it is to be young and ambitious and nothing matters but the road up."

"Maybe to you, Natalie, never to me. Nothing matters more to me than my friends. No, no, don't sneer like that, it's true. If you weren't a bit high, you'd know that I'm telling the truth."

"I'm not high."

"I can *smell* it on you. Come on, Natalie, the whole agency knows you're drinking too much lately. Hell, woman, you even said so to me last week. You're in deep trouble, lady. You must know that! Everybody knows it. Listen," she said after taking a deep, harsh breath, coming up very close to Natalie. "Listen to me. I'm *not* after your job. The proof is, I don't have it. Because, believe me, lady, if I wanted it, I could have it— like *that*." She snapped her fingers. "Like that," she repeated. "Your job is on the line, Natalie. I'm telling you like the friend I am, you are in deep shit, and Peter is just waiting for his opportunity to dump you. If I were you, I'd look at myself in the mirror, and I'd decide to get my act together. Otherwise, you are gonna be one sad lady. I'm sorry, but that's the God's honest truth."

Natalie's throat was too constricted to answer, and in any case, Martha J wasted no more time, but stalked out, slamming the door behind her.

"Go fuck yourself," Natalie whispered.

❧ 21 ❧

Wine and Nibbles with Natalie

There were three messages on Natalie's desk when she got back from the art department. She'd gone out at four o'clock, thinking it would take only a few minutes to discuss changes in layout; but Joe Hernandes had been more stubborn than usual and it had taken close to an hour. She came rushing back, annoyed, because today was the day she'd invited everybody to come in at five o'clock for wine and nibbles—like in the old days, when her group just naturally used to gravitate to her office every morning for breakfast and every evening for a bit of the red and the white.

Well, here it was, nearly five and Larry nowhere to be seen. Oh, shit, she thought, and then saw the three neatly arranged memo slips on her desk. They were all in Larry's neat block lettering. Number one said, "In test kitchen, getting vino." So that's where he was; good. Number two made her mad. It was from Jake. A client had just blown into town and he had to wine and dine her. So sorry.

She stuck her tongue out at him, long distance. If he didn't want to make up, he didn't want to. But it was too bad; it had left a bad taste in her mouth, the way they'd been that weekend at Paradise. That was one of the reasons she was having this little do: to make up with him. With him, and several other people she could mention, like Martha J for instance. Like Barbara, for instance. Like Peter, for instance. Well, she'd just have to try again with Jake.

Number three message was a helluva lot better. Carl Stern ... well, well, well, after all this time? It took him long enough!

225

She smiled as she read through the message. "Stuck in Chicago. Would love to see you this weekend but can't. Raincheck?" Her heart gave a little lift. So, life was not quite over for her. Good, good. Yes, she'd give him a raincheck. She only wished he'd left a number so she could call him back. But okay . . .

"Here it all is!" Larry was at her door, lugging a case of wine, not even puffing a little. Well, why should he? He lifted more weight than that every evening at his health club. "Where do you want it?" He put the case down and slid a glance at her. "What's up? You look . . . happy."

"Nothing, nothing." Wasn't it awful, how that one message from a man could change her mood? But to hell with feminism. That call from Carl Stern told her that at least one person out there in the world still cared.

She heard Barbara's voice, caroling something or other to Larry, before she saw her. Barbara came bustling in, all smiles, hefting a large and unwieldy wooden tray of canapes.

"Hello, hello!" she cried in a cheery voice. "Shall I put these on the table? in the middle? Yes, well, I thought finger food, finger food. Who needs sticky things and little plastic forks?"

She babbled on cheerily; but this was not Barbara; this was a polite and pleasant stranger, making social chitchat. Natalie wished she could hold out her arms and say, "Barbara, I've missed you." But of course, she couldn't. Politely, she said, "Oh, aren't you wonderful, Barbara! Honestly, nobody is going to want to touch them, they look so beautiful!"

"Oh, lord, don't say that! I have thousands of them waiting in the refrigerator! I'm warning you, Nat, if you don't get rid of them, you're going to have to eat what's left for lunch for a week."

They both laughed, but there was such a false ring to their laughter, Natalie thought. She itched to pour herself a drink— she could use a drink right about now—but she had promised herself to take it easy on the booze. She'd been good all week— no more than one drink at lunch, no more than two at dinner. She wasn't going to mess herself up today, not with absolutely everyone she knew about to show up here.

Careful, that was the ticket. She had asked everyone to come today, even the account execs, because she'd been feeling so uneasy lately, feeling as if somehow she was losing her grip. Now she'd prove to herself that she was making it all up, that her friends were still her friends, that she could control her drinking if she just tried, and that her career was not about to go gurgling down the drain—making a rather nasty noise, as Jake used to like to say. And then maybe that little knot of anxiety in her belly would finally go away.

She only hoped Peter was being reasonable today. Let him see that she was in control of herself. For Christ's sake, she'd landed him his Heartland Dairies last week, hadn't she, in spite of Porter Charles and his overactive glands, his overactive hands, and his overactive imagination. There was nothing wrong with her executive abilities! Dammit, at this point in her life, she shouldn't be having to play these goddamn little-girl games in order to prove she was one of the boys!

Now there was a burst of activity out there next to Larry's desk, and she recognized that peal of silvery laughter as Debbie's latest achievement. Debbie was a wonder. Somehow, in the past four years, she'd shed twenty pounds, her Brooklyn accent, and two or three young men who'd been very eager to move in with her. She had gone from being Natalie's perfect secretary to sophisticated copywriter with a minimum of bumps. What was really smart about Debbie was that she never stopped improving herself. A lesson to us all, Natalie thought.

A minute later, in Debbie danced, flinging her long curly hair around and grabbing one of Barbara's little pinwheel canapes as she walked by. "Fastest hands in the East," she quipped, giving Barbara a kiss and then coming to Natalie. "Hi there, boss lady. God, don't you ever get older?"

"Bless your lying silver tongue, Debbie. I knew there was a reason I hated losing you." It was so nice to have old friends and protégés around. Barbara was one, she was another, and here came two more. Eve Soloway, the divorcée she'd interviewed several summers ago and had passed right on to the accounts department, telling Tommy Thoms that she'd make a super saleswoman. And she had, she had!

But the one she was *really* interested in today was Martha J, right behind Eve. Natalie was a little nervous about Martha J, after their little scene in the test kitchen. It was doing herself a kindness, calling it a little scene, when in actuality it was a major temper tantrum thrown by a hysteric. Anyway, she'd gone back to her office, her temples pounding, and poured herself a large straight vodka on the rocks. Then she'd locked her office door and sat at her desk, drinking and crying, feeling very goddamn sorry for herself.

It took until the next morning—well, actually four o'clock the next morning—for her suddenly to feel awash in shame and horror at what she had done and, especially, what she had said. It took a prize idiot to allow Peter's poison into the brain. And she'd done it; she'd taken it whole and vomited it out without thought. She sat in her bed at four o'clock in the morning, writhing with self-loathing. It had taken every ounce of strength she had not to dial Martha J's number right then and there. She had waited, awake, watchful, anxious, until six-thirty, when she knew Martha J would be awake and showered, already finished exercising with *The 20-Minute Workout* on television, which she did every workday morning without fail.

She couldn't remember now exactly what she'd said. She only remembered her feelings at the time . . . how she'd squirmed inwardly as Martha J gave cool responses to what Natalie strongly felt were babblings and lame excuses. How did you *ever* apologize sufficiently for having been so vituperative and, worst of all, so unfair. And when she hung up, and she thought about it, she realized that Martha J's calm, "Not to worry" and "No sweat" were *not* what she had been hoping for.

She'd asked Martha J to lunch with her all last week but had been told she was all booked. And, even with the invitation to today's wine-and-cheese fiesta, she'd been rather tentative, saying she'd come if she could, that she was really sorry to be so indefinite but she couldn't help it, the Hasahnis were driving her crazy. Then she laughed and said, "Tell me the truth, Nat, you sicced them on me, right? You didn't want to deal with that cuckoo Paul any more, right?" And Natalie had hung up the phone, letting out breath she hadn't even realized she was holding. It was nice having her funny, sardonic Martha J behaving like herself—or close to, anyway.

But today was the acid test. If Martha J had really forgiven her, if they were back on their old footing, she'd know it within ten minutes. Hell, within *two* minutes.

"When Natalie entertains, the whole world shows up," Martha J said. "Debbie, I don't think I've seen you for three days. How the hell *are* you?" She and Debbie grinned at each other and Debbie cracked, "Working day and night and night and day for the eternal glory of the almighty client—as you perfectly well know, since it's all sitting on your desk waiting for your initials."

Natalie watched this byplay, her hands clasped together. Was there something just a bit forced about their banter? But no. Martha J had turned to her finally and was coming forward, her arms outstretched; and she was smiling her old smile, her real smile, the one that reached way back in her eyes. They embraced briefly, and while they were close, Natalie murmured, "I'm *so* sorry I said those stupid stupid things," and Martha J murmured back, "That makes number fourteen, lady. Don't you think that's enough apologies?"

They stepped apart, smiling at each other. "Look," Martha J said earnestly, "I understand. I know what Peter can do to someone's head. And besides, I said a few things, myself. So we're even. Okay?"

"Except for one little item." Martha J was back on her side! She wasn't going to lose absolutely everyone, after all. "I still don't know *who* Peter has panting for my job."

"Agh!" Martha J waved one languid long-fingered hand in dismissal. "He could make it all up, you know that. He's a sadist. Hell, we *all* know *that*."

"Who's a sadist, Martha J darling? Tell me and I'll take him right off the client list!" Oh, lord, Peter.

"Christ!" Natalie muttered, as Martha J quickly answered, "Ears like a lynx, Peter, as we all know. It's only the punch line of a not very good joke."

"Dirty joke?"

Martha J laughed. "In the offices of Marcus & Morrisey Advertising, Inc.? Of course not!"

And then Tommy Thoms and Jeff came in right behind Peter, and Tommy said, without even having heard what went before, "Of course not . . . not at Marcus & Morrisey." Because that's the kind of guy Tommy was: a bit dim, more than a bit stodgy, not of the very swift, and always *always* ready to be agreeable.

As usual, he could not understand the hilarity that often greeted his remarks. He didn't even waver when Natalie smiled at him and said, "We were just saying that at M & M we try very hard never to please the client, Tommy." He gave her a look—he knew her from the last movie, the look seemed to say—and said mildly, "Oh, now, Nat. I'm not quite dumb enough to believe that," and once again looked bewildered when everyone began to laugh.

Tommy was, in a way, their *idiot savant*. They found him incredibly dense, yet somehow he always made the clients very happy. He might be a fool, old Tommy, but he was *their* fool. And woe betide the man, woman, dog, or child in the advertising business who dared to deride or belittle him to anyone from M & M.

Now there was another flurry of arrivals, and as Peter stepped in, she saw that he had not come alone. For just a moment, she was furious. She hadn't invited Bambi Hirsch! What did Bambi have to do with M & M, anyway? . . . This was a party for her very own special people, and Bambi was not one of her very own special people. Dammit, just because he was the boss, that didn't give Peter the right to invite whomever he pleased!

And then, she calmed herself right down. Hey, what difference? He and Bams, which was the disgusting nickname he called her, he and Bambi, in any case, were always together these days. There were even rumors he was going to, of all the goddamn things, *marry* her! Well, they deserved each other; they certainly seemed very compatible . . . the Silver Fox and the Blond Mink.

No way she could make a fuss about Bambi's presence. He'd just widen his eyes and say, "But, Nat, I *told* you." And then, dammit, she'd be unsure, because, let's face it, her memory was not exactly one hundred percent these days, was it? Best not to say anything. *Had* he told her? Was there a bit of a memory of it somewhere in the back of her head? It wasn't worth worrying about. It was time for a glass of wine.

She had barely picked it up and turned back to the group when Bambi hurled herself across the room, to the window, a whirlwind of leopardskin print and high-pitched cries of delight. The truly remarkable thing about Bambi was that she never ran out of things to say, just kept going on and on and on, about absolutely nothing at all. Natalie waited patiently.

"Oh, I just love your office, Nat. What taste! And your plants!" Well, at least she had straightened up and turned around, so now Jeff could stop drooling over her round little bottom. "I can never get jade plants to grow for *me*! And just *look* at yours! What's your secret?"

"Jade? Is that what they're called?" Natalie nearly laughed aloud at the sudden blankness in Bambi's busy little eyes. "My green thumb is my secretary, Larry," she explained, gesturing with her head to where he stood at the ready, by the bar. Bambi followed her glance, blinked, blinked again, looked even more stupefied, and then it dawned on her. That *man* was Natalie's secretary. With interest, Natalie watched the thoughts slide over Bambi's expressive face, one after the other: A man. Oh and look, a good-looking man. And that's a very good haircut. A good-looking man who can afford a very good haircut. A man who can afford that and is still just someone's secretary. A nobody.

"Aren't you the one! Who else," Bambi caroled, "would have a male secretary? Only Nattie Simon!"

Natalie longed to snap that only her very closest friends called her Nattie. But alas, she was forced to be on good behavior, and oh, Christ, if Peter married Bambi, she'd have to keep her mouth shut for the rest of her life!

She turned from Bambi, saying, "Let me greet my lord and master."

Bambi giggled, and came back with "*Your* boss . . . *my* lord and master." There was just no dealing with that woman, without her turning it into a contest.

She turned to where Peter was holding court, with Bob and Renée, her two copywriters. As soon as he saw her he said, rather too loudly, she thought: "Natalie *darling*. What a wonderful idea, having a party for absolutely no reason at all except to drink. I mean, it's so like you." Now how was she supposed to take *that*? Martha J was right; he was often cruel. He didn't used to be, did he? "I've just been telling Bob and Renée, how you instituted S.H.I.T. at the agency, so many years ago."

Bambi had come up, linking her arm in his and leaning into the curve of his body. "S.H.I.T.?" she cried, laughing. "Oh, Peter, you're joking! What does it stand for?"

"Well . . . you know about T.G.I.F.—Thank God It's Friday. Nattie here invented S.H.I.T.—So Here It's Thursday. Isn't she the clever one?"

"Oh . . . and it *is* Thursday!"

Dryly Natalie commented: "Isn't *she* the clever one?" And instantly regretted it. Bambi was Peter's property, and one knew *never* to disparage anything that belonged to Peter Marcus. "And aren't *you* clever, Peter darling, to remember. Lord, those S.H.I.T. sessions were years ago!" So saying, she reached out to give him an embrace.

Peter hugged her, kissed her cheek, and murmured into her ear: "Started boozing early, I see." And when she stiffened at the unexpected attack, he added: "I can tell. It's loosened your tongue."

He released her, still smiling broadly, as if he hadn't just given her the knife, and continued: "And, like I was just telling Bob and Renée here, it's a wonder you have time for parties, you work so hard. You work *too* hard, Nattie. Like I said to Bob and Renée, the creative director shouldn't be burdened with working on accounts . . . no, no. The creative director should be directing creativity."

Natalie put on a big tight smile. "We've been through this before, Peter. And you have agreed with me: It's a damn shame that someone who makes it to the top by dint of her writing should find at the top that she hasn't got time to write anymore.

I like to keep my hand in. I like to do some of the writing. I think it keeps me fresh."

"Well, now, I think it's too much, Nattie darling. And that's my final decision."

Natalie felt nausea rise in her throat. The bastard! The human thing would have been to call her in and discuss it with her in private, instead of pulling the rug out from under her here in front of her own copywriters. Goddammit, in front of *every-body*, including the lady who wrote a gossip column about the ad business!

Her guts churning, she stretched her smile even further. "Oh, look, there's Jeff. I must ask him what the results were on the egg questionnaire. You'll want to know, Renée."

"*Eggs*-actly," the dark-haired copywriter said and bowed to the groans and moans that greeted this terrible pun. "Sorry, sorry, can't help myself," she said. "It's what happens to you if you work for Nat Simon."

From where she stood, across the room, Barbara watched Natalie as she chatted with Peter and Bambi. Lord, Nat was tense: so taut, she fairly quivered. Even from this distance, it was obvious. But maybe only to her, to a good friend. Barbara certainly hoped so. She knew Peter Marcus well enough to realize that if he ever caught on to how nervous Nat was, he'd home right in for the kill. Barbara went to the bar and held her empty wineglass up, waiting while Larry refilled it. Was Nat right? Was Peter really meaner to her lately? But why? Barbara couldn't see any reason for Peter to have it in for Nat. She was his most valuable player. But Ben had scoffed at that. He'd said someone like Peter doesn't need a reason for anything. "Spoiled rich kids like Peter just get used to doing what-ever occurs to them . . . and to hell with everyone else. Believe me, I *know*."

Ben! Just thinking about him was enough to make her sud-denly happy. He was like a gift from the gods, a surprise package, a present she hadn't been expecting. She loved him. She loved him and he loved her and it was all happening just naturally, without hassle, without worry, without angst, without

agony. With Mark, she'd always been scurrying around, trying
to please him. With Hal it had not been much different, had
it? She had thought so because his manner was so different
from Mark's, warm where Mark was cool, mild where Mark
was harsh, gentle where Mark had been insistent. But in fact,
she had ended up trying very very hard to please him; and
trying very very hard to convince herself that she didn't mind
trying so hard to please him because after all didn't he try to
please her and after all, nobody was perfect, were they, and
after all, he loved her and after all . . . And after all was said
and done, she had felt very married to Hal and feeling married
was what she wanted.

He had arrived one evening after work with a secretive smile
and a folder of reservations for a trip to Caneel Bay. "We'll
have a cottage to ourselves, on a private beach, and the dining
room is an open-air pavilion."

"Oh, Hal!" she'd cried, throwing her arms around his neck
and hugging him. "Our first vacation together! Oh, how lovely.
. . . And did you realize that our reservations begin on Valentine's Day?"

He'd grinned, so pleased with himself. "It's a double play,"
he said. "You get your Valentine—the trip—and I get mine:
you."

It was going to be perfect. Not just the trip, but everything.
Now she was able to admit to herself that being single was
something of a strain for her. It didn't seem to come naturally.
It felt good to think in twos again.

But right after the winter break, Jennifer began calling from
school. She was not happy. She didn't know why exactly: yes,
her friends were fine; no, she hadn't broken up with a boy, but
. . . she felt— "I dunno, Mom, kinda blah." Barbara suggested
vitamins and said, "In my day we called it senior slump and
don't worry."

And then, a few days later, another call. And then, a few
days after that, another. And then another. And each time, Jen
sounded more and more morose. It had gotten so that Barbara's

heart sank every time the phone rang. The night of February tenth, Jen called to say, "Mom? I'm dropping out."

"Now wait a minute, Jennifer. Don't do anything drastic. Not when you're so close to graduation."

"Too late. I've already been to the dean."

"I'll call the dean and say to wait! Tell me why, Jen! Please!"

It was a wail: "I—I can't! Oh, it's so awful!"

Her next move had come without thought or volition. "Jennifer, I'm coming up to Boston. Don't move. Don't you dare move."

As soon as she'd hung up she'd turned to Hal. "Something's very wrong. I have to go to her."

"What now?" He made a small face. "I don't have to ask who. Who else pushes your buttons like Jennifer?"

"I've got to find out what's wrong."

"That's what the long-distance telephone is for."

"Hal! She's dropping out of school!"

He'd shrugged. "She *says*. If you ask me, it's just an excuse to get you all upset . . . to see how fast you'll jump and run."

"Hal, why are you so grim? I'll only be in Boston a few days, a week at the most."

To her utter amazement, he threw off the quilt and flung himself out of bed, speaking through gritted teeth. "There's a little matter of a trip we are supposed to be taking. Aha! I *thought* you'd forgotten; you should see the look on your face! It had been my impression that this trip was as important to you as it is to me."

"Oh, Hal—!" She was instantly regretful. "You know it's important." He turned deliberately away from her. And just like that, her regret turned to cold fury. "How dare you! As if I had a choice! Come on, Hal, my daughter *needs* me! Surely you understand that!"

"I understand only that you manage to completely forget all our plans—*all* our plans!—in about ten seconds, just because your daughter moans and whines like a baby!"

Barbara had taken a deep breath. "Let me see if I can make you understand, Hal dear. I'll probably be back in time for us to leave. But if I have to spend some extra time in Boston . . .

well, that's what I have to do. And anyway, what's the big deal? We'll go the *next* week. Stop shaking your head, next *month*, then!"

"Caneel Bay is always booked solid. It's one of the most exclusive resorts in the world. No way could we get a different date!" His lips were tight and bloodless.

"That *is* too bad. But . . . look. I don't care."

"Well, *I* do! I went to a great deal of trouble, and spent a great deal of money—"

"Well, if time and money are more important to you than me—"

His fists clenched. "Barbara, that's not fair!"

"Well, you're not being fair, either!"

"I tell you, Barbara, if we don't go on this trip, as planned, then we don't go *anywhere*."

"Well, Hal, if you can't see that my child must come first with me, then I don't want to see *you* ever again!"

She had thought for an instant that he was going to hit her; he certainly looked as if he wanted to. But he only got himself dressed in silence, stormed out of the apartment, and slammed the door behind him so hard it made all the glassware rattle. That was it. She'd never seen him again. Too bad he was too selfish to understand what it was all about. Your child had to know she could count on you forever, no matter what. And if Hal didn't know that, then she didn't want to know Hal!

She never did call him, not even to say "Jen had mono, you know," not even to say "You left a few things here," not even to say, "I miss you. Don't you miss me even a little bit?" They had never talked to each other again. Never.

She'd filled in that aching emptiness with her work and her friends and her garden, and after a while, she felt her life beginning to normalize. She still cried each morning when she allowed her mind to wander while she applied her makeup; but she was no longer waiting for him to call. Of course, she didn't seem to be meeting other men, but she was going to have to learn to live with that. After all, she wasn't a kid; the supply of men of a suitable age wasn't endless. Even after Nat invited her to share the house in Fire Island with all its implicit promise of romance under the stars, she warned herself, reminded herself that even a house on Fire Island was no guarantee. She might not meet anyone, not even there . . . and she had prepared herself to deal with that.

And then, out of the blue, along came Ben DeLuria. Who would have thought that she'd fall in love at her advanced age? Wasn't that feeling reserved for college girls? The heart beating faster, the flutter whenever she caught sight of him, the anticipation complete with wobbly knees and constricted chest whenever she knew she was going to see him? All those corny symptoms of love at first sight—she had them all! She dared not admit it, not to anyone.

Barbara sighed inwardly, still following Natalie with her eyes. Dammit, she wished she could talk about her feelings with Nat, as she always had. Natalie knew men, that was for sure. What was more important, she knew Barbara.

But Natalie was angry with her over Ben. As soon as Barbara found out he and Nat had been dating, she went running to Natalie to explain, saying she was sorry, she would never have horned in if she'd known, etcetera etcetera. Nat was a bit disdainful of her apology, a bit dismissive. "No problem," she had said, "I saw him only two, maybe three, times. No big deal."

But something had been amiss ever since, something subtle and unspoken but very definitely there. She hated these silent misunderstandings, hated being at odds with anyone she loved, hated feeling she had to walk on eggs all the time. Dammit, she was going to have to talk to Nat, *today*. Right after everyone had gotten high and gotten out, she'd stay on.

For another hour, she circulated, sipping very slowly her glass of wine, laughing at all the witticisms and wishing Jake were there. She remembered back when this kind of gathering took place nearly every evening in Nat's office and Jake was a fixture slumped in a chair in a corner where he could hold court comfortably. Oh, dear, that was four years ago, *four years*. So much had changed. She'd been such a big baby, then, holding down her first real job: peeling potatoes for Millard, and trying to juggle her husband's growing hostility and her children's growing pains with her growing need to be herself. How different she was now, in charge of the test kitchen and in charge of her own life.

And she and Nat, who had started out as disciple and mentor, had, over the years, become friends and equals. Unlike so many people in this business, with Nat Simon, what you saw was what you got. It would be sad to have that friendship jeopardized by, of all the things, a man! They had never competed, she and Nat, not in the office, not at the dozens of parties they'd attended together, never. It just never happened. Later, Barbara realized that on several occasions, Natalie had given up a man she was flirting with, and when they talked about it, Natalie laughed and said, "The greater need, Barbara! No, don't look like that, there are hundreds of men out there for me if I want them. I'm so safe, Barbara. I'm *married*. . . ." And then she laughed and added: "It says here." Barbara thought she saw sadness in those dark, mischievous eyes. But if she did, it was gone in an instant.

No, dammit, she was not going to let a man come between them! She'd just have to make Natalie understand that this time was different. If only *she* could.

Normally, she wouldn't have to worry this way. But lately, there was Nat's drinking: Every day it got worse. Everyone had noticed it. Of course, she was very good about holding her liquor . . . most of the time. But every once in a while, she slipped. Just the other day, at lunch with a large group including Barbara and two of their food clients, she'd had a bit too much and had begun to hassle the waiter in a voice that was just a touch too loud and just a touch too hostile.

She was still feeling uncertain when the room emptied and she found herself alone in the littered office with Nat, facing her across the room, each of them with a glass of wine.

Barbara raised her glass. "Good party, Nat. As usual. It brought back a lot of nice memories."

"Oh, really? All I'm thinking is thank God it's over."

"Oh, Nat! You shouldn't. It was lots of fun."

"Fun! You thought it was funny, maybe, when Peter suggested I need a vacation? *I* didn't." She refilled her glass, and Barbara bit her lips to keep from saying, "Don't." Instead, she made her voice as mild as she could—Nat would hate even a hint of pity—and said, "Well, anyway, I'm very glad we have a few minutes alone, because we need to talk."

Natalie paced over to the window. "*Need* to talk? My God, Barbara, we talk all the time! Weekdays *and* weekends. Nonstop, practically. I think they're going to award us the gold medal in conversation."

"Natalie, please. There's something wrong between us."

"Don't be ridiculous. We're fine. Aren't we roomies?" But she never looked directly at Barbara and kept striding around.

"It's Ben," Barbara forced herself to say.

"Where? And I thought you meant *he* was between us. Now *that* might be fun! Only kidding, of course."

"Natalie, stop it. Stop prancing away every time I try to talk seriously."

Now, to her amazement, all the nervous motion stopped. Natalie poured herself another drink and looked up, this time calmly, this time looking right into Barbara's eyes.

Quietly Natalie said, "When Jake does it to me, I give him hell. I hate it. I'm really sorry. I'll talk to you. What's the problem?"

"I told you. There's something between us and it has to do with Ben."

"I told you, that's no problem."

"Well, excuse me, Nat, but I think you're not being totally honest with me. There's been such a bad feeling between us—oh, neither of us has *said* anything, but there's a definite chill."

"You say that? To *me*?" She had turned to look out the window; now her head swung back belligerently and she scowled at Barbara. "You say there's a chill? Oh, how strange, Barbara. How wonderful that you should notice it—considering you're the one who turned it on."

"Natalie!"

"Don't bullshit me, Barbara! You're on my case, just like

everyone else around here! Everyone laughing when Peter says his nasty little things about me! Jesus Christ! Can't any of you leave me alone!"

"Leave you alone? Natalie, I'm trying to fix up whatever's wrong. I'm not out to hurt you, for God's sake!"

Natalie took a big gulp of her wine. When she spoke, the harsh tone in her voice gave Barbara a jolt. "You're not, huh? Oh, really! That's very goddamn adorable, Barbara. You think if you say you're not out to hurt, that makes any goddamn thing you do to me okay? That it?"

Barbara was too stunned by this outburst to do more than hold out her hand and take a step forward.

But Natalie was having none of it. With a swipe of her hand, she waved her off. "You're a liar, just like the rest of them. A goddamn liar! You call yourself my friend. Well, a real friend is loyal!"

Now she found her voice. "But, Nat, what have I done to you?"

"But Nat, what have I *done* to you?" Natalie repeated in a nasty falsetto. "Oh, nothing, nothing at all. First you took Jake away from me...."

"I *knew* that was—"

"You knew nothing, nothing at all! It never was the same between us, never again. It never will be. I lost the only man I ever loved and it's thanks to my 'good friend' Barbara. Oh, but don't worry about it. It's all water under the dam, as Jake would say.

"I thought we had worked it all out. I thought that was the end of the whole business. And the minute I invite you to share my house, you go and do it again—walk in, look around, and walk out with *my* guy!"

"That's not true, Natalie! He wasn't yours; you said so yourself. One or two dates, that's what you said."

"So I lied. Or maybe I didn't. It doesn't matter. You did it. You did it to me not once but twice. Well, I'm not giving you the chance again."

Oh, God! Barbara thought. She's hysterical. Or drunk. Maybe both. She didn't dare approach her, didn't dare put even a pinky on her. There was no point in trying to reason with her, not now, she could see that.

"Natalie, listen. Let's not talk about it now. I think you should go home."

"Oh, you do, do you? And why is that, Barbara dear?"

It took all of Barbara's willpower not to turn on her heel and march right the hell out of there. Patience, she told herself. Natalie doesn't *want* to be snide and cruel; she can't help it. Maybe the proverbial dash of cold water... "Why do I think you should go home, Nat? Because you need to sober up."

"Fuck off!"

"Natalie, please, don't do this. Please. I told you before; I had no idea you and Jake were involved. And I had no idea that you even knew Ben. Hell, Nat, you kept him a *secret*. I mean, it's your fault that I didn't know."

"Oh, sure! My fault! Everything's *my* fault!"

"I didn't mean it that way, and you know it. It's just... Look, Nat, you know me. If I had known you were seeing him, you know I'd never have started up with him. I'd have said, 'No thanks, I don't date men who are going out with my close friends.'"

"Oh, really, Barbara? You'd have done that for poor little forsaken, hard-up, wrinkled, old, dried-up, sexless me? How sweet! You don't think I believe that, do you?" Her laugh was ugly, and she followed it with another hefty swig out of her glass. "Isn't it every woman for herself and to hell with friendship, out there in Singles Land? Ah, I thought so, I thought so."

"You thought *what*?" Barbara felt completely dazed.

"The look on your face, Barbara. It says guilt, just as clearly as the spoken word." She leaned over, refilled her glass yet again, drank from it thirstily. Barbara felt rooted to the spot, a core of icy coldness in the center of her being.

"I'm leaving," she said, willing herself to move.

"Wait, wait..." The eyes slitted and the voice became purring. She looked, Barbara thought, exactly like a sleek cat, getting ready to pounce. It was horrible, horrible. "You wanted to have girl talk. Okay. I've changed my mind. Let's have girl talk. So tell me, Barbara, how do you like fucking Ben? Good, isn't he? A bit on the primitive side, a little tough, but his cock—"

"Natalie! Don't!" Now she did turn and managed to start for the door.

And that sardonic voice followed her. "Oh, you don't like fucking Ben? I know you liked it with Jake, because you said so, remember? You thought he was a helluva lover. Think Ben is better than Jake? No answer, Barbara?"

Now Barbara was by the door. All she had to do was reach out, turn the knob, and let herself out. That's all she had to do, and this horror show would be over. As she put her hand on the knob, Natalie said: "Think he's a better fuck than Mark, Barbara? I don't."

A thick silence followed, while Barbara tried to think. Wait a minute, does she mean?— The blood was drumming in her ears.

"That's right, Barbara," Natalie went on. "That's what I said. I think Mark's better than Ben. That's right. I had it off with Mark. While you were still married." And when Barbara, her heart hammering, whirled around to face her, she laughed and said, "And the next day you told me he had come into the house and picked a fight with you, one of the worst fights of your marriage. So you don't have to pity poor little me, Barbara. You aren't the only one who can take men away!"

There was a humming sound in Barbara's ears that seemed to be filling her entire head. Little red and green spots danced in front of her eyes. "Natalie, it was so long ago. Why couldn't you keep it to yourself?"

"Why should I? Why should I be the only one to suffer around here? Oh, you were always so superior. You had the perfect marriage, the perfect husband, the perfect house, the perfect kids!"

"You're so wrong! Just because I never—oh, skip it! Why am I defending myself? You're the one who's just betrayed our friendship!"

"Friendship! You're a fine one to talk about friendship, when every man I've ever cared for, really cared for, you've just snatched away from me. And you needn't put on your Virgin Mary act. I ain't buying!"

Barbara suddenly felt exhausted, used up. The image in her head of Mark and Natalie, entwined, writhing, pounding at each other! She couldn't bear thinking about it. What a horrible thing to have done! "You'll probably never understand this, Natalie," she said, emptying her voice of any emotion, "but telling me is so much worse than the act itself."

"Oh, really? And what if that's not *all*? What if there's more?" Abruptly she stopped talking and turned away. "Oh, shit. Just get out of here. Goddamn it, *go*!"

She went. As soon as the door closed behind her, she heard the awful sounds of Natalie, weeping wildly, sobbing. Poor Natalie, she thought. And then, angrily: Oh, hell. Poor *me*.

❀ 22 ❀

Barbara and Ben

Ben ran his hand up the curve of Barbara's flank and bent his head to her breast, growling a little in his throat. He loved her breasts, the softness of them and then the hardness of the erect nipples. But this time, her body was cool and unresponsive. She was not moving in closer, like she always did.

He stopped making love to her, peering at her in the dim light of his bedroom. Was her cheek wet? He put out his hand, and yes, she was crying. She was crying! Why was the woman crying of all the damn things!

"Barbara? What's the matter, baby?"

No answer. But now she allowed herself to sob openly. "Barbara. Please, honey. Tell me. Is it me? What did I do? Don't just lie there and cry, please." He kept smoothing her hair with his hand, hating to hear those sounds. He loved this woman, he really loved her. Jesus, he hadn't loved a woman like this in twenty years. He wanted only that she be happy. What had he done? "Barbara," he pleaded.

"You had her here!"

He was stunned. "Who? Who did I have here?"

"Natalie."

Oh, shit. The couple of times he'd laid her were meaningless, so pale next to what he felt with Barbara that he literally had wiped the memory out of his head. "Why now, Barbara? You knew I saw her. I told you."

"You didn't tell me you slept with her." Now she sat up, shaking his hand off.

"So I slept with her. You knew I wasn't a virgin, Barbara."

"Don't make light of this, Ben. It's very important to me."

He sucked in a deep breath. God alone knew what the hell was in her head. He'd never understand women, never. They came up with stuff at the damnedest times. But with this one, he was going to be patient. He was going to make it work. "Okay, honey, then tell me about it. Okay? Why does it make you unhappy? It was meaningless. It was a roll in the hay. For her, too."

Her voice was muffled. "Don't you understand how that hurts? That you were here, with her, doing all the same things, saying all the same things?—"

"Hey! Whoa! Unh-unh. Not true. Where'd you get the idea I ever was here with her doing the same things? This is so much different."

"From her."

"What—from her?"

"You asked where I got the idea. She told me, that's where. Yesterday afternoon, after her office party. 'How do you like fucking Ben?' she asked me. 'Good, isn't he?' That's where I got that funny idea that maybe she'd been here."

Ben took in another gulp of air, thinking very hard. He didn't want to say the wrong thing; he had the feeling that saying the wrong thing might send her flying out of here and he didn't want to lose her. "Look, Barbara. Yes. I laid her. No, it wasn't the same. I love you. I'm in love with you. She? She was a woman I met by chance and we were both horny and we did it and that's all. Jesus, I'm sorry she turned out to be your friend, your coworker, your goddamn roommate, for Christ's sake. But I didn't plan it! And I told you about it. You gotta admit that."

"Ben. Listen to me. She put pictures into my head. I guess I knew, without really thinking about it, that you two probably had gone to bed together. But now I *have* to think about it. It's so clear and so plain and so vivid, I can't help but think about it. And tonight, I thought it was going to be okay, but when you began to caress me, the thought just came into my head, 'Did he do this to Nat? And this?' And I just couldn't go on."

"I get it. I'm sorry. But first of all, I never had her up here, in my room. Never. Okay? So she's never been in this bed and you never have to think that again. Next: I didn't make love to her the way I make love to you because I didn't feel about her the way I feel about you. Period. I don't know what else I can say, Barbara. All I can do is hope you believe me."

There was a long silence and then she whispered, "I believe you. No, no, don't hold me yet." Another silence, while she sat there all huddled in on herself and he sat next to her feeling like a lump, feeling miserable, wanting to hold her, wanting this sick feeling in his belly to go away, wanting to take Natalie Simon and throttle her, the bitch. Couldn't she keep her mouth shut? And it struck him.

"Hey," he said. "I thought you two were such good friends. What the hell was she up to, telling you something like that?"

"Oh, God, I don't know. She was drunk. She's always drunk lately, it seems. No, that's not fair. She's always been a big drinker. She just can't hold it like she used to."

"Hey, I'm telling it how it was. If I say it, it's so," he interrupted and she waved her hand at him impatiently. Well, she'd just better believe him. There had to be trust between them or there was nothing.

"It was horrible! She looked like a witch, her face all twisted. And she looked like she was enjoying hurting me! It was so awful! And the way she described you . . . it just hurt so much." Now he reached over and pulled her into him. Goddammit, he didn't care if she said don't, she needed him. And this time, she didn't say anything. She let her head drop onto his chest and she said, "Mark, too."

"What about Mark?"

"She . . . made love with Mark. While we were still married."

He tried very hard not to feel jealous, but he did anyway. Well, he wasn't gonna show it. So he made his voice very bland. "Does that bother you? After all this time?" Did she still care about that s.o.b.? They'd been divorced for so long. Still, some women never got over their first love, and Barbara had told him that Mark was the first man in her life. Well, if it still mattered to her, he didn't know what he was going to do. And the sick feeling down in his gut just tightened up.

"It's not Mark so much," she finally said and he felt sick with the relief of it. "It's not even that they did it; it's so long ago. But why did she have to *tell* me? You know, Ben, my marriage with Mark was far from perfect. But I always felt there were certain aspects of it that were good. I could have good memories. I could feel I had not failed. And our sex life was one of those areas. And now, suddenly, to have my best friend destroy it all! It's so cruel! Now I don't even have that. When I look back now, I have to feel totally stupid, do you understand that? I blush for my dumbness, whenever I think of it. I'm blushing now. I want to sink into the ground. She did a terrible thing when she came on to him, because even then she was my friend."

Ben took in yet another deep breath. Should he or shouldn't he? Jesus, what a mess. He didn't want to hurt her any more; but hell, neither did he want to go to bed with the ghost of Natalie Simon between them! Or of Mark Valentine, either.

Carefully he planned his words. "Honey, you shouldn't be so angry with Natalie, you know that? No, no, hear me out. First, she's a mouth, right? You know her. And I've seen her high, myself, and she *is* likely to get out of control. But listen, it probably didn't happen the way you think."

"What do you mean?"

Now he had to be *really* careful. "It takes two to tango. Maybe she didn't come on to him first."

"It had to be! Because Mark—"

He interrupted her, quickly. "Mark bragged to me, just before you and I met, Barbara, that he never went on a business trip where he didn't get laid. *Never*, that's the word he used." Now he waited for it to sink in.

"But"—she sounded perplexed— "wait a minute. I was just thinking, Well, he's a divorced man, why not? But . . . but he went on plenty of business trips while we were still married. . . . You mean—"

"I think that's what *he* meant."

"All those years? God. Of course, all those years. I *have*

been naive, incredibly naive and stupid. He never allowed me
to go with him!"

"I'm sorry," Ben murmured. "I'm really sorry. Maybe I
shouldn't have said anything."

"No, no, I have to know! I can't go on forever believing
in a quote happy marriage unquote that never really existed."
But he could hear that she was starting to cry again, and he
held her tighter. "He always had such logical reasons," she
said, her voice trembling, "always such *good*, sensible reasons.
I never doubted him. He called me every night and told me
how much he missed me. And all that time!" Now she was
silent for a very long time, her body shaking. Ben just kept
holding her, waiting, trying very hard not to press her.

He heard her take in a deep breath—exactly the way he'd
been doing all during this—and heard her let it out. And when
she spoke again, her voice sounded very different, lighter somehow. "Okay," she said. "Now I know. It's hard, but I'll have
to deal with it. But not right now. Right now," she said, curling
her body tightly into his, her hand stroking his chest and belly
in a way she knew he loved, "right now, I want you to know
that I'm deeply happy and grateful that I'm with you, here, in
your bed, here, in your life."

If he'd had the nerve, he would have stood up and cheered.
She loved him. She loved him. It wasn't over! He bent to her
mouth and their lips met in a kiss so tender, so sweet, he felt
tears spring into his eyes.

❀ 23 ❀

Interoffice Memos

MEMO FROM THE DESK OF
Natalie Simon

August 3rd or maybe 4th, I don't have the calendar in front of me,
anyway it's Monday.

Barbara dear, I've been wanting and wanting to talk to you for the
past week, ever since we had that spat in my office . . . but you
won't have any.

I'm sorry you feel that way and I hope you haven't already ripped
this up.

Are you still with me? Good. Because I feel terrible about this.
You're right, you're absolutely right. I never should have told you.
I like being honest with my friends, but I guess, no scratch that,
I realize that I went too far.

I'm sorry. I'm really sorry, Barbara. I'm sorry right down to my
toenails. I'm so deeply sorry I can hardly express it. But in my
own defense, I had no idea it would hurt you so much, I mean,
you've been divorced for three years and I thought you were finished
with him. Not that that excuses my saying what I said . . . but, you
know, you had hurt me and, well, it was childish of me, but I guess
I was trying to get even.

Can you forgive me for being high, being childish, being stupid?
I don't want to lose you as a friend. Last weekend in Paradise alone
in the house, it was terribly lonely. I really missed you.

In fact, right here in my office, I'm missing you.

Can't we talk?

Nat

MEMO FROM THE DESK OF
Barbara Valentine

August 5. Right now, no. We can't talk. I'm sorry too, but what you did was so cruel that I'm not sure I'll ever get over it.

For now, while I try to work it out, I think it would be best for me to stay away at the office and stay away from the house.

B.

❦ 24 ❦

Long Distance Calls

She must have been dozing; she couldn't remember, exactly. All she knew was, when the phone began to shrill, it made her jump in the chair. She was fully dressed, except for her shoes, which she had apparently kicked off, because they were halfway across the room. And when she moved her hand, it knocked over a glass on the floor; next to it was a half-empty bottle of vodka. She let the phone ring a couple of times, wondering what day it was, what time it was. She was totally disoriented. Dammit, she was too tired to talk; let them get discouraged. But they did not get discouraged. The phone kept on ringing and ringing and ringing. Finally, she pulled herself up and staggered out into the kitchen. Her head was spinning; God, she felt awful! "Hello? Hello?" she croaked.

"Nat, goddammit, now you've gone too far!"

Jerry. Jerry? Wasn't he on the coast? She squinted over at the big wall clock. Three. Three o'clock? In the *morning*. It must be; it was dark outside. "Why are you calling me at this hour? Do you realize what time it is?"

"I don't care what time it is, Natalie. Not when it concerns my daughter."

Her head was beginning to clear a little. "*Your* daughter," she informed him in haughty tones, "is in France."

"She was right!" Jerry said. "You really *are* out of it."

"What are you talking about, Jerry? And make it fast, please, I need my sleep."

"You need more than sleep, Natalie dear. You need help."

"Just what's that supposed to mean?"

"You really don't remember, do you?"

"Jerry." She tried very hard to keep the impatience out of her voice; but it was difficult. Her mouth tasted like the bottom of a bird cage and her head was thumping painfully. All she wanted right now was four aspirins, a little hair of the dog, and sleep. "Please don't play games with me, okay?"

"Natalie, don't you remember speaking to Melissa? Just a half hour ago?"

As soon as he said Missy's name, a vague memory floated into her head: the phone ringing, Missy whining and fussing, and her own efforts to stay calm and dispassionate.

"Oh, yes," she said now, frantically searching her memory for details which kept eluding her. "Of course I remember. She wanted to come back . . . more of the same."

"You really are sad, Natalie." She hated that superior tone. "Melissa called from France to tell you she's in the hospital, sick with some kind of fever."

Why couldn't she remember? She hadn't always been the most enthusiastic mother, but she loved her child, loved her and cared about her! "She didn't tell me about any fever."

"You're a liar. You're a liar and a drunk and a very pathetic person. Why do you think she called you? Even angry with you because you wouldn't let her come home, you were the first person she thought of. Her *mother*. Some mother!"

"Oh, fuck off!"

His sigh was heavy and dramatic; she could visualize the look on his face, the droop of his mouth, and the sad, droopy eyes. She squeezed her eyes shut. It must be true; she had talked to Melissa, and now, all she could recall was answering the phone and hanging up. She couldn't remember one single thing they had said. A cold chill ran over her, and at the same time, she began suddenly to sweat.

Shivering, she said into the phone, "Jerry, I'm not feeling well. Let me get some sleep and I'll call you."

"Never mind, Natalie. I don't need you to call. Melissa told me *she* doesn't ever want to talk to you again. I'll be back in the city next week, and I'm telling you right now, I'll get a court order to keep you away from her. Do you hear me? Are you sober enough to understand what I'm saying?"

"Jerry, for Christ's sake!" But all there was now was the hum of an empty line.

She slumped against the wall, letting the receiver dangle down, her arms wrapped tightly around herself. Tears leaked out of her eyes. She could hide it no longer. She was turning into a lush. It was one thing to forget a few details over a business lunch; hell, she could always cover herself. But to blank out an entire conversation with her child, her sick child, thousands of miles away, alone—and *sick*? Oh, Christ, Jerry was right; it was disgusting.

What was happening to her? Was her whole self slowly unraveling—first the business woman, then the wife, then the lover, and now the mother—all slowly disintegrating?

She stood, eyes closed, and behind her lids she saw baby Melissa, not yet two, chubby, head of dark curls even then, wide, trusting eyes. That's when she had been staying home with visions of motherhood dancing in her imagination. She was going to be Perfect Mommy with Perfect Baby. She was going to spend her days in harmony with her child, reading books and cuddling in front of the fire and toddling to the zoo. And the reality had turned out to be an extremely active baby who vaulted out of her crib in the middle of the night, wide awake, who had—this particular gloomy, gray, dreary November afternoon—already opened a five-pound bag of flour and arranged it on the kitchen floor, unplugged all the lamps in the living room, pulled books out of Natalie's shelves, and eaten a half-written letter to an old friend.

Natalie was wishing herself anywhere but there, was wondering why she had been so eager to get pregnant, was fighting the urge to take this child and shake her until her teeth rattled. Motherhood! Nobody had told her there would be days like this, when her housekeeper was sick, her husband was tied up in interminable meetings at the office, her friend Jake was out of town and unavailable for conversation, and the weather was too awful to go out and find other mommies with *their* toddlers. Nobody had warned her. She was sick to death of Melissa!

"Mommy! Mommy!" What now? she had thought wearily. But there was no ignoring that cry and, steeling herself for yet one more disaster, she hurried down the hall.

The baby was standing, awestruck, in the middle of her room, staring at a pool of sunlight glowing on her rug. The dark gray clouds had parted suddenly, leaving just enough space for this narrow shaft of light, and there it was, in all its shining glory, a circle of pale yellow in the center of the blue carpet.

"Mommy!" baby Melissa said. "What dat?"

Relieved and amused, Natalie relaxed. "Why, that's sunshine, sweetie pie."

Melissa regarded her and then squatted herself down to see it better, reaching out one careful, chubby finger to touch it. Then she looked back up at her mother. Natalie would never forget the look of absolute trust on that round face.

"Is it mine?" Melissa asked.

Natalie had been flooded with such love, it almost took her breath away. "Of course it is," she said and reaching down, picked up the baby, hugging her tightly, pushing her nose into the soft fragrant neck. "Of course it is. All yours, all yours." And, she added silently, the moon and the stars and the flowers and the trees and anything else you want. Mommy will get it for you.

What happened to that woman? What had become of her? What had happened to those feelings? How had they become so perverted that she could forget an entire conversation? What the hell had she said to Melissa? It was horrible, not knowing.

She licked dry lips with a thick tongue, wishing she could sink into the earth. She was a drunk. That nearly empty bottle of vodka in there on the floor next to the easy chair: It was full when she got in tonight. Everyone had been trying to tell her lately, saying, didn't she think she had had enough? They didn't know the half of it! They had no idea, the quantity of booze she put away each day. She'd lied, even to Carl Stern. Half a quart, some days, she'd told him; and he'd shaken his head and said, "Oh, Natalie, that's a helluva lot of booze. Here." And he'd printed out a phone number, and a name:

Nancy. "This lady runs a group for . . . ah . . . women who are having problems with drinking."

"Alcoholics, you mean!" she had flared up. "I happen not to think I'm an alcoholic!"

He held up his hands in surrender. "Whoa, lady. You tell me half a quart and you tell me you're bothered by it and I'm telling you that whenever you want, you call this lady. She's available any hour of the night or day."

It was now three-thirty in the morning. She couldn't possibly call anyone at three-thirty in the morning. And anyway, once she got some sleep, she'd be just fine.

And then she drew in a deep, shuddering breath. It was time to stop telling herself stories. Her child had cried out for help, and she had been too drunk to respond. Would Missy ever forgive her? Again, tears seeped out from under her lids and crept down her cheeks.

Any time of the day or night, Carl had said. Very well, then. She dialed the number and after only two rings, a sleep-tinged voice said, "This is Nancy. Can I help you?"

❀ 25 ❀

Two Lunches

"Jake Miller! Yoo hoo, Jake!" It *was* him, wasn't it? Nobody else on Madison Avenue was tall and skinny with a mop of curls like that. He turned quickly—rather too eagerly, she thought—and gave her a big grin. Poor Jake. It must be awful to be an out-of-work executive. You couldn't go through the "Help Wanted" pages, like one of the secretaries. Even her own classified section didn't carry anything higher than a group head. He'd really opened up that time on the beach; he'd given her a whole new insight into the problem.

Well, lucky for him she was a people person; she understood what he was going through. And now, lucky Jake, she had a nice surprise for him.

"Think of the devil!" she caroled, tipping her face up for him to kiss. He laid his cheek against hers briefly; and then said, "Were you thinking of me? No wonder my toes were tingling."

"Oh, you Jake!"

"So tell me, Bambi . . . why were you thinking of me?"

"Oh, it's too wonderful to just say, out here on the street. Can we go somewhere and talk?"

"Sure. I've just come from being at lunch with a guy who made me a promise. Why not?"

"Made you a promise?"

He made a wry face. "'Maybe I've got something for you, Miller. Out in Jersey.'" He laughed and then changed his voice slightly, putting on an accent: "Maybe Murray has something for you. Maybe my wife's cousin ... Agh, you know the kind of thing."

Meanwhile, he was steering her into a place she'd never been. "How cute!" All Art Deco: black and silver and pink and streamlined.

"Cute's the word," Jake said and saluted the bartender. "Two of my usual, Tony. And see what the lady'll have."

"Oh, you Jake! Of course I'll have what you're having."

"You heard the lady, Tony. Two egg creams. Just kidding, Bambi, just my little way of keeping the demons at bay. Is the bar all right?"

"Of course." They sat side by side, and she regarded him as he bantered with the bartender. He was a very attractive man. Not handsome, not at all, but there was something about him. Something boyish and charming, something young and playful. She loved to play.

"You know, Jake," she said, when their drinks were in front of them and they weren't egg creams at all, of course, but gimlets, "if I hadn't met Peter first, I think I'd make a play for you." Let's see what he'd do with that.

"In fact, Bambi," he said solemnly, lifting his glass, "if Peter hadn't found you first, I was about to make a play for *you*." And he drank to it, his eyes twinkling mischievously over the rim of the glass.

How exciting, how positively fabulous! Peter didn't exactly own her, did he? But what if he found out! Oh, God, he'd dump her in a minute ... in a *second*. But why would he find out? He need never find out. Her eyes searched Jake's and her heart speeded up a bit. But Jake only grinned at her and said, "C'est la vie! The best man won ... I guess!"

Thank God she hadn't made an ass out of herself, saying something stupid just then. He was only kidding! And yet, she could have sworn ... Damn the man, you couldn't tell!

"But that's not why you brought me here, right, Bambi? You said you had something to talk to me about."

"Oh, I do. You know the Diebers?"

"Sure. Sam and Bob, both graduates of BBDO."

"Right. Well, I got a scoop that they're going to handle a

major Japanese car account—no, I can't tell you which one, not even its initials—and they're in the market for a talented group head/VP."

The expression on his face changed instantly. He was now totally alert, totally serious. "Bob Dieber and I used to work together. Of course that was ages ago, but still . . . we always liked each other's stuff, always had a ball."

"Well, Jake, in fact . . ." Oh, this was the part she loved! "In fact, when Bob and I were talking earlier this morning, I mentioned you and he got so excited. . . . See, he was out of town the week my item about you ran in *The Ad Game*."

Jake took a careful sip of his drink. "Got . . . excited? *How* excited?"

"I mean excited excited. He said, lemme see, he said, 'Really? Jake's on the loose? Are you sure? Do you have his number? Hell, I'll call him at home; he must have an answering machine.' Do you have a machine, Jake?"

He grinned. "Would you excuse me for a moment?" He strolled over to the phone booth and a few minutes later he was back, really grinning this time. "In answer to your question, Bambi, yes, I have a machine, and yes, Bob Dieber left a message, and yes, he sounds excited, and yes, I will kiss you." And he did so, a nice firm kiss on her lips.

When he sat down again, he said, "How will I ever be able to repay you, Ms. Hirsch?" Then he waggled his eyebrows and twirled an imaginary mustache. Was he coming on to her, or what? God, she wished she knew, because if she knew, she'd go for it. Hell, Peter would never find out, and if he heard something, she'd just deny it. He was getting to be a bit too much of a bully, anyway. It would serve him right.

"We'll think of something," she told him; and was rewarded with a huge laugh.

"I take my hat off to you, Bambi," Jake said, signaling to the bartender for another round. "You do get around, on Mad Ave."

"I do my best." She hoped she wasn't blushing. It certainly felt like she was blushing.

"It must be constant work."

"Well . . . all I can say is, it isn't as easy as some people would like to believe. I have to keep my eyes and ears open all the time, even at parties, when everyone else is just having fun and getting smashed."

"I'll bet. It sounds almost impossible." He was bent toward her; he was very intent on what she was saying. He understood, he really did. Not like Peter, who loved to condescend to her. Jake knew how to really listen.

They talked for quite a while before he looked at his watch and said he had an appointment in five minutes ago. He was so funny; it was such fun to talk with him. She felt quite pleased with everything.

As they were leaving, he said, "By the way . . ."

"Yes?"

"No, I guess nobody would know. Well . . . maybe *you* would, since you have your pretty little ear to the ground."

"What, Jake?"

"Just wondering if there's any truth to the rumor that Peter's trying to raid Steinberg & Epstein, the big PR agency."

That Peter! Swearing her to secrecy. Everyone must have heard, if Jake had it as a rumor. He hadn't even been working, the past few weeks! For it to get as far down as him, the whole darn world must know! She could've printed it weeks ago and scooped everyone!

"Oh, I wouldn't know about that, Jake," she lied. "I have to say, read my newsletter and find out."

But as soon as he had rounded the corner, she headed right for the nearest phone booth. She knew someone pretty high up at S & E. . . . . She'd soon find out what was what!

"It was the damnedest thing," Natalie said. She toyed with the stem of her glass, twirling it around and around, watching the reflections change pattern on the white tablecloth. The restaurant was already mobbed and it was barely noon. She had decided five minutes before not to be too impatient for her food. And anyway, the meal was secondary. She needed to talk to somebody and who better than her lawyer? Her lawyer: what a strange new way to think of Paige Thompson. Paige was

Barbara's lawyer. Well, now she was Natalie's. They had, in fact, just come from Paige's office, where they had discussed the twenty-seven ways in which Jerry Weber was dragging his heels, slowing the inevitable process of separation and divorce— in spite of his anger at her. Paige found it terribly amusing because he did it in such a ponderous almost soft way . . . nothing openly aggressive. And yet, he managed in that soft way to bring things to a screeching halt. Natalie did not find it—or him—amusing in the least. Now that she'd really made up her mind, she wanted it done and over with.

"What was the damnedest thing?" Paige prodded.

"Oh. Yes. Well, it was two weeks ago, on a Thursday . . . a very dreary Thursday evening. There I was, with a new swain, holding hands, gazing into each other's eyes . . . and he's pitching me AA."

Paige's voice was carefully noncommittal. "AA?"

"Alcoholics Anonymous. Do you *believe*? Me, in group therapy?" She rolled her eyes and laughed. "That's what it is, you know. It's amateur night in a church basement. But apparently it works." She gestured at her glass, filled to the brim with clear liquid. "I'm still stunned that this is water and not vodka . . . me, the biggest boozer on Madison Avenue!"

"This guy, is he in advertising?"

"No, no. Didn't I mention? He's a lawyer, Peter's lawyer in fact. He's on the other side of that pond dispute out there in Paradise that was in last week's *Times*."

"The artist, the ringleader—Lovall. He must feel you're going over to the enemy."

"He doesn't know. And that's funny. Carl, Carl Stern, said very much the same thing. He made it a joke, of course. He said something about consorting with the enemy. What's up, Paige? I didn't say anything funny!"

"Oh, lord. Carl Stern. No, no, it's not funny. Just amusing to think of you and Carl Stern together."

"Oh, you know him!"

"Only by reputation. And of course I've heard him speak at DA conventions and that sort of thing. You know, don't you,

that he's called The Hawk, when he's not called The Blade or
The Killer?"

Natalie laughed. "I'm not surprised. He's a tough cookie.
But underneath, he's really warm and sympathetic, nice. I don't
know how he did it, exactly, but he convinced me. I mean,
Paige, I didn't *want* to go; I didn't *want* to stop drinking; I
didn't *want* to hear what he was saying. And he somehow got
through all those defenses, and in the end, dammit, when push
came to shove, I wanted to do what he said." She laughed
again, ruefully.

"It's my understanding," Paige said, "that The Hawk never
lost a case when he was in Morgenthau's office, an Assistant
DA. And, by the way, just because he's called The Killer or
The Hawk, that doesn't mean he won cases by being vicious.
All it means is that he always won. I found him a brilliant
speaker . . . very compelling."

"Yeah, well, he compelled me all right. Of course . . ." She
paused and sipped her water, making a little face and smiling.
"Of course, nothing is more convincing, in its way, than a
person who's been there."

"And has come out on the other side. You know, now that
you mention it, I remember hearing stories about his drinking
and how he could come into the courtroom skunk-drunk and
still win. And, then, if I remember correctly, he got a little
reckless and got called down a couple of times by the judge.
I don't know exactly. As I said, I never really knew him and
it's just gossip. Anyway, I'm glad you're taking care of yourself. Barbara was very concerned about you. . . . What's the
matter?"

"Nothing. You mentioned Barbara and . . . well . . . she's not
speaking to me these days."

"Oh, really? I thought you two were great friends. And I
saw her recently and she didn't say anything."

Luckily, just then, their waiter appeared with the chef salads.
They dug in and ate for a few minutes and then Paige looked
up and said, "But I never did ask: What is it with you and The
Hawk? Anything interesting?"

"I don't know, Paige. To tell you the truth, Carl Stern is

something of an enigma to me. I've never known a man like him before. They've all been very much like me, you know, with the same kind of humor and standards. Slick and glib. He's . . . different. Rougher. Tougher, for sure." She paused, and took a mouthful of food, chewing it carefully. "You know what it is? I don't know what to expect from him. I've always felt, by and large, that I could tell what a man wanted even before *he* knew. Kind of like mind reading. Can't do that with Carl Stern."

Paige smiled. "Sounds like an ideal man for you."

"Yes. Maybe. But he's a little too . . . candid, too smart, too aggressive."

"Typical trial lawyer. Especially the DAs. A nickname like The Hawk is typical too, and what's worse, they love it. They think it's wonderful. Well, isn't that most men, really? Thinking that winning is *It*."

"Not Jerry, you know that, Paige?" Natalie put down her fork. "I never thought of it before. He's very daddylike: gentle and approving. God, how guilty I felt all those years, for taking him away from that sweet, dull, drab woman he was married to when I met him. . . ." Her voice trailed off. "Jerry was never a heavy."

"Having second thoughts?"

"About the divorce? Hell, no!" Natalie said. But inside, she wondered. Was a man like Jerry what she really wanted? Carl Stern at times made her feel angry and disturbed, in a way Jerry never had. Was she making a terrible mistake getting divorced so fast? Panic gripped her. She took a deep breath. And then she thought of big lumbering Jerry, who always called her sweetheart but never made love to her, and she shook off her doubts.

"Hell, no," she repeated. "No way!"

❀ 26 ❀

The Ad Game

When Natalie got back to the office from her lunch, she surprised Larry at his desk. He was reading something and as soon as she said, "Hi," he guiltily closed it and slid it under a pile of work. Only then did he remember to put a smile on his face.

"Okay, Jordan, let's have it."

"Have what?"

"Whatever you just hid."

"Natalie . . ."

She began to laugh. "Dammit, Larry, don't make me play a scene from Grimm's Fairy Tales! I'm not the wicked stepmother, for Christ's sake!"

"You don't want to see this. I swear you don't." He was really agitated, she realized. How strange. Usually Larry was the picture of stoicism and calm, the exact opposite of her own self, in fact. Now she *really* had to see what was putting him in a twit.

It was a copy of *The Ad Game*. She reached for it, saying dryly, "Maybe I *should* wait thirty minutes after eating. Mom always warned me about cramps. Actually, Mom never bothered with all those cautions; she was always too busy with her own stuff. But what the hell . . ."

It was already open to page three, neatly folded, in fact, to "Galley Proofs," Bambi's gossip column. "Oh, of course," she murmured, scanning the closely set type, skipping from one ellipsis to the next. And then, she found her own name.

"Nat Simon, Creative Director of M & M, and hubby Jerry

Weber are in the thick of divorce proceedings. All of their friends are wishing Nat would come to her senses. She and Jerry began way back when, working together. . . . Rumor hath it they were always a terrific team. Too bad they couldn't work this out together. Could it be the cause is Nat's well-known weakness for the strong stuff?" She let the paper fall back onto the desk as her eyes flew up to meet Larry's; and he sorrowfully shook his head.

Was that all? She snatched the newsletter up again. It wasn't all. ". . . Her predilection for the multimartini lunch has gotten her into hot water more than once; and the word is that she'd better cool it if she values her job."

"The bitch!" Natalie threw the paper down and began to pace. "Do I call her? Do I kill her? Or do I take a shortcut and just go kill Peter?"

"Don't joke about it!" Loyal Larry. "I'm mad as hell!" he spluttered. "How dare she? How dare she stick her cute little nose-job into your life?"

"Oh, Larry!" She wanted to laugh; it was really a very good line. But she was too furious. She could feel her heart pounding against her rib cage so hard it hurt her chest. "Dammit, you're right! How *dare* she? The rotten little—! Not only to make a judgment on me, but to print it in her stupid little gossip sheet."

"That everyone reads," Larry added.

"Exactly. That everyone reads. That . . . everyone . . . reads. The bitch! Broadcasting my problems up and down Madison Avenue! I'll sue her. I swear I'll call my lawyer and sue her for defamation of character and for libel and anything else I can think of. . . . But first, I think I have some business with our dynamic young president."

"Go for it, Natalie!"

"I hope you mean the jugular." Out she went, stone cold sober and ready to do battle. It was a new feeling, marching down the hall on her way to Peter's office without that old alcohol buzz, without that old alcohol-induced belligerence. This time, by george, she was going to do it on sheer brain power and real anger, no help from the bottle. She smiled tightly to herself, imagining Peter's astonishment to find her in such

good shape. He'd really been on her case lately, checking up
on her lunch dates and snooping in her desk drawers after she'd
gone home. Doing it clumsily, too, in a very obvious way. Did
he think she'd stopped thinking *completely*? Or was he working
on her, hoping to make it so uncomfortable for her she'd be
forced to leave?

By the time she got to the *sanctum sanctorum*, she'd worked
her anger up to a boil, nicely under control mind you, but
enough to let him have it. Outside Mary-Claire's little outer
office, she drew in a deep breath, preparing herself for the
onslaught. Then she marched right by, straight into his private
quarters, pretending not to hear the squawks of protest that
followed her.

She found him sitting at his desk, writing something on a
piece of yellow copy paper. More gossip for Bambi? She
slammed the door hard and his head came up with a jerk.

"So, Natalie." His voice was pure ice.

"No 'darling' this time, Peter?" She planted herself in front
of the desk, her hands flat on its glossy surface, leaning across
it, as close to him as she could get. "Well, I'm not surprised."

Now he smiled his nasty little smile. "You've seen *The Ad
Game*."

"Peter, I don't know what to say to you. You've gone beyond
the pale. You s.o.b.!"

"Careful, *bubbeleh*. You're talking to your boss, remember?"

"It happens my boss is a nasty, mean son of a bitch who
hasn't grown up any since he was fourteen."

"Nattie! I'd be very careful, if I were you."

"If you were me, my dear Peter, you'd have a knife stuck
into your heart. Which you would deserve! 'Could it be the
cause is Natalie's well-known weakness for the sauce?' I ask
you, Peter! After all these years, never mind the years you and
I have known each other, never mind what I've done for you
personally—how about the years I've given to this agency!
. . . How could you say those things about me?"

Again the smirk. "I never said a word, Nattie darling."

"Bull Shit!"

"Oh, not really. I'm not the only one who knows what a lush you are!"

She held a fist up, watching her arm tremble and then, frustrated, brought it down, pounding on the desk.

"See? Out of control, as usual. Drunk. As usual."

Natalie sucked in air. She had to maintain dignity. "Wrong, Peter darling. Dead wrong."

He peered at her, sniffing the air. "Yes, you are. I recognize all the signs. I know you, Nattie dear."

"You little punk! I saved your rotten hide, not to mention your reputation—and your goddamn agency, in fact!"

"That's ancient history. I've paid you for that, over and over and over. Well, I'm finished paying for one tiny moment of indiscretion."

"One tiny moment! In case you don't remember, Peter, you were stoned regularly, back then. You were a goddamn loony-tune, driving everyone nutso with your crazy mood swings! Not to mention cooking the books. If I hadn't taken over for you, you would have come back from Wyoming to *zip*."

"That's right. You took over. Nobody asked you. Nobody *wanted* you."

"Oh, really?"

"That's right, Nattie dear. You blackmailed me, pure and simple."

Goddamn him, it was close to true. But not really; he'd been promising her the job for over a year, holding it out like a carrot on a stick, and then withdrawing it whenever he felt like it. Goddamn him.

"Oh, no answer," he went on. "Don't tell me I've actually made the famous Nat Simon shut up for once in her life! Will wonders never cease! If you kept your mouth shut more often, you wouldn't get into trouble so often in your work. Like now."

"And what trouble am I supposed to be in?" She'd brought in that new campaign for the egg people without a hitch. What in hell was he talking about?

"You ruined my deal with Steinberg & Epstein."

"What the *hell* are you talking about?"

Again, that self-satisfied little smile. "I got a phone call not

ten minutes ago. From the chief stockholder. The word is out
that the cousins were all set to sell their shares to me. In a
week, I would have done it; I would have been the majority
shareholder and M & M would have been twice as big. And
you, you and your boozing and your damned diarrhea of the
mouth, *you* shot me down! I don't forgive people who do me
in, Natalie. You should have thought of that before you blabbed
all over Madison Avenue."

"I never said a word. I gave you my promise and I kept it."

"You're a goddamn liar, Natalie. Oh, don't bother. The call
proves it. He said they all had wind of it and that they were
celebrating their escape! He already had his majority . . . damn
you! You've really done it this time, Nat! You've done the
unforgivable thing."

"I have said zippo. In fact, Peter, you told one third of the
known universe the same time you told me. If anyone around
here has a mouth, buddy, it's you and your gossip-mongering
little girlfriend."

"*You* drink."

"Not any more, Peter darling. I haven't had a drink for two
weeks, for your information. I'm in AA. Say, how come *that*
item didn't appear in *The Ad Game*? Was she too busy spreading
her poison?"

"Leave Bambi out of this! We're talking about you. We're
talking about how the sweetest deal of my lifetime just got
wrecked by a loose-lipped slob! I was counting on it, goddamn
you! They have cash, Nattie, they're rolling in it. I *need* that
cash . . ."

In a flash, she knew. The property in Paradise! "What did
you do, Peter, 'borrow' money from the agency? *Again?*"

"I don't have to tell you anything! It's none of your business!" He got up abruptly from his big padded leather chair
and turned his back. To hell with him; she'd yell at his back.

"Maybe not. But how about your one hundred forty-seven
loyal employees, Peter? Isn't it *their* business? Jesus, are you
ever going to learn how to handle money?"

He wheeled, glaring at her, his face suffused with rage. "I
never want to hear that old story again, not ever! You've been

holding that one mistake over my head for years! You think that keeps you safe, don't you? Well, I guess today's *Ad Game* proves it doesn't!"

"So! You *did* tell Bambi to print all that garbage!"

He pressed his lips together and folded his arms tightly across his vest. Natalie felt dizzy, but she knew she had to stay on top of this thing. She must not faint or anything else feminine and weak. She dragged in air again. Very very softly and very very calmly, she said, "Peter, listen carefully. If that little blond bitch prints one more word about me, she will be one sorry lady. That is a promise from Mr. Simon's little girl, Natalie."

Peter's face twisted into an ugly sneer. "Hold your tongue, Natalie! That woman is going to be Mrs. Peter Marcus!"

She couldn't help it; she began to laugh hysterically. The unctuous tone of his voice! It was too much, too much! Mrs. Peter Marcus, indeed!

"You dare to laugh!" His voice quaked with his anger. "You've been jealous of Bambi right from the beginning. She's been very aware of it. Yes, Natalie, jealous. Jealous and competitive."

"That's a scream! What in hell would I want to compete with *her* for?"

"She's told me plenty of stories. You just can't stand it when men consider her more attractive than you . . . and that she has her own business, her own *successful* business."

"Is that what she told you? Well, she's out of her mind. And never mind looking daggers at me, Peter. I say she's a *liar* and what's more, I'll say it in court."

"You wouldn't dare!"

"Oh, wouldn't I! Let me tell you something. It'll give me *double* pleasure to sue her as Mrs. Peter Marcus if she ever prints one single syllable about me, ever again!"

"You'd never win . . . since it's all true."

"Not if you're referring to my drinking . . . and I have two people as witnesses, two people who know exactly when I went on the wagon and why."

He waved her words away and gave a chilly little laugh. "Oh, you mean Carl Stern? Aha, surprised you, didn't I? Well, who do you think sicced him onto you, huh? I told him, 'Hey, Carl, there's a lady whose soul you can save from the demon rum. If you can straighten her out, I won't have to fire her. And furthermore, I told him, she's a helluva lay. She'll fuck just about *anyone*." How she longed to slap his smug face! He grinned at her. "Couldn't you have figured that one out? Why else would he go for an old broad like you? My God, he must be ten years younger than you!"

Now she smacked him, loving the sound of it in the air, the sting of it on her palm, and the mark of it on his stupefied face. For several long moments, they stared into each other's eyes.

"Remember those one hundred forty-seven employees I was talking about before?" she said, finally, feeling a surge of sudden elation. "Well, Peter darling, as of this moment they have become one hundred forty-*six*. I quit!!"

She couldn't remember turning, she couldn't remember opening his door, running out—none of it. The first thing she recalled was his voice, thick with outrage, echoing down the hall:

"Good! Go! I need your office!"

❀ 27 ❀

On the Telephone

"I bought a bottle. On my way home."

The female voice at the other end said, "But you don't want to drink it. You know you don't want to drink it."

"Nancy," Natalie said, her voice quaking a little, "that's why I'm talking to you. I know I shouldn't, but I want to. Oh, God, do I ever want to! I've left M & M. I'm out of work. For the first time in my life, I don't have a job! Do you know how many years I've worked in that place?"

"But," the patient voice interrupted, "there are no answers in the bottle. You've already found that out. You might forget for a couple of hours, but when you wake up..."

"I know. I know. I'll still have the same problems." She was sitting in the tiny living room of her sublet, none of the lights turned on, just the light from the hall dimly illuminating the edges of things. Like the bottle of vodka, for instance. Standing on a table across the room, beckoning to her with its tacit promise of forgetfulness, of oblivion. Two or three slugs. Oh, hell, she knew better than that now. Now she knew that there was no such thing as two or three drinks for her. She'd start with two or three, but when she woke up, the bottle would be empty and she wouldn't remember drinking it all. "Still..." she said.

Now the voice took on a firmer tone. "Natalie. Listen to me. You're stronger than that. You'll find another job. You're very talented, you're still young, you have your health. It only happened today; you haven't even given yourself a chance. You have to take it one day at a time. Natalie? You there?"

"I'm here. Where the hell else am I going? I don't have a home anymore, I don't have a marriage." And then she couldn't help it; she began to laugh. At least, it *started* as a laugh. And then it turned into a sob. "You know what, Nancy? I'm full of self-pity tonight. But you know what else? I think I deserve it. I know it's my own doing, but, Jesus, I've lost a lot of friends lately, I've lost my marriage, my home, and frankly there are times when I think I've lost my mind."

"Natalie. Listen to me. Where is that bottle?"

"Across the room. I don't want to touch it."

"I want you to go get it and bring it back with you. Will you do that? Come right back. Promise."

"I don't want to touch it," Natalie repeated, feeling like a child. "I'm afraid." Nonetheless, she obediently did as she had been told. She then picked up the receiver and said, "I'm back."

"Yes. You're good and you're strong and you're smart. That's why you're going to open that bottle and pour it right down the drain."

"All of it?"

"Every drop. You can do it. You know you can do it."

Natalie eyed the bottle. It looked just like water. It looked just like nothing. She was so filled with dread and anger and sorrow and hopelessness. If only she could have a drink, she'd feel so much better. She thirsted for that drink, hungered for it. Her brain was clamoring for it. She couldn't stand to feel her thoughts one minute more. She couldn't stand to *feel* anymore.

"Natalie?" The voice, even and calm, had a definite edge to it. "Natalie. Open that bottle and pour it out. Now."

She wrestled with herself for a minute. How easy it would be just to hang up and have a drink. But of course, Nancy would then call her back. How simple, then, to leave the receiver off the hook.

"Three weeks, Natalie," the voice said. "Come on. Take it a minute at a time. You've already managed three weeks of minutes. Do it."

"Yes. Okay. I'm on my way. Hang on. You there, Nancy?"

"I'm here as long as you need me."

A minute later, she was back. "I did it."

"You must feel terrific."

Natalie thought for a minute. "I guess I do, actually. Not terrific exactly, but as if I'd won something."

"You have. Now I think you ought to reward yourself. Go out and get yourself something delicious and gooey . . . like a banana split."

Natalie laughed, and this time it was a real laugh. "Forget *that*, Nancy! I don't want to use food as a substitute for booze. If there's one thing this world believes is worse than a woman who's a drunk, it's a woman who's fat. And anyway, a banana split isn't what I need. What I needed is . . . TLC!"

"Isn't there someone you can call on for that?"

"As a matter of fact, Nancy, no. But it doesn't matter. Really. It doesn't matter. I don't even *want* a drink anymore." Not quite true, but she could handle it.

After she hung up, Natalie looked around the apartment, looking for something she could do for herself that would make her feel better. There was nothing here, nothing. Maybe she should go out to a movie. But she didn't want to see a movie; she doubted she could concentrate. And she didn't want to see a play, either, or go to a concert. Dammit, she didn't want anything uplifting; she wanted to get laid, dammit! She wanted a man to put his arms around her and tell her how wonderful she was. Hell, at this point, she'd settle for just being told she was terrific and never mind the rest.

At which thought, she naturally began to dial Jake's number. Jake would make her feel better, she knew it. He might not want her to be his lover anymore, but he'd be willing to give her ten minutes of conversation! He couldn't turn her down for that!

When he heard her voice, there was a small moment of silence; and then he said, "Nattie. I must say, I'm a bit surprised to hear *your* voice." At first, she didn't know what he meant; and then, suddenly, she remembered. "The last time we were together," he went on, "was not exactly wonderful, if you recall."

"Oh, Christ, I'm so ashamed! It hasn't exactly been my summer and ... I was drinking too much. But of course, you knew that!"

"It wasn't what you might call a secret, Nattie."

"Well, I'm in AA now."

"AA? Alcoholics Anonymous, you mean?"

"None other than. Yes, Jake, after all our jokes about cheapie therapy. Well, it works. At least it works for two weeks and a day, which is how long I've been on the wagon."

"Do I congratulate you?" He laughed. "Maybe there's a market for a whole group of greeting cards for impossible situations. You know, congratulations for joining AA ... best wishes upon completing your therapy ... continuing success with your birth-control pill ..."

This was more like it. Now she was laughing and really meaning it. "What a terrible idea! Do you think we could do T-shirts, too?"

"Nattie, Nattie, drunk or sober, you're my best audience."

Bless him. She *knew* he'd make her feel alive again. It was so good, just talking to him. Why? Because he was funny. Yes, but that wasn't all. Because she'd known him for so long. Because they had a shared history. Because, when the chips were down, she knew she could count on him.

"Guess what your best audience did today?" she asked him.

"I'm breathless with anticipation."

"Quit."

"Quit what else? besides drinking, I mean."

"My *job*, you nit! What else? My goddamn job! Even as I talk, I find it hard to believe. I told Peter to take his lousy executive vice-presidency and shove it!"

"Terrific! It's time you moved on! That place was getting to be a womb. Hell, you should have done this five years ago. The more I think about it, the better it sounds. Where are you going?"

"Going? What makes you think—?" She stopped, taken aback. He thought this was a well-planned and neatly-executed maneuver on her part! "Weren't you listening to me, Jake? I quit. I mean, this afternoon I read Bambi Hirsch's nasty-poo column and there it was in black and white: my entire personal life history and some snide asides about my quote drinking problem unquote—all supplied by darling Peter, of course."

"Oh, shit, really? I never read the damn thing today."

"Well, there it was! And let me tell you, it was awful. I *couldn't* stay, knowing he'd been putting knives in my back, behind my back."

"Oh, come on, Nattie. Nobody who counts takes that kind of gossip seriously."

"Wanna bet? When I start making the rounds of agencies looking for a job, I *know* it'll be uppermost in everyone's thoughts."

"I don't think you'll have a problem, not the famous Natalie Simon."

"I did have one thought, Jake. We could team up for a while, offer our services as a dynamic duo. Waddaya think?" And when he didn't answer, she said, "What's the matter, Jake? We've worked together before!" and her voice came out much sharper than she wanted.

"Take it easy, Nattie. I'd like nothing better. But . . . well, the fact is, I've had an offer from Dieber that I think I can't refuse."

"Even better! You can hire me!"

The silence went on so long, it rang in her ears. Then, in very careful tones, he said, "You know how I feel about your work, Nat. You can write circles around the dummy kids they get nowadays. And when I think of the way we used to read each other's minds! It would be wonderful, all things being equal."

"I gather from your embarrassed tone that all things are *not* equal." She let some more silence slide by and then added: "Look, Jake, I really *am* committed to being on the wagon."

"Aw, Nattie, it's not that! Hell, if I cared about your drinking . . . I mean, come on, too much water's gone over the bridge for me to start becoming soberer-than-thou. No, no. But you really hit it, Nattie. Things wouldn't be equal. Come on, you wouldn't want me to be your boss."

"Try me."

"No thanks. I know damn well what would happen. Remember how it was for the last three months you were *my* boss?"

"This is different. You should pardon me for saying so, I'm not you. I could be your underling. No problem."

"Nattie, Nattie." Now—she could hear it so plainly she could have drawn a picture of the pain on his face—he was becoming impatient. "You couldn't. Believe me, your friend for lo these many years. You couldn't. Listen. Remember Neil Chapman? Wrote a book, got on the bestseller list, wrote a movie, made a million, left his agency job, spent a million?" She grunted; yes, she remembered Neil Chapman. He had been the subject of many he-just-lucked-out conversations, when was it? seven, eight years ago? "Well, he wrote another book, it bombed, he wrote another one, ditto. The upshot is, out on the coast, he came to me for a job. I knew it was a mistake, but I couldn't stand saying no, realizing that his wife and babies were all going to starve or something. So there he was, Nattie, and let me tell you, it was awful. Every time I blue-penciled his copy, I could see his back going up. He began to snarl at me and I heard from the other guys that he complained about me all the time. I had to let him go."

"So it didn't bother you in the end that his wife and kiddies would starve?"

"That's right. I hardened my heart." He laughed. "It taught me a lesson, Nattie. Never hire a friend."

Later, she'd weep a few bitter tears over the perfidy of her old friend. Right now, it was very important that he not know how desperate she felt. So she made sure her voice was lilting and light. "Okay, so no job. So how about taking me out to dinner, so at least *I* don't starve?"

"Gee, Nattie, what a shame. Love to, of course, but no can do. I'm having a few people over in a little while."

In vain, she waited to be included and after a few awkward seconds, she brightly and insincerely wished him a happy evening and hung up, and shed her bitter tears right then and there. Goddammit, was she never going to learn? When he needed her, he was always available. And when she needed him, she could just whistle through her ears. Well, there were other people in this world who cared about Nat Simon.

She dialed Jerry, almost hanging up when she heard his voice. She'd made up with Melissa—she *hoped*—by phone and by mail and by money order. She'd dealt with Melissa and with her drinking, both. But who knew what Jerry's reaction might be. "Hi, it's Nat," she said.

"I recognize your voice, sweetheart."

Immediately she was sorry she hadn't put the receiver down before speaking. There was a tender note in his voice, and it irritated the hell out of her. The idiot actually thought she was calling to make up. She knew that tone in his voice, all full of understanding and forgiveness. Well, goddammit, she didn't want his forgiveness!

"I just wanted you to know, Jerry . . ." Jesus Christ, what *was* it she just wanted him to know? "I just wanted you to know that I've joined Alcoholics Anonymous."

"Oh, darling, that's such good news. Melissa will be overjoyed. As am I. As am I. May I say that I've been hoping and working for this, for a long time."

Damn him to eternal hellfires. She hoped he roasted slowly and in agonizing pain throughout the rest of time. Other than that, she felt perfectly fine about him.

"It's so good of you to tell me that, Jerry," she said with false sweetness. He either didn't hear the sarcasm in her voice, or chose to ignore it.

"Well, after all, I'm still your husband, aren't I? And I care about you. As does Melissa, you know."

"Jerry," she said, as calmly as she could manage. "I have been in touch with Melissa. I don't need you as a go-between."

"Are you aware how disappointed she is with you? She calls *me* every three days from France. Believe me, sweetheart, it's a pretty penny."

Natalie grit her teeth. "First of all, Jerry, you could have taken her to California with you, but never mind. Just stop telling me what a rotten mother I was not to let her come back."

"Have I said one single word that sounded like rotten mother to you? I think it's a guilty conscience speaking, there, sweet-heart."

"Well, sweetheart would be delighted to pay you back every single pretty penny for those phone calls, but sweetheart can't. Because sweetheart quit her job today."

"Oh, Natalie, you didn't!"

"Oh, yes I did. Aren't you proud of me?"

"Proud? Are you crazy? Do you know what the job market is like for a woman your age?" Damn him to *two* eternities of hellfire, one roasting, one sautéeing! "Sweetheart, sweetheart, you've done yourself a terrible disservice."

"You don't know what's been going on."

"Natalie, I *know*. Didn't I work there all those years? You think I don't know how difficult Peter is? I know how difficult he is, believe me. We both know him. When did you quit?"

"About two and a half hours ago."

"Let's see, if you give him another half hour, he'll be miss-ing you. Yes, another half hour. That should do it."

"What do you suggest I do, in another half hour?" But she knew, she damn well knew. She could have said the words in unison with him and, in fact, she mouthed them as he answered.

"Why, *call* him of course. Use your best feminine manner. You know how to handle Peter Marcus. Didn't he used to fire you regularly? And didn't you used to get yourself rehired right away? I'm sure that hasn't changed."

"*I've* changed, Jerry, and if you're interested, I no longer grovel to a spoiled little Jewish American prince." He was answering her as she very gently put the phone back into its cradle.

She sat, looking at the phone, undecided whether to laugh or cry. Oh, hell, it was a long evening, maybe she'd do both. In the meantime, she had one more phone call to make. She hesitated, wondering if perhaps there was a strong masochistic streak in her somewhere. She hadn't done too well for herself with the phone tonight, beginning with pouring that expensive Stoly down the drain and ending with Jerry Weber pontificating. However . . .

She dialed, let it ring six times, and was about to give up when that familiar voice inquired, "Hello?"

"Hi, Sandy," she said, all at once knowing exactly what she was going to do. "Guess what? I'm giving up on the city and moving out to Paradise."

✤ 28 ✤

Reentry

When the phone rang, Natalie was deep into her resume, juggling dates, trying to remember all her clients, and wondering who she could use as a reference. Surely not Peter, and Jake was no good until he was really set somewhere. And then the phone rang and her whole train of thought was interrupted and she reached for it, annoyed. Her "Hello" sounded peremptory and strange in her ears.

"Guess what, Natalie?"

She was absolutely in no mood for guessing games. "Who *is* this?" She stared out of the sliding glass doors onto the deck where everything was gray, gray, and gray; and what looked like tons of water was streaming down the pane. Just her luck, the week she decides to leave the city and spend all her time on the beautiful sunny Fire Island beach, a low pressure system settles in and it rains every goddamn day.

"Natalie, come on! What's your problem? It's Sandy, of course, and you'll never guess where I'm calling you from."

"Sandy, I was working. I can't guess anything right now." Suddenly she remembered: They had a date for dinner. Had he come to the door and knocked and knocked and she never heard him? "What time is it?"

"Seven oh two. That's why I'm calling. I know I'm supposed to be there now, to start cooking, but I can't." He sounded gleeful. "Come on, you have to make one guess. I'll give you a hint. This is the one phone call I'm allowed."

"Sandy, please don't play games with me. I'm not in the mood."

Now he was totally exuberant. "I'm in jail!"

"You're what?"

"In jail. On the mainland. Isn't that wonderful? It'll be in all the local papers and maybe a TV station'll pick up on it. And then we'll get some attention! Black, please."

"Black what?" Natalie asked.

"Coffee."

"That's some incarceration, with room service," Natalie said, licking her dry lips with a dry tongue. She could use some coffee, herself. What a night out there! Wet and gloomy and raw and absolutely deserted. Damn it, why didn't he stop yammering and get to the point!

"Well, I'm not *exactly* in jail. But I am in custody and I'm in the sheriff's office waiting for my lawyer. I want them to lock me up, but they won't. Natalie? You still there?"

"Where else would I be?"

"Well, you didn't say anything."

"What shall I say, Sandy? I hope they lock you up?"

"Well . . . yes. I mean, you do want us to get publicity, don't you?"

"Yes, Sandy." She yawned. Seven o'clock. And she'd been at her desk since four-thirty.

"They got me for trespassing, isn't that a scream? I had this great idea early this morning—that's why I didn't call you. I took a pup tent and put it up on Peter's property, right next to the pond."

"In the *rain*, Sandy?"

"Of course in the rain."

"God, you must be crazy."

"Nope. Just muddy. I had to wait hours for someone to call the sheriff." She heard murmuring and then he said, "Okay, just a minute more," and then he said, "I have to get off the phone, Nat dear. I'm sorry about dinner; I'll cook for you tomorrow." Now he laughed. "I'm giving you a raincheck!"

Very cute, she thought, hanging up and feeling a curtain of gloom drop over her shoulders, as heavy as concrete. Very goddamn cute. But here *she* was, all alone in a damp house on a rainy Friday with a refrigerator crammed with assorted fancy items, but nothing *she* knew how to deal with. And she did not love his assumption that he could just break their date and make it tomorrow. He shouldn't take it for granted that she was free all the time. Oh, shit, why fight it? Did she have anything better to do tomorrow night? No. In fact, she had nothing to do tomorrow night. In fact, she had nothing to do *tonight*.

She forced herself up and tottered out into the kitchen. Damn, she hated feeling so grouchy. It was not her usual style. It was this horrible weather, that's what it was.

Nothing possible in the refrigerator, just as she had thought. She finally grabbed a peach and nibbled it, walking back to the glass doors and staring out into the dismal scene. The very ocean was thirteen shades of drab. Even the foam on top of the wavelets looked dingy, and the surf slapped onto the wet beach with a heavy, despondent sound.

God, how depressing. Or maybe it was her state of mind. Changes in the weather usually excited her; even electrical storms didn't faze her. She loved to go outside on the deck and watch the lightning play over the water. But she had been feeling very down about every goddamn thing, good or bad, since that stupid argument with Barbara.

Barbara was being unforgiving, unrelenting. Well, of course she was. It made Natalie cringe, every time she remembered the way she had mouthed off. "I fucked Mark!" Oh, wonderful, Natalie, very goddamn kind. Well, if she remembered correctly, she had been provoked. She heaved a great sigh. Goddammit, the trouble was, she didn't know if she remembered correctly. Then she had still been drinking.

She remembered Barbara's cool, superior stance; she remembered feeling the rage, the self-righteous anger, rising in her throat. She remembered thinking about Jake running into her office all those years ago and rhapsodizing over the beautiful blonde he'd been following down the street who wonder of wonders had ended up right there in the offices of Marcus & Morrisey . . . her feeling of utter panic that day, that certain sure knowledge that she had just lost him, her own, her special, her Jake. To be fair, Jake had gone after Barbara. Natalie knew that. She just wished she could recall exactly why she became so enraged so many years later.

She'd apologized. She'd written Barbara a perfectly marvelous warm note, asking for forgiveness. And what she got in response was so cold, so implacable, that she had crumpled it into a ball and thrown it away without reading it a second time. She couldn't believe it: All this emoting over a marriage that ended four years ago? And Barbara kept saying that she no longer loved him, no longer cared very much about him, and was happy to feel that way. So why all the fuss? Wasn't she overreacting? Natalie thought so. Jesus, what if she'd told her about *Scott*? But luckily, even half in the bag, she'd had enough sense not to breathe a single syllable about *that* little episode.

All right. This was her second weekend alone in the house. Enough. She didn't like it. Maybe it was the rain, maybe not. She was not meant to be all by herself; she needed other people. She had asked a couple of friends if they wanted to come out on Saturday or Sunday, but everyone already had plans. God, you'd think people would *jump* at the chance to come to Fire Island! And now her Friday night date had dumped her for a night in jail. If that wasn't sinking about as low as you could get!

To hell with it. Was she going to stand there in the darkness all evening, feeling sorry for herself? And maybe, heaven forfend, begin thinking affectionately about the bottle of cooking sherry? No, she was not. She was going to go downstairs and fix up her face and slick up her persona and then—? Then, she'd think about it.

She was all done, in ten minutes, right down to the bright toothpaste grin, looking in the mirror and wondering whether she could really face Bob's Bar with only a glass of Perrier to sustain her. Why not? Listen, you, she told herself, you're Natalie Simon, the indomitable, the unsinkable...

And then she heard the pounding on the front door. Who the hell? She ran up the stairs, aware that she was a little nervous because she was alone. Some indomitable, some unsinkable, when you couldn't be by yourself in your own house.

Nevertheless, she hollered "Who is it?" through the closed and bolted door.

"Carl Stern!"

Of all the people! Well, well, imagine that. Carl Stern, who'd been sent by Peter to save her sodden soul. Maybe. *Maybe*, Natalie, she reminded herself. And maybe Peter lied.

"Hey!" Carl was shouting, "What's the problem? You want me to drown?"

"I'm not so sure I want to see you," Natalie said, opening the door, letting in a gust of chilly rain-laden wind.

He was soaked to the skin, in spite of an umbrella which he was propping against the wall, and water dripped down his face. "Hey, Natalie! How you doing?" Something must have shown on her face, because he peered at her and said, "What's the matter?" And then, a moment later, added, "Hey, whatever it is you think I've done, could we talk it over inside maybe? And I wouldn't look askance at an invitation to sit by your fire."

"I don't see how I can refuse a man who uses the word 'askance' without blushing," she said, making up her mind all at once. "But if you want a fire, you'll have to make it yourself."

He came in, slamming the door shut. "Jesus, what a night!" And he shook himself like a big shaggy dog.

Oh, hell. "I think I have a big towel downstairs. I'll go get it."

"And *I'll* make the fire," he answered. "You may not know it, but you're dealing here with a genuine Eagle Scout."

As she trotted down the stairs, she was planning how to bring up the subject with him. Blurt it out, get it out in the open? Or hint around? Be subtle? She grabbed the towel and headed back up, deciding that up front was her way and to hell with it.

In the living room, he was kneeling by the fireplace, doing stuff with logs and sticks in a very assured manner. In fact, a cheerful little fire was already beginning to blaze away.

"You do good work, Mr. Stern," she said.

He looked up, narrowing his eyes at her. "Why do I sense a certain chill in your voice?"

She handed him the towel. "Maybe you're imagining it."
Hey! Hadn't she just decided to deal with it right up front?
Some up front! As he clambered to his feet she just dove right
in. "No, you're not imagining it. Yes, you detect a certain chill.
You detect it because it's there."

"You want to tell me why?"

"Stop dripping all over my floor. Yes, I'll tell you why. I
had a little conversation with Peter...."

He paused in the middle of rubbing his hair dry. "Yeah?
And?"

"And he told me...well, he told me about you." *There*,
she thought. But he still looked perplexed.

"Yeah? And?"

"He told me all about it, Carl. Stop pretending. He told me
all about enlisting you in the cause of sobering up Nat Simon."

"What? *Months* ago, when he first hired me to deal with
this property. Well, you *were* drinking pretty heavily. He was
concerned. That's to be expected; you were his second in command, right? If I remember—and I didn't pay very close attention—he said he thought your drinking was escalating and he
asked me for advice. I told him about AA and that was it. So?
Why would that make you mad? I thought we were beginning
to really like each other."

That made her mad. What did he mean by that, anyway?
"Really like each other!" she repeated in bitter tones. "Oh,
sure, so did I. But that's not the way Peter tells it!"

He stood right where he was, feet planted apart, still toweling himself off as best he could, still calm and unruffled. If
he was feeling guilty, he sure didn't show it. Well, of course,
he had been a trial lawyer. Everyone knew what good actors
they could be. "How," he asked gently, "exactly does Peter tell
it?"

She took in a breath and let it out. How to say it? "He says
he told you I was an easy lay, a sure thing."

Quietly: "No, he didn't."

"That's what he told me!"

"I understand that, Natalie. But he was lying to you. He
never said it, and if he had, I wouldn't have listened. Hey!

I'm not a teenager, Natalie. I have too little time to play games. I particularly don't waste it schlepping in a downpour through the dark to beg admittance at a lady's door." He cocked an eyebrow at her, a half smile curling his lips. "Well?"

He was very convincing. And she knew Peter was capable of saying *any* damn thing! Dammit, she wished she could know for sure. And, as if he could read her mind, Carl Stern walked over to her and, putting one finger under her chin, tipped her face up so that they were looking into each other's eyes. "Natalie," he said, "I'm going to prove it. I won't even touch you . . . see?" He backed off a little, still smiling, and held both hands up. "Look, Ma, no hands. We'll just sit by the fire and talk. How about it?"

"You're on." And anyway, she thought, it was certainly the most novel offer she'd had from a man in a very long time.

But an hour later, deep in conversation about fathers and the fast-track and expectations, she found herself wondering how his thick springy hair would feel under her fingertips, how those firm lips would be, whether she ought to just reach right over and take his hand, like she wanted.

"Carl?"

"Yes?"

"I think I've had enough proof."

He laughed and reached out for her, holding her face in his big warm hands, and kissed her very slowly, very expertly, caressing her lips with his. Now her eyes flew open and she said, "Then you must be married."

"What does *that* mean?"

"When it's this good, there's always *something*."

He chuckled. "Not guilty, this time. Not married."

"Not that I mind, Mr. Stern."

"I'm glad to hear it, but I'm still not married. Divorced for seven years."

"Good for you. Now kiss me again."

"I can kiss you because I'm single?"

"Oh, no! Because it feels so good. . . . I don't care if you're married, Mr. Stern."

"Funny," he said, covering her lips with his again and moving closer. He lifted his mouth for a moment and said, "*I* do. I never fooled around when I was married."

"I did. Not very liberated, are you?"

"We'll see about that, shall we?" Then he shifted so that they were very close, and this time when he kissed her, he pressed his tongue into her mouth.

The next time she was able to put two thoughts together in coherent fashion, they were entwined on the rug, stark naked, he had just collapsed over her and she was thinking "Oh, shit!" It had started so nicely; he kissed beautifully, and she was very excited. He undressed her and she undressed him and it seemed that they couldn't get rid of the clothes fast enough. And then he said, "Natalie, look, the first time is going to be fast." And oh, Christ, he wasn't kidding. He was becoming quite heavy on her, and she wished he would get the hell off and get the hell out. She grunted and moved her body. "You falling asleep there, Carl?"

He lifted his head and gave her that sly smile and said, "No, ma'am, I am *not* falling asleep. I told you: the first time is fast. Well, did I tell you about the second time? It isn't." And before she had time to do more than take in his words, he had lifted himself up and turned her onto her belly.

Now he straddled her and began to rub her back with slow sure deep movements, using both his hands. He was very strong, but gentle, and she allowed her body to relax and go limp under the warmth. He moved his hands slowly down her back, pushing and massaging rhythmically. Every muscle in her body was loose and her skin tingled. As his hands worked their way down to her buttocks, she found her breathing quickening. His did, too; she could hear it, ragged and excited. She could feel his erection hard and hot against her thigh, and she wanted it, she wanted it. She struggled against the weight of his hands, trying to turn over. But he only chuckled and held her down, his hands firm on her buttocks.

Then it began: a systematic teasing that had her screaming and writhing. He pushed his cock up against her, pushing lightly, moving in little circles; but he would not enter. She arched her back, desperate to force that rod into her wetness, to ease the heat in her cunt. "Please, please," she heard herself begging, but he only laughed and reached under her body for her breasts, pinching playfully at the nipples. He would not let her turn over to face him. It was excruciating, it was diabolical, it was wonderful. He was totally in control, in the nicest way, building her pleasure so slowly, so surely.

He would *not* let her turn over, and he would *not* give her his cock; he was the unseen, the invisible male force, making her crazy, moving his hands to explore all the places that made her explode, over and over. She wanted to see him, she wanted to hold him, she wanted, she wanted. After a while, her body was electric, trembling desire that was not quite fulfilled.

"Oh, God!" she heard herself panting. "Oh, God! Have mercy, please!" By this time, she was pure sensation. She had forgotten her name, almost. There was nothing else in the universe save the weight and length of the male body behind her, the male hands that toyed with her, and the need that burned within her.

Then she heard him whisper something and, holding onto her belly with both hands, he plunged deep into her, filling her at last. She let out a groan of pure pleasure and pushed her rear end into him to meet his slow, steady thrusts. Then he turned her onto her side, grabbing a breast in each hand and began to push in and out, faster and faster. From a distance, she heard the sound of her own cries as she erupted again and again into orgasm. And then, with a mighty grunt, he came, pulsating, clutching her tightly, and it was over. Her heart was hammering against her chest with great thumps, and she gulped in air, holding his hands tightly. They lay on the rug, curled up together spoon-style, sweating, breathing hard, drifting.

After a while, she stirred and said, "Carl?"

"Yeah?"

"Peter was right, wasn't he?"

He chuckled and hugged her. "You think that was *easy*?"

This struck them both as wildly humorous. In the middle of their laughter she rolled over to face him and gave him a big hug, feeling suddenly very very good about him, about them, about everything.

✿ 29 ✿

A Visit from Martha J

The day was bright and the bay was as still as glass and the little ferry seemed to skim over the water without touching it. Martha J leaned on the rail and watched Fire Island appear on the horizon as if by magic, a large hazy bump with a flagpole sticking out of it, the banner fluttering in the breeze. Yes, it was the right decision. A house on Fire Island, amongst the Pretty People. Well, dammit, she and Calvin were pretty people, weren't they? And they came complete with tan, too. Her wonderful husband . . . God, she was lucky. She was just about the only female executive left at the agency—if not the world— who was still married. And loving it. Oh, they had their battles and storms, she and Calvin; but they always seemed to come out of them, just a notch or two better than they had been before. And now, there was Paradise. Nat stood there on the dock, frowning just a little as she scanned the passengers. She looked fit, somehow tightened up. And tan! Her long dark hair was twisted up and she was wearing white shorts and shirt and running shoes and she looked, Martha J thought, as if she could take off and fly without any effort at all. Martha J let out a sigh of relief and then laughed at herself. She hadn't even realized that she was tense over what she might find. She had imagined a Natalie depressed and desperate and down.

"Hey, lady!" she called. As soon as Nat spotted her she began waving both arms and grinning, like an excited little girl. From this distance, she might be thirty, or even twenty. Of course, close up, you could see she wasn't any twenty-year-old chickie, but a grown woman. "You look absolutely fabulous," Martha J said, giving Natalie a big hug. She smelled good, too. "God, am I glad to see you!"

"No, am *I* glad to see *you*!" Natalie said. "Remember, I'm the one out here in exile and you're the big-city kid come to give me the good word."

Martha wrinkled her nose. "Lady, there is so much to tell you, I hardly know where to start. Maybe I'd best stop in at Margie's and make a date with her to look at those houses tomorrow."

She finished with the real estate agent in about three minutes. Nat waited outside, chatting with the guys who lived next door. And then they headed up the boardwalk, the little red wagon clattering behind them.

"It's real nice here," she said, "unlike a certain ad agency which shall remain nameless."

"Except that its initials are Marcus & Morrisey?" Natalie finished.

"You got it, lady. It is a grade-A, class-A mess. I mean, Peter's done some screwball things in his time, but this . . ." She rolled her eyes.

"Oh, lord, what's he done?"

"You aren't gonna believe your ears, lady. He's replaced you."

"So soon? Ouch. That hurts." Natalie laughed. "And here I was, thinking I was irreplaceable." There was a very brief pause and then, in the lightest imaginable tone, she added: "With you?"

"Natalie, you oughta know better than that. No," she said, giving Nat a grin to show she was only kidding. "No, it's much much worse than that."

"*Bambi Hirsch!!*" Natalie guessed. Martha J couldn't help it; she had to laugh. The look of horrified disbelief on Natalie's face was funny; and it was even funnier because it was the twin of Martha J's own reaction when she was first informed.

"Yeah, that's what *I* said when Peter sent the memo around. This past Monday. And I've been saying it every hour on the hour, ever since. I mean, that lady don't know nothin', Nat. She's totally ignorant. What the hell does he think he's doing?"

"Saving my salary, it looks like."

By this time, they had reached Nat's house. It was a *very* nice place, she had to admit. "Yeah," Natalie said, looking around with a look of pride, "this house is my declaration of independence. You know, Martha J, this is my very first piece of property, ever. The apartment is in Jerry's name, my office always belonged to Peter, the house I grew up in was my father's, and that dreadful depressing sublet belongs to somebody else, of course.

"But this . . . this is *mine*! Now I know how it feels to be lord of the manor. You actually walk around telling yourself *This is mine, all mine*. You actually *do*!" The phone rang from inside the house and they hurried up the ramp.

As Nat spoke to her friend, Sandy, Martha J walked around, looking out at the ocean, admiring the view, trying not to listen to Nat's private conversation. But it couldn't be helped; she heard it. And it struck her that it sounded like the chat of an old married couple, or a couple of pals. No juice, no . . . passion. And she didn't even lower her voice. Whatever was going on between them, Martha J Jones knew it wasn't high romance, no way!

When Nat hung up, she said, "Now you have to tell me everything. Ohmygod, Martha J, it sticks in my throat, to call that little blond bimbo by my title."

Martha J laughed. "Wait'll you hear what she's done." And while they changed into their bathing suits, she told. And told and told and told.

She told Natalie about that first Monday. She'd never forget it. There was a call from Larry, who sounded strangulated. Martha J couldn't figure out what was bothering him; but she soon found out. It seemed she was to report to Ms. Hirsch right now, on the double. "On the *double*?" Martha J joked. "Is *that* what she said?" "I'm afraid so," Larry answered, and right then and there, she got a feeling that there was trouble.

And was she ever right! There was Bambi Hirsch, seated behind Natalie's desk, swiveling in Natalie's chair, and smirking. She was dressed for success in a man-tailored cotton suit, shirt, and tie. Martha J, who usually wore Calvin's ties around her waist or maybe as a headband, wanted to burst out laughing.

But laughter was not to be part of this meeting. Bambi, looking very very serious, told Martha J that she was talking to each group head individually to tell them that she expected a daily report from each of them, by five P.M.

"Report? On *what*?"

"Are you making fun of me, Martha? Because if you are, you should know that I don't put up with insubordination."

Well, excuse *me*! Martha J thought, but wisely did not say. "Making fun, Bambi? Absolutely not. I really want to know what it is you want me to report on every day."

"Why . . . why . . . what's been accomplished each day, that's *What?*"

"Excuse me, Bambi—"

"Ms. Hirsch, Martha."

You'll pay for that one, lady, Martha J thought. Not this minute, but eventually. She put on her sweetest, most reasonable expression and said, "Well, you know, Ms. Hirsch, that's a little difficult to do in this business. Because we aren't turning out widgets, so I can't make a progress report saying today we turned out so many widgets but a certain percentage of them had to be rejected or anything like that, see? We work with ideas and we work against deadlines and—let me see how to explain this. Some days, for instance, Debbie turns out absolutely perfect copy easily, and some days, she has to rewrite and rewrite and it still doesn't suit. But that doesn't matter, because—"

"Well, it matters to me!"

Jesus, but the woman was stupid. Too stupid to know when she didn't know something, the worst kind.

"Well, okay, what will you want to know? How many phone calls to client? How many pages of copy? How much research? How many layouts? How many hours we spent in the library? *What?*"

"Dammit, Martha, now I'm sure you're just being difficult. I'm sure you know what's required in a daily report. Just see that it's on my desk by five o'clock each day."

Martha J struggled not to reach over, pick her up by the scruff of the neck, and shake her good. "Anything else?" she finally said tightly.

Bambi swiveled and smiled a little smile. "As a matter of fact, Martha," she said in saccharine tones, "I'd like to discuss with you your . . . ah . . . unusual mode of dress."

"And do you believe?" she demanded of an openmouthed Natalie, "the woman had the utter gall to tell me that I had to start dressing like *her*? Do you believe it? That little blond runt who wears the cookie-cutter version of what the *New York Times* says everyone has to wear to the office?! Do you believe *she* was trying to tell *me* how to *dress*?"

"Oh, shit!" Natalie said. "And I'll bet you weren't even wearing that silver jumpsuit with the cutouts all over it, were you?"

They both began to laugh. "No, ma'am, I was wearing my most conservative African scarf costume . . . and I didn't have on my shark's-tooth bib either!"

And then Natalie, suddenly sober, said, "She's really incompetent, isn't she?"

"Incompetent isn't the half of it, Nat. She's downright *mean*. You know the kind, stupid mean. Jesus, she went into the test kitchen and immediately started telling Barbara how she ought not divide the work, but that she and Jessica should always work together. And when Barbara managed to ask *why* she should do that, Bambi mumbled something about how she knew damn well why and not to get fresh. And then she turned on poor Jessica and told her she needed a haircut. I mean . . . *unbelievable*!"

Later, on the beach, they were still talking about The Disaster, which is how Martha J had come to think of Bambi. She told Nat how Bambi yelled at Tommy Thoms and called him Thomas. "My God, she didn't even have enough sense to look up his real *name*! And then she tried to tell Larry to get rid of his earring. . . ."

"What did Larry do?" Natalie said, grinning. "Did he deck her?"

Martha J couldn't help smiling. "What did Larry do? He said, 'Okay, baby, no more earring. And no more Larry.' And he walked—no fuss, no muss, no nothin'.''

"Good for him!"

"Wait, you haven't heard the worst yet. The worst is yesterday, Friday, right after lunch. She called us all in, every group head, every account exec, every art director. And you know what she said? She said she knew we were in cahoots with each other. She waved this big bunch of papers, all of our reports, and I guess everyone had done what I did, which was make it all up." Martha J giggled. "One day I reported hour by hour, everything we all did, including visits to the ladies'. And she told us she knew we were all covering up our gross inefficiency and that we were taking advantage of Peter with our cushy jobs and our very high salaries and, by God, she was going to see to it that production went up and, oh God, Natalie... It's her attitude, that's what's wrong. She's managed, in one short week, to put us all on the defensive, make us all despise her, and make it extremely difficult to turn out the work. Oh, I forgot to tell you, she's on the phone to me at least twelve times a day, with one goddamn thing after the other. Checking up on me."

Natalie said, "I hate to be so delighted at someone else's failings, but I hope to hell Peter realizes pretty soon what a mistake he's made."

"You said it, lady. He'd better realize it, or there ain't gonna be anyone left at M & M. Hell, there ain't gonna be an M & M! I knew love was blind, but I didn't know it was a moron. Oh, Nat, I wish you would come back. You *could*."

They were strolling along the water's edge, letting the little wavelets break over their bare feet. "Yeah, I have that feeling, too. All I have to do is grovel. But, you know, Martha J, I think my groveling days are over."

"Aw, hell!"

"Oh, I have my moments, when I break out in a cold sweat, convinced that nobody in the business will ever want me again and that my safest course is to get on the horn to Peter and grovel, grovel, grovel. But then I quickly come to my senses."

"Oh, my God, and I almost forgot!" Martha J pummeled Nat's shoulder in her excitement. "It was wonderful! Full-page picture of her on the front page of *Ad Game* and a description of her as *Ad Game*'s Choice for the Most Exciting New Executive on Madison Avenue! I mean, Nat, *Ad Game*'s "choice"? When she's the editor of *Ad Game*, the *owner*? Who did she think she was fooling? It was embarrassing!"

"I'll bet she believed it," Natalie said. She shook her head. "Poor Bambi," she said, "trying to convince herself she's somebody."

"Poor Bambi, nothing! Poor *us*!"

"Oh, Martha J, she's bound to hoist herself with her own petard—whatever *that* means. Do you know what a petard is, Martha J?"

"Matter of fact? Yes, I do. But you don't want to know." And, laughing, they turned around to go back to the house for their lunch.

Nat had bought a delicious cold chicken curry and they were both starving, so they just concentrated on eating for a few minutes.

When the phone rang, Natalie jumped up, saying, "It's probably Sandy again. That man checks in about four times a day. Say, maybe he ought to work for Bambi. She'd love it."

Maybe Natalie *didn't*, thought Martha J. But this time, Natalie's voice sounded very different. When she said, "Well, hi there!" there was a lilt to it, a tiny note of excitement. And this time, she turned away from Martha J, walked as far as the cord would allow and spoke softly. Martha J took pity on her and walked out onto the deck. She'd bet it wasn't Sandy this time; but that it was a man, she had absolutely no doubt.

When Natalie poked her head out the door and said, "You can come back in now," Martha J gave her a big grin and said, "Who is he?"

"How'd you know—never mind, you're a witch."

"Come on, lady, anyone could've told you were talking to

a M-A-N! Your voice got that flirty sound. I mean, I do it, too."

"Speaking of Calvin . . ."

"Oh, no you don't! You're not changing the subject on me. I wanna know about this guy!"

She colored a little. "Well, his name is Carl Stern, he's Peter's lawyer, and that's how I met him, would you believe? He's very attractive, a bit tough. Oh, stop grinning that way, Martha J. I know everyone thinks that's just what Nat Simon needs, a man who'll boot her around a little; but I'm not so sure. Anyway, he's the one who sent me to AA."

"Good for him."

"Yeah, good, I know. I was feeling very good about him. But then, the day I quit, Peter told me a story . . ." And she gave Martha J a blow-by-blow, ending with, "Well, I didn't know whether to believe him or not."

Martha J shook her head. "No, no, no, and no," she said firmly. "First *and* last, you can't *ever* believe something like that from Peter. You've known him long enough to know that!"

Nat threw her hands up. "Too long, too long. And that's why I'm not going back, ever. I know it's different for you."

"In fact, it's not. In fact, my darling Calvin wants me to beat it out of there. He's ready to set me up in business specializing in the Black market, maybe. So. What do you think?"

For a few minutes, Natalie just stared at her. Then she said, excited: "Martha J, do you realize how you could tap into that market? I think it's a *wonderful* idea!" She laughed. "Can I have a job?"

"Can you have a *job*? Are you kidding me?" Didn't Natalie realize what she was being asked? "What do you mean, a job? I'm asking you to come in with me, be my partner." She paused. "Like we already discussed over lunch . . . only this time it's for real. Oh, Nat, isn't it exciting?"

Natalie came over and threw her arms around Martha J, laughing. "Oh, Martha J, if you only knew what you just did for my head! When I asked Jake for a job, he gave me such a song and a dance about how it would never work and I'd never be able to take such a comedown, and there I was, saying,

'Look Jake can't you give me some work so I don't starve,' and he's giving me lectures instead!" She pulled back then and all of a sudden looked serious. And sad. "I only wish I *could*, Martha J."

"Well, why *can't* you?"

"Hey. I'm broke, Martha J. I have some profit-sharing coming to me, if Peter ever lets it go, but I have a feeling by the time I get it, it'll be 1994 and the lawyer's fee will have taken it all. So I can't be anyone's equal partner."

"Lady, you don't understand. Money's no problem either." Didn't Natalie understand that little Martha J Jones didn't have the nerve to go into business all by her lonesome? Didn't she know how badly she was needed? "Come on, Nat. Say yes."

But Natalie was shaking her head. "I'm not saying no, Martha J. Listen, I *want* to. But I'm telling you right now that I'll only come in if I can put in my fair share. So, give me a little time to figure out if I can do it. Okay?"

"Sure. Okay. But . . . I really want to go *now*. I need to get out of there. So . . ."

"So, okay. I get it. I'll move as fast as I can. Be a little patient. I'll think of something. . . ."

❀ 30 ❀

At Sandy's

"Here I am—at last!" Natalie said lightly. Keep it light, that was her motto. She didn't want to scare Sandy Lovall off. She'd been wondering all summer what in hell was up there in his private preserve that made it off-limits—and when in hell he was going to take her up there and go for it. He was quite obviously interested in her. And there had been those kisses, those warm delicious kisses that hinted at a slumbering sexuality. So? she kept asking herself. And so . . . at long last, here she was. "It's really very nice."

"What were you expecting?" Sandy laughed. "A dusty mess, with blobs of paint everywhere and canvases stacked to the ceiling?"

"I don't know." The room was huge, the size of three normal rooms, with beamed ceiling, an entire wall of windows, a few chairs, and a bed the size of Rhode Island. The view of the bay with its distant misty horizon and the reflection of the setting sun from the ocean side, was breathtaking. "It's perfectly lovely," she finished. "It's so"—and she laughed—"you should pardon the expression, *artistic*."

Sandy laughed. "What else, my dear? What will you have to drink?"

Natalie gave him a look. "My usual."

"Vodka and what?"

Natalie laughed. "Sandy. You *know* I've stopped drinking."

"Surely not altogether!"

"Absolutely altogether. No more drinking period, finished, the end."

"What a bore. I don't see why."

"Because I have what is known in the trade as a drinking problem."

"Well, *I've* never seen you drunk. . . . No, really. A little high, perhaps, but we all get a little high from time to time. I mean . . ."

In a warning tone, she said, "Sandy . . ." and he said, "Okay, okay, okay. Club soda and lime it is." And a minute later, he presented it to her with a flourish and a bow and no further comment.

Natalie took a sip and said, "You have this enormous room with maybe twenty, maybe twenty-five pictures hanging on the walls . . ."

"Twelve," he said.

"Okay, twelve. But where are the Alexander Lovalls?"

"Oh, them!" He blushed just the littlest bit. Again, she knew she had pleased him. Did pleasing him please her? Well, she certainly liked verification that she hadn't lost her touch. "They're downstairs," he said, "on display. I don't have to look at them, once they're finished. No . . . up here, I have all *my* favorite artists and my favorite pieces. And here, next to my bed, is the most favorite one of all."

He led her over to the expanse of sleeping platform, heaped with pillows, tented with mosquito netting, and made up with crisp white sheets that smelled divine . . . like sheets from her childhood, when her mother hung them out on the clothesline to dry in the sun. He put his arm casually around her shoulders—well, that wasn't so unusual, but up here, with that oversized, opulent bed dominating the entire space, it made her a bit self-conscious.

"Isn't that funny? And wonderful? I just love it." It was a David Levine caricature, signed with the artist's scrawl, and it was Sandy to the life . . . well, not exactly. It was Sandy to the *inner* life, with certain little things, like his incipient paunch, and his pouched crinkled eyes, exaggerated with great humor.

"Yes, it's wonderful," she agreed, and waited for his next surely inevitable move. Would he, she wondered, push her down onto the bed? Or would it be more subtle? Would his arm now tighten around her and his soft lips descend to her waiting mouth? Or, would he invite her to the dance, as it were?

And the answer was: none of the above. They admired Levine's work for a minute and then his arm dropped away and he turned toward the window and said, "Let's have some nibbles and watch the sun go out in a blaze of glory. Look, look at the sky this minute."

Feeling very much off-balance—when in hell was this man going to make his capital M Move, for Christ's sake?—she went. The sky was a blaze of pink and orange, shading down to a kind of hazed plum near the horizon. In a minute and a half it would fade to pale peach and dusky purple.

"And how do you like my sunset?"

She laughed. He really was a very cute man. Why, she wondered, did it always take her by surprise? He was cute just about eighty-seven percent of the time. "It'll do, until tomorrow anyway."

"It'll do even better," he countered, his usual blandly good-humored expression tightening to a look of controlled disgust, "once *that's* gone and we can get the pond back to normal."

She had been finding his constant propagandizing a bit excessive lately. It seemed you couldn't talk about anything without having it turned back to his beloved Halfmoon Pond and the desecration being perpetrated upon it and so forth and so on. She agreed with him in principle, but it was becoming boring, frankly. Peter owned the property, that was the fact. And he really wasn't doing anything illegal. Just being unpleasant.

And from up here, she had to admit, it looked *most* unpleasant. From here, you were looking nearly straight down upon it and there were no tall grasses to hide the piles of lumber and stone, and the big gaping holes that had been dug, and the dying vegetation. From here you saw it in all its ugliness, like a blot upon a beautiful canvas. She could understand from this vantage point what made Sandy run.

"Oh, Sandy, how awful for you."

"Well, I'm glad *someone* understands."

"You're talking to someone who's had to deal with Peter Marcus for fully half of his life! Yes, I understand."

"Oh, Natalie, it's so good to talk to you about these things. We're so much alike. You're such a comfort!"

A *comfort*! Again, a clever answer rose to her lips; but she said nothing, as she noted his eyes misting over. He gave her a smile of unutterable sweetness. And nothing else? Alexander Lovall did not exactly have the most active libido in the Western Hemisphere. Under normal conditions, this would be the moment she went and put a hammer lock on a guy, wrestled him to the floor, and had her way with him. But, no, for some reason, she didn't want to do that with him.

"What further word from Martha J?" he asked, bending over to spread caviar and onion on a slice of bread.

"Oh, she's looking for office space. She really means it, I guess. And she can really do it, too, which is more to the point. At least one or two of her clients will follow her, wherever she goes."

"That sounds very promising for you, too. If she can pull old clients, surely *you* can, after all your years in the business. Why don't you sound more excited?"

"Hey, Sandy. Since three days ago when we last discussed this, my financial situation hasn't changed any."

"Oh, yes it has." And he gave her a shit-eating grin such as she hadn't seen since she was a teenager.

She couldn't help smiling back at him; he was obviously so damned pleased with himself. She was working on a couple of mailing pieces for his next show and it must be that he had more work for her. Or maybe he'd found her a really big account. Well, terrific. But why make such a big mystery out of it? Just tell her who and when and what and where . . . and she could begin to think about it, start to have ideas on it. She only hoped it wasn't a catalog; God, how she hated catalogs, with their precise word counts and exact line counts and never enough space to say what you wanted to say. She'd been writing a catalog for Selma's client list all this week, and it was a royal pain in the butt. "Come on, Sandy," she cooed. "Tell a lady in distress how you're planning to rescue her."

He gestured to the big couch. "Come sit with me."

She plunked herself down next to him, very straight and prim, hands folded in her lap, and turned her big brown eyes full on him. "Okay, Sandy. What?"

He cleared his throat and took hold of her hands. "Natalie, I want you to know I care very deeply for you."

Yes? Natalie thought. And?

"I want you to have the money for your partnership. As a gift. No, no, don't shake your head yet. As a wedding gift." And when she didn't respond immediately—because she was saying to herself, What is he getting at, anyway?—he added, a bit impatiently: "I'm asking you to marry me."

What to say? What, in the name of all that's holy, to *do*?

She had to say *something*. She couldn't just sit here and not respond to an offer of marriage. He was still holding tightly to both her hands and his eyes were soft with his emotion. Jerry, she almost said, and gave an involuntary gasp. Sandy Lovall was just a nicer, cuter, richer, more energetic Jerry Weber.

Sandy took her gasp as some kind of assent, for he pressed her hands even harder and said, "Oh, my dear Natalie, my very dear Natalie." And *still* the man hadn't so much as kissed her!

"If you'll pardon a cliché, Sandy," she said, "this is so sudden."

He smiled at her. "I love your sense of humor, Natalie. It's one of the reasons I feel we'll do very well—"

"Whoa, Sandy. Really. Let's take it a bit slower, okay?"

"I've known ever since I first met you, Natalie, that we could have something wonderful. Surely, you felt it, too. You certainly haven't shrunk from my company. I'm offering you a good life. You'll be my wife, my hostess, my companion. We'll travel, we'll entertain, we'll have a marvelous time! And, if you'll pardon my frankness, I'm also offering you the chance to do your own thing. I doubt there are many men who could say the same."

"Ummmm," she murmured noncommittally. He kept on talking, about weddings and guest lists and his Great Aunt Nora and family heirlooms and such, but she wasn't really listening. She felt quite unreal—not the way a blushing bride-to-be should feel, not at all.

I really like him; but on the other hand, he doesn't turn me on.

But on the other hand, sex isn't everything.

But on the other hand, it's something.

But on the other hand, so is security.

And, in case you hadn't thought of it, poor little abandoned Natalie, you'll be set for life. He'll take care of you.

And, in case you hadn't thought of it, you'll be Mrs. Alexander Lovall and that's not a bad thing to be in New York City. In a flash, she had a vision of a life that was shining, magical, exciting, glamorous. . . .

And he was going to give her the money she needed. No more grubbing, no more thousands of fruitless phone calls, no more resumes to mail out by the gross lot, no more subtle begging and not-so-subtle rejection. The end of her problems!

She eyed the broad, tanned, pleasant face with the crinkles around the eyes and the mop of curly graying hair and felt a surge of affection. If only there were more of a spark, some of that delicious high excitement. Oh, hell, he was a shy boy and what could a lady do except do what she always did—make the first move!

So she freed a hand and reached up and pulled his head down, lifting her lips to his; and almost immediately wondered why in hell he hadn't done this himself. Because he so obviously was loving it and his kissing was eager and expert. His mouth was warm and seeking, his tongue was warm and searching and she began to become excited.

After a few minutes, when he lifted his head, smiling down into her eyes, she said softly, "I think it's time we made love, don't you?"

She felt him cringe, saw his lips tighten just a little. "The physical side of a relationship . . ." he said and then made a little face, "I've never felt it was all that important."

What the hell could you say to *that*? She said it: "Oh, really?"

"Do you realize," he said with much more heat than was usual for him, "that at the moment of orgasm, someone could stick a knife into a man's back and he wouldn't even *feel* it?"

She was at a loss. It was so bizarre! Normal people didn't think of orgasm as dangerous, surely!

He was going on. "You're so vulnerable at that moment, so unprotected." He gave a shudder. "And it sucks you dry, drains you, takes away your life forces . . . ugh, no. We can do very nicely, on a higher plane than *that*. We're soulmates, Natalie. We don't have to rely on animal instincts."

She was unable to look at him directly, filled with a mixture of feelings she couldn't—or wouldn't—put a name to. She felt frozen, from the inside out, like a person turned to stone. She had to save him, extricate herself, excuse herself, and get the hell out of there, before he exposed himself any more.

But wait a minute. What was he talking about now? Something about her needs? "Of course I will understand, dear Natalie. I'm a man of the world, after all. I know that you have needs. All I would ask is total discretion."

Was he actually inviting her to marry him and fool around? Yes, he was. Would she go for something like that? Again? She didn't know; that was an honest answer. She didn't know. He could be her ticket out of trouble and despair.

She patted his arm and hoped she looked pleasant. "Let me think about all this, Sandy. It's . . . well . . . it's overwhelming." The understatement of the century! She got herself up and she bustled about, all cheery and social and tactful and ladylike. So fucking well behaved that it was a shame Jerry wasn't there to see her and applaud.

She even smiled when he gave her a husbandly hug and peck and murmured, "Think about it, Natalie, have sweet dreams about it, and give me your answer soon, dearest."

Dearest! Outside, in the gathering darkness, a darkness for which she was grateful, she allowed herself to shudder and shiver with distaste. But Christ, it was so creepy, so damned bizarre, it set off all kinds of alarms in her brain. She half walked, half ran, telling herself to calm down.

The man was, after all, not a kid, he was in his fifties. And he had a sexual problem, okay, so what else was new in the world? She could always get laid, right? *If* that's what she wanted. But what was the tradeoff? That was the real question. What was she going to have to give him in return for his implicit promise that she wouldn't have to grow old and ugly alone?

And she had no answer, no answer at all.

❁ 31 ❁

In the Office

Bambi went clicking down the hall, enjoying the brisk tap-tapping sound of her own busy feet. She loved M & M, just loved everything about it. The art department with all the ADs in their white jeans and tailored shirts . . . the chalky smell of the place and all the wolf-whistles and teasing that always followed her as she walked through. The copy department with the dozens of typewriters all going at once and spitballs flying around—they were all just a bunch of big babies; well, a lot of them were fresh out of college. It was all so alive and New York and she just loved it!

Most of all, of course, she loved her office. Natalie hadn't done anything to it, really, just *threw* it together. Well, Natalie Simon was the type who thought all you had to do to decorate was toss a few plants and some wicker around. Careless. Well, didn't Peter say she was a big drinker? She had become careless with just about everything and everyone by the time Peter got rid of her.

Bambi let out a sharp sigh. Just thinking about the mess Natalie had left behind her made her tired. Honestly! she'd had hardly a minute to spend on her real job, which was overseeing all the creative efforts. She ought to have been looking over layouts and consulting with group heads about concepts and seeing to it that the results of brainstorms got back to her right away for review. Instead, she'd had to spend all her time straightening out little things.

Why, even today she hadn't been able to settle down at her desk. She'd had to go into the test kitchen to read the riot act to Barbara Valentine. Oh, she knew Barbara was miffed. Of course, Barbara didn't dare say anything, but this was Bambi she was dealing with, not her old crony Natalie; and, whether she knew it or not, Bambi Hirsch was nobody's fool. She knew when she was being diddled. And she was not afraid to confront the situation. Well, if Barbara hadn't known it before, she knew it now, Bambi thought with satisfaction. The nerve! Bambi had asked her a very simple thing: a taste test for Archer Pudding's two new flavors, to see which one adults would like, since that had been Natalie's rather dumb idea: to sell pudding to adults, most of whom (it had said in her memo to the client) had loved pudding as children; so why not now? Well, she, Bambi, thought it was a dumb idea, but Peter had given her That Look and had said, "It's a *fine* idea, Bams. The client loves it, see? and that makes it a fabulous idea."

Well, anyway, fine or fabulous or lousy, she was stuck with it. You couldn't make everything right all at once, could you? So, she told Barbara to run a test of pina colada flavor against rum raisin. And Barbara had the gall to turn around and give an important job like that to her assistant. Why the girl couldn't be much over twenty-one years old. Sloppy and inefficient, that's what Bambi called it; and that's what she had just now told Barbara. And Barbara's lips had tightened and her cheeks had flamed and Bambi just knew she was dying to say something nasty. But too bad, she didn't dare, or she would be following her friend Natalie right out of here! She had to learn, just like all the others. You couldn't mess around with the new creative director!

Bambi began to hum happily as she rounded the corner and headed for the ladies' room. Gloria, the receptionist, was there, and gave her a respectful "Hello, Ms. Hirsch." At least she knew who was who and what was what. Well, she ought to; Peter had chosen her himself years ago.

She waited until Gloria left before taking out her cosmetic case. Underlings shouldn't see what she did. She started with her face, darkening the eyeliner and renewing the blusher and putting on fresh lipstick. The mascara was still okay, and her hair just needed fluffing up. There!

And now, for the most important thing. She took out the vial of perfume, the one Peter had given her because, he said, he loved the way it enhanced her own natural scent. *Madame* by Carven. She wasn't exactly crazy about it; it was a little heavy for her taste. She liked *Pavlova*. In fact, *Pavlova* had been her signature, and every other man had found it delicious. But if there was one thing you had to learn when Peter Marcus was your lover-man, it was that what he wanted had just better be what he got. If you didn't do it his way, it made him depressed and on edge. She, for one, wanted him happy. So good-bye *Pavlova* and hello *Madame*.

As she thought it, she dabbed it on all the places he liked to smell it: in her armpits, at the base of her throat, in the cleft between her breasts, on the insides of her thighs, at the backs of her knees, in the arch of her feet. As she rubbed the stopper here and here and here, she smiled to herself, anticipating her "meeting" with him in five minutes.

Oh, she knew her Peter! It would end up being what he liked to call a "special meeting," probably with her on her knees, adoring his body. Oh, she knew there were women who would denigrate this . . . women who would tell her she was demeaning herself. But she knew better. Loving her Peter's beautiful cock was *not* debasing, not a bit. She loved doing it for him. And she was a free spirit; her philosophy was anything goes in a truly loving relationship. Peter could have just as many special meetings as he wanted, and she would always be there for him . . . gladly. As a matter of fact, it was getting her a little hot right now, just imagining what was going to happen in just a few minutes. She winked at herself in the mirror and then held up her left hand, wiggling her fingers around so that the humungo diamond caught the light, fracturing into a thousand bright sparkling shards. She especially loved the way it threw rainbows onto the mirror. Five carats! Well, that was your reward when you were clever little Bambi Hirsch and knew how to handle a complex man like Peter. She deserved it.

And now she was ready. Down the hall she went, paused in front of Peter's suite, licked her lips, sucked in her tummy, and then marched in, pausing for a moment to say hello to Mary-Claire. You had to be nice to the little people. "As you were!" she sang after she'd asked about Mary-Claire's mother and her cat and her begonias. She knew how to get on Mary-Claire's good side, which you had to do or your messages never got to Peter and you weren't allowed in the door. Mary-Claire was entirely too possessive, and Bambi had told Peter that his secretary's behavior was just going to alienate everyone. But he just laughed and said, "Bams, she adores me! Every man needs at least one woman who thinks he's perfect! And as long as she feels that way, Bams, it'll take an atomic bomb to get her out of here." Every once in a while, Bambi got an image of Peter and Mary-Claire in a special meeting of their own, and it gave her heart a little lurch. She'd even asked him, once, but all he would say was, "Now, there's an idea!" and laughed and laughed. She hated when he laughed at her, even more than when he got that cold look and that hard voice.

Did Mary-Claire give her a strange little triumphant kind of smile today? Bambi took in a deep breath before she went into Peter's inner office. He'd called this meeting, and she knew he was going to tell her how pleased he was with her work so far. So to hell with Mary-Claire and her funny little smiles. They didn't mean a thing.

What counted was all the good things she'd done so far. Straightening up the mess in the test kitchen was only part of it. She'd given Natalie's accounts to Bob and so of course Renée's nose was all out of joint, but too bad. But she'd handled that one with style and grace. She'd taken Renée out for a very expensive lunch and had explained. "Clients like talking to *men*, Renée. I mean, you and I know that's nonsense, but . . ." And when Renée had said, "Really, Bambi? That's funny, because I had those accounts for two years before Bob was hired and they didn't object to talking with me then." Well, what could she say except, "I've made an executive decision and I guess, Renée dear, we're just going to have to live with it."

Only three weeks, and she'd really accomplished a great deal. All the group heads were now turning in their daily reports

. . . well, all but Martha Jones, of course. Oh, she handed one in for every day; but it was either late, or it was some kind of childish joke, or *something*. Well, what could you expect? She was another one of Natalie's little pets, so of course she'd *have* to try to sabotage the new director. Not that it would do her any good!

She opened the door and gave her beloved her very best smile.

"Come in and close the door. You're late." Something was wrong. But what?

"Only a couple of minutes—"

"Late is late. After you've worked here for a while, Ms. Hirsch, you will learn that when Mr. Marcus asks for a meeting at one o'clock, he means one o'clock and not a couple of minutes after . . . not even one minute after. Is that understood?"

"Yes, but—" Oh, dear, his face was set in his grimmest expression, and he had his hands splayed on the desktop, leaning forward, as if ready to attack. She knew how to soothe this beast. She moved toward him, allowing her hips to swing just a trifle, just enough, opening her mouth a little, and smiling, smiling, smiling. If she could just get close enough so he caught the scent of her perfume . . . if she could just get close enough for him to put his hand around her leg . . .

"What do you think you're doing?" Peter snapped, and she instantly came to a shocked halt. What was his *problem*? Every single workday since she'd come to M & M, he made an appointment with her, and always, he gave her a great big grin, and when he said to come in and close the door, it was in a very different voice. And every single day, he swiveled his chair around as she walked over and spread his legs and said, "Well, Ms. Hirsch, do you have anything for me?" And that was her signal. And every single day at about five after one, Peter Marcus got the blow job of his life. He said it just calmed him down for the rest of the day. So what was it? Bambi stood very still, thinking as fast as she could, trying to figure out what was on his mind.

"Sit down, sit down," he ordered. "I don't have all day. And I have a lot of things that you have to hear."

Well, at least now he'd get to the good stuff. He couldn't deny what she'd done for M & M already.

"Goddammit, Bambi, can't you do *anything* right?" What! She had already sat down; otherwise she'd probably have fallen.

"Whatever do you mean, Peter? What did I *do*?" Oh, if he was going to get into one of his crazy moods, she didn't know what she was going to do. When he got that way, almost anything could put him straight into a rage, and she just didn't want to have to deal with Peter in a rage.

"Do? Barbara Valentine has complained four times already. Evan has been telling anyone who will listen that you had a bloody nerve, telling him he didn't look right. I mean, Bambi, the man is our group head on men's wear! You cannot—"

"Oh, Peter, I only suggested he'd look wonderful in pleated trousers. I mean, my God, Peter, the man looks like something out of the fifties!"

"The clients happen to like the way Evan dresses *because* he's so conservative. And anyway, it's not your job to tell anyone in this agency how to look or act or behave. You've overstepped badly."

"Well, I'm sorry, Peter, I really am. I was only trying to help."

"And stop pouting. It's not professional. Your entire demeanor, in fact, has been a grave disappointment to me, Bambi. I expected the editor in chief of a publication to understand the subtleties of management." He held up a hand. "And there's more. Mary-Claire says you patronize her. And Eve Soloway is threatening to quit." His voice softened, but she could tell by the look on his face that his attitude hadn't. "Now, Bambi dear, tell me . . . what did you do or say to Eve Soloway, my most promising new account executive?"

"Eve? Eve? I don't remember anything . . . oh."

"Oh?"

"Well. I only made a little joke—about how often I come upon her, standing around and flirting with the men in the agency."

"Goddammit!" he thundered and banged his fist on the desk.

"Well. I only made a little joke—about company ink and

stuff. Well, Peter, I mean, every day after work, I'd see her at the Silver Streak with three or four of the account executives! Every day! I only told her it might be misunderstood, that's all."

"Dammit, don't you realize that's the way people who work together cement their relationships? They go out together after work! Goddammit, don't you know *anything* about business?"

She wanted to cry; oh, how she wanted to cry, but she wasn't going to. Not now she wasn't. "I'm sorry, Peter. I'm sorry I haven't pleased you. I tried."

"Well, you'd better shape up very quickly, my dear, or someone else will be in that office you've spent so much money redecorating."

Bambi stood up, her heart hammering in her chest, an empty sensation at the pit of her stomach. Why did he get like this, every once in a while? If everyone had been complaining about her, why didn't he tell her right away? It wasn't fair. In fact, it was mean.

And in fact, there was that little gleam in his eye and just the tiniest quirk of a smile. Oh, yes, he was pleased as punch to make her feel bad. She ought to take off that diamond and throw it at him. She ought to turn right around and walk out of there. And she would, only she understood him so well. He lost his mother at such a young age, he really was a dummy when it came to women. He just didn't know what to do with them. What could you expect? He was scared to death of their intimacy, poor darling. Well, he wasn't dealing with just any lady; he was dealing with Bambi Hirsch!

Now she was her old self again. She gave him a demure smile. "I'll be good, Peter. You know I'm your good good girl. And I have a lovely present for you . . . if you'll only let me come over there and give it to you."

His face didn't change, but an eyelid twitched and after a moment, he said, "Well . . . maybe."

"Shall I come over there and show you what I mean?" Her voice had deepened and softened, and from here, she could hear him swallowing. He was turned on, yes, he was, and now he had crooked a finger and was gesturing her to come to him.

Bambi smiled as relief washed over her. One of her worst dreams was that, one day, Peter would suddenly decide in that way he had that it was all over. Before he married her. Every once in a while, she let her mind drift to that horrible thought, and she could imagine him just turning totally away from her, telling her to get lost, to get out. And she would turn absolutely cold. It mustn't happen, it mustn't!

Well, as long as she took care of all his needs, she thought, crawling over to him, watching as the heat rose in his face, yes, as long as she satisfied his deepest wishes, he would remain forever her darling boy.

❀ 32 ❀

Bob's Bar, Labor Day Weekend

By now, the wind had already risen and was blowing fast and fitfully, pulling up sand and saltwater and bits of trash and flinging them against the sides of houses and into people's faces. In spite of this, there were quite a few people out, in Paradise, all heading in the same direction, toward the bay, where the normally still water was churning and frothing in agitation. Above, the clouds had thickened and darkened steadily since early in the morning; and now the sky was a strange yellowish black, casting a weird other-worldly light below. Behind this solid wall of cloud were ominous rumblings and flickers of lightning that skittered silently across the sky. Flocks of gulls screamed as the wind blew them about.

Natalie, bent against the stinging wind, rounded the corner to the entrance of Bob's Bar and, with relief, flung the door open. It slammed behind her, as if pushed by an unseen and angry hand. Now she lifted her head, spitting a few grains of sand from between her lips, letting the rain poncho slide off her shoulders.

"You often have tropical days like this?" she called out; and Irving laughed. "Always in September," he answered. "In Paradise, we like to end the season with a bang." And, right on cue, there was a clap of thunder outside.

Now everyone in the room laughed—rather nervously, Natalie thought. She looked around. Noontime and the place was packed. Well, signs were up all over the place that anyone who didn't feel wind- and water-tight in their house should come here for the duration of the storm. Those who needed instruction on how to prepare for a hurricane were to come also. And, an hour ago, the local Long Island radio station announced that the hurricane watch had just changed to a hurricane warning . . . and that meant that the storm was *sure* to affect Fire Island. That's what had sent Natalie out of her bed and out of her house, after first taping the big glass sliding doors.

Sandy had told her to do that, and he had also told her to come to his house. "You're too close to the ocean," he warned her. "In the hurricane of '38, a whole oceanside street in Beach Haven was carried off to sea, houses, wagons, pots and pans, everything. On Fire Island, darling Natalie, we take our hurricanes seriously."

Well, all right, she'd go to his house eventually. She almost had to. She hadn't yet given him an answer to his proposal; and in fact, after two weeks of trying to sort it all out, she had found herself unwilling even to think about it. She had avoided him quite a bit, dreading another encounter. She had to admit that, when it came to her relationship with Sandy Lovall, she was conflicted. To put it mildly. What she did was bury herself in work. God knows, she had enough of that, at least for a while, between Sandy and Selma. Speaking of whom, she was out this weekend and staying with him and what a weird threesome *that* would make!

A voice from the bar called, "Come on over, Nat, and I'll buy you a drink."

"I don't—" she started and then she realized who it was. It was Carl, that bastard. Why hadn't he called her to say he'd be out? Why hadn't he called her *period*? It had been nearly two weeks since she'd spoken to him at all; and the last time he did call, it was from a pay phone at the airport. Their so-called relationship, apparently, was to be a series of good-byes. Oh, hell, she shouldn't even care. She was about to be somebody's intended . . . maybe.

He patted the stool next to him, so she went and sat down. It wouldn't hurt to sit next to him. And maybe to get an explanation of why he hadn't answered her last message on his machine.

"So how are you doing? Still unemployed?" The rat wasn't even going to mention her message, which she had thought mighty clever.

"I'm freelancing . . . and trying to decide whether or not to accept a proposal of marriage." Let's see what he did with that!

"Are you going to? Accept it." Ball right into her court. Damn these men with their poker faces! Did it or did it not bother him?

"I don't know . . . yes . . . no . . . maybe . . ." She stopped, and Carl laughed, but he also looked relieved and it wasn't her imagination, either.

"A woman who knows her own mind, I see." He was right. She was uncharacteristically of two minds about Sandy.

The other night, she'd written a pro list and a con list and she'd been all set: The answer was "No, thank you very much." And then, Martha J called. "Come on, Nat," she said, her voice aquiver with excitement. "Say you'll come in. It's really gonna happen, it really is! I've got two clients, and there are two more I've talked to who say they'll give us a try if you're there. Lady, it's a GO, that's what it is!"

Instantly, Natalie's head had begun to whirl with pictures of herself back in the city, back with Martha J, back at work. Oh, God, it would be wonderful! Her mouth fairly watered at the thought of it.

Weakly, she had protested: "Rent for office space is sky-high, Martha J." But she got back a cackle of delight. "Oh, no! I found us a bargain, a beautiful office for us. It's called Calvin's den and the two maid's rooms. I'm not kidding . . . we're really set! So how about it?"

Natalie's heart had beat wildly against her ribs. Did she want to do it? More than anything!

Wasn't it every career woman's dream? To be free of the condescension of men, to be free of the constraints of trying to act like a man, to be free of the complaints you got when you did act like a man? Of course it was. What a strain on women, always to be working in what was a man's world, always to have to second-guess what was expected. If you were soft and gentle and "feminine," you obviously didn't have a brain in your head and you certainly weren't behaving professionally. If you were tough and aggressive and smart, you were a ballbuster.

Oh, hell, it was so true, it was trite. It wasn't even worth listing in her head yet again, all her grievances. It was the system and that was that.

But here was her way out! A business where all the bosses were herself. Dammit, there was no other way to free herself. Beginning with her father, her life was just one long list of men who had felt it their God-given right to lord it over her, give her orders and criticize her behavior. Old Man Marcus . . . Jerry . . . Jake . . . Paul Hasahni . . . Tommy Thoms . . . Jeff . . . Peter—all of them! Including every client, every salesman, every goddamn office boy who thought it was only natural to give her a pinch or a pat or a proposition!

And dammit, wouldn't she just be flat out of money. That's the only thing in the way: cash. Damn Jerry for never making her save. Oh, hell, it wasn't his fault. Poor Jerry, always taking the rap—she was a spender, always had been. She'd always figured she'd never run out of money just as long as she could work. She never figured she'd need so much money. Hell, she'd never thought she'd ever be out of work!

"Look," she finally said to Martha J, "I want to, you have no idea how badly I want to . . . Can you give me another week?"

"Okay, one more week. But, Nat . . . listen. Tell me now if you think it'll be no. Because I don't think I can face it alone."

"I'm going to move heaven and earth to make it a yes, Martha J. It's really what I want."

Now she said, to Carl: "Oh, I know what I want, all right. I want a guy who answers when I leave a message on his machine."

"Oh, yeah? And I want a lady who's home from time to time, when I call to answer her message."

"Oh. You called?" She sipped her Perrier.

"Natalie, I never figured you to be the kind of woman who gets miffed if a guy can't call. I mean, you're a professional yourself; you know what goes on. If you don't hear from me, so you call again. Am I right?"

She sighed. "Of course you're right. But in this case ... well, there's a little echo in my head, the memory of Peter saying, 'What would Carl Stern want with an old babe like you?'"

"You know the answer to that one: Anything I can get!"

"Well, for starters, you could get dinner this evening. I might even cook."

"You can't mean *here*."

"Remember? I'm living here now ... well, for the duration or the end of September, whichever comes sooner. Of course I mean here."

"What about Hurricane Harry?"

"My windows are taped and my battery-powered radio is at the ready and here I am, awaiting my final instructions." And then her voice dribbled out. This was not, she thought, the appropriate moment to tell him that she would then go to Sandy's because Sandy thought she was his bride-to-be. So she just added, in a brave voice: "I'm staying. This silly hurricane doesn't scare *me*."

"Well, it sure as hell can scare me. I'm scared that if I don't leave now, I'll miss the two meetings I have scheduled for this weekend back in the city."

Natalie made a face. Dammit, again a good-bye. "Do you always work weekends?"

"Usually. Although I might change my ways if I had a real good reason." He ran one finger down the side of her arm, sending a series of little chills right through her.

"Don't start with me, bud," she said, flip as she could be, "not when you don't plan to hang around."

"Next time."

"Sure. Next time."

"Hey." He put a finger under her chin and gently turned her head to face him. Dammit, she didn't want to melt. And then he put his firm lips over hers and she melted. "Talk to you soon," he said and was gone. Dammit.

No sooner had the door slammed with a fury behind him

than it opened again, letting in the eerie glare from outside. It was a yellowish gray world out there, with a hard wind blowing howling around the buildings and whipping the bay into a frenzy of choppy whitecaps. And blowing in with it, or so it seemed, was a short figure wrapped in a voluminous shiny black raincoat. Bang! and the door once again slammed closed. Natalie felt a little jolt. It was Bambi. This was actually the first time she'd seen the little bitch since she'd been handed Natalie's job. She and Peter had been out here, all right. But the pair of them had kept their distance . . . and a damn good thing, too.

But now, here she was, little as life. And now, here she came, right over. With a smile! And with her hand outstretched! Swiftly, Natalie decided unh-unh, no make believe! She was damned if she would shake the hand that had bit her.

Apparently something showed in her face, because Bambi had dropped her hand by the time she reached the bar. The smile, however, the smug, social smile was fixed firmly in place.

"I'm glad you're here, Natalie. I've been wanting to talk to you."

"Why?"

"Oh, dear . . . I was hoping you wouldn't feel that way. I only wanted to say no hard feelings."

"Well, I *have* hard feelings, so you don't have to bother." She started to turn away, but Bambi was nothing if not persistent.

"Natalie, I wish you could be more mature about this. I know you have a long history at M & M and that it must hurt, not being there any more—"

"Actually, Bambi," Natalie interrupted, "it feels wonderful. As you undoubtedly know from experience, Peter is not easy to deal with." She smiled as she watched Bambi struggle to answer that one in a way that would not reveal anything. She couldn't, and after a moment or two, Natalie decided to let her off the hook. "Anyway, I couldn't care less about the *job*," she went on, her voice carefully even. "No, Bambi, it's having my personal life smeared all across the pages of that two-bit newsletter of yours . . . *that's* what I couldn't stand and that's why

I really don't care to continue this conversation—or any other conversation with you, for that matter."

"Everything I printed was true!" Bambi flared. "I can't help it if the truth hurts! I mean"—she flashed a cruel little smile at Natalie—"I wasn't going to say this but . . . I mean, Natalie, here it is, just past noon, and where are you? At the bar, and with a drink. I mean . . ."

The nasty little monster! "For your information," Natalie said, "you stupid little bitch, this drink is sparkling water. . . . And here's the proof!" And she flung it right into Bambi's face.

Bambi spluttered, startled and swearing. "You'll pay for this!" she promised. And away she flounced.

Go print *that* in your stupid newsletter, Natalie thought. For about two minutes she felt real good, triumphant almost. And then it faded and once again, she was left with the feeling that she was all alone. She sneaked a look across the room to where Barbara and Ben were seated, shoulder to shoulder, probably holding hands. She really missed Barbara. If they were speaking to each other, she could discuss all of it with Barbara. Honestly. Completely. She could talk about her fears at being alone. She could discuss the deal with Martha J. She could ask her advice about Sandy Lovall—and most important, she could tell Barbara, in as much detail as she liked, exactly what had transpired. Or not transpired. She could bitch about Bambi and cry about Carl. She could brag about staying on the wagon and admit how often she wanted to fall off. She could be totally herself. God, what a luxury that was!

Suddenly Barbara's eyes lifted and met hers. Calmly, Natalie thought. Without hostility. Not real warmth, but without anger, either. Maybe, she thought, just maybe her dreadful words need not hang forever between them, palpable. Maybe, just maybe the time was approaching when Barbara and she could sit down and talk it out and maybe just maybe make it better.

Barbara watched Natalie stride away from the bar and thread her way through the packed tables. She was looking good: fit and healthy and alert. Martha J had mentioned that she was on the wagon and it suited her just fine.

She missed Natalie, missed her at the office and missed having that nice, close, tell-her-anything-at-all relationship. She had been devastated, absolutely destroyed, when Nat blurted out about sleeping with Mark. She had wanted to murder Natalie right then and there. But she'd had time now, time to think it out and talk it out with Ben and really, if she was going to be furious with anyone, hadn't she better be furious with Mark? Of course, Natalie had been a party to it, but it had happened years ago, it was ancient history now, and even though she'd never again feel exactly the same way about her friend, well ... Maybe it was time to at least discuss it with her, see if they could salvage something. She just wasn't sure she could do it. Somewhere inside her, it still hurt.

And now the sheriff was banging a glass on the bar to get everyone's attention. It took a minute or two for the place to quiet down, and as soon as the murmur of voices had ceased, they could all hear very clearly the sounds of the growing storm outside and there was a little ripple of fright through the room.

"Now then," the sheriff said. "Before the winds get too strong and nobody is able to leave, I'm going to run down what everyone should have. One: a battery-powered radio. If you don't have one, go to a house that does. Two: a flashlight. Candles. Anyone here doesn't have candles, we're handing them out, two to a customer. Same with batteries for your flashlight.

"Okay? Now. Here's what you should have done in your house. One: tape the windows, an X is the most efficient."

Barbara let her mind drift. She didn't have to listen. Ben had lived out here his whole life and knew exactly what to do, and she, thank heavens, was with Ben. Her eyes roamed the room, and she was fascinated by the wide variety of expressions on the upturned rapt faces. It was fascinating, too, to realize that she recognized quite a few of those faces. If she married Ben, she'd probably get to know even more. Stop that! she ordered herself. You're not going to think about geting married again, not for a while, remember?

She went back to people watching. The locals, she noted, were almost to a man and woman, serious and concerned; whereas the summer people seemed excited more than anything else. She'd be willing to bet any amount of money that you could sell tickets to New Yorkers to come out to the island and see a hurricane in full force and they'd pay.

And her eyes lit on Sandy Lovall, sitting up front at his usual table, Natalie on one side of him and Selma, resplendent today in a Day-Glow pink raincape, on the other. When did Sandy come in? She must have missed it. Honestly, it was enough to make you laugh, to see the three of them. Sandy's arm was flung across the back of Nat's chair and his finger rested in a proprietary way on her shoulder. As she looked, Natalie's lips tightened and she made a sharp movement, shrugging off his touch. She quickly bent over, as if to tie a shoelace or something; but Barbara recognized that move. God, she ought to; she'd seen Nat do it often enough, with Jerry. Natalie did not want that arm around her and did not want that person touching her. That's what that was all about and Barbara knew it as a certainty.

Well, hadn't she warned Nat? Hadn't she pointed out that Sandy Lovall was just another Jerry? Soft, mushy, baby men totally turned *her* off. She liked them lean and muscular, demanding and cool. And now that she thought of *that*, was that so wonderful? Should she be proud of herself? Look what she'd done with her great taste in men. They were all the same: handsome, clever, athletic, sure of themselves, in charge. It was her preference, but was it *good* for her? She really had to think about it, and think seriously. All very well to be crazy about Ben DeLuria. But he was the exact same type.

As she turned to look at him, to check it out again, to see that rugged face, he raised his hand and boomed out, "I have one of the largest, most solidly built houses in Paradise, on high ground. Anyone who doesn't feel safe is welcome to wait out the storm there."

Immediately there was movement at Sandy's table and he was on his feet. "As you all know, I live in the original Lovall house," he said, "which is *actually* the largest house in Paradise." He made a mock bow. "With all due apologies to my brother."

There was a scatter of applause and catcalls and boos and laughter, and a couple of shouts of "Siddown, Sandy!" The sheriff banged his fist on the bar and called for order.

"Listen, everyone," he thundered. "If you follow all precautions, you should all be able to stay in your *own* houses," and he once again went through the rules of hurricane safety.

Barbara couldn't help but notice that as the minutes went by, he had to raise his voice more and more. The wind was howling like three hundred lost souls out there, and she suddenly wanted out. Apparently a whole group of people were electing to stay right here, but she, for one, hated the way the walls shuddered and the heavy shutters rattled.

"Okay, folks, I've got my own house to check in on. Don't be foolhardy and we'll all be just fine!"

There was a surge of movement during the last phrase, and quickly groups began to move out, everyone leaning heavily against the door to keep it open for the people behind them.

Ben and Barbara were in the middle of the crush; Barbara had thought she might ask Natalie where she would be staying ... maybe ask her if she'd like to come with them ... but she only caught a glimpse of Nat talking animatedly with Fred and then they were lost in the crowd.

It was now dark and beginning to spit rain. Barbara shivered and Ben's arm tightened around her. Thank God for him!

As they staggered against the wind, a rain-soaked boy on a bike came careening around the corner. He let the bike just fall to the ground, leaping nimbly away from it.

"Last boat, folks! Last ferry for the mainland!"

❀ 33 ❀

Hurricane Harry

"I just love this kind of weather!" Natalie shouted, grabbing onto her deck rail. Her hair whipped around, stinging her cheeks. The wind, heavily laden with saltwater, was blowing wildly now and the sky was a glowering charcoal gray.

"Me, too!" Fred's face was all but hidden under the hood of his poncho, but his voice mirrored her exhilaration. "It's exciting when it gets wild like this! Except, of course, if you're out there in a small sloop...then it's a little *too* exciting." They both laughed; and Natalie quipped, "Nothing can be *too* exciting, as far as I'm concerned, Freddie!"

Fred grasped her upper arm and leaned in toward her. "Yes, I've noticed that about you. You're a gal who craves excitement, aren't you?"

There was a smoky note in his voice that she immediately recognized. Well, well! Fred Nextdoor, who had maintained a careful distance since their one date early this summer. Coming on to her now? It must be the electricity in the air, charging him up. She found it charming...why the hell not? Carl Stern certainly found it very easy to turn his back on her and go off! The more she thought about it, the madder she got. He was just a big tease, making with the boyish charm and then taking off.

"I like to *make* excitement," she said to Fred, letting herself lean a little into him. Her heartbeat was quickening with the delight of the mating dance. It had been quite a while and really, he was a cute guy. She had thought so when she first met him. *He* was the one who had lost interest!

"And *I* like to make excitement, too." Now he was definitely coming on to her. They were moving closer and closer to each other, and in a minute, he'd be kissing her, she just knew it.

"You had your chance in June, remember?"

"I regretted that. But . . . well, Joanna came back—we'd been together for three years and apart for three months—and . . . well, we decided to give it another try."

"So where's Joanna now?"

"Out of town," he murmured, bending his lips to hers, and speaking against them. "Isn't that nice? And isn't *this* nice?" And then he *was* kissing her; he had a nice mouth and an even nicer tongue and knew how to use them. Her response was, as always, immediate. He lifted his head to say, "So? How about it?"

Well, it was ridiculous to stand outside in a gale, smooching, so they went inside and without a word, both began to strip.

He was eager, he was well built, and he knew all the right moves. His hands and his tongue were busy on her, and Natalie lay on the couch, absolutely unmoved. She was stunned by her own lack of response to an avid, young, erect, uninhibited male. What was happening to her? She faked some moans, but somehow, she couldn't get into it, not at all, as he expertly made love to her. It was awful. He sucked her and licked her and kissed her and caressed her and all she could think was, When will he ever finish?

Was it because she was stone cold sober? Had all her casual amorous adventures been lubricated by liberal doses of booze? Maybe her intense sexuality had been an eighty-proof illusion. But there was Carl. There *was* Carl, wasn't there? Yes. And she had made love with *him* sober. Maybe her days of falling into bed with whomever, at a moment's whim, maybe those days were gone.

In the meantime, her feet were freezing, her butt was getting rubbed raw by the coarse fabric on the couch, and she was totally bored with the whole thing. God, would he never come?

At last. He collapsed onto her, breathing little endearments into her ear, prepared, it seemed, to spend the next hour with her. Well, he could just think again.

"Fred, I'm getting nervous," she said.

He lifted his head, smiling at her. "That's what you say to a guy who just did his damnedest?"

She kissed two fingers and held them to his lips. "You did swell, Freddie, but in case you forgot, there's somebody named Harry on the way and from the sounds of the rattling windows, I'd say he's due any minute now. No kidding, Fred, it was real nice, but Sandy's expecting me and frankly, I don't think it's safe this close to the ocean."

He lifted himself up and peered out the sliding glass doors. "Jesus," he said. "You are so right. Do you think Sandy would mind if I came, too?"

It wasn't her favorite idea, but how could she say no? He might get killed down here. She didn't want to deal with him at all now. She felt grubby. Why the hell did she have such round heels, anyway? What had made her think she wanted to fuck him? And why did she feel nothing? It frightened her.

There was quite a crowd in Sandy's studio, all in a holiday mood. Why was everyone so exuberant? Only Annie was nervous, prowling back and forth.

"Isn't anyone scared around here?" Natalie demanded as she and Fred came in. It got a laugh and Margie said, "Hell, no, we natives are used to it. This is just another one of our friendly hurricanes!"

And someone else added, "And we're drinking to it!" More laughter. There was a flurry of hello's to Margie and Selma and a few other of the locals. "Where's Jay?" Sandy asked Fred as he draped a casual arm across Natalie's shoulder.

"On a business trip. I'm here all alone for the Labor Day weekend."

"Well, there's the food and there's a drink. Sally has just introduced us all to the tequila bullshot. You wouldn't believe how smoothly it goes down."

"I will once I try it." And Fred was gone to the bar. Had Sandy's possessive gesture sent him away? Natalie wondered. Or was he as relieved to be able to leave her as she was to see him go?

"Come, darling," Sandy said. "I'll make you a drink. It really is unbelievably good."

"I am ready," she said sweetly, "to believe anything. I'll even believe seven impossible things before Hurricane Harry. But I don't drink, remember?"

He had already steered her to the bar and was beginning to mix two drinks. "Oh, Natalie. You do have a tendency to dramatize."

Tightly, she said, "I'm an alcoholic."

"Oh, you're not, either! I've known plenty of alkies and you're nothing like! So stop it. I don't know who talked you into that."

"Sandy. Quit it. I'm an alcoholic. It's the first thing, after your name, that you have to admit, when you join AA. Believe me, it sticks in the throat." She spoke very earnestly, as if by her tone of voice she could convince him of the truth of her words.

"I've never seen you drunk. Come on. This is a very light drink."

"Dammit, Sandy, if admitting you're an alcoholic is the toughest thing to do, then the next toughest is having to fight off people who keep forcing booze on you."

"What's the problem?" Margie, who had just walked up for a refill, asked. "Don't like liquor in your soup? Me, neither. Sandy, you can't force what you like on everyone."

"I'm not forcing, Margie. But this darling girl here has been sold a bill of goods. She's been on the wagon for a couple of weeks and okay, why not, but she doesn't *need* it. She's no drunk. Look at her. Does that look like a drunk?"

Once again, he slung his arm across her shoulders. It weighed a ton. How dare this man condescend to her? How dare he not believe her? He was unwilling to allow her her own existence; she had to do and be what *he* wanted, or else! She looked down at the floor because she couldn't bear to look at him, at that soft, smug, sure-of-itself face.

Through her teeth, she said, "I'll have plain tonic, please, with a slice of lime." And lucky for Sandy, Margie just butted in—the woman was no fool, she probably sensed trouble brewing—and in a bright voice said, "I'll make that for you, Nat. Sandy, your presence is required across the room. Selma has your stuff all set up. Go on now, Sandy, shoo!" Natalie could have hugged her, tight corset and all.

Now she noticed the easel in front of the huge window wall. Sandy had seated himself, and everyone was gathering around as he prepared to paint. Holding her tonic, Natalie drifted over to look out the window.

"Whitecaps on the pond!" she murmured. "Jesus!" And someone said, "That's Mother Nature" and someone else quipped, "running amok!" and then there was a discussion about whether one person could run amok; or whether it had to be a crowd.

"Lord, I had forgotten how fathinating it could be," Selma remarked. "It'th tho long thinth the latht hurricane. How many yearth, Thandy?"

"Five, I think . . . and that one veered away at the last minute."

Natalie laughed a little. "You sound as if you were disappointed."

"I was! Believe me, I was!" He was busy putting blobs of paint on his palette, looking up every few seconds to check the scene. "You've no idea how long I've been waiting for a really good storm. The last time I was all set up. I'd even called the gallery to tell them they'd be getting a Lovall Hurricane Series . . . And then, the damn storm decided to go out to sea! Well, that's not going to happen this time!

"*This* time," he went on, "I'm going to *get* my hurricane. Annie, over here!" The dog, quivering but obedient, hunkered down, leaning against her master's leg.

Natalie gazed out the window, staring half in fascination and half in fear at the wildness of the scene. The sky was now the color of a bruise, bluish gray with purple overtones, and it cast an eerie dim light. "Like the end of the world, ithn't it?" Selma said. The wind was howling louder and louder, and now there were branches and leaves and scraps of paper flying about. And now the gulls, swept here and there in the darkness, were screaming. Like the end of the world? Yes. The walls of Sandy's big substantial house were shuddering as each gust slammed against them. She said a silent prayer to the gods of the winds that her poor little house not be blown over, please.

"I'm grateful for Mr. Edison and his electricity," she said aloud. "The light makes me feel . . . I don't know, safe somehow." And, as if by signal, the lights all went out suddenly, and they were plunged into a weird half-darkness that was colored yellow and violet. Sandy, on his stool by the big window with its huge Xs of tape, swore and shouted, "The oil lamp, Sel!"

But the big woman had already started to move and in a moment, there was a faint pool of golden light on the coffee table. And then she lit the other lamps and other candles. Natalie stood where she was, feeling disoriented and stupid. Also superfluous. Hell, Sandy was so intent on his art, and when there was a problem, he called for Selma. So that's what he needs me for! she thought. To run around and wait on him.

She eyed him, sitting there, all his energy focused and directed to Mother Nature's extravaganza out there. Could she live with that . . . with *him*? God, she was tired of thinking about it. Then Fred called her from the other end of the room, where a profusion of finger foods had been laid out, and so she went over there and let him serve her a celery rib filled with cheese and a slender slice of pâté.

"Come on and be my partner in Trivial Pursuit," he said; but a game didn't appeal to her right now. And anyway, it seemed to her that throwing a party while a storm raged outside was enough of a trivial pursuit.

She was standing there alone, looking at the array of food and wondering why she had no appetite, when Selma walked over.

She gazed at the spread and sighed noisily. "It lookth tho good. I really shouldn't. But"—she giggled—"ath we damn well know, I *will*." And she helped herself to a handful of cashews and raisins. Swallowing a mouthful, she turned to Natalie and said, "Oh, Nat, your brochure . . . The printer thent over the proofth the other day. Beautiful! Thimply beautiful! You're tho talented."

"Thank you. I need those kind words."

"You're a very nithe perthon, Nat. I'm very fond of you. Ath ith Thandy . . . but you know that." She laughed.

"He's very nice."

Selma turned to stare at her. It was hard to read her expression; the oil lamp on the table cast deep inky shadows. She was a shimmering hot-pink bulk, redolent of musk and flowers. At last, she said in a low voice, "Thandy tellth me he wanth to marry you."

"Yes."

"Tho?"

"So? So . . . I don't know, Selma. Look. How long have we known each other? A couple of months, that's all. How can we possibly know we want to spend the rest of our lives together?"

"Well . . . if it maketh you feel any better, he propothed to *me* after ten *dayth* . . . although we didn't actually get married for two yearth. And the reathon we thplit . . ."

Hastily Natalie said, "Oh, please, Selma, I don't need to know."

Selma frowned. "I thee," she said. "He'th thtill . . . you know, the thame. Too bad."

Natalie was startled. She hadn't thought of this big soft shape as sexual. She stared at Selma, who laughed and said, "Yeth, even a very fat lady can do it, Nat. And like it. And need it. And want it."

"I didn't mean—"

"Of courth you meant. It'th okay. I'm uthed to it." She embraced Natalie. No wonder, she thought, so many men go for fat women. What comfort, it's like being in the middle of a cloud . . . or a featherbed. She hugged Selma back, as well as she could, considering her arms wouldn't go all the way around, thinking, So he's *always* been that way! Can I deal with it on a permanent basis? Do I *want* to?

"Oh, I hope you decide yeth," Selma said, releasing her. "It would be tho nithe to have you in the family."

Natalie thought, Why do we think of fat people as not quite human? I've been thinking of her as a big soft doll without any real depth or any real feelings.

Then, "Lithen to that thunder," Selma said in an entirely different tone. "Thoundth like a lion growling in hith throat, getting ready to thpring."

And from the window, where he was working feverishly, Sandy called out, "Oh, God, Selma, I love it when you get poetic. Nat, I've told that woman time and again that she ought to write. Now, aren't I correct? Shouldn't she?"

"And put me put of a job?" Natalie shot back. "Not on your life!"

The wind now shrieked like a banshee, and every gust hit the house like a bulldozer, shaking it so she could hardly walk across the room. Nervously Natalie said, "Are you sure we're safe up here? I mean . . . what if the window breaks?"

"The window will not break. Don't worry, Natalie. Selma and I have been through many a storm out here, haven't we, sugar cube?"

"Oh yeth . . . but I don't remember any tho violent."

"Oh, yes, you do. Come *on*, Selma!" He never put the brush down for a single instant; nor did he turn his head from the window, just kept talking as he painted. "Look, if any of you people want to go downstairs and hide out, be my guest. But I think that would be silly. It's absolutely gorgeous out there, gorgeous! Look, look!"

"I'm looking. I'm looking," Natalie said, coming to stand behind the easel. All the sea grasses near the pond were flattened out by a slanting curtain of rain. The window was flooded with water, coursing in thick rivers; and when Natalie said "Oh, Christ," it made Sandy laugh. "City kid!" he twitted her. "You'll get used to it after you're here a couple of years!"

He had turned his head to give her a reassuring smile, so he wasn't looking—as she was—when the rain thickened into a great gray force. With a sound like the sky ripping apart, it slammed against the window. As she watched, a huge pile of lumber down below was picked up and flung about like so many pick-up sticks. "Sandy!" she cried, but he had already turned to look. Now the wind grew in fury, shrieking and roaring like a giant animal. And then she gasped involuntarily, as it all fell apart, all of the framework for Peter's house. It was like watching a silent explosion as it all went spinning out into the air. In split-seconds, there was nothing left but the foundation. Now the sky darkened swiftly, and the world was plunged into darkness.

"Oh, my God!" Margie cried from across the room. "Just like in '38!" And Natalie called to her, "Do you think my poor little house is safe?" and Margie came over, saying, "That's a sturdy little building, and it's dug into the dune. So you have a good chance."

Now everyone had left whatever they had been doing, to gather around at the window, doing their best to reassure each other.

"Don't worry about your house, Natalie. Your house will be just fine. You're safe; that's the important thing. It's a magnificent storm. Enjoy it, why don't you?" said Sandy.

"Enjoy? That's not exactly the word I would choose," Natalie said; and there was a murmur of agreement from the others.

"I, for one," Fred said, "am scared out of my gourd. Hey, I'm used to the big city! Frankly, Sandy, I don't know how you can just sit there and paint. It reminds me of Madame LaFarge knitting while everyone got their heads chopped off."

Sandy laughed. He was obviously enjoying his superior stance. "Everyone calm down. We're going into the eye right now."

And sure enough, the inkiness was giving way to a dark gray which lightened minute by minute as the wind calmed. In a little while, there was nothing left of that elemental force, just a drizzle and some tatters of dark cloud scuttering through the sky. And, amazingly, two figures swathed in raincoats, scurrying around.

"There's Bambi," Fred remarked. "Undoubtedly dramatizing this into a personal blow from the gods upon her beloved."

Of course. Bambi. "And Peter," Natalie said aloud, at which Sandy gave a chortle that could only be described as triumphant.

"At last!" he gloated. "That little twerp gets his comeuppance! That'll bring his price down, right, Margie?"

"What price?" Natalie said. "You mean he's selling?"

"Not yet! But he will! He didn't figure on Sandy Lovall! Ha! I knew if I held it up long enough . . . And now here comes good old Hurricane Harry to help me out. That modern monstrosity was never meant to be! And this just proves it!"

"Sandy! That's nonsense! A hurricane is an Act of God!"

"Precisely!"

He couldn't be trying to say that God was on his side, could he? Yes, she decided, he could.

"Your delight is somewhat unbecoming," she ventured.

He just laughed again and said, "But justified. That man has put me through hell this summer."

"And how about the hell he's going through now?" She didn't wait for a response, just went for her raingear.

"I, for one, am going to go down there and at least offer my sympathy," said Fred.

"You and me both."

In the end, they all went, even Sandy, who tried in vain to hide a self-satisfied smile.

❀ 34 ❀

Peter

Bambi held tightly onto Peter as they inched their way through the debris, wishing he hadn't insisted they come down here. Something was wrong with him, something was badly wrong, and she didn't know what it was. All she knew was that it was scaring her; it was making her heart beat so fast, it hurt.

He was sick . . . or something. Since yesterday, he'd been sweating and vomiting and he could hardly talk most of the time, he was so out of breath. He shouldn't be out in this weather! He'd catch pneumonia. But when she said he should stay in, he told her to shut up. And when she insisted that at least he ought to see a doctor, he got absolutely furious and yelled at her and then had to lean back to catch his breath; and he looked so dreadful, so drawn, that she hadn't said another word.

She wished, though, that he'd let her take care of him. She wished he wouldn't attack her when she tried to help him. But, face it, that was Peter: man of many moods. Actually, she was getting better and better at figuring them out in advance.

He was limping a little now and that made her even more worried; that and the lack of color of his skin, just awful. His face was slick with sweat and rain, and he kept making these little moans all the time. Well, poor Peter, she couldn't blame him for feeling sick. The scene was sick-making: everything gone, every last bit of what they'd built. Just totally wrecked and all the lumber splintered into pieces. All that money, down the rathole! He kept muttering "Fuck! Fuck!" and then breathing hard, and every time he had to rest against her, he felt heavier.

If there was anything Peter didn't need, it was a whole troupe of spectators. But they came anyway, a whole gang down from Sandy Lovall's house, gathering like vultures on a corpse.

Natalie among them! The nerve, coming down here to enjoy Peter's misfortune! She thought he would blast Natalie, at least tell her to get out. But when she said hello, he nodded.

"Can't you say hello to me, at least, Peter? I did come down here to see if you needed help!"

Bambi glared at her. Just look at her, like a tough little boy—nothing feminine or soft about Nat Simon!—her hands fisted, challenging him, yelling at him. Didn't she realize he wasn't feeling himself? A fool could see it!

But he didn't argue with Natalie. Bambi couldn't believe it. She could feel the muscles in his arm where she held onto him getting all tight and tense. But not a word. Well, she knew her Peter, and Natalie would not escape his wrath forever. Even now, out of work and down on her luck, she was still a showoff, lording it all over everyone. Just who did she think she was?

Well, if Peter wasn't going to answer her, *she* would. "This isn't your property, Nat Simon," she said. "In fact, you're trespassing."

"Hush!" Peter's voice sounded tight and choked and once again, that feeling of dread filled her stomach. She'd just love to tell that wiseass Nat Simon that he'd been faint and nauseated for the last two days; that he'd been lying there, fighting the sick feeling, all through the storm; that he'd dragged himself up, saying, "I already feel better, much better" because he was brave and strong; and that she had a hell of a nerve, coming down here and attacking him.

Bambi had argued with him about taking that long walk to his property, but he had told her she was stupid. He wouldn't talk that way to her unless he was sick! "As soon as this feeling passes, I'll be fine, Bams. It's just a bad bug." Well, she didn't know about that. At first, he had thought it was indigestion, insisted it was indigestion. She couldn't understand that: They'd had the same food. It occurred to him, too, and he turned on her. "We ate the same meals. How come *you're* not sick?" he said, and turned his head away, as if she'd done it deliberately and should be punished for not being sick, too.

Now, though, he wasn't mad at her. He leaned on her, really leaned. "What do you want from my life, Nat?" Even his voice seemed weak.

And then that nasty Sandy Lovall came over, laughing and saying, "Well, Marcus, now you're really up shit creek, aren't you?"

Peter made a strangled little sound in his throat and turned even paler; but he didn't answer.

"You're going to have to start from square one. And did you notice? All of the drained areas have filled up again!"

"Fuck off," Peter whispered and at the same time, Margie hissed, "Sandy! Now's not the time. Can't you see the man's suffering?"

"Yes!" Bambi shouted. "Isn't it enough that everything here has been destroyed? Isn't that good enough for you, Mr. Lovall? Do you have to come here and gloat, you and your girl friend?" God, it felt good to let it all out!

"For your information," Natalie said icily, "it was *my* idea to come down here, to see if Peter needed any help."

"You?" That was Peter. Bambi's head whipped around because suddenly his voice was strong and full and his cheeks were stained pink. "You expect me to believe that? You've got to be kidding. You, help? That's a laugh! When have I ever been able to depend on *you*?"

"Always!"

He laughed bitterly. "Never, you mean! You quit, you walked out on me, just when I needed you the most. And now, you're taking Martha J from me, my protégée, my best, my brightest! You're a damned ingrate and a traitor!"

Bambi felt his whole body stiffen and then he made a strangled sound in his throat. Alarmed, she turned. His face first turned purple, then drained of all color and he began noisily to gasp for air.

She wanted to say, "Let's go home now," but she never got

the chance. He stopped suddenly, clawing at the air, his face twisted and contorted and she could see sweat suddenly pouring, matting his hair. It all became slow motion, like in a dream, his knees giving way beneath him, and then he pulled away from her and sank to the ground. What was happening? It was awful, awful, and she didn't know what to do!

It came to Natalie in a flash of memory as she watched Peter turn waxy and begin to sweat horribly and then choke on his own voice. She knew what this was.

"Heart attack!" she shouted. "Get a doctor somebody! Oh, my God, he's having a heart attack! Like his father." Just like his father. Pure panic swept over her, leaving her icy cold. Old Man Marcus had died in her arms, just this way. On the corner of Madison Avenue and Forty-sixth Street, he had clutched first his chest and then the air around him, he had gasped for air, he had choked out her name, and he had slowly sunk to the pavement. By the time she'd knelt by him and cradled his head in her lap, his eyes had turned in and he'd given a funny little gurgle and died.

All the time the pictures were flashing through her head, she had been running. She found herself suddenly cradling Peter's head in her lap, found herself weeping and yelling for a doctor, a doctor for God's sake before this man dies!

But Peter did not make that funny little gurgle. He groaned, he muttered words she could not make out, but he breathed, he kept on breathing, while Bambi fluttered around and everyone else stood aghast, immobilized and silent.

It seemed like forever and then Ben DeLuria appeared. "I know CPR. Let me have a look. No, he's not fibrillating. I've had training, I'm with the rescue squad. Don't worry, Natalie, I know what to do. He needs a hospital. Peter, you're going to be okay. You're having a heart attack. I'm going to take you in my Jeep now, and I'm going to get you to the clinic where there's a doctor. . . ."

He kept talking as he wrapped Peter in a blanket—where in the world had he gotten a blanket?—and he lifted Peter in his brawny arms, carrying him as easily as if he were a child.

His voice was calm and soothing and underneath it, her thoughts kept racing.

She sat where she was on the damp ground with the drizzle soaking slowly into her hair, hugging herself, telling herself to calm down.

But all the memories of that dreadful day—she'd just been a kid then and it was her first face-to-face meeting with death—came racing back in all their painful detail. She'd had nightmares about that for years and years. It felt like a bad dream starting again.

Someone hunkered down next to her and put arms around her. She opened her eyes. It was Barbara, Barbara with wet hair, a smudge on her cheek, and understanding eyes. "Oh, Nat, how awful for you! Don't worry, he'll be okay. Ben says so, and Ben knows. He'll be okay."

"Maybe I shouldn't even care, the way he's been treating me!" Natalie tried for a flippant grin; but it was all too much and with a sigh, she gave up being brave and allowed herself to sink against Barbara's soft warmth, crying for all the lost dreams and all the lost pieces of the past, while her friend—*her friend!*—stroked her hair.

Somewhere behind her, she heard the bleat of Bambi's voice: "Peter! Peter! Oh, my God, my God, what's going to happen to me now?"

❀ 35 ❀

Natalie and Barbara

It was a glorious morning: bright blue skies, sparkling sunshine. Even the ocean was extra calm, just one lazy wave breaking on the beach every minute or so. From Natalie's deck, which had miraculously escaped any real damage, it all looked serene and picture-postcard perfect. Of course, when you went down onto the beach, you could see that it was littered with flotsam and jetsam of all kinds and there were deep puddles in the sand in odd places, some of them inhabited with poor stranded starfish. All over Paradise, there were messes to be cleaned up and litter to be swept away.

Her own kitchen window had been smashed by a flying railing from the house next door and she had spent half the day yesterday mopping and cleaning the kitchen and taping pieces of plywood over the holes. The only local glazier, a man known as Smitty, had to come by boat from Bay Shore and was in very high demand. He reckoned he might get to her window maybe next Wednesday, maybe Thursday. "And what am I supposed to do in the meantime?" she had asked. His answer was right to the point: "Pray for no rain." And then he told her to use plywood. It made the kitchen very dark, but what the hell. As Barbara said, "Dark is better than wet."

"You were so good to stay with me last night," Natalie said for the tenth time. She and Barbara were picking their way down the beach, as were half a dozen other people, looking at the damage. Not bad, not as bad as expected.

"I couldn't leave you alone, not when you were so upset," said Barbara. "Anyway, that's what friends are for."

Natalie laughed. "To take advantage of. As Jake has often said. But I feel bad . . . you know, keeping you from the arms of your beloved." -

"What's one night in a lifetime?"

Natalie gave her a sharp look. "A lifetime? Are you trying to tell me something?"

"We're not talking marriage. But, yes, I feel that this is the big one." She paused and then added in a cautious tone: "Nat? . . . I'm really happy with him. *Really* happy."

They walked on for a moment, not looking at each other. Then Natalie said: "Isn't it funny? . . . How it always takes a *man* to make us happy?"

"Oh, Nat, that's not quite true!"

"I don't mean just regular happy. A raise or your kid doing well can make you regular happy. But for a woman to be really happy, in that particular tone of voice . . . that always means there's a man in her life, fulfilling her, filling her time, and filling her house. -

"You know what I discovered about myself, the weeks I've been living here alone in Paradise? I take long walks, by myself, right? To do my hard thinking, right? And I'm telling myself, Look how well I'm doing all by myself, walking down the beach alone, thinking my own thoughts, and planning my own plans. Oh, yeah? Meanwhile, I've got the shoulders back, the gut sucked in, and I'm playing a little game called How Many Men Are Looking at Me? And I'm giving myself points for every turned head, for every interested look, for every raised eyebrow."

"Oh, Nat! Every woman likes to be looked at."

"I'm not talking about just being looked at. I'm talking about *rating* myself by a man's response. Don't you see, Barbara, that's bullshit! It doesn't have to be an important man, just *any* man. Oh, and when it *is* an important man, oh, well, then it gets even worse.

"This guy Carl Stern, for instance. He interests me, yes. And stop looking at me, Barbara. I say a man interests me and I see wedding bells in your eyes!" She paused to join Barbara in laughing and then she said: "But seriously. I like Carl and

Carl likes me and I guess we'll be seeing a bit of each other. That's the reality. But already I find that, without even thinking about it, I have changed my life to accommodate his schedule, his needs, his habits, his absences. No, wait, let me change that, Barbara. I have changed my life to accommodate what I *guess* is his so-on-and-so-forth. I've always done it and so have you. So has every woman in America. We don't plan it. These guys don't ask us to do it. We do it. *We* do it."

"But, Nat." Barbara came to a halt, squinting into the sun. "That's what a relationship is about: accommodation."

"Read my lips, Barbara. Carl doesn't accommodate; *I* do. Okay, okay, I can guess your next sentence. Maybe he can't accommodate and I can. But that isn't the point, either. The point is: I'm doing it automatically. I'm making myself available to him, neatly, quietly, efficiently, secretly. I change a meeting here and a lunch there and a dinner there."

"Like you say, we do it automatically."

"Oh, Barbara, we're in such different spaces! I don't know how to explain this to you. When I switch plans around . . . when I sit home to wait for his call . . . I'm not living *my* life, I'm living *his*. I'm forty-four almost forty-five years old. It's time I stopped waiting for a man to come along and make my life worth living."

"Oh, Nat! I guess you must think I'm weak and stupid. Because I don't feel complete without a meaningful relationship in my life . . . and I admit that means a man. But, in my own defense, it has to be the right man. And it's not as if there's nothing else in my life."

Natalie stopped now and took Barbara's hand for a moment. "I'm not asking you to justify your feelings, Barbara, really I'm not. I'm only wrestling with my own, out loud. As it happens," she added after another pause, "you turn out to be the only person I can talk to about this stuff."

"Oh, Nat!" The two women stood, looking at each other, smiling. "That makes me want to cry."

"Don't you dare. If anyone sheds one tear in front of me today, I'm going to run away." She consulted her watch and said, "Eight forty-five. Let's go see if the phones are finally working. I want to tell Martha J . . . about Peter."

They started back and Barbara said mildly, "You know, Nat, we've talked and talked and mostly about men, as usual, but there's one man's name that hasn't come up."

"Who, for God's sake? I thought we'd covered the past five years quite well since last night."

"How about Sandy Lovall? I mean, he *is* hoping to marry you, isn't he? That's the word around town."

Natalie wrinkled her nose. "I wish he hadn't talked to quite so many people, because . . ."

"Because?" Barbara prompted.

"Because, I can't seem to decide either yes or no."

"Do you love him?"

"Oh, Barbara, I wish it were that simple. It should be, shouldn't it? I love you and you love me and so we get married and live happily ever after. . . . But it isn't. It never is. In this case, in any case, love has very goddamn little to do with it. Agh, I don't want to talk about it!"

"Okay, okay. But one of these days?"

"One of these days, I'll tell you the whole thing."

When they reached the house the phone was ringing.

"So," Martha J said, when Nat picked it up. "Finally! What's this about Peter?"

"You took the words right out of my mouth, Martha J. I was just about to call *you*. The phones were all down yesterday. Hurricane Harry."

"So tell me. I got a call from Bambi—all the group heads got a call from Bambi. But she's so hysterical I don't know what to believe."

"What did she tell you? I haven't heard anything since he was taken away. They were supposed to be helicoptering him over to a hospital in Bay Shore."

"They did. At least, that's where he is, at Mother of Mercy in the coronary care unit. It was a quote major heart attack unquote, but he is quote stable unquote. That last word is straight from the CCU nurse."

"Turns out, Martha J, you know more than I do. Hold on." And she repeated it to Barbara. "Barbara's here with me."

"So you guys are talking to each other again. Good. Because, well, that's my other reason for calling you, Nat. I've got a contract! A black cosmetics line—God, they need everything, including a name for their product. And I've got an account that makes dolls, would you believe? Dolls in colors, Nat, like the Sesame Street characters. They look just like real babies, but they're green and purple and orange, isn't that great? And I've got an almost-commitment from the Hasahnis."

"Almost! After everything you've done for them? Those ingrates!"

"Oh, they want to come with me. But they want *you*, too."

She couldn't help it; she was thrilled at the words. "They do?"

"So you see, you *have* to. You're holding up the works, lady."

"And *you*, Martha J, are laying a guilt trip on me."

"I'm doin' my very best!"

They both laughed and then Natalie muttered something about money and Martha J said, "Oh, pooh, Natalie. Calvin can loan it to you. I'll bet *Jerry* would be glad to loan it to you. Or how about a bank! Come on, Nat, you can find it, I know you can. Hell, *I'll* lend it to you."

"Give me until tomorrow."

"Tonight. I have to call Paul Hasahni tomorrow first thing."

"He really insists I have to be part of it?"

"He really insists. He says I'm terrific, but you're the one who *understands* the pita business."

Natalie groaned. "You are a tough taskmaster, Martha J."

"Well, lady, I learned it from an expert. Why don't you discuss it with Barbara? I want her, too."

"Poor Peter."

"You mean because all the rats are deserting the sinking ship? Well, sorry about that. But he deserves it. I'm sorry for his heart attack, but he never should have dumped you and put his lady friend in your place! It's really her doing. Listen, I'm only the first of the exodus."

"Really?"

"Everyone's busy dusting off their resumes."

They hung up then and Natalie turned to Barbara. "Everyone's leaving the agency. Jesus . . . after all those years. It makes me feel very sad."

"Excuse me, Natalie. Who was talking just a few minutes ago about living her own life? Look how long you've been accommodating Peter—even when he was hopped up on pills! Even when—"

Natalie held up a hand. "You're right, you're right. I mustn't become overly nostalgic. But that isn't even the point anymore. The point is . . . damn that Jerry, anyway!"

Barbara burst out laughing. "Poor old Jerry. How is he to blame?"

"Money. If it weren't for him, I could buy in."

"What did he do?"

"What did he do! Cheated me, that rat in teddy bear's clothing! Supposedly, we were sharing all expenses. So I have no money, but it turns out he has plenty—money he socked away without bothering to tell me. Paige discovered it somehow and he told her it wasn't community property and I wasn't entitled to a penny of it and then she said cough it up or we go to court and he said we go to court. So everything has come to a halt while she tries to convince him it'll cost more to take it to the judge than to give me my fair share."

"It's hard to imagine Jerry being stubborn and difficult; he presents such an easy-going image."

"You've just told the story of my life, Barbara. Honestly, when they say it's a man's world, they know not how true it is. Men own every goddamn thing, including their wives. Just look at me. I've been working my whole life and yet, here I am, dependent on three different men, for Christ's sake! Peter won't come across unless I crawl. Sandy won't come across unless I marry him. And Jerry won't come across *period*. Working my whole life and in the end, I have *nothing* to show for it!"

Barbara raised her hand. "'Scuse me?" she said in a meek

little-girl voice. "Wadda ya call *this*?" And she flung her arms out.

"Call what?"

"Your house, dummy. Your *house*."

"My house is the only thing I've ever done for myself by myself. It's my only home, goddammit!"

Barbara laughed. "Now I know what I learned from all those years with Mark Valentine. I learned that a house is not a home. No, no, Natalie, first and foremost, a house is an *investment*. Don't look so perplexed. It's worth *money*, Nat, get it?"

Natalie felt stunned. "Where has my brain been? It's so obvious . . . now that you've told me! But, Jesus, of course, of course!"

She would sell her house. Yes, she would! Yes, she loved it. Yes, she adored it. Yes, it gave her a good feeling. Yes and yes and yes, but yes, she would sell it. She would make a profit besides—houses in Fire Island never went down in price, never—and with the proceeds—she wanted to sing it aloud as her dear old friend Jake surely would have done—with the proceeds she would buy into the biz with Martha J! Oh, my God, it was so simple! She stood stock still in the middle of her living room—her *salable* living room—grinning and clapping her hands like the village idiot.

* * *

Margie the real estate lady walked right in without knocking, singing out, "Hi there! Where are you?" Not bothering to wait for an answer, she sailed through the living room and out onto the deck, where Natalie was leaning on the rail, looking out to sea and dreaming a little. "Sorry I'm late. Bambi Hirsch called just as I was leaving. It seems he may need bypass surgery. And in the meantime, his doctor has told him to take it easy, not to work, and not to get upset. So, of course you know what *that* means."

Natalie had to smile. First, there was Margie's presumption that you knew exactly who she was talking about. And then, there was the assumption that you knew as much as she did.

But nobody could. Margie had eyes and ears everywhere.

"Tell me," Natalie said.

"Well, of *course*. He'll be selling that property. And of course, Sandy's already put in his bid with me. And I guess that means he'll get it because nobody else, God knows, would want that swamp . . . not to build on. And of course, it's perfect for Sandy because he doesn't *want* to build on it, he just wants it *there*. So he's as happy as a clam."

"I can just imagine he is," Natalie said dryly. "But I'm a bit surprised he feels he can afford it now."

"Oh, well, I guess I can tell *you*, seeing how things are. Peter Marcus needs the cash, so it's priced to move. And Sandy says he's putting the property in trust for the town of Paradise so he'll get a good tax writeoff. And I'll have sold it twice in one year, so everyone is going to be happy. I've known Sandy since he was a little boy, and he's always considered the pond his, so you can imagine his emotions."

"I can imagine. He must be ecstatic."

Margie gave her a sharp look and said, "I don't want you to think we enjoy making a profit off somebody's bad luck. I'm not making much on this deal. I want you to know that."

Natalie pushed away from the railing and turned her back on the spectacular view. It wasn't going to be as easy as she had imagined, giving up the house, the view, the summers, the freedom, the fantasies. The fantasies were the hardest. She had envisioned a summer filled with endless time and endless sunshine, endless bronzed men in swimsuits paying court, endless nights of love in rhythm to the regular beat of the surf. Like childhood for grown-ups—no responsibilities, no work, no hard facts to intrude on the fun.

It had not happened that way. Not quite. Everything had intruded: her divorce, her marriage, her job, her work, her drinking, her destructive behavior. God, she thought now, you name it, I had it to contend with this summer. It was a wonder she'd been able to get a tan.

"Margie," she said now, "*I* have a commission for you and I think it'll be a good one."

If a stocky woman with gray hair could be said to bridle girlishly, that's what Margie did. She even blushed. "Oh, I know what you're talking about."

"Really?" She had to smile.

"Oh sure," Margie said, nodding wisely. "And I'll be very happy to handle it for you. Well, of course, we all expected it." And when Natalie raised an eyebrow, she said quickly, "Well, of course. When you're married to Sandy, you'll live in *his* place, I mean"—she laughed loudly—"we wouldn't expect the lovebirds to have separate nests!"

Now it was Natalie's turn to laugh. Right after Barbara left this morning to meet Ben, she had spoken to Sandy. He wasn't quite the last one to know, but close. And it turned out not to be as difficult as she had imagined. She had walked over to his house, insisting that he come outside.

"What's the big secret? It's only Selma there!" Sandy said.

She took a deep breath. "I . . . I have something to tell you. . . . Oh, hell . . ." She'd better talk fast because his face had just lit up and he was smiling broadly. "The answer is no. I can't marry you." His look of confounded perplexity was almost comical; but then it changed to petulance and she knew she had done exactly the right thing.

She put a hand on his arm. "I'm very sorry," she lied. "But we really wouldn't do well together, you know. No, don't shake your head. Think about it. You'll see that I'm right. We'll do much better being just friends."

She wanted to get away so badly; she just prayed he wouldn't make a scene. He didn't. He pouted and he said, "But I thought—" But, when she interrupted him and gently turned him around and gently said, "Sandy, why don't you go back in to Selma now. We'll talk . . . soon." He went. He just went, docile and gentle as a little lamb.

And now she really *was* free. Free, free, free! Now she didn't walk, she ran, she flew, she skimmed the earth, on her way back, to her ex-house. Not bad in one stroke: ex-fiancé and ex-house. She knew her first move, and as soon as she was in the door, she did it. She called Margie.

"What's the joke?" Margie said now.

"Sorry. It's not really funny. But, you see, Sandy and I aren't getting married."

Margie's face fell. And Natalie quickly added: "So you see, yes, I do want to sell, but no, it's not because I'll be moving into the Lovall house. Oh, Margie, don't look so stricken. We're both much happier with this decision. Honestly."

"I'm just surprised. I thought it was all set. Well, of course it's none of *my* business. My business is selling houses, and I'll be happy to handle this for you. Of course"—she touched Natalie's arm—"we'll all be sorry to lose you as a neighbor. I hope you know that."

And then she was gone—at last—and Natalie looked around, testing herself. You're all alone, she told herself. You're divorcing your husband. You're selling your house. You're taking a terrible chance going into a new business, using every cent you own. You don't have a full-time lover, a full-time housekeeper, or even a full-time child anymore. You are on your *own*, lady! And what do you say to that?

And, dancing around the living room, flinging her arms out wide, she answered herself: So what else is new?

❀ 36 ❀

Natalie and Melissa

"Fu's Rush Inn!" Melissa said disdainfully. "Oh, *cute*, Ma! Real cute."

Natalie fought a feeling of irritation and said calmly, "The food's wonderful and you're talking to an old advertising lady, remember? So the name tickles me. I think it's fun that the owners were willing to take a chance like that. I admire that kind of chutzpa . . . Chinese chutzpa!" She laughed.

Melissa didn't crack even the littlest of smiles, just repeated, "Oh, cute!" in that same semidisgusted voice.

They sat, not looking at each other, ostensibly discussing the menu. Melissa, while not crazy about anything they offered and anyway, she wasn't hungry, finally deigned to try a shrimp dish, a chicken dish, and a lo mein, oh, and maybe a spring roll and come to think of it, spareribs. After Natalie had given the order, she looked across the table at her daughter, and dryly said, "Yes, I can tell you're not very hungry. You didn't order anything in column A."

Wonder of wonders, Melissa began to giggle and then really gave way and, throwing her head back, laughed at herself. The ice was now broken, Natalie knew. She sat smiling at this self-possessed and really good-looking young woman. She had striking light-colored eyes, but in every other way, she looked exactly like Natalie. She looked, in fact, Italian or Greek. Mediterranean. The boys must love her. Did they? Did she dare ask? At sixteen, what were they like, girls? She could barely remember herself at that age, only that she was so ready, so ripe, for sex. It was all she could think about. And those

were the days when nice girls didn't. Anyway, she felt she was
so homely that no boy would ever look at her.

"What are you laughing at?" Melissa said.

"Myself. I was looking at you, thinking how beautiful you
are, and what a strange little ugly duckling I was at your age."

"Oh, Mom, you were never ugly!"

"Oh, yes I was, and I knew it. The nose . . ."

"Your nose is fine. And anyway, I think you're super looking. I wish I had your legs!"

Natalie waited a beat or two and then she asked, very carefully, "How about my company? Do you wish you had *that*?"
And before Melissa could answer, she added: "I'm talking about
you being so angry with me. It's because I left, isn't it?" No
answer, but Melissa had dropped her eyes in confusion. "It *is*
because I left. Well, I'd like to talk about it. I thought I had
explained it, when I first went, and I thought you understood.
But it's becoming plain to me that you *didn't* understand."

Stubbornly, Melissa put in: "I understood, all right."

"Okay, you understood. But it's obvious that it bothered
you a lot and *that* you never told me. If I remember correctly—
and I'm sure I do—your exact words were, 'It's cool, Mom.
I'll like it better staying in my own room and going to school
with my friends.'"

Melissa burst out: "You think you know everything! Well,
you don't!"

"Granted. Would you like to explain that? No, Melissa,
really, I *want* to hear what you think. I have to know. Let's
take this opportunity to talk woman to woman."

"I'm not a woman; I'm your daughter."

Natalie knew damn well she was being given a message.
Okay, at least Missy was talking. It was much much better than
her stiff silence and very much better than the wild accusations
she'd screamed over the transatlantic phone lines.

"Of course you're my daughter. I'm very proud that you're
my daughter. You should hear the way I talk about you. And
above all else, I don't want bad feelings between us. I want
you to try to understand why I left and Daddy didn't."

"I know why you left. Dad said you were drinking too much to be much of a mother. I heard it!"

"Oh, Missy! What a shame! I'm so sorry. But, you know something? He was pretty much right. I *was* drinking too much. I've joined Alcoholics Anonymous. I don't know if he told you that. No? I thought not. But I'm not drinking anymore, not at all."

Melissa gave her a wary smile. "Oh, I hope so. I hope it lasts."

Each word from her child was like a knife in the belly. God, had she been that bad? She must have been; she had never thought so. "Was I really that awful?" she managed to say.

"Oh, Mom, you weren't *awful*, exactly. I mean, you didn't actually *do* anything. But when you were drinking, you weren't *there*, if you know what I mean."

"God, I'm sorry. I really am. I hope this year we can see a lot of each other and I'll make it up to you, Missy."

A strange look passed over Melissa's face. "Oh. Well. Um," she said. "Actually, Mom, I was going to get to that. See, I want to go back to France and study this year. Daddy says fine and my school has a program with a school in Nancy and I love my French family and it'll be terrific and there's a boy named Jean-Jacques..." As she continued, she talked faster and faster. This amused Natalie because Melissa had done the exact same thing when she was three years old. The more she wanted to convince you, the more her words tumbled over each other in their eagerness.

"Rather sudden, isn't it?" Natalie said, thinking very quickly. How did she feel about it? Fine. It was a strange feeling, thinking of her little girl an ocean away; but at the same time, what an opportunity. When she was sixteen, she'd have given her eyeteeth for such a chance. "Not that I object..." And that was absolutely true; she didn't object. She loved Melissa, but she didn't have to have her around every minute to be happy; she never had. That was the honest, open truth of the matter. She had never been half the "mother" Jerry was. The maternal instinct did not run strong and deep within her. And anyway, Melissa was not a baby. She was sixteen, on the verge of adulthood. And a damn good kid, too, in spite of her mother's having gone back to work before she was three.

Yes, by God, Natalie thought, gazing at the rosy-cheeked girl sitting across from her, her curly black hair cut in the latest bob, wearing three pairs of earrings, a jumpsuit and four belts and looking what could only be described as *au courant*. Maybe she didn't want to talk woman to woman, but woman she was. And a pretty goddamn together woman, at that.

"I was homesick for a while, in France," Melissa said.

"I remember."

Melissa colored. "I know. But I couldn't help it; I was really homesick and you wouldn't let me come back. I was mad."

"I remember that, too."

"Well," Melissa allowed, "I guess you were right. I had to give it a chance and it worked out just fine. But I really suffered, Mom! It was awful, and you wouldn't listen!"

"I'm sorry. That makes about seven times I've said I'm sorry this evening. Can we leave that now and get on with it, two women out for a Chinese meal?"

"I'm still a child, you know. I'm not as grown-up as you think."

"Well, Missy, I happen to think you're wrong. I happen to think you've grown up just beautifully."

"What I wanted to ask you," Melissa said, abruptly changing the subject, and not looking her mother directly in the eyes, "was, see, I'm not going to start until second semester and . . ."

"And?" Natalie prodded after a very long pause.

"And. What if I want to live with you, instead of Daddy, for now, I mean?"

Natalie thought very fast. "You'll have to wait at least until I find an apartment," she said with a light laugh. But she didn't feel light, and she didn't feel amused, either. She felt trapped. She wanted to say, "No, Melissa, not now. I need space, Melissa. I need privacy. I need to find my own way back to myself." But of course she couldn't say that. She couldn't. Instead, she said, "But I'm looking right now, and as soon as I'm settled in, if you decide you want to come live with me, of course you can. Of course you can. What's with this 'what if' business? I'm your mother!"

"Well, I've been wondering about that!" And to the surprise of both of them, Melissa began to cry.

"Missy!" Without even thinking, she reached across the table and grasped both of Melissa's hands. She was glad she had, because Missy just clung to her, squeezing her hands hard, gulping and sniffling and trying very hard to stop the flow.

"You know I love you, Melissa."

"Yes . . ."

"Your happiness is very important to me. And, you see, I thought it was in your best interests for me to leave the apartment. And, Missy, I only went crosstown. I talked to you every single day. And you never once told me how you were feeling!"

"Stop blaming me!" Melissa sobbed.

"Oh, God, I'm not blaming you for anything!" She felt so frustrated, so stupid and frustrated. I am ready, she thought, for this motherhood thing to end. I have had enough of motherhood. She's sixteen, for Christ's sake; she's intelligent! Why can't she seem to understand the simplest thing I say to her? "I'm not blaming you, Melissa. Stop crying, Melissa. Please stop crying, okay? I love you, sweetie pie. I love you the best I know how."

Feeling very weary and impatient, Natalie got up and slid into the seat next to Melissa and put her arms around her daughter. Letting her head fall onto the top of Melissa's curls, she murmured, "I love you," over and over. Melissa's hair smelled of baby shampoo, and Natalie felt tears prick at the corners of her own eyes. "Melissa," she said, taking in a deep breath, "I'm going to bawl in a minute, if you don't stop. And what will they do, in Fu's Rush Inn, with two crying women?" She wished she didn't feel so used up. "I love you, Melissa," she said. "Okay? Okay, Melissa?"

"Okay," Melissa said in a muffled voice. "Okay, Mommy."

I wish it all were really okay, Natalie thought wearily. God, how I wish it. Mommy. The very word brought with it all the responsibility for Melissa's happiness. But I can't be! Natalie thought. How can I be responsible for her happiness when I'm not at all sure I know how to find it for myself?

❀ 37 ❀

Alone at Last

"In just a minute," Carl called from somewhere in the depths of his apartment, "you are going to get your just deserts!" His laugh, Natalie thought, could only be described as x-rated . . . and she found herself becoming all fluttery, like the ladies in all the romance novels: *Natalie, her heart aquiver with anticipation, sat trembling on the edge of the soft down cushion, looking about her at the elegantly appointed apartment of the arrogant, handsome, rich attorney who was about to come out of his bedroom and* . . . What? she wondered hopefully. Like that. God, you know what? she said to herself. Maybe I ought to try my hand at one of those romances. I'll bet I could do it.

She was feeling very very good. He had presented her with a delicious meal—"hot from Eli Zabar's E.A.T.," he explained—at the little round table next to the window that looked out over the entire Upper East Side of Manhattan. He had plied her with Evian water and ginger ale and a fabulous strawberry tart and fresh-brewed espresso. And he had been witty and charming and affectionate and very interested in her new business venture, and all in all, she was feeling about as up as she had in months.

His apartment had been a nice surprise: filled with art, beautifully decorated, not at all what she had expected from a man she thought of as a diamond in the rough. He was a lot smoother than he let on. And when she faced him with that, he laughed and said, "That's right. You ever hear stories about Clarence Darrow, with his galluses and his drawl, convincing juries they were only dealing with a simple country lad who happened to be a lawyer? Well, I'm a rough 'n' tough city kid with street smarts who happens to have graduated from Harvard Law. It fools them, every time. People believe what they damn well want to believe, Nat. You, for instance." He leaned back in his chair, narrowed his eyes, and squinted at her. "Put on more makeup and a frilly dress and high-heeled open-toed shoes and anybody would take you for a dumb housewife."

"Oh, really? Well, for your information, I don't have to change my style for *that*. All it takes, as far as I've ever been able to ascertain, is to appear at a meeting and be female. Every man in the room is convinced women are dumb, period."

"Not this man. And most of the guys I know don't feel that way. A few years ago, maybe. In fact, back when I was in law school, we were all convinced that the few—and I mean one or two—women in the class were dykes. We liked to say that they were women who weren't content to merely marry men, they wanted to *be* men. But not anymore!"

"That's what you think." But it warmed her heart, that he even thought about this. He was much more interesting than she had thought. What a snob I am, she scolded herself. A Stella on the wall, nice leather furniture, an expensive meal, and all of a sudden he's so much sexier? That's bullshit. Well, maybe it was bullshit, but it was true. And then a thought struck her, an amusing thought.

"Who decorated this place, Carl?"

"My sister . . . Why are you laughing? Don't you like it? I thought she did a terrific job. Well, she's an interior decorator. Will you stop laughing, please? I don't see anything funny."

When she could finally speak, Natalie said, "What's funny is that I was becoming very interested, in your sister, apparently."

Carl got up from his chair then, came around the table, pulled her to her feet, and held her close, nose to nose. He said, softly, "I don't care who it was. It sounds good to me." And then he kissed her lightly and excused himself, saying he had a surprise for her. And that's where he'd been for ages. Well, not ages exactly; when she checked her wristwatch she could see he'd been out of the room for exactly three minutes. Am I falling for this guy? Is that possible?

Now he came out and gestured to her. "Okay, young lady, we're ready. C'mere..." Natalie smiled at him. He was buck naked save for a rather skimpy white towel wrapped around his loins.

"A bit overdressed, aren't you?"

His answer was to whip off the towel. He was grinning broadly, she noted, and semierect.

"Well, okay," she said and, swaying a bit, as if to music, began very very slowly to take off her clothes. He started to come to her, but she held up a hand, slowly unbuttoning her blouse, twisting and turning a bit. Next to come off was the skirt, slowly slowly unzipped and then allowed to drop. She was standing there in her tan and a wispy pale blue bra and bikini, and he licked his lips, growling in his throat, heading toward her again. Natalie laughed aloud and shook her head. He was now fully erect and she licked *her* lips. "You have to wait," she said, and he shook his head. "No way, *no way*."

He covered the distance between them in about three long strides, the stiff penis seeming to nod at her, as if it were saying, Hi there, Natalie! She laughed and then Carl grabbed her, wrapped his arms tightly around her, and bent his head to hers, kissing her hungrily, his tongue pushing deeply into her mouth... and all rational thought came to a halt. His mouth felt and tasted so good to her; she strained, up on her tiptoes, to get more of him. His hard cock was like a ramrod against her belly, and she wriggled frantically, helping him as he pulled at her panties. Off, off, she repeated to herself mindlessly. There was only one thing she wanted in the entire world and had to have and that was to feel him, hard and hot and eager, pushing into her, just as his tongue was probing her mouth.

She couldn't figure out how they got onto the living room floor; but there they were, she on her back and Carl, his face suffused with heat, on his knees above her, and then he rammed it and she took in a deep rasping breath of delight.

"Tell me, does it feel good to you? Does it? Tell me. You like my big cock inside you? You like it gentle, like this?...

Hard, like this?. . ." As he suited his actions to his words, she stared up at him, murmuring, "Yes, yes, yes, yes, yes, yes . . ." Over and over. Yes, it felt good, it filled her, it completed her. And now he moved up on her body and wiggled his hips from side to side, putting delicate tantalizing pressure on the clitoris, and she began to scream. Wave after wave of sensation coursed through her, and she could feel the climbing of the heat in her chest, the flush that presaged her orgasm. And then it exploded, like the waves breaking on the shore, and she could hear herself crying out, like the calls of the gulls.

His face twisted and his teeth bared in a grimace. "I'm sorry," he grunted out. "Sorry . . . too fast, but . . ." And then he began pounding rhythmically into her, and all too soon he was pushing into her at frantic speed, groaning through his teeth and then they lay entwined on the floor, panting.

After a minute, Carl said softly into her ear—an easy task since his lips were right there—"It's not over yet . . . remember?"

"I don't know . . . It was so long ago. Why don't you remind me?"

"In a little while," he said, pulling her in even closer to him and burying his nose in her neck. "Little while . . ." he repeated drowsily and snuggled into her.

She must have been dozing because it seemed to her that he was suddenly rock hard again and instead of lazily nuzzling her throat was biting and licking at her. Her eyes flew open, and she arched her back as his lips sought out a breast.

And then he pulled himself away from her. "Hey!" Natalie protested. "Who told you to stop?"

"Who's stopping? We're about to play a game."

"A game?" She reached her arms up for him, but he wiggled away, chuckling.

"Treasure Island. You'll love it. Listen . . . You're the island." And he drew rivulets and mountains on her quivering belly and chest with one fingertip. "I'm the pirate—see my sword?— and I'm just going to have to search and search and search and search for the hidden treasure that's buried somewhere deep in the island." As he spoke he walked his fingers down the length of her body, hesitated by the nest of curly hair and then delicately probed, only to withdraw and march up again. By this time she was gasping for air and begging for mercy.

"No mercy, my girl! I'm the pirate chief and I *never* show mercy! Let me seek it out . . . not here. So let's just see. No, no, not there . . . oh. There? Yes? Yes, I think I've struck gold, I think I've struck gold, I think I've found the hidden treasure!"

And he had . . . oh, lord, how he had!

❀ 38 ❀

Partners Three

"Here's where the horses stayed," Calvin said, "and over there, the grooms. And that's about it. That's the grand tour of Partners Three, Ltd. and, incidentally, my home." There was a ripple of laughter from his audience: and then they dispersed for the bar or the huge buffet table over near the fireplace.

Natalie stood at the archway leading into the huge main room and nodded her head in satisfaction. It was going well. There must be over a hundred people here already. It was hard to tell because the proportions of the room were so oversized. There was a baby grand piano, three oversized couches, and several trees—and still room enough left over to give a play. Even with all these people, all chatting and laughing and trying to impress each other, it didn't seem crowded. Which was just as well, since they had invited a lot more. She should know. She and Barbara and Martha J had hand-addressed three hundred seventy-two cream-colored engraved invitations to this party, right after signing their partnership agreement.

The three of them had been here today since seven-thirty in the morning, checking last minute details and overseeing the caterers as they set up. Of course then the room had been empty. Empty and echoing. All she'd done was go home to change from jeans and sweatshirt into a cashmere dress and high-heeled boots—much more suitable for a partner in Partners Three, Ltd., Advertising and Public Relations. And in the forty-five minutes she was gone, it looked as if half of New York had descended upon the renovated carriage house in

Greenwich Village, all of them talking at once. Calvin and Martha J's living room was no longer empty and no longer echoing. Instead, there was the steady, low-pitched buzz of a party just getting underway—a combination of voices and the clinking of ice against glass, punctuated occasionally by a burst of laughter or a loud greeting.

It was going to be a good party, Natalie thought. In fact, it looked like it was well on its way to being a *terrific* party. In any case, she was going to enjoy it, because it was the celebration of the opening of their agency tomorrow. Bright and early Monday morning, P/T Limited would swing into action, in a little wing in the back of this house, a great little setup with a reception area and three small offices, its own entrance, and—as of this morning—a gleaming brass plaque engraved in big block letters with their names. The name of the new corporation. Their new business. She savored those words. Unbelievable! But true, she reminded herself, hugging her happiness to herself.

Now, an *obbligato* accompaniment to the party sounds, she heard the sophisticated tinkling of a piano expertly played. Something just the least bit obscure from the jazz repertoire, something often played but not often sung, something that nagged on the edge of your memory. Exactly, Natalie realized, like something Jake Miller would choose to play, something that would give him an edge on the rest of the world.

And of course, it *was* Jake, hunched over the keyboard in his characteristic posture, head down, eyes closed. She made a beeline straight for the piano, and when she got there, bent over and whispered in his ear, "'A Ship without a Sail!' Gotcha!"

Startled, Jake looked up, blinking. Then he grinned at her. "Wiseass," he said. "Remember, I taught you everything you know."

"Don't get too smart," Natalie said. "You're talking to an independent business person, my dear, a partner, an *owner*."

He never stopped playing. It was one of the things about him that never ceased to amaze her, how he could carry on a conversation and modulate chords all at the same time. And never miss a beat either. He was the eternal boy, she thought, the gray in his hair notwithstanding. Wonderful at a party, mighty good in bed, and pretty goddamn useless in any real relationship. Would she ever stop loving him? Not a chance. They had too much history, she and Jake.

As if he were reading her mind, he slipped into "Friendship," making up his own lyrics as he went along and then, bored with that, segued into a ditty of his own devising, "Simon and Jones and Valentine, those three most beautiful girls of mine . . . If you need words or good design . . . they will fix it up just fine . . ." Natalie laughed and when he paused, nodding to her, she sang: "I think you're handing me a line." Everyone around the piano laughed, and Jake moved smoothly into something or other by Cole Porter.

Natalie kissed him lightly on the top of his head and ruffled his curls and looked around to see whom she should be greeting. There were Paul and a few other assorted Hasahnis over in a far corner, surrounding Eve Soloway, who looked, Natalie thought, a bit nonplussed by this profusion of hot-eyed sheik types. Since Ali Baba Bread was the linchpin of the new agency's client list, it might be a good idea to sashay over there and pinch Paul's cheek or something.

Oh, and there was her ex. Her almost-ex. Her soon-to-be ex, please God. She eyed Jerry Weber, big, bearlike, comfortable looking in his stretched-out tweed jacket, holding the ever-present pipe in one hand while with the other he kept touching the arm of a very nice-looking young woman he was talking to. She was all dressed for success in a man-tailored suit, shirt, and glittery tie. They were both very intent, and the girl's face, turned up to Jerry's, wore the rapt expression of a woman who thinks she's found something likely. Little does she know, Natalie thought; but what the hell, maybe he'd be more sexual with something new. More active. More alive. Did she care? No, she did not. She was just surprised she didn't know the woman . . . couldn't remember ever having seen her before. Well, Martha J had said, "It's our party, it's for us, for our business, so most of the people will be clients—past, present, and future. But since Calvin's paying for the whole thing, that darling man, there may be a few of his contacts."

Maybe the little lady was someone of Calvin's. Sooner or later she'd better get ahold of Martha J and check up on who was who. There were three black couples out in the garden, regaling each other with stories that were making them all double up with laughter. Were they perhaps the black cosmetics people— God, they looked gorgeous enough to be—or just friends of Martha J and Calvin? Couldn't tell the players without a score-card. Well, for now, she'd check in with Paul.

On her way over, she thought, Funny, how once upon a time, she'd have headed straight for the bar, no question about it. She slowed down, asking herself if she missed it. Some-times, a whole lot. She prodded herself, testing, but no, not today. It was a glorious, crisp, still-warm golden autumn after-noon, a lazy Sunday, and they were partying to the beginning of a whole new venture, a whole new opportunity. Today, she didn't need booze. She hadn't needed it yesterday, nor the day before, nor the day before that.

She *had* had one horrible night when she woke at two in the morning, weeping, feeling alone and deserted and fright-ened. Like a naughty child, looking over her shoulder for the adults who would surely come and make her stop, she took the cooking marsala out of the cupboard, uncapped it and put it to her lips. Maybe twelve drops slid down her throat and then she slammed the bottle down onto the counter, so hard that it shattered into pieces. It had taken quite a while to clean up the mess of sweet, sticky wine and shards of glass. And in that time, she had strengthened her resolve. Never again. So she swept and she mopped and when it was all done, she picked up the kitchen phone and dialed Nancy, and she had agreed that the thing to do was to go to a meeting and talk about this.

Well, in any case, that was weeks ago and it hadn't happened again. Nancy had warned her that it might: "We're never really safe, Natalie," she said. "For instance, we both know you hardly ever cook, so how come the cooking wine, huh? Think about that." And Natalie had to admit she was right; it had been an excuse, a reason to have it around . . . just in case.

Now, crossing the sunlit space, surrounded by Martha J's lovely things and by people who wished all three of them well, she took in a deep breath, looked over at the busy bar with its array of bottles, its two tuxedoed bartenders with their big smiles and their deft hands, at the lines of sparkling glasses. Looked at it, looked at the cluster of people, chatting and joking while they waited, and said, to herself, But not for me, that's all. Not for me.

A hand touched her shoulder and she turned to see the handsome, sun-tanned face of Scott Valentine. She was stunned all over again by how terribly well built he was, how terribly young and gorgeous, how terribly tempting. And there was no doubt what his intentions were: strictly dishonorable, she'd bet any amount of money. There was that gleam in his eye and something caressing about the way his hand curled around her shoulder, a little extra pressure for a little extra moment.

"Hi there, Scott. How you doing?"

"Much better now."

"Oh, have you been sick?"

He grinned, the devil. "Just lonesome. I've thought of you often, Natalie."

"Oh really? . . ." Who did he think he was talking to, some little college girl? After their one incident, he'd disappeared totally. He'd been out to Paradise, working with his father's crew, and once or twice she'd seen him at a distance, always with some little girl his own age. Maybe the same one, they all looked alike to her. He hadn't given elderly Natalie Simon a single thought. She knew that. So what now? And why? He was about as subtle and understated as a Mack truck.

"So? . . ." Scott murmured.

"So what?"

"So how about it? Shall we try it on again?"

He was beautiful and there had been a time, not very long ago, when she wouldn't have hesitated. She felt an actual wrench somewhere in the depths of her insides as she shook her head and said, "No, Scott, we shall *not*. It wouldn't be right and you know it. Your mother and I are now not only dear friends, but business partners. In brief: no way."

"You sure? You don't want to think it over?"

"I'm sure. I not only don't want to think it over, I want to forget it ever happened."

He shrugged and let go of her. "Fair enough. Anyway, Mom put me in charge of Jennifer." He made a face and gestured with his head to somewhere in back of him. "I'd better get back before she floats away. Weirder and weirder," he added, rolling his eyes.

Natalie turned to see Jennifer, like a little white ghost, standing, hands folded in front of her, quite alone, her eyes vacant and her lips moving. Her mantra no doubt. Natalie looked at her, remembering her as a wispy but still normal teenager, trying out every new idea she came across. What had happened to her? Look at her: weirder and weirder, just as Scott had said.

And now, to get to Paul. But Paul was no longer with his brothers and cousins. He was, in fact, heading for the bar, a hand tightly around Eve's upper arm, his dark sleek head bent cozily to her. No doubt about it: Paul was coming on to her, as only Paul could, something Natalie was familiar with from experience. It had happened, between her and Paul, a long time ago, longer than she wanted to count. She stood still for a moment, looking around the room, which was becoming more and more crowded with every passing minute, and wherever she looked, she saw people she knew: old clients, old friends, old husbands, old lovers . . . yes, indeed, old lovers. Good lord, she said to herself, I've been to bed with just about every man in this room except Calvin! She didn't know whether to laugh or cry, so she decided to go to the nearest comfort station to pee, instead.

Even the bathroom was splendiferous, practically the size of the so-called master bedroom in her new little apartment, complete with whirlpool tub, the john in its own little stall, wall-to-wall marble, twin sinks, dolphin faucets—the works. She locked the door behind her, thinking, Maybe Martha J could rent this to me.

A few minutes later, there was a knock on the door and when she called out, "In a minute," Martha J's voice answered, saying: "Can't wait. I'll explain later."

Natalie unlocked the door and Martha J breezed in and

breezed by, calling out, "Don't go away. In fact, lock that door and maybe we'll get a chance to talk. Isn't it exciting?" The john door was left ajar and Natalie called back, "The most exciting thing I've done in years."

"Not counting the last time you saw your boyfriend?"

"Not counting that, Martha J. No, but really, it's like getting a reprieve. Like being rescued. I feel . . . I don't know . . . just as if I'm embarking on a brand new life, not just a new career, but a whole new life."

"Yeah," Martha J said and came to stand in front of the mirror, straightening out the wide flowing legs of her satin pajama outfit, appraising herself. The satin was a dusky mauve and she had done her face in various shades of plum and lavender. If she said so herself who shouldn't, she was a knock-out.

She chuckled at her reflection. Her mama had known immediately, just by looking at her. "You're pregnant!" she had announced. "Hallelujah!"

"Mama, are you a witch? How'd you know? I just found out for sure myself, yesterday. I was coming over here to give you a surprise." She stamped her foot, and her mother had come over to give her a big warm hug.

"There's a look in the face, Martha J, a look of softness, and you've got it. And I'm a happy woman cause I'm going to have me a baby to spoil and sing lullabies to."

Martha J leaned closer to the mirror, studying her lean coppery face with the prominent cheekbones. Softness? She couldn't see it and neither could anybody else. But Mama had been right and there was no arguing with that. She was pregnant. *Pregnant*. And she was happier than she'd ever thought to be. Every morning when she woke up, feeling nauseated, she was nearly smothered by her joy. She couldn't figure it out, couldn't understand why a little speck of life, no bigger than her thumbnail should be able to light her up this way. And Calvin, the same! The man was beside himself. Well, he'd always been the one who wanted a real family, and it was she who had circled around and around, not willing to say yes, not willing to pronounce no never, not knowing what the hell she wanted.

She had not stopped using the diaphragm, telling herself she didn't need someone else to take care of. And it had happened! It had happened anyway. And then, to her astonishment, the moment she knew for sure, she realized she could not—not now, not ever—get an abortion. To do away with something that was part of Calvin, part of herself! She just couldn't. So when Natalie burbled about a new life beginning, she didn't know the half of it!

Now she turned to Natalie and answered her. "You don't know the half of it, lady!" she said, and laughed at her own secret joke. She'd tell, she'd tell, probably today. She was bursting with it. "Did you meet Sarah and Luther Wisdom? The cosmetics people?"

"Is she elegant and wearing white and is he slim and dressed like a banker?"

"The very ones!"

"I only saw them. I just came back from changing, to find three thousand people here suddenly. And anyway, I think you'd better do the introductions."

"You'll like them, Nat; they're smart and they don't make fusses over nothing. They're going with us because they know they need our expertise to market their stuff."

"I've been thinking. How about Moonglow or Moon Maid . . . as names for the product line?"

"Gee, Nat, it sounds awfully good. But . . . you know . . . awfully *pale*."

"Oh, shit! like *white*, you mean. God, I'm sorry."

"Hey, no problem. I'm not all hurt and tremble-chinned. I'm just stating a fact. You'll have to learn to think black to do that account just like you had to learn to think man back when you did tire copy. Just like I'm—"

She was interrupted by a knock on the door and sang out, "Hang in there! Two ladies are putting on their faces so it shouldn't be more than a year or two!"

It was Barbara's voice that answered. "Depends on which two, doesn't it?"

Martha J ran over and unlocked the door. "Hey, partner! Join us!"

Natalie, applying eye shadow, slid her glance sideways and smiled hello. "We might as well take a meeting while we're all here. Right, partner?"

Martha J clasped her hands and grinned mightily. "Oh, lord, you don't know how good that sounds. We're really partners, all three of us!" She paused, looking from one to the other, her face full of delight. "Five, almost seven, clients already and we haven't even opened our doors officially! I can't believe our luck, ladies. I can't believe *my* luck, that I actually have the great Natalie Simon with me . . . and the delightful Barbara Valentine who is about to become the best living account exec in New York. Oh, lord, it is so wonderful! And I love our offices."

"Calvin's den," Natalie put in.

"Calvin's ex-den," Martha J agreed, "*and* the maids' rooms." She threw her head back and laughed. "Oh, Mama didn't like that, when I told her. 'In the maid's room! That's going backward! That's awful!' But I joked her out of it. And my sister Loretta said she'll be receptionist/secretary/general helper . . . isn't that terrific? The good news is that she's smart and organized and eager to learn. And the bad news is that, next year, when she's finished with NYU, she'll be quitting. Sure you don't mind it being my sister? Lord, I never thought about that—"

"Nepotism is a fine old tradition," Barbara laughed. "And if we'd minded, we'd have told you when you first suggested it."

"Well, if either of your kids needs a job, later on. . . . I saw them, Barbara. It's been years. They're so grown up. . . ." Her voice faltered.

Barbara made a face and sighed. "You don't have to pretend, Martha J. I know what Jennifer is like. She's strange. Oh, no, don't argue with me, she's strange, all right. I'm just grateful I'm able to say it to you two. With most people, I just smile and make believe she's just like any other flaky kid who'll straighten out any day now. But I don't have much hope."

"Well, Scott seems fine," Martha J said. "He's a doll!"

"Yes, he is. He's an extremely handsome young man. But

he's a junior edition of his old man! He spent his entire summer chasing after girls. In fact, he seems to spend *all* of his time chasing after girls. The more the merrier, apparently . . . just like Mark . . ."

Martha J didn't like the look of pain on Barbara's face, but she was at a loss as to what to say. She put a hand on Barbara's shoulder, and good old Nat came to the rescue, talking very fast about her own daughter: "You're right, Barbara, they're sometimes more trouble than they're worth. Thank God Missy has decided she wants to spend the year in France—yes, you heard right, in F-R-A-N-C-E, as in across the ocean, far far away. It's a terrible thing to say, I know, but I'm so goddamn grateful. All those months, somebody else is going to be responsible for her welfare! I won't have to think about her or worry about her or argue with her. Or *live* with her. It's going to be a *reprieve*! Isn't that awful? I do love her. But I'm so tired of being a mother!"

"Hey!" Martha J protested, laughing but feeling just a bit uneasy. "Don't talk like that! You make it sound horrible, having kids, and here I am, just beginning!"

Two pairs of eyes rounded on her, both wide with amazement. "Just what does *that* mean . . . I think!" Natalie said.

She couldn't help it; the chortle came bubbling up out of her throat. "Don't bother looking at my belly," she said. "It's a little too soon for that. I think this child is about as big as your finger . . . if that. But yes, that's right, I'm gonna have a baby!"

Both of them fairly flew to her, hugging her and squealing in excitement. "Oh, Martha J! How exciting! How wonderful! When's it due?" Their questions tumbled over each other.

When she was finally able to get a word in, she laughingly said, "June fifth! And I thought you-all were down on kids. Yet, the minute I say pregnant, you both light up like a pair of Christmas trees."

"Oh, they're a pain," Barbara said, "but, you know, having my babies was the most intense and important experience of my whole life."

"If you're a woman," Natalie said very seriously, "and I do

believe we all are *that*—it's an experience you shouldn't miss. After all, it *is* the one thing no man can ever ever do. We can have babies. They can't. So you might as well do it at least once, that's how I feel. But, like any other executive position, there's a certain amount of burnout."

"Amen! After fifteen years, it's time for a change. And you *can't*. Once you're Mommy, you're Mommy forever," Barbara said. Then she laughed and hugged Martha J again. "I hope we're not discouraging you."

Martha J patted her flat tummy. "Nope. Here it is and here it stays. And, anyway, anything you two old pros say is welcome after the way Calvin's been carrying on. He follows me around, making sure I eat right and strand right and sit right and do right. You'd think I was sick, instead of just pregnant."

"Excuse me for asking, MJ," Natalie said, frowning just a little. "But . . . what are your plans after the baby is born? I mean, for the business?"

"Same as they are now! See, the difference with women of my age is we think we should have it all and, personally, I'm *determined* to have it all. And I'm *going* to have it all. The offices are right here, where I live. I'm going to hire me a nurse and I'm going to be able to see my baby whenever I have a minute and I'm going to work like the dickens. And you know what? If I turn out to be wrong, fifteen years from now, so sue me!" And they all laughed together.

They let themselves out of the bathroom, giggling a little at the picture they must make: grown women, going to the ladies' room together, like teenagers out on a triple date. And then, without a word being spoken, they split, arrowing off in three different directions, the three equal partners, each doing her own part.

Three *equal* partners, Barbara repeated to herself with enormous pleasure. Equal: That was the important word. What a feeling! Her own woman—at least in the business world. She glanced quickly around the room—it looked as if a hundred new guests had come in while the three of them had been gossiping in their conference room—and decided that now was the time to chat up Gus Whitaker, Mr. Lovin' Oven. He was, as it happened, standing by himself, gazing out at the garden, nursing a drink, and, Barbara guessed, wishing to hell that someone would come and talk to him. It was going to take a crowbar and about a million words to convince Whitaker that he should move his account to P/T. But he *had* mumbled something or other to Martha J about Natalie coming up with good ideas and Barbara having her head screwed on straight, so there were two very good sales points. She knew she could talk him into it, just *knew* it. And that was heady, indeed, this knowledge that she could live by her wits and her tongue, not necessarily by being pretty and motherly and knowing her way around a stove.

And just in the nick of time! Another week at the new and rapidly-demoralized M & M, and they would have come to put her in a rubber suit. She glanced over at Gus Whitaker, noted that his drink was white wine and that his glass was nearly empty, and stopped off at the bar. It wouldn't hurt a bit to bring him a fresh drink. See? Only a few days out of M & M and already thinking like an AE.

She smiled, thinking of Bambi's tight-lipped rage when Barbara came in to give notice. "Well, I must say," Bambi snapped, "the rats are all deserting with great speed. You're giving me two weeks notice? I say to hell with your two weeks notice! Peter Marcus gave you the chance of a lifetime and this is the thanks he gets—"

As gently as she could, Barbara said, "I hate doing this while Peter's still recuperating, I really do. I wish you wouldn't give me that look, Bambi. I wish you would at least do me the honor of believing what I say. I'm not a liar. I had hoped to stay at M & M indefinitely, in fact, but frankly, I don't think you and I can work together."

"Well, you're right about that, at least! Here I am, all but buried under all this detail—dammit, Peter left things in a total mess, *total* mess. . . ." Her voice faded and then she sucked in a deep breath and the hands on the desktop clenched into fists. "I'm getting no help from anybody around here. I have to do everything myself. No wonder Peter was driven to a heart attack."

"Whoa, Bambi! You can't be saying that we had anything to do with that!"

"Oh, can't I! Well, my poor Peter was under such stress, from his employees undermining all his efforts and being so uncooperative and unprofessional—"

Barbara took two steps forward. "Bambi," she said in tones of ice, "I'm going to tell you something. Everything was fine until Natalie was forced out and you came in. If you don't want to believe me, check it with Peter, why don't you?"

The two little fists slammed down on the desk. "You can take your two weeks' notice and shove it, Barbara! I don't want it. What I do want is for you to pack up your stuff and get out of here!"

"Today?"

"This minute!"

With pleasure, Barbara thought but did not say. She wheeled and nearly ran out, her heart beating very fast but with a smile on her lips. Dealing with Bambi was unpleasant, but on the other hand, this was the last time. Thank heavens!

The desk outside the executive office was empty. Mary-Claire had left in a huff, not two days after Bambi moved herself into Peter's office, announcing that she was president *pro tem* until further notice. It was to Barbara that Mary-Claire had come running that very first day, tears in her eyes, saying: "Well, I won't put up with it! I won't, that's all. I don't have to. The nerve of that woman, putting herself in Peter's chair, in Peter's office! She's been the ruination of a splendid man who was once so creative, so full of life, so loving—" And she had burst into noisy tears, and Barbara of course had to come over and say "There there," a lot, for a long long time. Not that it did any good. By lunchtime the next day, after Bambi had given her a list of personal errands she wanted done, Mary-Claire had had it. "Never!" she had cried, so loudly that the entire art department could hear it. "I'm *Peter's* executive, personal secretary, not yours! And I never will be!" That was two weeks ago and the last Barbara had heard, Mary-

Claire was resting at home under the care of her mother while she settled what she called a nervous condition and circled ads in the *New York Times* classifieds.

That was Mary-Claire's way of coping. Tommy Thoms wandered about M & M looking lost and sounding plaintive. Jeff had gone right out and got himself a new job at Doyle Dane. Eve was looking for something. And the art department contented itself with setting up a giant blowup of Bambi's face and using it for a dart board. Apparently, art director jobs were scarce.

Before she had been approached by her new partners, Barbara had been having her own little *crise de nerfs*—more like a "*crise de calories.*" She had found herself ravenous, all the time, day and night. Nothing seemed able to fill her or satisfy her. And it was back to baby food for her: anything soft and slippery that you didn't have to chew, something that would slide right down. How many grilled cheese sandwiches had she eaten? How many ice cream cones? How many bowls of chocolate pudding? Even oatmeal—with plenty of butter and brown sugar, of course! She'd put on five pounds . . . okay, seven; and then she'd finally said to herself, Enough! And that's when she decided she just had to leave her safe little nest at M & M and test her downy little wings. And *that's* when Martha J and Natalie had rescued her . . . snatched her from the jaws of Creative Cohorts and all the other employment agencies she really didn't want to deal with, ever again.

She took two glasses of white wine from the bartender, smiled at him, got a dazzler in return, and headed once more for Gus Whitaker and her mission. How lovely it was to have this kind of autonomy. Well . . . almost autonomy. The hard truth was that, equal partner though she might be, she wasn't, not exactly. It wasn't her money that had bought her share; it was Ben's. Not her idea; his. But when no bank wanted to take a chance on her, she'd had to.

God, how she wished it didn't have to make a difference. But the day he'd written her the check and kissed her on the top of her head, she'd sensed a subtle but unmistakable change in his attitude toward her. There was a soupçon more condescension, she thought, a pinch more paternalism. It was as if, by accepting his loan—and she made sure he knew that's what it was: a loan, with interest—she had somehow sold him a piece of herself. No, scratch that . . . *all* of herself. Suddenly he was behaving as if he *owned* her, assuming it was up to her to make all their social decisions and up to him to offer her all kinds of business advice, in spite of the fact that he knew less than nothing about advertising.

And last night, they'd had the most stupid argument! It had begun calmly enough with Ben jokingly saying, "Who's gonna cook dinner if you're working late all the time!" Of course, he insisted he was only kidding, only kidding, honey; but immediately afterward he'd whirled on her, saying, "And you can't tell me that a lot of that working late isn't those guys trying to make time with you!"

"Ben!" she had cried, unable to believe her ears. "That's ridiculous! No, it's positively antediluvian! That doesn't happen . . . well, at least not much. And it certainly doesn't happen to me. And if it should, don't you think I'd know how to handle it?"

"Oh, yeah? What could *you* do against a two-hundred-pound guy with sex on his mind?"

"Oh, yeah?" she echoed, watching his lips tighten at that. "And what do you think could happen in the middle of a restaurant?"

"You know what I mean, Barbara! I'm talking about not liking my woman being out alone with dozens of guys while *I* sit home alone, like a good little housewife, waiting!"

"Ben, for God's sake, we don't even live together! And listen to yourself: You sound like an old-fashioned husband, giving the business to his little woman! You'll be in your house on Fire Island during the week. What's all this about waiting?"

"Well . . . I'll know you're out and I'll be worried. Dammit, Barbara, I just get crazy thinking about it." His expression softened and he held out his arms. "I'm just crazy about *you*, that's what it is." Oh, yes, she'd gone into his embrace. Gladly. Joyfully. She hated it when they fought.

And there he was now, coming into Martha J's living room,

and immediately her heart gave such a lurch. He looked so
good to her! So damn good, so big and solid and beautiful and
hers. To hell with Gus Whitaker for the moment. Ben was here.
Seeing him, she chided herself for always overdramatizing their
differences. She knew why: She was scared to death that he
was like Mark. She was terrified of doing what all the articles
on the subject said divorced people invariably did: get seriously
involved with someone exactly like that first mistake. She was
desperate not to, that's what it was. How unfair to continually
find fault with him when he was one of the winners in a world
full of men who were unwilling or unable to commit. Look at
Jake. And there were plenty of others and not just the ones
she'd dated. Any time she talked to younger single women,
still in their early thirties, all she heard was despair and depression because they were all getting older and there were no men
for them.

Dear sweet Ben. She loved him. How could she be angry
with a man whose fault was that he loved not wisely but too
well? She made her way over to him where he stood searching
the room with his eyes as he chatted with Calvin and handed
him the glass of wine meant for Gus.

"There you go!" she said without preamble, and was rewarded
with an instant grin of such blatant pleasure that she vowed
then and there never to be angry with him again. He put an
arm around her shoulder, squeezing, and said with obvious
pride to Calvin: "Like I was just saying, Calvin. This is the
smart lady I've put *my* money on."

There went another vow. The rage that rose in her chest
was so hot and huge and sudden that there was no way she
could control it. Never be angry with him again? The bastard,
who in hell did he think he was? Who, in fact, did he think
she was? She knew the answer to both of those questions, if
she was willing to be really honest with herself. He thought
he was the lord and master and she was the servant and slave!
Just like . . . but she was not going to allow that thought to be
thought.

She had to calm down. Calvin's living room was not the
place to reenact the Battle of the Sexes. And besides, she had

no business becoming so enraged. It wasn't as if his attitude came as a surprise. On the contrary. She'd been noticing little things lately, nothing too terrible, but indicative. He made fun of her list-making. Well, how did he think she kept track of everything? It annoyed her, it was so damn patronizing. *And* none of his business, besides. And another thing: He was always saying, "Whatever your heart desires," but he never meant it. It was just a polite phrase to throw out when the decision didn't really matter to him. Sometimes, she really *wanted* a discussion, and then there was nothing more maddening than to have him smile upon her and say, "Whatever your heart desires." Not to mention his habit of thinking he had a God-given right to switch the radio station or the television channel the minute he came into the room—without ever saying a word. How many times had she said "Hey! Who said I wanted that changed!" He always gave her a look of such amazement that she knew it hadn't occurred to him that what she wanted mattered!

It was crazy, absolutely loony, for her to be standing there in the middle of her celebration, seething about Ben DeLuria. First of all, it reminded her too much of all the years of doing likewise over Mark Valentine, while he just blithely went along doing whatever he damn well pleased. She hadn't divorced him and made it on her own, just to put herself into the hands of another man just like him! Had she? Oh, no! They weren't the same man. But more important, *she* wasn't the same Barbara. This time she knew she had options. She didn't have to smile and behave and take it.

She made herself relax—all this time, his arm had remained encircling her shoulders—and she decided she would take that as a sign of what this relationship was all about. He was there for her, he loved her. What's more, she loved him too. If she was angry, the thing to do was to talk it out. And if he wouldn't talk, she'd shout. And if he still wouldn't listen, she'd get him into counseling if she had to drag him herself. This time, she wasn't going to sit and snivel. This time, she was going to make sure it worked!

*   *   *

Natalie was very glad when Sandy and Selma made their entrance and she was finally able to get away from Jerry and his oh-so-slow-and-deliberate explanation of how he was going to arrange the division of their property. She had tried, without success, to catch the attention of Barbara, to rescue her. She simply didn't have the patience to listen to him pontificate—he could never talk about anything without giving a lecture!—and he wouldn't let her go. She kept saying, "Listen, Paige will be here in a little while; she said she was coming. If she doesn't mind talking business on a Sunday afternoon, why don't you discuss it with her?" And he looked horribly wounded and said, "Now, sweetheart, I thought you'd like to have input." And then there was a murmur all around them, and when she turned to look, there was Selma, and no wonder everyone was staring. She was wrapped in a huge black satin cape, lined in scarlet, with a large collar that stood up and framed her face; and she blazed with diamonds. She really was something to behold, and for a moment or two, everything froze as she was beheld, by one and by all.

And then she spoke and broke the spell: "Ithn't thith jutht wonderful! Natalie! Barbara! And beautiful Martha J! Come right over here and let Thelma kith you all!"

Oh, bless Selma, Natalie thought. She was such a marvelous character. Natalie took herself right over and allowed herself to be enveloped, as did Barbara and Martha J.

"I think," Natalie announced, "that you're going to be our only client who regularly hugs and kisses us."

And everyone laughed when both Paul Hasahni and Luther Wisdom said, as one, "What about *me*?"

When the room quieted down from that one, Selma put a beringed hand on Sandy's shoulder and said, "And we'd like to announthe, Thandy and I, that we're getting married. *Again!*" Even those who had no idea who she was or who Sandy Lovall was, applauded at the word "again." And once more there was laughter. And once more, there were kisses all around.

"You can all see," Sandy said, "why this woman is my business manager as well as my wife twice. There isn't a better press agent in this world!"

"And I'm tho vithible! Jutht ath Thandy'th new paintingth, which will be on exthibit tharting next week."

Natalie allowed herself to drift away. She'd be at Sandy's exhibit, for sure. She'd still be handling his catalogs and press releases, of course, and her presence would be obligatory. Not that she minded; it was amazing to her how quickly she had been able to put their personal relationship behind her, to all but forget it. When she looked at him now, across the room, she saw a tall, bulky, nice-looking older man whom she knew rather well but not intimately. It was hard to believe she'd ever even, for one moment, considered *marrying* him! It was hard to believe she'd ever, for one moment, considered screwing him, too.

As a matter of fact, it occurred to her, she hadn't considered anyone for that particular job, lately. She had noted several men today, in passing and not in passing. There was a very handsome young black man, who as a matter of fact, had been giving her certain looks all day. He was doing it now. And there was Paul Hasahni, who'd murmured something about picking up where they'd left off . . . "and I don't mean advertising either, Natalie darling." Not to mention the white-haired gent slouching in the corner, talking to Eve Soloway; he looked interesting. Not to mention Scott.

It amazed her, just amazed her: In the past, even in the recent past, at a party like this where she was without escort and where Jake was pointedly ignoring her, she would have been frantically hunting down somebody who would take her to bed. Anybody! And drinking plenty too. All the boozing she'd done! All the men she'd needed! She found it difficult to believe she'd ever been that desperate, that hysterical.

Was it because she was more or less regularly seeing Carl Stern? No. Because regularly, with Carl, meant less rather than more. Earlier, Martha J had asked about him. "Why didn't you bring him?"

"He's out of town," Natalie had told her.

"Again, out of town?"

And Natalie had shrugged, saying, "What do you mean,

again? Out of Town is his home address! He's always out of town!"

It wasn't quite accurate, but close enough. Carl wasn't her beloved, just her beliked, really. He was a nice guy, the guy she slept with when he was in town. And it was okay, it was fine. She didn't need him. Dammit, that's what it was all about: She didn't *need* him, or anyone else, to prove to herself and the world that she was attractive, or sexy, or all right, or young, or desirable, or normal, or worthy, or *anything*.

She drifted over to the window overlooking the pretty little garden with its bubbling fountain and Japanese maple with its blazing red foliage, and stared out. A strange new feeling was overtaking her, and she stood very still, trying to understand it. And it came to her, what she felt: Joy. Pure and simple joy. Tears formed behind her eyes as she realized it.

She was free, really free, for the first time in years. No husband, no child to care for, no Peter, no Jake, no position at M & M, no house, no nothing from her past to bind her or hold her or hurt her. It wasn't given to too many women of her age, to shake free from everything and have the chance to do whatever she wanted, *whatever* she wanted, wherever life led her. So many choices, so many new doors to open, so many new places to explore, so many new things to try. The future she had thought so set and settled was gone like a wisp of smoke and in its place was . . . anything, *anything*! She loved it. She felt lightened, ready to fly, ready to soar.

It was wonderful, wonderful! She was free to do any damn thing and to hell with running around trying to act like she was still twenty-three. She was forty-four and proud of it. Well . . . she smiled to herself . . . okay, more like forty-five. But who's counting?

❀ *About the Author* ❀

Marcia Rose is not a real person. She is *two* real persons—two women who met as young mothers and began to write books together (much to their surprise) ten years ago.

Marcia of *Marcia Rose*, a divorcee, has two lovely daughters, and lives in a lovely coop apartment in Brooklyn Heights, NY. She enjoys good music, theater, and the company of people with the initials HC.

Rose of *Marcia Rose* is married, has two delightful daughters, a cuddly cat, and lives in a hundred-year-old house in Brooklyn Heights. She enjoys travel, skiing, and theater.

They both love a good laugh, a good cry, and a good book.

Marcia and Rose have written every word of their novels together. After so many years as a team, it no longer comes as a surprise when they think of the same thing at the same time, in the same words. What *is* a surprise is that something that is so much fun has turned out to be a full-time career.